Temple of Love

Laurelei Black

Asteria Books

Martinsville, IN

Temple of Love by Laurelei Black © 2009, 2013

Asteria Books

ISBN: 978-0-9857734-4-1

Cover design by Natalie Black, featuring "In the Days of Sappho" by John William Godward.

Temple of Love

Laurelei Black

Prologue

The world has forgotten. People have been prim, prudent and aghast at the mere mention of the priestesses of the Goddess. "Sacred Whore" is an oxymoron to most, because they fear their own skin and the power of a woman's desire. To us, she has always been the "Holy Virgin," bound to no man.

They have turned their faces from all the guises of the Goddess save one, whom they call virgin indeed and hide her behind the son. For too long, they have forsaken the Maiden, the Hag, the Avenger, the Whore, the true Mother who took pleasure in her own body to beget, bear and bring forth her precious fruit.

The people have forgotten, forsaken and feared the Goddesses of Old, but the Goddesses have forgotten nothing. Their ageless beauty, wisdom, honor and power have been preserved – within marble, bronze, oil on canvas, ink on papyrus. They have been kept within the earth, water, stone, trees, and air that still sparkle and flutter with the laughter of nymphs and satyrs reveling in grotto temples.

And we remember, dear sisters – priestesses who have been recalled to service in all the ancient forms. Our line has long been broken. We have been cast out of the ruined temples for centuries upon centuries. The roofs have collapsed, the columns have crumbled, the altars were broken to prevent our worship. But the foundations remained. They wait for us to come and discover their long-kept secrets.

The Golden One herself will whisper in our ears, bathe us in her pools, and touch our most secret places with Divinity. Kypris, most beautiful, will initiate us again into her Mysteries and remind us that not all has been lost through neglect and destruction. Much has been preserved – hidden in poetry, pottery, plays. Even the crumbling classical architecture longs to whisper its secrets, if we will only stop and listen.

Come, dear ones, and learn who you are. You are the priestesses of the new temple, and your training will begin to rebuild what was lost. The temple is indeed being erected anew – not of marble upon the acropolis, but within our flesh, our hearts, our souls. Listen to the stories of the priestesses whose names we haven't forgotten, though their true natures have been veiled by history. We are daughters of Aphrodite, you and I – her priestesses reborn. Come, dear sisters, and claim your place in her worship. We were once consecrated by Psyche, Hero, Helen, Dido, and Sappho.

Lift Sappho's veil and remember ...

Figures from Greek Myth & History

Aglaea – Grace of splendor

Akidalia – an epithet of Aphrodite meaning "of the bath"

Apollo – God of the sun, music, arts, healing

Ares – God of war

Artemis – Goddess of the hunt, youth, and wild places

Bacchus – an epithet of Dionysos

Cheiron – the ferryman who takes souls across the river Styx and
into the land of the dead

Chryseis – epithet meaning "golden one"

Daphne – a water nymph pursued by Apollo; she was turned into a
laurel tree in order to escape hime; in Greek, daphne means
"laurel"

Dionysos – God of wine and theatre

Erato – Muse of lyric poetry

Eros – God of romantic or sexual love; Aphrodite's son

Euphrosyne – Grace of mirth

Euterpe – Muse of lyric poetry and music

Eileithyria – Goddess of childbirth

Fates – Goddess of weaving, life, and death

Helen – wife of Menelaus; later, wife of Paris (of Troy); most
beautiful woman in the world

Helios – Apollo's son; responsible for carrying the sun on its course through the sky

Hestia – Goddess of the flame, especially the temple and hearth fires

Hera – Goddess of marriage, queenship; Zeus's wife

Hero of Hiera – a female runner mentioned in one of Sappho's fragments

Hermes – God of communication, messages, and magic

Hesper – the evening star (planet Venus); hespera meanings "evening" in greek

Hesperides – daughters of Hesper; guardians of a sacred apple grove

Hylas and the nymphs – a mortal man who was drowned by water nymphs

Jason – hero from Argos; captain of the ship Argo

Kalliope – Muse of eloquence, epic poetry; mother of Orpheus

Kinyras – ancient king of Kyprus; father of Adonis

Kharites – Graces

Klio – Muse of historical and heroic poetry

Kypris, Kypria, Kypriana, the Kyprian – an epithet of Aphrodite, meaning "from Cyprus" (one of the islands claiming to be her birthplace)

Kytherea – an epithet of Aphrodite, meaning "from Cythera" (one of the islands claiming to be her birthplace)

Ladon – the dragon who assists the Hesperides in guarding the apple grove

Melpomene – Muse of theatrical tragedy

Morpheus – God of dreams

Muses – the nine daughters of Zeus who inspire mortals with the arts and education

Odysseus – Greek hero of the Trojan War; known for his cleverness and his extremely long voyage home

Orpheus – a famous singer; son of Kalliope; went to the underworld to bring his wife back to life

Ourania – Muse of astronomy; also an epithet of Aphrodite meaning "heavenly"

Ouranos (Uranus) – Titan of the sky

Pandemos – an epithet of Aphrodite meaning "of all people"

Paris – awarded the golden apple to Aphrodite and took Helen as his prize, thereby igniting the Trojan War

Persephone – Goddess of the underworld

Phryne – famous Greek courtesan; Praxiteles's model for a famous statue of Aphrodite

Polyhymnia – Muse of sacred song and dance

Praxiteles – famous Greek sculptor

Psyche – Aphrodite's daughter-in-law; the wife of Eros

Scylla and Kharabdis – two sea monsters Odysseus overcomes in the Odyssey; Scylla has many heads, while Kharybdis is a devouring mouth in the sea; the passge between the two is very narrow

Styx – the river that marks the boundary between the living world
and the underworld

Terpsichore – Muse of dance

Thalia – Muse of theatrical comedy; also a Grace (Kharite)

Zeus – God of the sky; king of the Olympians

Characters

Sappho's household

Anassa – Sappho's second stepmother

Atthis – Sappho's friend from childhood; Tessa's daughter

Damara – Sappho's first stepmother

Desma – servant of Kleis (the mother)

Doran – Sappho's half-brother; Damara's son

Eurygius – Anassa's son; Sappho's half-brother

Iantha – Sappho's youngest half-sister

Kastor – a servant in Antti's house

Kharaxus – Anassa's son; Sappho's half-brother

Kleis – Sappho's mother; also her daughter's name

Larichus – Anassa's son; Sappho's half-brother

Nilo – Tessa's son; Atthis's brother

Reah – the nurse to Sappho's baby

Scamandronymus – Sappho's father

Tessa – Sappho's nursemaid; Atthis's mother

Zeta –Anassa's daughter; Sappho's half-sister

Zoe – a kitchen servant in Sappho's family home

Temple

Adara – daughter of the priestess Adesia

Adesia – a priestess; caretaker of temple children

Agueda – a priestess

Alkaeus – famous Lesvian poet and aristocrat

Anactoria – student at the thiasos

Daphne – a priestess

Dica – student at the thiasos

Errita – a priestess

Eugenia – a priestess and hiereia

Eunice – student at the thiasos

Frona – apriestess

Hermione – a priestess and teacher at the thiasos

Kallista – student at the thiasos

Kastalia – a priestess

Malva – student at the thiasos

Melanthe – student at the thiasos

Milesia – student at the thiasos

Rhodia – a priestess and teacher at the thiasos

Sanura – priestess and teacher at the thiasos

Timas – a priestess and hiereia

Mytiline

Andronikos – Atthis's husband

Eranna – a woman in the marketplace

Fotis – a young neighbor boy

Hymenaeus – Dica's husband

Kerkolos – one of Sappho's lovers

Phaon – one of Sappho's lovers

Pittakos – political and martial leader of Lesvos; one of the "Seven
        Sages"

Platon – a poet

Voyage

Eustis – Pittakos's partner

Larissa – Pittakos's housekeeper

Glossary of Greek Words

adelphe – dear one (feminine), dear sister

agora – marketplace; central gathering place

andron – the men's quarters; a place for entertaining guests

demos – village; people

epaulia – bridal shower

fibulae – pins used for fastening garments

gamos – wedding/marriage

gyneaceum – women's quarters

hetaera (pl. heterae) – courtesan

hiereia – high priestess

Hiereia Aphrodites – title; high priestess of Aphrodite

hierodule (pl. hierodulei) – literally "sacred servant;" most often used
  in reference to sacred prostitutes

hieros gamos – sacred marriage; the sexual union of divine partners

himation – large piece of cloth used as a cloak or veil

hydrophoros – water-bearer

kallisti – "for the fairest"

khaire – a greeting of joy and blessing

khiton – a sewn garment held in place by fibulae at the shoulders

Kytherean – from the island of Kythera

maenad – one of the wild women who follow Dionysos

miasmos – wrongness, uncleanness; being ill-prepared for contact
with the sacred

odeon – ancient Greek building for singing exercises, musical shows,
and poetry receitation

omphalos – navel of the world; sacred stone beneath Apollo's temple
at Delphi

orchestra – literally "dancing place;" it is the stage of the Greek
theatre

pallake – concubine or common-law wife

peplos – folded and draped garment; one side is open; held at
shoulders by fibulae and at waist by a girdle/belt

pompe – procession, usually for a religious or civic ceremony

pnyx – an open-air auditorium of stone nearly enclosed by short wall

proaulia – part of a wedding celebration that focused on the bride
and her female relatives/friends

pythia – oracular priestess of Apollo

temenos – sacred place, like a temple or grove

thiasos – school; community of people devoted to a similar
philosophy or deity

symposia, symposium – men's drinking party that usually involved
political, artistic, and philosophical discussions

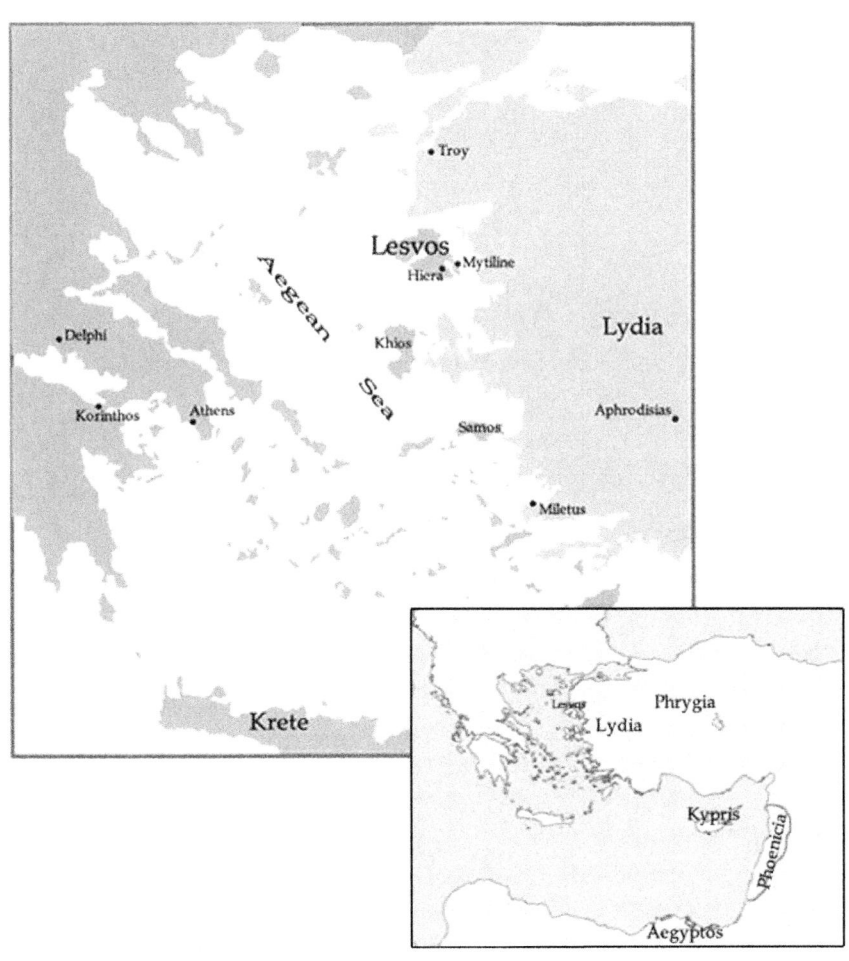

Invocation

Come now, gentle Graces and fair-haired Muses,
Come hither, foam-born Kyprian Goddess, come,
And in golden goblets pour richest nectar
All mixed in most ethereal perfection,
Thus to delight us.

– Sappho

Chapter 1

"A sweet-voiced maiden – loved, lovely, loving, beloved. The one you carry is truly Kypria's daughter." The words came through and around the prophetess as she uttered the voice of oracle. Her eyes were blank and her face expressionless, sitting rigid in her high seat, unaware of her own body's discomfort or the expectant eyes of her petitioner. Unaware, even, of the attendant Priest whose work it was to see to the needs of the *pythia's* body and monitor the passage of the fumes which kept her mind and spirit only vaguely in contact with that shell. It was also his responsibility to record her oracles and to put them in verse, in the rare instances when she spoke in prose.

The priestess of the oracle in Apollo's temple at Delphi seemed beyond human to the mystified noblewoman who awaited her words. The young priestess was somewhat plain in natural appearance, but so strong was her connection with Apollo that she radiated something beyond mortal beauty, a cultivated intellect and innate bond with the Divine. Her voice was at once soothing, melodic, clear, distant and enveloping. She was disconnected from everything in the physical realm except her own power of speech, and yet somehow in touch with every spirit in the temple – not the least of which was its patron, Apollo.

Kleis was dizzy and queasy, overwhelmed by the power of the *pythia* and the sweet fumes of her trance. *How will this affect my child?* The child! She had only half begun to suspect she carried a life in her womb the day before she and her husband, Scamandronymus, made preparations to visit this temple.

She had come to Athens with her husband because her brother-in-law had fallen ill. Scamandronymus himself was not particularly close to his brother, but since his brother had no children or other trusted relatives to tend his interests during and after his death, Scamandronymus had responded obligingly to the summons. Kleis had never met any of her husband's family. Scamandronymus had left Athens a decade before, when his father was killed, and hadn't returned until now when her sister-in-law, a nervous and fragile woman, had sent a message of desperation, calling on Scamandronymus's sense of honor and family duty.

Kleis wanted to like her sister-in-law, but she found herself being grateful that the relatively unconnected woman wouldn't be returning with them to Lesvos. Scamandronymus had made the offer to make his brother's widow part of his own household, but she had declined, preferring to stay with her own sister in Athens under the care and supervision of her nephew. Scamandronymus helped her make the financial preparations for her own livelihood while simultaneously taking care of his brother's business interests in the city. A certain amount of money, naturally, would secure the remainder of his widow's days with the necessary provisions, and even a modicum of luxury. However, all of his brother's existence, outside that small domestic sphere ruled by his wife, was now in Scamandronymus's hands for the managing.

It was for this reason that he had brought Kleis to Delphi, the navel of the world, to seek guidance from the oracle. The prophetess was generally sought for guidance in making the best choices. Where should the village be established? What offerings should be made? What course of action should be taken? They had arrived early in the day so that Scamandronymus could gain counsel in dealing with his brother's holdings. They were arranged into a line with the other seekers to wait their turn to enter the temple.

High-ranking officials, heads of state, and foreign dignitaries were given places near the front of the line. Mere heads of household, such as Scamandronymus, were relegated to the end of the line. Kleis didn't mind the long wait that followed, though. The grounds of the temple were awe-inspiring. The sanctuary was situated on the southern slope of the mountain, surrounded by high cliffs. As they stood and sat on the grounds, talking with those near them in the queue, the petitioners were at liberty to view the wealth and splendor of the temple. Monuments and treasuries had been donated by the richest of the past visitors to seek the *pythia's* wisdom.

As Helios drew his sun-chariot across the sky, the visitors meandered their way to the terrace, getting ever closer to Apollo's inner sanctum. They progressed from the terrace to a ramp that lead up to a colonnade, through a set of double doors and into the temple proper. Women from Delphi tended a fire upon which the petitioners burned incense and other offerings as they entered. It was upon this constant fire, too, that the sacrifice of a goat had been made that morning to ensure an auspicious day for prophecy.

After making their own offerings, Kleis and Scamandronymus had descended into a space that sat below the level of the temple floor in which they saw a great, golden statue of the God and the stone that marked the center of the world, the *omphalos.* Beyond this was the chamber of the *pythia* which was not to be entered except by her. Beyond the golden veils that secluded her somewhat from those seeking her audience, she sat upon a high tripod stool that straddled a crack in the temple floor. Though most of the vapors seeping up from this fissure stayed within the veiled chamber, Kleis drew her own veil over her nose and mouth to block out the smell of those sickly sweet fumes. Her stomach was ready to leap, and again she thought of the child only now being announced to her and Scamandronymus.

"Her arrival coincides with a departure, and she is well-provided for. Her skillful touch will long be felt upon the soul of the world. Make offerings to Aphrodite *Ourania* to guard and guide her." The prophetess said no more about the child, but spoke instead of the best course of action for liquidating Scamandronymus's brother's estate and making the appropriate offerings. More detail than this Kleis did not hear. She was far too focused on the new nature of her own flesh, keenly aware of a tingling in her stomach that was either illness or excitement.

Of course, the sensation wasn't entirely pleasant. In fact, it seemed connected to a lump she now felt in her throat and a wobbliness in her knees. Still, the knowledge that she carried her first child buoyed her spirit enough to carry her body in a dignified way through the remainder of the interview. Her hand rested protectively on her womb as she thanked Aphrodite for sending her a daughter and thanked Apollo for sending her the news.

She wondered how Scamandronymus was responding to the news. His face showed nothing, save grave interest and respect for the instructions of the priestess. Would he be disappointed that their first child wouldn't be a son? Surely, he would be grateful that she had conceived at all. They had been married a year, and this was the first sign of childbearing that Kleis had received. She had started to worry that she would never have a child and would be set aside as a broken and unwanted vessel. After all, she had been taught since her own childhood that the role of a respectable wife was to please her husband, run the home and produce fine, strong sons.

She was sure that Scamandronymus was pleased with her, in general. She was educated and charming, a fine wife for entertaining guests and business relations. She was beautiful, kind and well-schooled in making her husband feel like a man. The temple of Aphrodite across the bay from their city was well-known for instructing girls to be the kind of wives that any man would prize. Kleis didn't feel that she had given her husband any cause for complaint, but she had been surprised several months ago that she hadn't begun to show the outward effects of the passion with which she embraced him. Now that she knew she carried a girl, she hoped he wouldn't be annoyed that she hadn't given him a son.

What does it matter? she thought. *I am young and healthy. I will bring forth as many sons as he could wish. This daughter is for me.* Already, she began to think lovingly of the child within her. As they began the long journey back to Lesvos, she had lovely daydreams of a young girl with laughing eyes whose shining hair she would comb and twist and finally let fall in soft waves upon her back. She saw a girl with skin like milk and eyes as azure as the sea around the island, singing as they rested together under the acacia trees outside Mytiline on a warm summer day. These visions of the daughter

Aphrodite had sent her fed her when she was too unsettled to eat, steadied her when she was too faint to walk and enlivened her when she was too tired to journey.

In fact, the journey home was considerably slower than planned. Scamandronymus didn't want to strain his wife. He hadn't been around many breeding women, but she seemed more delicate than most. He had come to love her in their year as husband and wife, and he appreciated the brave face she wore, but her discomfort and sickness were undeniable. She wretched every morning before he and his servant were fully awake, and she couldn't eat much during the day unless the same fate came upon her. He would have thought that she got no nourishment at all except that her servant had identified a handful of items she could eat after the queasiness of the morning subsided. He wanted to ease the journey for her, and, at the same time, get home as quickly as possible. He felt she would be most comfortable there in familiar surroundings, no work to be done, and more of her own women to tend to her. Furthermore, a midwife could be employed, someone who was trained in such matters and would know more of what to do and say than he did.

"It's no great cause for alarm, sir," the servant woman who had accompanied them on the journey had tried to assure him. "Some women are tenderer than others in the first few moons of their carriage. Some babes are more demanding, too, and put their poor mothers through worse than my lady is getting. I know some herbs that will ease her stomach when it rebels, and it won't be too long before her appetite returns. By the time two more moons have waned, so will her nausea have lessened."

"Do you think the journey is safe? Should we rest until her strength returns?"

"It might be wise to find suitable accommodations until the new moon, sir. I think by then that the greatest danger of losing the child will have passed and she will be strong enough to travel safely."

Though she was pale and weak, on the morning of the new moon Kleis felt well enough to push toward home. The time at rest, with no business to attend to, had quieted and calmed her. It had given her time with Scamandronymus alone to discuss their gift from the Golden Lady, to learn his thoughts, and to learn to take pride in her changing body. Soon, she would start to become round and the other women of Mytiline would know that she was to experience the Mysteries of motherhood. There would be a rite at the temple of Aphrodite when she got home, and another after the child was born. The priestesses would give her protection while she carried the babe and cleansing after she was delivered. She would make offerings every month at her own shrine during the time she would have menstruated, thanking Aphrodite for keeping her blood within her body to nourish the child. She would be seen as Scamandronymus's full wife with no impeachment laid to that title and no rival to threaten her, though such jealous and paranoid thoughts surprised her when she had them, knowing Scamandronymus's fondness for her.

Kleis was determined and eager to return to Lesvos and the city of Mytiline. With the help of Desma, the servant woman, and the understanding of Scamandronymus, Kleis felt strong enough to journey to the farthest island in the world. She knew she could at least lie quietly in the covered sedan Scamandronymus had arranged for her and Desma, listening to the other woman's stories, keeping cool and still and sleeping. Kleis purposely stayed awake at night, walking a short way in the cooler air with her shawl wrapped around her, so she would be more inclined to sleep her way through the daytime travel. And with this rhythm, they eventually arrived at their home on the island of her own birth.

Chapter 2

Kleis found it necessary to rest much of the two weeks following her arrival back in her own dwelling. She was exhausted in every limb and had no energy or inclination to move from her bedchamber. She laid in her bed, and her women brought her some food that she found palatable, cool water and soothing oils that they used to massage her aching body.

After a time, though, she found that she wanted to take walks again in the cool morning and evening hours, and so she began to regain some of her strength. She also recalled her desire to visit the temple to make offerings of thanks and ask for protection during this pregnancy. She asked leave of Scamandronymus to make a donation of gold to the temple and made arrangements with Desma to gather other items for a more personal offering to the Goddess herself. It was a day near the full moon, and Kleis wanted to take advantage of this auspicious time for giving to the Goddess.

She rose the next morning and began to make her way with Desma and Scamandronymus toward the temple. Hiera, the sacred site of the temple, sat just across the bay from Mytiline, but the night would be spent near or at the temple for this particular visit. It was for Kleis' safety that Scamandronymus came as well. Nor did he mind that he would be afforded time to worship Aphrodite in his own way with another of the priestesses. Indeed, Kleis' nighttime hours would be spent with Aphrodite's priestesses, though just in what way was not to be foreseen by the first-time mother.

When she arrived at Hiera, she made use of the well to wipe

the dust and sweat from her face, though the roughest portion of the short journey for her had been the patchy crossing of the bay on the ferry and not the short time spent on the road. The cool water on her skin and in her mouth refreshed her and made her feel presentable. She had once spent a great deal of time inside this temple and within the dwellings that were a part of its campus when she was one of its pupils. She knew several of the priestesses personally, having studied with them in their earliest maidenhood trainings. She wondered who would be the priestess who would give her the blessing of the Goddess within the temple, and if she would even know the woman.

She and Desma had brought sweet herbs to throw on the fires and red roses to lay at the feet of the statue within the temple. They had also brought a length of fine blue linen and another length of white silk to present to the priestess of the temple who would wear the face of the Goddess for her this day. As a gift to the temple itself, she brought several pieces of fine gold jewelry, one of which was a bangle she had worn on her wedding day.

The temple was exactly as she had remembered it. Though, in truth, not enough time had passed to warrant much change in a place as timeless as a sacred site. The marble still gleamed; the masonry was as solid as ever. The air within the temple was hung with sweet perfumes and punctuated with the sweeter song of the priestesses who intoned hymns to the golden daughter of Ouranos. Rose petals of every hue were strewn around the altar. Rich gifts and offerings of gold, jewels, and fine fabrics were piled into baskets waiting to be added to the temple treasury. Offerings of food and drink, Kleis knew, would be taken to the storehouse immediately to keep from spoiling. She placed her own gift to the temple within one of the baskets, vaguely wondering which priestess would eventually wear the silk and whether or not the gold would be melted and made into coins or some sacred tool or if it would be kept as jewelry to adorn one of the priestesses during a rite. Of course, it might just as likely be used to trade for the practical necessities required to keep three-thousand priestesses fed and in clothing, to keep the temple's fires and lamps supplied with wood and oil for burning and to provide for all the details of staging sumptuous rituals for the initiates and priestesses. Kleis understood that it didn't matter how the offering had been used, so long as it was given freely and with love to be used however it was needed for the Goddess.

Kleis and Scamandronymus approached the statue of Aphrodite that stood upon the plinth. Desma lingered a few paces behind. The marble figure wore a *peplos* that accentuated the graceful curves beneath while holding a drape that hung loosely from one hand to the floor. The other hand lingered delicately between her throat and breast. Her gaze fell in front of her at the level where her petitioners would stand, as if addressing them directly. Her expression was one of interest and, Kleis thought, sublime intensity. For a moment, Kleis wondered what her husband and servant were thinking as they gazed at this figure, but they were quickly replaced in her mind by the urgency of her own need in coming to this place.

Beautiful Lady, Kleis began to form the prayer in her mind, *you are Daughter, Wife, Mother, Lover and Friend. I come to you, Kypriana, to thank you for the blessing you have given me. You have sent a child into my life, and I already burst with the love I bear her. She is your child, Lady, and I thank you.* She felt her eyes sting and water as she envisioned all the dangers that could snuff out the glittering bliss of motherhood. *I beg of you, Lady, to protect me as I carry this babe. Let her be born healthy and strong. Let no mischance keep me from smiling into her face at the hour of her birth.* Kleis felt as if she had been wrapped in a soft embrace, comforted, and protected. The knowledge formed clearly within her mind that the great function of her life was to bear this child and alter that destiny. She knelt before the altar and offered now the sweetest gift to the Goddess, her tears of thanks and joy and encompassing devotion.

When she was ready to rise, Scamandronymus and Desma helped her to her feet. She went with them to the place where they would be led to individual priestesses for more private devotion. A building adjacent to the temple provided a shaded resting place and a spectacular view of the area from a terrace. Several cushions had been arranged along the terrace for the devotees to sit on as they waited. There were a few other men and women waiting, but not much patience was required today – nor ever, given the number of priestesses in service at so large a temple. Presently, a slave girl with dusky skin and thick, curling black tresses approached them and asked their needs.

Kleis spoke first. "I am here to ask the blessing and protection of the Lady upon my unborn child. Any *hierodule* may serve." *hierodule* was the name for any priestess of the temple, if one did not know her birth name. It was also considered disrespectful to call any priestess by another name while she performed her role in service to the Goddess.

"I am here for private devotion," Scamandronymus began, "and humbly request Timas as *hierodule*." The girl turned and began walking toward a courtyard between the priestess houses, beckoning them to follow. Kleis had forgotten that Timas had always been his choice in priestess. She supposed that some women might be jealous of their husbands paying such passionate respect to the Goddess through the body of one of her chosen women. True, there were mysteries involved of which she would never be fully aware, not being a man; but Kleis herself was trained at this temple and knew the sanctity of touch and ecstasy, and she could not begrudge her own husband his desire to touch the very source of Love and Beauty through the form the priestess.

The people of Lesvos, in general, were aware of the need for this form of divine expression. How else would the temple district here have become so large? In truth, the temple and *thiasos* of Aphrodite on this island were the largest ever founded to that particular Goddess, larger even than that on Korinth. They were so grand, in fact, that they looked and operated more like a small village than a temple. A sacred city.

Most wives of this island had no insecurity regarding their husbands' visits to the temple. They made their own visits and paid honor in the same fashion. If anything, the women of Lesvos had a greater number and more intimate dealings with the temple priestesses than did their men. Women, after all, have more to share with each other than just their bodies.

Kleis remembered Timas from her time as a student at the *thiasos*. Timas had come there a few short years earlier to begin her training. She had just begun her novitiate when Kleis arrived. Kleis remembered the young priestess's voice as being one of the most beautiful she had ever heard from the times when Timas sang for rituals.

The girl ushered Kleis and Desma to smooth stone benches under the shade where they would wait again for a time. Scamandronymus brushed his wife's cheek with his hand and pulled her body close to kiss her before departing. Kleis noted the sweetness of his mouth and the excitement that was growing beneath his *khiton*. He turned to follow the slave into one of the buildings and disappeared within its shadow.

Desma and Kleis sat on the bench and became more aware of all their senses. The beauty of the courtyard pleased their eyes, as did the fresh smell of the nearby sea mixed with the sweet scent of roses from Hiera's gardens. The sun had warmed the smooth, hard stone of the bench and the walkway, and a warm breeze caressed their bare shoulders. They could hear music being played on a lyre and the soft voices of several girls singing, mixed with the gentle rustle of bay leaves and the urgency of someone's lovemaking in a room a little distance down the path. Lately, Kleis had been overwhelmed by sensation to the point of becoming woozy and disoriented. But today, in this place, she found comfort and pleasure in so much food for her senses.

The slave girl returned quickly and led the two women to a private chamber near the rear of the priestess dwellings. The room was not large, but it was furnished with a beautiful copper mirror, a bed with a thick cushion and many pillows and a fresco painting of

Aphrodite holding her son Eros on one wall. There was a basin with a pitcher of water on a table and two clean linen tunicas folded on the bed. "You should wash and change into these. She will be with you soon."

They did so, and soon a priestess was with them. Kleis didn't recognize her. She was tall, with reddish hair streaked from the sun, blue eyes like a forest pool, and creamy smooth skin that seemed to glow and shimmer from the touch of the Goddess. The room was filled with her presence and the scent she wore on her skin. Kleis stood before her and then knelt in reverence. "You bear your first child, daughter of this temple. In the course of a few moons, you will be initiated into the mysteries of motherhood. Now is a time of preparation, and you are in need of protection and also of fellowship. Tonight, in this sanctuary, you will be given such protection and blessing."

Kleis felt at once comforted and excited. The priestesses were going to bless her. "*hierodule*, how shall I prepare for the rite?"

"You have cleaned yourself and put on clean garments. Food will be brought to you soon. Take nourishment for the night ahead. Pregnant women do not fast for purification, though your woman should observe the fast until evening. Rest. We will be awake late into the night, and you will need your strength. Focus on your child, Aphrodite and the bond of women. Beyond that, I will say no more."

Kleis rested and ate and looked forward to the coming evening in anticipation. She had asked about Scamandronymus and was told that her husband would be informed and taken care of. She vaguely wondered what that might mean, but then let the thought slip away. It was enough that he would be happy. Their plans weren't changed in any way, since they had originally thought to spend the night nearby before returning home. So instead of thinking of her husband, she let her mind drift to the life of the growing person inside her, the connection between herself and the women in and around the temple, and the face of Aphrodite as she had always seen her. She drifted in and out of pleasant dreams and stretched on the bed like a cat. When the day had passed, and night was settling around the island, the *hierodule* who had come to her before pushed aside the curtain that hung in the doorway and stepped just inside the room.

She said nothing, but Kleis and Desma both reacted to her presence by rising and preparing to follow her. The priestess wrapped Kleis in a perfumed and soft embrace, then held her at arm's length to look upon her with a smile, as if congratulating a sister on her great joy. Then she turned, and the two women followed the priestess into the night air, through the courtyard and then into a smaller temple than the one they had visited earlier.

The smaller temple had cushions littering the floor and a fog of incense smoke billowing from censers that were suspended from four columns. There was another altar here, and behind it stood a statue of Aphrodite more beautiful than any Kleis had every seen. She had only been allowed in this temple on one or two rare occasions as a student, but she remembered the icon that showed Aphrodite in a tender embrace with a beautiful young woman. The woman wore her hair down, falling gently onto her shoulders, and a *peplos* that left one breast exposed. She had laurels in her hair and her hands rested on Aphrodite's hips. The Goddess herself was covered from the waist down, with her entire torso exquisitely exposed. There were a few columns hung with oil lamps whose glow through the smoke gave the temple a softness that was ethereal. The priestesses were chanting in a rhythm and harmony that almost sent Kleis into a trance. This place felt outside of the bounds of the world as she had always known it, and the women themselves seemed as Goddesses to her. Goddess-Sisters, and she herself was divine.

Chapter 3

Kleis screamed again with the pain. Surely Eileithyria, the Goddess of childbirth, had come to her chamber. But instead of helping her, the laboring woman thought the Goddess must have been torturing her with the flame she carries.

"You'll tire too quickly," the midwife said soothingly. "You must try to rest between pains. Focus on your own breath when the fire comes. Try to open the gate to your womb."

Kleis did not feel comforted by the midwife's reassurances. As the heat of the pain began to ebb away, Kleis felt her energy leaving, too. She sank down into the straw that had been brought to the women's chambers of her home to soak up the blood. She was naked and sweating, her hair frizzy and damp. There was a mixture of awful smells in the room, emanating, she guessed, from her own body. There was incense burning to ward off the evil spirits and, she thought ruefully, *to hide the odor of life coming into the world.* She began to wretch, and she realized she had focused too long on those scents. As she wretched, another pain came upon her. The combination was ferocious. She was sure she would be torn in two. She struggled to catch her breath and felt the spasms and panic of hyperventilation. The midwife put a fragrant oil into a bowl of water and held it under Kleis's nose.

"Inhale this."

Kleis could smell the scent in the water with the sharp intake of her next breath, though she still had no control over her breathing. The water smelled pungent but clean. It looked cool and clear and undisturbed by the struggle for life happening around it. Her chest relaxed as her belly let go of the cramp.

"They are coming soon now," the midwife explained. "This is good. We are getting close to the end."

Close to the end. Kleis could think of nothing in the world that she wanted so much as the ending of this torture. She couldn't imagine how women were expected to do this and survive. She wanted to be done with the pain, done with the wretching, done with the stink. She longed for sleep, even if that sleep would never see a sunrise. She was too exhausted to care.

She slumped into the straw and closed her eyes. She begged for sleep, and something *like* sleep came to her. She felt as though she had been lifted from her own body. She stood up and walked lightly away from the heap of straw where she had been lying. No one seemed to notice that she had stood up and walked away. She couldn't feel the pain of her body, but she could still hear the women talking to her. She could hear her own voice moaning behind her, but she felt no desire to turn and look at the wracked husk that she knew she had momentarily left. In waking, a description of this experience would have seemed lunacy to her. But right now, it made complete sense, as with the logic of dreams.

There was a woman standing in the room with her, one she didn't recognize from the house or as having been one of the midwife's assistants. In fact, this woman looked too clean to have been in the birthing room long. Kleis studied her and was not surprised when the woman met her eyes.

The other woman was beautiful, the most beautiful creature

Kleis had ever seen. She was tall and stately, with cascades of silky, wavy locks. Her eyes were as green as the sea, her skin a golden honey. She smiled. Her lips were the color of coral, and her teeth as white and smooth as pearls. Her smile was like sunshine.

This is no mortal woman. Kleis knelt before her, daring only to look at the pools of blue silk made by the Goddess' *peplos* as it rained down to her feet. "Hail, Aphrodite!"

"I bring you little comfort, though you do me great service." Aphrodite smiled, but offered no apology for the tidings she brought.

"I do not understand." Kleis almost turned to look at her body, but the Goddess touched her cheek to stop the woman's head from moving.

"If you look at yourself lying there, you will immediately be back in the midst of the pain and labor your body is feeling. You have precious little time left with the flesh that struggles in the straw and blood. Stay away from the pain as long as you can," Aphrodite Kypria advised.

"Am I to die in childbed, then?"

Kypriana spoke gently as she asked, "Are you frightened of leaving this place?"

Kleis thought for a moment. Her life was pleasant. Her husband was kind to her, and they had a fondness for each other, but she couldn't say that their love was so consuming that she wanted to brave the torture her body was sure to experience in bearing another baby.

In truth, the horrific labor was no surprise to the midwife,

Kleis or her women when she considered how torturous the entire pregnancy had been. She suffered with nausea throughout most of the nine moons. Her face, feet, and ankles had swollen to grotesque proportions. She had leaked blood and water for the last few days, so that she had suspected she and the baby would not make it through so trying a transition.

"I do not fear leaving. Instead, I fear that I have no reason to stay. I fear that my death will mean little to anyone because my life has meant so little to all but myself."

"Do not judge the value of the thread that is your life. The Fates weave all together in a pattern that you cannot see from where you stand." Aphrodite's eyes hinted at some secret amusement behind the mild reprimand. "Your life makes another life possible. You have made a great sacrifice to bring this daughter into the world."

"If I die, I will not get to hold her," Kleis felt sadness greater than any she had ever known.

"You have held her for nine months, longer and closer than any mother does once her children are born."

"I'll never see her face or hear her laughter. I won't be able to rub my cheek against her downy hair or feel her tiny fingers grasp mine." Kleis felt sorry for all the mothers who had lost their children, for all the mothers who had lost themselves and had never seen their children. "I'll never hear her voice calling me 'Mother' or see her married or hold her babes in my arms."

"Some things I cannot change for you. The Fates will cut your string soon enough, and your grandchildren are many years distant from this time and place. Your child, though, is here with you. You will not die before you see her. You shall not pass without smelling the sweetness of her skin, feeling the softness of her curls or kissing the face of one who will only know you from her dreams. The spirit of your child walks this room and attends on you as you labor to bring her new little body into life. She loves you already, little mother."

Aphrodite indicated the form of a woman who was stroking the hair of the mother struggling in the straw. She was humming a lullaby that Kleis recognized. Her own mother had sung it to her, and she had been humming it incessantly for the last few weeks. The other woman caught Kleis's gaze and kept it. The young woman stood and Kleis felt a swell of pride and love that she had never felt for any other person. Without either of them speaking, she felt she knew something of the spirit of the woman in front of her, her daughter. Kleis looked into her eyes and saw everything she needed to know about the child. In this place outside of place, and this time outside of time, her daughter's clear, dark blue eyes held all the answers.

Something happened in the straw that made both women look down. With the sight of her flesh so close at hand, Kleis felt herself immediately and abruptly reunited with it. She gasped as she felt the intensity of her desire to push. The midwife moved Kleis onto the birthing stool where she squatted and waited for her next chance to bear down. She could barely believe the power of her body's desire to bring forth the life within her, and for the first time in this day and night's long ordeal, her own will was in harmony with that desire. She desperately wanted to look on the face of the child she had just seen. More than her care for her own life, she wanted to hold her precious girl.

The struggle continued, but in time the babe came into the waiting hands of the midwife. Kleis felt the shock and delight at seeing a tiny body emerge between her own legs. The midwife cleared the nose and mouth, and the child gave a great cry as she drew her first stabbing breaths of air. In a moment, the babe was clean, bundled, and lying on her mother's belly. Kleis was looking into the same gemstone eyes that she had just met, and she found all the answers to her life's riddles in their sparkling blue depths.

Kleis nursed her child one time, though she knew Tessa would have that honor and responsibility from now on. She ignored the worried and sad faces of the midwife and her assistant, who knew how badly hurt she was. This was a moment of joy for her, not of sorrow. She kissed her baby's head, cheeks and lips again and again. She touched the soft curls and let them tickle her nose and mouth. She watched the beautiful eyes close in their first rest and then she closed her own eyes for the last time.

Hours later, Scamandronymus held the struggling newborn in his arms as he thought about his wife. Their marriage had not been one built on romance and young, girlish notions. He had come to care for his mate deeply, but he also saw the position of wife as a practical one that needed to be filled by someone in order to run a proper household. Kleis had done well at maintaining the home and keeping charge of the servants. She had been a pleasing lover for him, too. He had thought she would bear many strong sons, as well, but that was not to be. He had lost his young, handsome wife and had been left with nothing more than a baby girl.

Scamandronymus tended to hold the common Athenian view that girl children were of very little use. A father had to provide food, clothing, and shelter to a daughter until she was old enough to bear children. Then, he had to pay some other man to take responsibility for her needs. He knew the people of Lesvos, though, had slightly different views. They sent their girls to be trained at the temples of Aphrodite, Athene, and Artemis, to be educated just like the boys. It seemed a waste of resources to him, to give so much gold to a temple to teach a girl who would probably end up dying in childbed.

He thought of his wife again. Just such a fate had awaited her. Against his better judgment, he felt a twinge of sadness at the thought of her final hours of agony. He looked into the now sleeping face of his infant daughter. *She died giving you life. I should hate you. I should leave you outside tonight to die of exposure. I should have no place in my life for a motherless daughter.* The tiny girl opened her eyes and looked directly into her father's. He couldn't be certain, but he thought he saw a smile. She turned and nuzzled her head against the soft layers of his *khiton*. He sensed a veil had been lifted within his own heart and he seemed to hear a woman speak from an empty cavern there. *Do not be quick to throw away the gifts I give you. A child is a blessing from the Gods. This one is my daughter, as well as yours. Come to my temple and give thanks for the promise I fulfilled.*

Scamandronymus still looked at the tiny form cradled in his arms. He had never held anything so small, so in need of protection.

He would keep her, he knew. The tingle of emotion at the back of his eyes and the back of his throat made him uncomfortable, though. He looked up and saw one of the servants standing near. "Is there a nurse for this child?" Scamandronymus asked.

"Your wife had arranged for Tessa, my sister, to nurse her," the mouse-like woman reported.

"Take the babe to her right away, then," Scamandronymus instructed. He shifted his weight and looked uneasily at the pattern on the border of his *khiton*. "What is my daughter's name?"

The baby fixed her father with a sparkling, dark blue gaze.

"Your wife called her Sappho, sir."

Chapter 4

The day was wet and gray, hard and cold. Heavy, like a stone quickly sinking in a pond. The little girl's spirits were sinking, too. She had been scolded twice for disturbing her stepmother and the baby. She was now shuffling past their room in the *gyneaceum*, the women's quarters, stealing a glance at the woman and infant boy lying together in the bed.

Sappho didn't remember when her father married Damara. In truth, they hadn't been married for long – three years, perhaps. Scamandronymus's young daughter had been old enough to walk, but she only had twenty or so words in her budding lexicon on the night Damara had arrived at their door. Sappho still remembered the iridescence of her stepmother's veil in the torch-lit procession to her new home. Damara had been kind and loved the child more than Scamandronymus had anticipated. She had enjoyed playing with her, and she had delighted in the child's infectious laughter.

Everyone loved Sappho's sweet laugh. The little girl had an enchanting and heart-warming voice. The entire household smiled and cheered when she would sing one of her simple child-songs. Her voice brought them joy, as did the innocent, honest lyrics that she improvised to accompany her simple tunes. Sometimes the women would let their sewing or laundry drop into neat piles to join hands and dance when Sappho began the folk songs that they all remembered from their own childhoods.

The girl typified everything beautiful and joyous about being young. Scamandronymus couldn't think of a single person who didn't love her. Damara had loved her, too, almost like her own child. Scamandronymus had been grateful to his new wife for embracing his daughter so wholly right from the beginning. Indeed, he had been comforted to see that, though Sappho had lost the mother of her flesh within moments of being born, she had two women who had taken her deeply into their hearts.

Damara had fallen ill, though, since the birth of her son. Scamandronymus was starting to suspect that Hera had cursed him by finding wives who seemed healthy but couldn't walk away from their first confinement. Scamandronymus rejoiced in his first son, but he worried for the infant. He didn't seem as robust as little Sappho had been, though he had survived his first month of life already.

The strain of birth and new motherhood were debilitating for the gentle Damara. She was understandably weak for several days after the delivery. The women of the house knew her time hadn't been as tortuous as Sappho's arrival, but they were showing signs of concern that Damara hadn't found her feet again after all this time.

They could be heard talking as they washed the linens and prepared the meals.

"Weak and tender," a plump woman said as she nursed her own baby. Tessa had been employed again as the family's wet nurse. Her own daughter, Atthis, and Sappho had been weaned for the better part of a year, and she had just delivered her second, and probably, last child. "Gentle as a lamb. May the Gods give her the strength to see this one grown."

Another round woman added, "She can't be sick as all that.

Her labor was no worse than my first, and I was back to fetching water and scouring the cook pots long before a month had passed."

Tessa had heard this argument before. It seemed that many of the plain women, those who toiled in the service of the finer houses, mostly as slaves, begrudged the gentle ladies their luxuries and thought them to be weak and whining. Tessa herself had known enough women to die in childbirth or shortly after to see that a wife, in duty to her husband, was frequently called upon to exchange her own life to bring forth the sons of the house. Gentle breeding or rough, no woman truly knew if she would come away from her labor.

Damara was languishing. Whether she had weak resolve or weak constitution, no one could know but her. The fact remained that she was not thriving.

The women were somber as they discussed the probable fate of their mistress. Sadder still was the weakness of her new son. His cry was tenuous and thin, his appetite poor, his movements feeble. The women felt sure the child would not survive the winter.

Sappho found herself being shushed by the adults, or being nudged out of doors to play with Atthis. On a pleasant day, she and her playmate would sing and dance and race through the courtyard. Sometimes they would be allowed to go to the orchard, which was a short distance from the house and in plain view of the entrance, where they would pick apples and swing from the lower branches. But today was no day for sunshine and songs, and Sappho felt the sinking stone of the household's happiness within the pit of her own stomach.

Looking into the room as she skulked past, she saw Damara

adjusting the blanket around the baby. She stood in the doorway and watched, trying to see her brother's tiny, wrinkled face. Sappho thought he looked like an old man, somehow, which was wonderful to her. The toothless, bald, squinting boy was fascinating and strange. She longed to hold him, to stroke the silky smooth arms and inspect the miniature fingernails.

Damara saw Sappho watching her and could feel the longing that welled up in the young girl. "Come, daughter," she beckoned weakly. "Come sit with us."

Sappho was giddy at the invitation, but also timid. She hadn't been permitted to come very close to her stepmother or to her baby brother in several days. In such close proximity she could see how thin they both were, and she was frightened. The baby slept without moving, and the young child suddenly feared something was wrong.

"Are you sick, Damara?" she asked frankly.

"Perhaps," was the response. "I feel very tired. Too tired."

"Is Doran sick?"

"I do not know," tears welled in the woman's eyes as she thought about her helplessness in strengthening her child. She felt something was wrong with him, but she had no way of healing the problem.

"May I kiss him?"

Damara gave a nod and Sappho leaned on her elbows over her brother's forehead. He smelled sweet and milky, and she could feel the little fine hairs on his skin. His mouth twitched and his nose wrinkled, but he didn't wake up.

Sappho lay on the blankets next to Damara and Doran for a long time. Sappho watched her brother's chest rise and fall in the rhythmic pattern of sleep and saw, after a short time, that Damara had drifted back to sleep as well. Then, she crept off the bed and out of the room. Sappho was quiet and spent the remainder of the day watching the raindrops splatter on the stones and pebbles of the courtyard from a protected spot under an awning. It seemed to her that the Gods and Goddesses tiled into the floor's mosaic wept for her baby brother.

Doran died within a week, and the fire in the family's hearth was extinguished as Scamandronymus and his household mourned the loss of his firstborn son. Damara gave up any hope of leaving her bed, and died within another month. Tessa told the young girl only that her stepmother had become very ill and that she died because they didn't know the right medicine to cure her. Sappho need never know that Damara had sunken into a depression so black that nothing in her life held any joy for her, until finally she refused to eat and would drink only enough water to moisten her lips. When it had become clear that the woman would never recover herself, one of the women of the house made her a tea that would help her body die. Damara had taken it gratefully and blessed the woman for her mercy.

Little Sappho mourned the loss of her brother and stepmother. Damara had been a kind and loving mother to her, and the young child felt the loss very sharply. She often wept in Tessa's lap for the gentle lady who would not return.

Eventually, the family made a sacrifice and brought a burning ember from the civic fire to rekindle their hearth's flame.

Scamandronymus and Sappho bathed and put on clean clothes, and turned their faces back toward life. As Sappho's tears began to dry, her smiles and songs returned. She played every day with Atthis and the household's other children and spoke less and less of Damara. Only occasionally, when the rain streaked the colored pebbles of the courtyard mosaic, did she become melancholy and cry for the second mother she lost.

Chapter 5

Tessa's dwelling was a room in Scamandronymus's house. Small, with a doorway into the courtyard. It was on the ground level and across from the store room. Big enough for Tessa and her two children, Atthis and Nilo, a boy of about a year. Her husband had lived there with her since the time Tessa had been brought to nurse Sappho. He had worked in Scamandronymus's house from that time until his death over a year ago. A fever had seized him before the birth of his only son.

The room was furnished with one plain bed where Tessa slept with both children. It also had a chair, a stool, a small table with a jar that the small family used for keeping water on hand from the well in the courtyard, and a wooden bowl and plate. Some herbs and flowers hung from the rafters, a few that Tessa used frequently – to bring calm and sleep, to ease a headache, to clear the mind. There were a few less common ones that she found comforting to keep on hand. They had a few blankets on the bed, and a heavier one folded in a wooden box without a lid where their few garments and linens were stored.

An oil lamp sat on the table, its small flame offering a warm but weak light in the coming darkness of the settling night. Tessa sat near the flame, adding a few stitches to the *peplos* she was making from a fabric woven in the house last month. She had been given a length of the beautiful green wool that was easily long enough to produce garments for both her and Atthis, perhaps with some remaining that could be used later in striking contrast with another remnant to make a *peplos* or *khiton*. Tessa looked at her daughter and thought that such a cloth paired with a rose-colored piece would be very becoming on the young girl. For now, though, a plain green would suffice.

Atthis and Sappho were sitting together on a woven straw mat, playing a game they had invented with a few pebbles and a pair of crossed sticks. Atthis shrieked with victory and both girls laughed as they quickly gathered their stones for another match.

"Before you start again," Tessa got their attention, "Atthis, come here. I need to check the fit of this *peplos*."

The girl came obediently but kept her face turned toward her game. Her mother quickly stripped the child of the bright yellow she had been wearing and replaced it with the green. Sappho watched and saw the way the other girl's dark curls tumbled over the vibrant green fabric.

"It's too long, Mama," the little girl laughed as she wiggled inside her tent. "And too wide. I'll trip on the edge and the whole thing will fall off."

Tessa produced a length of slender rope from a pouch made by the folds of her clothing. "This will keep your clothes in place," she said as she cinched the girl's tiny waist. "If we pull up the fabric here," she tugged until Atthis had a pouf of fabric around her middle, "this garment can grow with you. See here?" She pinched the seams that fell on either side of Atthis' slender neck. "You can move your *fibulae* father out each time you require more room."

Atthis walked and then danced around the table, admiring the touch and movement of her new clothes. Sappho couldn't resist the opportunity to dance, too, and grabbed her friend's hand. Tessa clapped a simple beat for part of a minute before changing Atthis back into her yellow peplos.

"And in a year or so, if you take care not to rip or sully the fabric," Tessa grinned, "we can add a border pattern at the hems."

"A year? Why can't I have it now?"

"In a year, my impatient one, you will be old enough that I may teach you and Sappho to mix the dyes and apply them so they'll last." Tessa was folding the fabric to store in the box.

The girls talked about the patterns they liked best, comparing the ones worn by various women in Scamandronymus's house and beyond. They didn't generally see a great deal of pattern and trim on the clothes worn within the house, though, because most of the women who lived here were slaves. Scamandronymus's mother had lived with her other son in Athens, and both of Scamandronymus's wives had died. Damara had worn several lavishly decorated *khitons* and other garments, as had the women who had come to visit with her during the day. Sappho vaguely wondered what would become of Damara's beautiful clothes now that she was no longer here to wear them.

They were drawing patterns with rocks on the plain stone floor, the scratches barely visible in the shadows, when Tessa suggested it was time to take Sappho to her room to sleep. Both girls groaned in response.

"May she stay with us, Mama?" Atthis clung to her mother's skirts and petted her arm. The five-year-old's attempt at persuasion produced a barely repressed grin on her mother's face.

"It is more proper that she goes to her own room, where the women of the family sleep," Tessa instructed.

"She slept here with us when Damara was ill," Atthis countered.

"That was different, my dear. Damara needed her rest, and Sappho didn't sleep in their room so that she could have it."

Sappho looked forlorn and very small as she said, "Please, Tessa. My father won't care. I'm so lonely in that room. It frightens me."

Tessa thought about the deserted *gyneaceum* and her little ward sleeping there alone. It seemed cruel to force her to go to sleep in the room where her mother, stepmother and brother all died with no other female relatives close by to teach her how life continues. She pictured the room, darkened by the night, kissed by the cold moonlight. In this vision of the chamber, she saw little Sappho, looking smaller and more timid than she ever had in reality, peering out from under the rim of a blanket, shivering from the chill of midnight and the touch of pretended ghosts.

Sappho, of course, shared Tessa's and Atthis's bed that night. As they fell asleep, Sappho lying between Atthis and her mother, the girls held hands and whispered childish secrets, taking turns to stroke and twirl each other's hair.

Scamandronymus had no objection to his daughter's new sleeping arrangement. In truth, he only cared that Tessa took care of the girl and presented her properly before guests, when necessary. And so Sappho continued to spend both days and nights with Atthis. She kept her clothes and other belongings in her own room and would often nap there during the day, but she spent the long hours of the night in the warmth and protection of her nurse's modest chamber.

Her days took on a comfortable cadence and she found herself comforted by their predictable rhythm. She would wake in the morning and break the night's fast in the open air of the courtyard with Tessa and the other servants. Tessa would then bring her one of her simple garments for everyday wear, if it was a bathing day, while Sappho washed and splashed in the bathing pool in the courtyard. Atthis would sit on the stone floor next to the water and splash her friend, and sometimes she would join her. Cleanliness was very important in Scamandronymus's house, and even the servants bathed themselves on a regular basis, though not as frequently as their masters. Of course, neither child thought about the significance of the bath or the luxury of having it in their own house. They were far too involved in their game of the nymphs drowning Hylas, played in this case by a broken jug that produced a satisfying gurgle of strangled bubbles as it succumbed to its watery grave. If not Hylas and the nymphs, they were Scylla and Kharybdis destroying ill-fated leaf-boats in their frenzy.

The girls would spend the morning in the courtyard in lively play or conversation, inasmuch as childish prattle can pass for conversation, or else they would create games out of stones, twigs or whatever materials they could sneak out of the kitchen or away from the women as they sewed. A favorite game of theirs, when such supplies were guarded too closely for capture, was to imitate the adults of the house. Atthis was particularly good at this sport. Being a bit older than her friend meant that she had a sharper eye for the details of a person's manner and a keener sense of which gestures or phrases to impersonate.

On one such day, the girls pretended themselves to be two servants of the house. They began as Cook and Kastor, shooing imaginary children out of one area of the courtyard and alternately scolding and petting them until the invisible babes found fresh trouble and punishment.

The cook was a big woman with a shrill voice that sounded like tree branches scraping the side of the house in a storm. Worse than that, her meals were plain and not very good, and she tended to scold the girls if they even looked in her direction. This made her an easy target of impersonation for one of Atthis' performances.

Atthis was savvier than her friend, due mostly to an age difference of almost a year, but cleverness in a young girl still has its limits. For one thing, her impression of the cook was fairly unoriginal and missed many of the nuances that the adult servants in the house chose to mock. She widened her stride into a waddle and mock-scolded Sappho in the squeakiest falsetto she could muster. "Eat that fish, girl. I don't care if still looks grey. Take it and stay out!" Of course, Sappho laughed, being a fairly undiscriminating critic, and so Atthis had pleased her audience.

Where the lack of maturity was most evident in her mockery of the cook was not in the fact that she dared to mock her, or even that she did it clumsily, but rather that she did it at a distance not far enough removed from the kitchen. So, as Sappho's laugh halted and Atthis turned around, she was met by the narrow eyes and flustered cheeks of her humorless target.

"We'll see about that," she huffed as she marched off to find Tessa.

Tessa frowned. "Smart girls need more to do than find or make trouble in the house," she said. "I must give those little hands and minds something to do, though I can't expect much refinement in your work. With work of your own to do, you might value the talents of the women you seem so keen to mock."

With that, she produced two coarse pieces of linen and broken chunks of beeswax. She conducted the girls to the hearth and broke the beeswax into smaller pieces that she then melted in a bowl close to the fire. When the wax was soft enough, she scooped some out of the vessel with a thin, flat, smooth, wooden tool. She used this same instrument to spread the wax in an even band along the edge of the fabric before having each of the girls do the same to their own pieces of linen.

"Now, you must choose a design," she prompted. "Practice scratching it on the flagstones, as you do when you play."

The girls did as they were told, excited to be doing the work of the grown women. Tessa had them focus on simple designs like block-waves and straight line patterns, unlike the complicated patterning of experienced women. They spent much of the afternoon practicing their patterns on stone before carving them carefully into the waxed linen. Eventually, Tessa called an end to the lesson and the girls were sent back to their play while she went to help prepare the evening meal.

The girls' education in resist dyeing continued every

afternoon. They watched Tessa mix the dye and demonstrate the best ways to cover the exposed fabric in the wax. They followed all the steps to treat and remove the wax masking until they had finally dyed their first crude scraps. Then, they began the process again from the start. As they took breaks from their work, they would admire the swift agility of Tessa's hands and the intricacy and contrast of the patterns she created.

After the third set of dyed scraps were finished, Tessa taught the girls to make the simple lines that would form the base of a new design. This time, Sappho and Atthis were not etching into the wax on a shred of leftover linen, but instead they were being allowed to work on a very fine, rose-colored piece.

"This piece is big, Tessa," Sappho stated as she and Atthis scooped melted wax from the jar. "Too big to be a scrap to throw away after we have practiced on it."

"That is true," Tessa smiled in a way that made Sappho think she had a secret.

"But, Tessa, it's too small for a *peplos*. What will you make from this piece?"

Tessa kept her secret and her smile and only said, "Oh, a piece like this can be used for many things. Drape it one way, it's a *khiton*. Wear it around your shoulders, and it's a *himation*. Twist it around your waist, and it's a sash. Don't look too far ahead in the process." She walked over to inspect their work and said, "Just be careful about making your part clear and even."

The rose linen became quite an on-going project for Tessa and the girls. Tessa taught them how she made a complicated pattern with many lines, shapes, and colors, by working with one line and one color at a time.

When Tessa was satisfied with the dye-work, which covered a large swath along the fabric's edge, she began teaching the girls to work a pattern with needle and thread. Again, the girls were handed scraps of linen or wool and shown how to make two or three basic stitches. They filled their pieces of fabric with line after line of stitches, struggling to make them neat, even, and small. For weeks, they spent their afternoons making lines and chains, first practicing straight lines and then following simple waves and curves that Tessa marked on the fabric. As they got more secure in working the needles, Sappho would tell stories and sing songs, and Tessa would work on other embroidery.

When their stitches were reliable enough, Tessa laid the rose linen before them again. "Do you see this horizontal line here?" She pointed to a bold stripe and then to a narrow one. "And this one? Use this green thread to make a line along the top of each. It's just a straight line, remember. Nothing too difficult."

Again the girls spent weeks adding accents of colored thread to the dyed pattern. The season changed as they worked. The days got longer, hotter, heavier. Some days they left their project lying in its basket and went with the rest of the household to the festivals in honor of the Gods and Goddesses. During other days, Scamandronymus would claim the role of priest in his home, as was his right, and make an offering or sacrifice at the household shrine in the courtyard. And on some other days, the two girls were content to sit in the shade of the courtyard and make up new adventures about the famous heroes of by-gone days.

The last touches of embroidery were made from a golden thread that Tessa used to accent certain shapes in the great design. "Do you remember how this fabric began when I first brought it before you?" she asked the girls as she finished her work.

"It was plain rose," offered Atthis, a little unsure of the type of response her mother sought.

"I can barely remember how that looked, though. It's so different now," Sappho observed.

"Yes, little ones. We've taken this linen and made it into something more than it once was. Now, it is hard to imagine it as anything else." Tessa regarded Sappho closely and said, "Our lives change like that, too – woven by the Fates into a pattern we can't always guess when we see the plain linen or even the first line."

Sappho tried to understand the woman's meaning, but couldn't get past thinking of the beautiful fabric in front of her. "Do you know yet what garment this will be?"

"And more," said Tessa. "I know who will wear it and on what day."

The girls looked at each other and then back at Tessa as she unfolded the other two fabrics she had embroidered and dyed while they worked on this one. With pins, she secured a long blue *khiton* onto Sappho, clasping it above each shoulder. Then, she draped the rose linen over one shoulder and clasped in place under the other arm. The last piece was nearly sheer, a fine, misty green with shells bordering one edge. This, she carefully placed on Sappho's head with the rim of shells framing her face and providing a type of ballast to keep the veil balanced and in place.

Sappho was stunned. It was too beautiful. "For me? Why?"

"Because, dear one, on the next full moon, you must wear something appropriate to your father's wedding."

Chapter 6

Sappho had no idea how to react to the news of her father's impending marriage, and so she gave no reaction whatsoever. She was too young to understand how the adults hoped, or feared, she would respond. In all reality, the only person in the house who worried about Sappho's reaction was her nurse. To everyone else, the little girl's feelings were of very little consequence. Scamandronymus needed to remarry, a suitable wife had been arranged, and the emotions of a daughter from a previous marriage had no place in the decision.

Tessa was concerned for her little charge, though. This would be the third mother that Scamandronymus had provided for his only living child – fourth, if Tessa herself was to be considered. She knew Sappho would adjust with the ease that only a small child could demonstrate, but she also knew that too much had changed in the young girl's life already. She watched carefully for any reaction that the girl may have given, but was surprised to see very little. In truth, the closest that Sappho came to expressing her displeasure or concern was in her newfound ambivalence toward her beautiful clothes, which she no longer wanted to look at or try on.

Three days before the ceremony would begin, Tessa asked Sappho to wear the clothes again so she could check the length and be certain she had the ties and pins to fasten the garments properly. As she wrapped the fabrics around the little girl's frame, she noted the question in the child's eyes that was stubbornly refusing to form itself on her lips.

"How do you like these wedding clothes, little one?" Tessa smiled softly.

"Oh," Sappho was shaken from her reverie by the question. "They are wonderful – the most beautiful things I have ever had."

"And how do you like the reason for having them?" Tessa prodded.

"The wedding?" Her nurse nodded. The words were hiding from the child. She was afraid, though she didn't know what frightened her. She was sad and angry, though she didn't recognize her own melancholy and anger or the place inside herself that bred them. "I don't know." She still searched for the words to go with the fleeting shards of thought and emotion that filled her and felt her frustration rise at being unable to grasp the situation. As she felt assaulted by the icy heat of her confusion, she found it even more impossible to make sense of her apprehension.

"You have never seen an entire wedding," Tessa interrupted the tempestuous stream of thought coursing through the girl, and Sappho was glad for a new thought on which to focus. "You were present at your father's marriage to Damara, though you were far too young to recall it. For the other weddings that have happened in this town, you have been present only at the procession and the marriage feast."

"There is more to the wedding?" Sappho asked, the flush of her anger subsiding as she engaged in the dialogue.

"Oh, by Hera! There is so much more," began Tessa's explanation as she continued pinning and draping the fine fabric around Sappho. "A wedding takes three days to complete. The bride must go from being a child in her father's house to being the mistress of her husband's house. Such a process doesn't happen in one afternoon."

Tessa explained that the first day of the wedding rituals would focus entirely on the bride and her family. Anassa, the girl who was to become Sappho's second stepmother, would make a sacrifice of her childhood toys and garments at the ceremony called the *proaulia*. Her father would hold a feast in his home, and Anassa would offer the things of her childhood to the Gods and Goddesses whom she hoped would provide her with blessings in her new life.

"This is for two reasons," Tessa explained. "First, she is no longer a child and no longer needs the effects of her childhood. Second, she will want to ask Hera, Aphrodite, and Artemis to show her the way from child to woman." The older woman did not expect Sappho to understand the meaning behind what she said. It was enough to say it and know the girl would understand later.

The next day would be the *gamos*, the wedding day. On that morning, the bride would rise and be given a special bath in the women's quarters of her father's home. A certain child would carry the water for her bath in a type of vase that was only used for funerals and weddings. As the bride washed herself in this special bath, she would be purified by the water and made fertile so she could conceive and bear children.

Anassa would have a special woman, a relative and friend, who helped her with her tasks this day. This helper would assist the bride in putting on her new clothes, including her veil, which would obscure her face and form to the gazing eyes of her groom and the wedding guests.

With the veil secure, and her maid and female relatives leading her to the banquet hall in her father's home, Anassa would join the guests and her groom, Scamandronymus. Both Anassa and Scamandronymus would make sacrifices to Hera and Zeus for a strong and fertile marriage, to Aphrodite for joy and love between bride and groom, and to others besides. Their friends and families would join them in the feast and then watch as Anassa was unveiled and the couple began their procession to Scamandronymus's home.

Tessa explained that when Anassa and Scamandronymus reached their home, certain guests would stay in the house while the new couple spent their first night together. Scamandronymus would have chosen a man to stand guard at the door of the bridal chamber, and the unmarried women would stay awake all night and sing songs to help her be unafraid.

The third day would be the last day of the wedding ceremony, called the *epaulia*. The guests would give gifts to make Anassa comfortable in her new role as wife. Some gifts were blessings from the Gods; others were household conveniences.

"What do I do during these ceremonies?" Sappho asked.

"You will stay with the women during the feast, help us sing the songs, wear your new clothes and garlands of flowers," Tessa said. "You have a very important job, Sappho. You are the only member of your father's family who is still alive. You represent the good wishes and blessings of his entire family, whose blood is in your veins. Be clean, be beautiful, and be happy so he will know he has the blessing of his family and so Anassa knows she is being welcomed."

Sappho pondered these instructions and tried to set her will to work so she could accomplish them. She wasn't sure how so small a girl could perform all duties had just been asked of her, but she would try.

The household was busy with the preparations for the wedding, and before Sappho had time to take account of what was happening, she found herself in the banquet hall of Anassa's father. She was sitting with the women and girls, most of whom were dressed finely, with veils covering their hair and shoulders and golden jewelry shining from their wrists and throats. Libations had been made, as well as the animal sacrifice upon which they were now feasting. Sappho had been nibbling at her honey-sesame cake and listening to the singers who had been hired to entertain the guests. She had always been so fond of music, and she enjoyed hearing one musician compare her father and his bride to Zeus and Hera. Her father had always seemed powerful and important, and, though she hadn't yet seen her face, Sappho thought Anassa carried herself in a way that did credit to her name, which meant "queen."

The girl had spent a great deal of time during the feast trying to appraise her young stepmother, though her bridal veil and the thick company of guests made accurate judgments difficult, if not impossible. Anassa wasn't a delicate, fragile-looking woman despite her obvious femininity. She moved with grace and surety, and Sappho thought she noticed a change in the way her father stood or inclined toward her when Anassa stood near him.

By the end of the feast, Sappho was drowsing and ready for

her bed. She was immediately awakened, though, when Anassa's father stood and prepared to give his daughter to her groom before all their witnesses. He urged a young boy to come forward and begin disbursing bread to the guests from a basket he had carried.

Tessa whispered in Sappho's ear. "This boy stands in place of the son your father wishes to have with his wife. The bread the boy gives them also represents a baby being carried in the basket-cradle."

Anassa's father took her by the hand and said, loudly to Scamandronymus, "I give you this girl, in front of these witnesses, for the bearing of legitimate children." With these words, Scamandronymus seized his bride's wrist and followed the boy, the man chosen as guard to the couple, and Anassa's mother who was bearing a torch close to her daughter as if warding off attackers. They all climbed inside a wooden cart and were drawn through the streets toward Scamandronymus's house.

"I thought she would take off her veil," Sappho was almost whining with her impatience to see her stepmother's face.

"Sometimes here, sometimes later," was Tessa's answer. "We will see her at your father's house."

As the crowd walked through the streets, they sang loudly and carried their torches high to fight back the night and any evil that might offer to upset the union of bride and groom. Women carried vases filled with fruits and flowers that the guests would use to throw at the bride as she moved toward her new home.

As they reached the front wall of Scamandronymus's house, a great cry erupted from the assembled crowd – a great relief that the couple had endured their journey and were about to begin their lives as mates. It was during this paean when Tessa took Sappho to the door of her home and gave her quick instructions, "It is your duty to welcome your father's bride to the home and family. Normally, his mother would do this, but that cannot be."

At first, Sappho was stricken dumb. She stood at the gate of the house facing her father and Anassa, but nobody had noticed her yet. Then, as Scamandronymus lifted Anassa from the cart and led her toward the place where Sappho stood, the girl found her voice, small but strong within her. "I am the family of Scamandronymus, and I welcome you to this home." Anassa knelt to kiss Sappho in acceptance of the welcome, and, although Sappho couldn't see her through her veil, she felt dizzy with the fragrance of roses and some other sweet oils that lingered upon Anassa's skin.

Tessa pressed a quince into Sappho's palm, which she in turn offered to Anassa.

Chapter 7

Anassa was used to living in a house with several female relatives. She had come from her father's home where she had a sister, her own mother and paternal grandmother, and her father's *pallake* and her daughter. The women's quarters at her father's house were always bustling, always active. Women were continually coming to visit from other households, and there was always a flurry of needlework and gossip.

The young bride had also received her training at the temple of Aphrodite at Hiera. She had spent a few years there, learning the wifely arts and making friendships with the other girls in her *demos*. To say she was lonely in Scamandronymus's house would have been an understatement. The women's quarters were nearly empty with only the shades of the women who had come before sitting in the chairs and couches during the day. Luckily, as a newlywed, she rarely slept in the women's quarters at night.

Anassa expected Sappho to stay with her during the day, and she also enjoyed the company of Tessa and Atthis as they sat in the cool *gynaeceum* or in the shade of the courtyard. "Once I have borne a healthy son, I would not object to Scamandronymus acquiring a *pallake* wife so there is more company," she was heard to joke on more than one occasion.

The girl was fertile, too, because within a moon or two, she was indeed pregnant. Scamandronymus had chosen well in picking his bride. She was no fluttering flower that swooned and sweltered under the influence of her swelling body's rapid changes. Instead, she seemed to blossom and become more invigorated while the new life grew inside her.

With the cool of the autumn settling in, Tessa and Anassa chatted freely as they worked. Sappho and Atthis sometimes listened, sometimes talked quietly in another part of the room, and often practiced the new stitches or decorative techniques demonstrated by the grown women.

Listening to her stepmother, Sappho started thinking of the world as a place that existed outside of the walls of her own house. She had seen very little beyond the high walls of her own home, and she was curious about the few places the women went. Typically, the daughters and wives of a house were only permitted to visit with the wives and daughters of other respectable homes. Sappho had gone to the marketplace once or twice with Tessa, but she had never had a mother to take her to visit at someone else's home. She had been to a few of the festivals, but only the ones where children were permitted. She had never gone to a village or city outside of Mytiline.

Anassa seemed so well-traveled and experienced to young Sappho. She had engaged in the typical female visits in the *gynaecea* of other homes, which wasn't extraordinary in itself but seemed interesting to the little girl who had never had that simple pleasure. Unlike most other women, though, Anassa had been taught to read and write, to discuss politics and poetry, to cultivate beauty in herself and her home in ways that one can only learn from the Goddess of Beauty and her priestesses.

Sappho thought Anassa should have been a priestess of Aphrodite. She was beautiful, graceful, generous, endearing, and charming. Sappho watched her much of the time. She tried to move like her, walk like her. Even pregnant, Anassa moved with a grace and fluidity that seemed uncommon to Sappho, who had primarily been given servants and slaves as her examples of feminine carriage.

Sappho had noticed Atthis watching Anassa as well. She even caught her friend trying to emulate the way Anassa walked. Sappho couldn't exactly copy the walk either, but she knew it involved the hips in a way that the other women in the house had never attempted. Atthis had been embarrassed at first at having been seen, but Sappho's ready admittance of her inability to do it set her at ease. Together, they retreated to the far corner of the courtyard and practiced, advised, and giggled the remainder of the afternoon.

Anassa was also a talented and trained musician. She could sing like a nightingale, Sappho thought, and accompany herself effortlessly with the lyre. When Anassa would tire with her embroidery, she would frequently sing or tell stories of the Olympians and heroes. Sappho never tired of these and frequently asked her stepmother to retell her favorites.

"The Kyprian, golden Aphrodite, has forever been hailed most beautiful," Anassa would begin. "Neither mortal man nor immortal God is able to deny her charms. Her husband, the forge-master and patron of handicrafts, Hephaestus, once made her a golden sash that only adds to her powers of seduction. When she wears this sash between her breasts, no man or woman may reject her."

"She liked men *and* women?" Atthis asked incredulously.

"Of course," Anassa said simply. "The Goddess of Beauty

sees what is beautiful in both men and women. And the Goddess of Love is capable of loving both equally well."

As Atthis pondered this idea, Sappho accepted it readily and turned her attention again to Anassa, who had resumed her story.

"Aphrodite, like many of the other Gods, was married. Also like many of the other Mighty Ones, She chose to have many lovers. One of the most famous and long-standing of these was war-like Ares."

Now it was Sappho's turn to ask questions. "Why would the Goddess of Love choose the God of War? I don't understand."

"Ah," Anassa smiled secretively, "this is a Mystery that many do not understand. As you grow, though, I am sure you will see how closely love and war are linked. The greatest war ever fought was waged over the love of one woman – Helen, who served Aphrodite."

"Helen was a priestess of Aphrodite?" Sappho asked.

"Oh dear, yes! How could Aphrodite give to Paris something that was not hers to give? And later, Aphrodite commanded Helen to obey her in showing love and devotion to Paris. But I will tell you Helen's story some other day. Today, I speak of the net that ensnared the undying lovers.

"Hephaestus knew of Aphrodite's affair with Ares, and he was hurt and angry that she wanted anyone but him. He was so hurt, in fact, that he wanted her father Zeus to reclaim his daughter and return the gifts Hephaestus had made at the time of their wedding. Zeus would hear nothing of it, saying there was no proof. So the great master of the forge devised a web to entangle his wife and her paramour in the throes of their passion. His device worked perfectly, and he was easily able to capture them. Once in the net, they were unable to move.

"Hephaestus gathered the gods of Olympos together to show them the proof of his wife's infidelity and demand that Zeus dissolve his marriage to her. This plan was amiss, though, as the Gods didn't really care about these infidelities when they didn't affect them directly. They laughed at Hephaestus because he wasn't enough for his wife, and they laughed at Aphrodite and Ares for getting caught. Aphrodite and Ares were angry at their humiliation but vindicated that they were not punished. However, Hephaestus felt the most intense sting of the humiliation he had wished on his wife and her lover.

"As the Olympians were leaving, Apollo told Hermes that he thought Ares was the biggest fool, to risk such humiliation just to satisfy his carnal desire. Hermes, though, watching Aphrodite don her multi-colored, sheer garments and seeing the absolute beauty and perfection in her form and face, said that He would gladly brave such a humiliating display to lie with her just once."

Sappho liked this story, though she didn't understand all of it. The concept of lying with anyone had little meaning for her. She knew only a little of what it involved, having heard the servants of the house coupling with their mates or lovers in the late hours when she was sharing Tessa's room. As best she could tell, the men and women wanted something from each other. By the guttural sounds of their voices, she thought they wanted something desperately. And, when she stayed to hear the ending, the contentment they voiced let her know they had found whatever it was they were seeking.

Of course, their love-making sounded silly to the little girl, as well as sounding desperate. *Maybe that's why Aphrodite and Ares were embarrassed at being caught*, she thought, *because they were doing something silly and everyone saw them.* She reflected on this for a moment and thought of her stepmother. *She is beautiful like Aphrodite. If she wanted me to look silly in front of other people because it made her happy, I would do it.*

That night as they readied for bed, Sappho told Tessa about her simple interpretation of the story. The older woman smiled and said, "Yes, she is very enchanting – and very strong. Your father made a good choice. She will bear children and be a good wife. He is also very lucky because she is so much like his first wife."

"My mother?" asked Sappho.

"Yes, child. Your mother." When Sappho wondered in what way Anassa was like her mother, her nurse explained that Scamandronymus had cared very much for his first bride. He had married because it was the right thing to do, but he had been very fortunate in his choice. Kleis had also been schooled at the temple of Aphrodite across the bay, and she had been trained and taught the ways to love her husband. More than that, though, they had felt a connection in their hearts. Kleis had understood Scamandronymus, Tessa thought, in a way that none other had done in his life. When she died, he grieved for her more than most men do.

"Why does he never mention her?" Sappho asked.

"I imagine that he doesn't wish to appear weak," Tessa explained gently. "It wouldn't be fitting for him to pine for a woman that has been gone so long – not to just anyone."

"But I'm not *just anyone*. I'm his daughter."

"And in his care. He wouldn't want you thinking he was too weak to provide for you or make strong decisions on your behalf," advised Tessa. "Men do not always show their feelings, though you may see them if you have the eyes to see."

"I do have eyes," said Sappho, "and I have never seen what you say is in my father."

"Your eyes see only the exterior of things. Look deeper," Tessa was now looking Sappho directly in the eyes. "Have you seen your father pray and make libations at the family altar ?"

"How could I not?" remarked the child, a little stung at the realization that her nurse might know more about her own father than she. "The altar is in our courtyard, and he makes the prayers and libations there all the time."

"Have you noticed the times when he buries flowers or food in the earth near the altar?" The child nodded, very curious now. "Those are gifts for the dead. We bury our gifts for those who are in the Underworld, in Hades' realm. They hunger and thirst, and through the earth we can quench them." Sappho nodded. She had heard this before. "Your father has many dead to provide for now. His own mother and father, his brother who died the year you were born, Damara and Doran, and your mother. When you see your father bury a hyacinth, he is remembering your mother. She loved the purple of that flower."

Sappho lay in bed for a long time that evening, thinking of her father and the fact that he had genuinely loved her mother. *And she died in bringing me to him. It is no wonder he doesn't show me his grief. My own sorrow is as strong as his, though. At least he had her for a time.* And as she slid into her dreams, she saw herself burying a purple flower in remembrance of her mother.

Chapter 8

Anassa had married Scamandronymus at the end of the summer and had conceived shortly after. She spent the winter and most of the spring watching her body change and continually making adjustments to her balance because of her girth. When the summer was just starting to erupt around the island, Anassa delivered a healthy son whose lusty cries erupted throughout the house at all hours of the day and night. Though the entire household found themselves wakened several times a night in the beginning of Kharaxus 's life, nobody was upset at the disruption of their sleep. In fact, they were all too happy to hear the little master's call.

The only person in the home who didn't react with exuberant joy was Tessa. Truthfully, she was happy for Kharaxus 's arrival, but she was too tired for any happiness. Tessa had become sick in the winter, and even when the fever passed her energy didn't return. She rested more through the day than she had ever done, and she relied more on Atthis and Sappho to help her with needlework and caring for Nilo, Atthis' little brother. Nilo was just over two years old, and he was constantly finding trouble that Tessa didn't have the will to remedy.

On a bright, warm day, Tessa asked the girls to help her back to her room. When she lay down on the bed, she held the girls' hands tight and had them sit on her bed next to her. "You are big girls," she said to the two little worried faces staring back at her. Tessa fought tears and struggled to keep her voice steady as she said, "I ...when ...." She sighed heavily. "I know very few ways to tell you what you must know. I've waited so long. It was unfair of me."

Apprehension gripped Sappho. Atthis began, "Mother …"

"Darlings, I don't want you to worry. What I am experiencing is nothing to fear."

"Then why do you cry?" observed Sappho.

Tessa gave a grudging little laugh. "I cry because I will miss you, both of you, and Nilo."

"Where are you going?" Atthis begged. "Why can't we come with you?"

Tessa squeezed their hands more tightly. "You will come to me someday, dear ones, but not yet. I would not want for your journey in this place to end so soon."

"Where does your journey take you, Tessa?" Sappho asked.

"Across the river Styx, into Hades's land. I will join my mother and yours, and I will wait for you."

Sappho thought Tessa was very strong to tell them that she was dying. Atthis wept openly, but Sappho wanted to show this woman, who had been more of a mother to her than any other she had known, that she too could be strong. So, she saved her tears for a time when she could shed them freely, and she stroked her nurse's hair until the woman gave into her exhaustion and fell asleep with her own daughter curled beside her.

Sappho went to courtyard and knelt at the altar there. She dug a little hole next to it and whispered her mother's name as she poured water and honey into the tiny pit. "Kleis! Mother! The mother you left me with is coming back to you. Show her the ways of the strange world of the dead. Comfort her as she loses her children, and send comfort to us as we take our leave."

Tears streaking her face, she stood and turned to leave, to seek a quiet dark place where the darkness of the moment could overtake her, and she could feel the sting in her heart. Anassa was sitting on the other side of the courtyard holding the baby. He was sleeping on her shoulder, and she was fanning them both. Sappho was in no mood to discuss her heartache, but she could not refuse to come to her stepmother when she beckoned with her fan.

She tried to wipe her tears away before reaching the woman. "There is no need to hide the proof of your love, even when it hurts you," Anassa said gently. "Your eyes would show your sorrow even if they didn't leak." Sappho could feel the puffiness around her eyes and lips and knew that her face must look damp and splotchy. Sappho looked at the tile below Anassa's feet as more tears sprang into her eyes. "Tessa has told you, then?" The girl nodded. "I shall miss her, too." Neither of them spoke for the remainder of the afternoon, but Sappho sat near Anassa and accompanied her to the women's quarters later that evening.

Sappho spent the last nights of Tessa's life in the *gynaeceum*, though she still tried to help Tessa through the day. Frequently, she would play with Nilo in the courtyard while Atthis sat with her mother. And when Tessa's moment of final distress came upon her, Sappho stood with Tessa's children at her bed.

Tessa spoke so softly that she was barely audible. Atthis knelt close to her, and Nilo climbed on the bed to lay his head on her chest. Sappho stood behind Atthis, one hand on her friend and one hand on the bed near her foster mother. "You are all my children," she gasped. "Watch over each other." She wanted to say more, but she could only gulp the air. Atthis melted in a cascade of tears. Nilo became very scared, and Sappho pulled him close to her to reassure him. When she looked back at Tessa's face, it was empty and slack. Her struggle for breath was over.

Chapter 9

Tessa's funeral was held on a very small scale, only that which was fitting for an esteemed servant. The inhabitants of Scamandronymus's house observed a brief period of formal mourning followed by the requisite purifications – the rekindling of the fire, the baths, the clean clothes. Those closest to the woman felt her loss more deeply, and Sappho and Atthis had a particularly difficult time of transition.

The girls wanted to find comfort in each other's presence, but they fought more about petty issues than they had in the past. Sappho continued sleeping in the women's quarters, and Atthis and Nilo were given into the care of the fat cook whom Atthis had mocked. She was very fond of Nilo, fawning over the little boy and giving him chunks of cheese and sweets to eat while she prepared the meals. However, the woman seemed to have held a grudge against Atthis, and though she didn't beat the girl, she was not kind.

Atthis was no longer allowed to pass her time with Sappho unless Anassa made a specific request for her help with the sewing or some other task. She spent most of her day fetching water and cleaning crockery. She peeled and scrubbed vegetables, cleaned fish, and generally did all the foulest tasks that the cook felt like the child's hands could manage. She worked hard through the whole day and endured an exhausted sleep at night on a mat in the servants' rooms.

Sappho enjoyed the time she spent talking with Anassa, but she longed for the company of her friend and missed the woman who was most like a mother to her. On one afternoon, when Sappho was playing with the baby and Anassa was working on some new project, Anassa asked Sappho about her vision of her own life.

"I know you are young," she began, "and probably haven't given much thought to what your life will give you. Most girls do not get the opportunity to be taught in a school or temple. It is a possibility, though, for a girl of your standing in the community. Do you think you would like to be educated before you marry?"

Sappho hadn't spent much time thinking about such matters. It had only been since her father brought Anassa to live with them that she had even known that there was such a life to be found within the walls of the temples. Anassa had gone, as had Kleis, to study at the temple of Aphrodite. Anassa had also told her that other young women studied at other temples in Lesvos or in the homes of wealthy women. She was enticed by the idea of being as graceful and engaging as her stepmother, and the thought of learning to read and write poetry excited her further yet.

"I would like to go, I think," she said tentatively. "I would be afraid to leave this house to go live there, though."

"You would learn quickly to live with the other girls and women in the temple," Anassa said. "All of the girls who study in the *thiasos* are housed together, and you learn the ways of the temple from teachers who know that you are scared at first."

"*Thiasos?*" Sappho tried out the new word a bit haltingly. "What is that?"

"A *thiasos* is a group of people who study and are devoted to a particular God or Goddess. There are *thiasoi* for the heroes, as well," Anassa explained. "In the *Thiasos* Aphrodite in the temple at Hiera, you would learn how to let the love and beauty of Aphrodite guide you in making a home, being a wife, rearing your children. These are all things you would learn in any woman's house, or even here from me and the servant-women, but at Aphrodite's temple, you would focus on the special ways that she can be seen in those activities."

Sappho thought of the afternoons she and Atthis had tried to walk like Anassa. She imagined a line of young girls following a grown woman across a courtyard, trying to emulate her walk. She nearly giggled.

"I am not asking you these questions out of idle conversation, Sappho," Tessa said. "You are six years old. If you are to have an education, it must start soon."

"Atthis is a year older than I am," Sappho observed. "Will she also be educated now?"

Anassa had anticipated this question, knowing the girls' closeness. It was not customary to send servants to the temple, unless they were sent as slaves. Some families even sent their own daughters to the temples as slaves, to be utilized by the God or Goddess as the clergy saw fit. Families sometimes did this as repayment to the Goddess of the temple in fulfillment of an oath – one of the most dramatic votive offerings one could make. Other families did so because they were poor and unable to provide a dowry in order to secure a marriage for their daughters. There was no shame or dishonor in being given to the Gods in such a way, but Anassa imagined that Sappho would not understand her friend being traded like a pretty vase.

Anassa had also developed a friendship with the girl's mother during the short time they shared. Tessa had devoted her life to Sappho. Atthis was like a sister to the girl. In honor of the woman who had raised her stepdaughter, Anassa did not prefer to give Atthis as a slave, but to send her there as a pupil like Sappho. However, Scamandronymus didn't wish to make the monetary offering required to educate two girls in the privileged style he intended for his own daughter. Anassa wasn't sure how they would resolve the problem, but she was sure that Atthis would accompany Sappho to the temple in one way or other.

"As a matter of fact, Atthis will go wherever you go," Anassa said as Sappho smiled, "at least for a time."

Sappho bubbled with excitement until she saw Atthis later that afternoon. Atthis was filling a large jug with water for the third time in a row. Sappho was so giddy at her good news that she didn't notice how bedraggled and weary Atthis looked. Atthis noticed Sappho's energy and immediately began to resent her for it. The little girl was not yet accustomed to her new chores, and her weariness choked any bright feelings she may have had at seeing her friend. To worsen the matter, Atthis had also had a conversation about the temple and the plans for her to be sent there. The fat cook, however, was not nearly so informed or so caring as Anassa in relaying the information.

"Atthis!" Sappho cried as she saw her friend. She grabbed her in a tight embrace as she said, "I have the best news! We are being sent to the temple of Aphrodite." Atthis pried Sappho's arms away from her and scowled. Sappho didn't understand. "Why aren't you happy? This is the best thing that's ever happened to me."

"Yes, it's a blessing for you," Atthis said with a slice of malice in her voice. "Such a blessing to have a rich father! Such a blessing that he has something on hand to pay the temple so they'll take you."

Sappho was dumbstruck. She had no way of comprehending Atthis's searing reaction or the scorn in her eyes. "Why are you angry with me? You should be pleased."

"Pleased?" Atthis was shaking and nearly in tears. The words of her guardian rang in her ears as she hurled them at her friend. "I should be pleased that I am like a mule to be given to the temple? I should be glad that sweaty men will lie on me and hurt me, and no one will care? Should I be pleased that I am the price of your spoiled, rich girl's education?"

"What are you talking about? Anassa said you were coming with me wherever I went. I don't think my father would send me to a place like that."

"Cook said I am going," Atthis choked on her tears, "because a father has to send some kind of property along with his daughter to have her trained. If not, the girl is a whore in the temple and a slave. I'm the payment, she said. She told me I'm nothing more to him than an animal, and I would be used like one. She said I would get trained, all right. I would be trained to keep my mouth shut about what I didn't like and to moan like a prostitute when a man gave gold to the temple. I won't be allowed to wear clothes, she said, and if I do you will be able to see through them. She said …," and here the frightened child could repeat no more of what she had heard.

Sappho was terrified and disbelieving. She conjured pictures in her head of herself in clean, new robes listening to a singer playing a lyre while a monster smothered her friend in a dark corner. She threw her arms around Atthis and hugged her tightly as the other girl clung to her. A moment later, she was dragging her protesting friend into the women's quarters to face Anassa.

"Is Atthis going with me if I go to the temple to study?" she demanded.

"Yes, I told you so earlier," Anassa responded coolly. "What is the matter? Why are you so flushed and breathless?"

"Is she the payment?" she asked fearfully.

Anassa didn't respond immediately. "Where have you heard this?"

"It's true!" Atthis shrieked and was crushed to the floor under the weight of her despair. "I don't want to be a whore. Please don't give me away."

"You misunderstand," Anassa began, but her stepdaughter interrupted her.

"You can't! She is my friend. She is my sister!"

Anassa tried to calm the girls, but they were in a frenzy of terror and anguish. She learned what they thought would happen to Atthis, how she would be used. Anassa tried to explain that a temple priestess was not a prostitute, and that no girl would serve Aphrodite in *that* way until she was truly a woman and ready, but the girls were simply too young to understand the distinctions.

She also tried to assure them that she would do everything in her power to prevent a forced life of priestesshood upon the servant girl. She would try to convince Scamandronymus that some other arrangement could be made. She would also insist that Atthis not be left in the care of the cook who obviously took pleasure in tormenting the child.

With Anassa's reassurances in their ears, Atthis and Sappho retreated to a quiet corner of the women's quarters where they whispered their worst fears to each other until the shadows grew long and dim and they were chilled with apprehension.

Chapter 10

The journey had been very hot and tedious, and it seemed very long to the little girls. Anassa had stayed home with her infant son, fearing that a full day's journey in such sweltering heat would be dangerous for so young a babe. Scamandronymus agreed to take both girls to the temple in addition to the provisions he had brought as offering for them. In the end, Anassa had been successful in convincing Scamandronymus to treat Atthis as his own child and allow her to study in the temple in repayment of Tessa's many years of faithful service. He determined to regard Atthis and Nilo as the children of his *pallake*, though Tessa had never actually been his concubine. In so doing, he would have two daughters whose educations were to be bought, but he would also have two daughters to make profitable alliances through their marriages to important men in the community.

Scamandronymus pointed out various sites as he drove the cart carrying the girls and their goods to the ferry. Sappho was amazed at the number of houses and temples in her own hometown of Mytiline. She had only had a few excursions around the city, and had never really grasped how many people lived there. Her father made a point of showing the girls the large amphitheatre in the pine grove high on the hill on the other side of the town. Though they didn't have the time to stop, and the girls wouldn't have been permitted inside anyway, Sappho was disappointed that she couldn't look at it longer. She wanted to climb the hill and stand at the top of the terraced rows, to see the orchestra and the altar that she knew must be down in the center of the bowl.

They first saw the eastern side of Mytiline where it kissed the bay, as this was closest to Scamandronymus's house. Both girls were dazzled by the glint of sunshine on the water at the harbor. The sea was a glittering blue, alive and sparkling in the light of the morning sun shining before them. Scamandronymus told them that the land they could just see on the horizon where the sun was rising was Lydia and that the city of Mytiline ruled the cities on the coast all the way to a place called the Hellespont.

This was Sappho's and Atthis's first geography lesson, and they were overwhelmed by the size and scope of the world that was opening up around them. As they took the road that led to the mountainous area to the northwest of their city, Sappho marked the names of the towns her father mentioned. There was Moria, and past it, on the coast where they wouldn't be going today, was Thermi, which had hot springs and special baths that the people nearby used for purification and also to welcome visitors from the East.

"Hiera, the sacred place of Aphrodite's temple," Scamandronymus explained, "is also famous for its hot springs. You will both become very familiar with them during your time in the temple-village."

The company stopped for a brief pause in their little journey before approaching the ferryman at the large and beautiful bay that separated Mytiline and Hiera. Scamandronymus cleared his throat as if to make an announcement. "Atthis, you know I am sending you to the temple with Sappho to study." It was a statement, but Atthis thought she heard the hint of a question, and so she nodded. "There is little purpose in teaching a girl or woman, except in teaching her how to be a good and pleasing wife. You are both my daughters, by law if not by fact." This time both girls nodded, remembering what Anassa had explained to them of their new situation. "I expect that you will be obedient to me and to those in whose charge I place you. These few years in Hiera will make you both more appealing in the marriage bargain when I feel that time has come." More nods, but with less vigor. Neither girl could picture themselves as married women.

"Father," Sappho began somewhat meekly, "how long will we stay here?"

"Not long, I think," he was very curt. "In about eight years, you will be ready to marry." Eight years seemed like a life-age to Sappho. In truth, it was. She was just barely over six now.

"Will we come home or see you and Anassa at all during that time?" Sappho was feeling scared and a little homesick. Atthis was trying to hide the tears that slipped down her cheeks as she thought of eight years away from her little brother, her only true family. She wanted to turn back right now and return to the house she had always known. She was willing to be a slave in the kitchen for the rest of her life if it meant that she could be there with her brother and feel safe.

Scamandronymus considered his daughter's question carefully. "I am sure you will be with your family from time to time. The temple is not at so great a distance that we cannot come to fetch you, or at least come to visit. I make personal visits to the temple several times in the year, and I will be sure to check on you then. As for Anassa, I am sure she would be glad to come when she can."

His response relieved Sappho somewhat. She found that her stomach was twisted and fluttering, but she didn't think that her tension was due to dread. Rather, she felt a tingle of anticipation at the mysteries that lay ahead of her. She didn't know what to expect when she arrived or what her life would be like for the next eight years. But she did know that there was very little of interest, besides Anassa, at the home of her father. As far as she could tell, she would spend her entire married life penned into her husband's house, and the eight years in Hiera would probably be the only ones in which she could be somewhat free.

They crossed the bay in silence, each thinking private thoughts about the future. Sappho admired the water and the tree-covered hills and enjoyed the feeling of sunshine and light breezes on her face for so long a time. She thought she would never again be able to live a life bounded by walls, in which the only sky she saw was the patch above an interior courtyard, and the only wind she felt was what blew through the carved lattice of the windows in the women's quarters. She felt like some part of her spirit had grown wings on this little journey and that she wasn't actually gliding on a ferry but flying over the crystal waters.

They arrived at the shore where the temple and its many buildings stood. Sappho was surprised at the size and beauty of the complex. She had never seen a holy place that was so expansive. There was one building that was clearly the main temple. Sappho would later learn that this was the primary temple for public ceremonies, votive offerings, prayers, and such. It was primarily blue, though sections of the white stone used in its construction had been left exposed around the trim as an accent. The gilded inscriptions around the building astonished the girls. They couldn't read the messages, but they knew the words must be important to be put in such large gold letters.

Sappho didn't have time to examine the other temple she noticed, the courtyards or the many buildings that were laid out around the village as they were preparing to enter the temple. They walked up the steps to the terrace, and Sappho was struck by the thought that both her mother and stepmother had once mounted these same steps with their fathers carrying their tuition to begin their training for womanhood. She imagined the shadows of the countless little girls who had entered here before her watching as she sprinkled herself with water to be cleanse before entering the sanctuary. She could feel the eyes of the Goddess watching her as she approached the raised platform and the statue at the west end of the inner sanctum.

The temple seemed a palace to Sappho and Atthis, a treasure trove. The doorway into the temple was bordered by two large pitchers of cool, clear water strewn with rose petals. Oil lamps hung in brackets along the walls and gave a rosy glow to the whole interior. Fragrant smoke hung in the air like the breath of the Lady, and aromatic oils clung to the skin of the priestesses like the honey of Aphrodite's kisses.

Sappho saw the baskets of offerings left by other worshippers, precious metals and expensive fabrics heaped in rich piles on either side of the altar. The day was drawing to a close, and it was clear to Sappho that many people must have been here today for so many gifts to have been left in the temple. There were only a few worshippers now, and more priestesses lined the walls than there were guests.

Sappho counted five women who she felt sure must have been the women of the temple. They were draped in garments of green, yellow or pink with heavy doses of white. All were veiled, and most were singing.

Her father had bought a handful of incense on his way into the temple, and he now sprinkled it onto the glowing coals in a container on the altar. The sweet smoke rose, and Sappho thought she saw a sparkle in the green enameled eyes of the icon. He made a prayer that Aphrodite would accept his two daughters in her temple as students. In exchange for this favor, he offered the foodstuffs and other valuables he had brought with him. A veiled priestess clad in green and white robes stepped forward from her appointed station and greeted him. As she did so, she beckoned two other women to come collect the portion of the offering he had brought inside the temple.

The veiled woman made a gesture of welcome and ushered Scamandronymus and the girls toward the house of waiting where he and Kleis had stood years earlier. "You are most welcome here, sir," she began in a cool, even voice. "You wish your daughters to be trained among us?"

Scamandronymus gestured his salutation as well and responded, "I do. I have brought them here from Mytiline for that purpose."

"The hiereia will come to you shortly to discuss the arrangement," she informed him. "However, I am involved with the school and help the woman who runs the girls' house."

Scamandronymus made a gesture of respect to the woman and said, "I have brought other offerings with us in exchange for their admission to your school. I paid a man to watch them while we entered the temple."

"Have him draw your cart to this building so the hiereia may accept your gift," the veiled priestess instructed, and Scamandronymus left to carry out the task.

In the short time that he was gone, the priestess said nothing but watched both girls closely from beneath her sheer fabric. Sappho tried to keep her eyes cast down respectfully, but she was too curious about the woman and their surroundings. Her eyes roamed and stole sidelong glances while she tried to keep her nose aimed at the floor of the terrace.

As Scamandronymus dismissed his helper and approached the landing, a woman in a *peplos* of canary yellow with intricate gold trim glided up the stairs. She, too, was wearing a veil, but it did not cover her entire face. Instead, it covered her hair and shoulders and framed the oval of her distinctly beautiful face. Her features were strong, yet very feminine. Her body was pleasantly rounded, but not bulging. Sappho thought, in that moment, that she was the picture of womanly beauty. *This woman is Aphrodite,* she thought. Then she realized, *This woman is the high priestess, the* hiereia.

Chapter 11

The *hiereia* gestured her greeting to those present and then spoke to Scamandronymus. "I am told you wish to educate your daughters in our thiasos."

"Yes, Lady, this is true," Scamandronymus said respectfully, though Sappho noticed he wore a strange expression after having seen the face of the hiereia. "My wife and I believe they will be best prepared for their future roles if they are taught here."

The priestess considered this a moment, looking at each of the girls and then returning her gaze to Scamandronymus's face. "You are probably accurate in your belief, though their futures may not take the shape you plan for them." She blinked, and Sappho thought the woman's expression cleared, as if she had just recognized that she was in the middle of a conversation, though that impression lasted only an instant. "What provisions do you make for these children?"

Scamandronymus indicated the cart he had brought from Mytiline, which was loaded with food and other goods in payment of the anticipated tuition. The woman stepped closer and quickly looked over the quantities of barley, dried fruits, nuts, the golden goblet, and the fine linens. Sappho thought the hiereia hadn't looked at them long enough to adequately judge their value, but she would later learn that this high priestess, like so many before her, had learned the art of evaluating offerings, situations, and people both swiftly and precisely. Sappho would also later be taught that there was no set price for the offerings to be made in the temple for any devotion or request. Each offering was judged according to the weight of its sacrifice in the life of the giver. The *hiereia* must have found the sacrifice to be appropriate as a symbol of Scamandronymus's willingness to give deeply to Aphrodite because she motioned for her attendant priestesses to take the items to two large buildings behind and to the side of the temple.

"Your initial parting with your daughters must begin tonight," the *hiereia* said. "You may sleep on the temple grounds this evening if you wish, but the girls will be taken into the *demos* immediately. For the first year, they will remain here without any visitation from family." By the nearly wild, searching look on Atthis's face at these words, she seemed Scamandronymus's daughter indeed, fearful to be separated from a beloved father. Sappho could feel the fear emanating from her friend in frenetic pulses of tension. The priestess explained to them all that familial contact was discouraged in the first year so the girls could overcome their homesickness and acclimate themselves fully to temple life without any temptation to leave or otherwise reserve themselves from their studies.

The high priestess removed herself modest distance and turned to observe the goings-on in the open area below the terrace while Scamandronymus bade farewell to the two girls. The moment was awkward, filled with hope and tension and uncertainty. Scamandronymus spoke brusquely, "You are my daughters. Conduct yourself with the honor befitting my house. Anassa and I will bring your brothers when we come to renew your tuition in a year's time." He gave each girl a quick kiss on the brow and turned to go. An older priestess led him away from the terrace and he turned back to the bay to begin making the journey back to Mytiline alone.

The girls stepped closer together and clasped hands as their connection to home walked away and the H*iereia Aphrodites* turned her gaze upon them once more. "Are you frightened, little ones?" Sappho shook her head no, while Atthis merely cast down her eyes. "What is your name?" the priestess gently inquired.

"Atthis," the girl whispered.

"My name is Timas, which you may call me some day, if you like," said the *hiereia* soothingly. As a product of their extreme youth, Atthis and Sappho were both rather surprised to learn that the highest-ranking priestess in this temple had a common name like them – that "*hiereia*" wasn't her name. Judging their shock by the looks on their faces, and having experienced the same reaction from other little girls new to the temple, Timas explained, "My title is H*iereia Aphrodites*. It tells those who come here what my job is and how much I am responsible for. It is appropriate that those who come here on pilgrimage or to worship call me by my title. It is appropriate that you should call me this as well, unless you take initiation into the mysteries of Aphrodite and serve as of her priestesses. Should that time come, you will share something so special with me that you may call me by my given name. You may even learn other names for me that are secret."

Sappho was fascinated by the idea of secret names. She had secrets that she shared with Atthis and a few that she shared with Anassa. There were secrets she kept locked deep inside her own young heart, and she had a secret hiding place in the courtyard of her father's house. But she had never known that a name could be a secret. In her mind, a name fell into a category that was the exact opposite of secret. All knew a name. "You have secret names?" she couldn't hide her curiosity.

"I do," said Timas.

"Why are they secret?"

"They are secret," Timas began, "because they reveal a truth about me. Names show the true nature of a thing or a person – or a God or Goddess. Aphrodite has given me names that show a truth about me, and that is powerful knowledge. Only my initiated sisters within the temple may know those truths – just as only those whom Aphrodite has initiated may know the truths she wishes to reveal to them."

Timas knew the children wouldn't comprehend most of what she had just explained. This was their first lesson in the temple, and their first test. The truth behind names was commonly accepted among adults, most of whom had been told this as part of their own educations. However, it was a mystery that only a few individuals truly comprehended. This was a lesson with which the girls would need to be familiar. After all, Aphrodite was known by a wide range of names – usually based on places or her attributes – and the girls now had some background knowledge for understanding why people sometimes called her Kypria, Aphrodite *Ourania*, or *Pandemos*.

However, the *hiereia* was also testing the new pupils. She wanted to gauge their curiosity and aptitude for studying the mysteries of the temple. As Timas made arrangements for the girls to be taken their house, she continued evaluating them. Atthis seemed to have already accepted the new information as fact and was awaiting her next instruction. This girl would be a good worker, an obedient wife, a solid member of whatever community she inhabited. Sappho was frowning slightly, lost in her thoughts. She was still chewing on the mystery Timas had partially revealed. It wasn't enough for her that an adult, a priestess – even the high priestess – had said it was so. The girl clearly wanted to feel the truth in her bones. She wanted to *know*. Timas thought to herself, as the girls left with two priestesses adorned in green and white, *This little one has come to us for a purpose. She has the makings of a priestess.*

Chapter 12

The priestess who had initially greeted them led Atthis and Sappho toward the *thiasos* and its dormitory. The temple they had been inside a few moments ago was situated so that it welcomed the morning sun through its open doors. The terrace faced the southeast and offered a view of the sloping hillside down to the iridescent bay below. The girls stepped down off the terrace and followed a flagstone walkway behind the temple that led to the northern side of the sacred village.

Just to the west of the temple, directly behind it, was a large courtyard where several women were talking or sitting and enjoying the last warmth of the day. Several trees dotted the edges of the spacious lawn, providing an indulgent amount of shade for the stone benches that nestled beneath them. There were several paths that led up to this courtyard, but none of them crossed it. It was as if the stones didn't dare to interrupt the pristine green of the verdant grass. There were, however, several large rosebushes that dotted the expanse of green, lending their lusty reds and pinks to the pleasant picture of cultivated beauty. Similar rosebushes punctuated the walkways through the parts of the temple grounds that the girls could see, including a few on the path they followed.

The guiding priestess spoke. "This is the central courtyard for the holy village of Hiera. There are a few times in the year that the women of the temple gather here for festival celebrations or some other communal gathering, and it serves many of the functions that the *agora* serves in other cities." They stopped and faced toward the

97

southwest. As the priestess pointed, she explained, "That tall, square building on the hill over there is the storehouse. All of our food stores are kept in there. Behind that are the pens where we keep the animals – livestock brought to us as offering. There is a gate in the wall further to the west where we can lead the animals to a pasture on the gentler slopes of the hills." Sappho could smell the odor that accompanied sheep and goats, though the perfume of roses and other flowers hung in the air and helped cover the scent.

Then she pointed to another large warehouse building that she said was the temple's treasury. Women were carrying the baskets Sappho had seen in the temple into the building. All of the valuables were stored here until such time as they were needed to buy necessary food or supplies for the maintenance of the grounds and the priestesses who dwelt there. "Some of the gold," she offered, "is taken to Mytiline where it is minted into coins with Aphrodite's image. We have considered bringing the mint here, and may do that some day, but it is close enough just across the water."

"I saw baskets full of beautiful fabrics in the temple," observed Atthis. "Do they also get stored in the treasury?"

"No," answered the woman. "We have too many women to clothe. It would be unwise to keep the fabric locked away when there is always someone who needs it."

As they rounded the corner to emerge on the northern side of the temple, Sappho noticed a wall that began a short distance from where they now stood, its opening protected by a heavy gate. She followed the line of the wall first to the north and then to the west, where it disappeared with the declining sun behind the many hills and the houses that dotted them. There were several of these homes, apple and olive trees shading the buildings, and more roses offering sweet welcome at their doors. The buildings bordered the northern and western edges of the courtyard and mounted the hills as they got steeper.

"What are all these buildings?" she asked.

"These are the priestess houses," was the reply. "Each room has its own small window," she said as she pointed at the nearest building. Sappho looked at the windows peeking out of the nearest house. There were so many little windows in that block of a building! On the first floor alone, Sappho counted six windows on each wall. "These houses are unlike the houses you are accustomed to seeing in some ways. There are bedchambers on the first floor, lining each side of the interior courtyard, along with a kitchen and an *andron*." The priestess saw the look of surprise on the girls' faces. "Yes, even in a house occupied only by women, we have a special room for men to gather, talk, and be entertained." Continuing with her description, she said, "There are two floors in each house, with bedchambers for individual priestesses on each floor." She let the effect of her words sink in. She knew the girls did not have the math skills to comprehend the number of rooms – and women who inhabited them. She also knew that the number of rooms they imagined to be there overwhelmed them.

"There are so many!" exclaimed Atthis. "These buildings remind me of the beehive I saw once at home."

"Exactly right," said the guide. "There are around three thousand priestesses at this temple. This is Aphrodite's largest temple. We are larger than the temple in Korinth, which only has one thousand priestesses, and larger than the temple to the east of us whose temple-city is called Aphrodisias. And our grounds are like a beehive in many ways. People are always coming or going. Everyone has a task to perform. Priestesses are even known by a general name that means 'bee.' The common title for a priestess in this type of organization is *melissa*."

Sappho was still curious about the remainder of the grounds. "Is there anything beyond these houses? Or does this wall just include what we see here plus the houses?"

"There is more," the priestess smiled in appreciation of the girls' curiosity. "Our most sacred places lie beyond the cloister. But enough of this tour," she redirected their attention to the northeast. "It is time to show you your new home."

They walked along the flagged path toward the smallest building Sappho had yet seen on the temple grounds. It was made of stone and plaster, the way Sappho's father's house had been built, though it had more windows set into the outer walls than his. Bushes of delicate pink roses flanked either side of the arched entry, and garlands of vines and flowers had been hung across the arch itself. The house had two floors and an open courtyard, like the girls' childhood home, but there was a distinct difference in the atmosphere. This place was clearly a place of femininity. The girls and women were everywhere and weren't relegated to the women's quarters. Sappho wondered if this house even had a *gynaeceum* since there were no men or boys to share the dwelling.

The courtyard was buzzing with girls busy with the work of

preparing their evening meal. A couple of grown women were supervising and directing the tasks of the thirty or so girls who were in various stages of cleaning, cooking, and arranging the tables to accommodate all of the diners.

Sappho saw that the tables were arranged along the long sides of the courtyard under an awning of exposed beams that were entwined with ivy and honeysuckle and hung with oil lamps. At the far end of the courtyard stood an altar that supported a large clamshell, a shallow golden cup, a mirror, several roses in a vase and a dish of smoldering incense. The altar had been painted bright white and decorated with a pink and red rose motif just under the top molding. The same pattern was echoed in the tiles on the floor around the altar's base. There was a well to the right of the altar, and Sappho saw several golden trinkets glittering around its edges.

"I will direct you to your rooms, where you can freshen up a bit before dinner," said the priestess. "You will not be sharing a room, as I am sure you have done all your lives." Sappho felt Atthis stiffen slightly. "We prefer that you each have a separate room and that sisters sleep in different corridors. This will help you meet other girls more easily, and it will also allow you some privacy for the work you will be asked to do during the next several years. Much of what you will do involves reflection and quiet thought, which I am sure you will find easier in the privacy of your own room."

The girls followed her around the edge of the courtyard to a small hallway at the back of the house. In the middle of this hall, she pushed aside the curtain that hung in a doorway on the right. This was to be Atthis's room. When Sappho turned to follow her guide to her own room, Atthis was sitting on the edge of her bed looking blankly at the plain wall ahead of her.

Sappho then followed the woman to her room, which was on the second level. She noted with some satisfaction that her window looked out on a beautiful, large tree that provided her room some shade as it spread its limbs over a small lawn below. The lawn, Sappho saw, was positioned between the house and the temple and featured a series of curved benches arranged around a small circular platform. It reminded Sappho of a miniature amphitheatre.

"You may rest here for a few minutes, if you like," her guide advised, "but dinner will be ready soon. There is water in the basin near the window that you may use to wash up. When you are ready, come to the courtyard again and I will introduce you to the *thiasos*. Do you have any questions for me?"

Sappho asked, more timidly than she had intended, "What is your name?"

"My name is Hermione," she said. "Anything else?"

"After dinner," Sappho began, "I don't know what to do. What is expected of me?"

"You have no duties yet and there will be no lectures until tomorrow," Hermione said. "After dinner, you are free to do as you like for a time. You may begin the process of getting acquainted with the other girls, spend some time in your room, or explore the house and the grounds nearby. Later tonight, there will be a ceremony to welcome you to the house – to invite you and your sister into the *thiasos* at its most elementary levels. Then you will come home to your room, sleep, and awaken in the morning to breakfast and your first lessons."

"Do we all have the same lessons together?" Sappho asked.

"Some lessons you share with all the girls," Hermione explained. "However, that is rare. There are now twenty-four of you in the house, and few classes work well with so many students. The *thiasos* is sometimes divided in half, according to age or skill-level, but it is more common that lessons are taught to a quarter of the girls at a time. Generally, half the girls are in a class while the other half are either preparing for a lesson or carrying out their duties in the house."

"Will I have duties?"

"Of course," Hermione smiled. "Every girl must contribute to the physical needs of the home. Your chores will be determined based on your age and ability. Tomorrow, you will learn what work the youngest girls are responsible for, and you will begin to help them with it."

"What about my studies?" Sappho found that each explanation lead to another question. "What will I be learning first?"

"Enough questions, little one. There is no need to rush. Everything you need to know will be made clear." Hermione enjoyed bright, inquisitive girls. It was their enthusiasm that kept her role as teacher fresh and alive. "Tonight, you will be paired with a mentor – an older girl who will help guide you. She has many of the answers that you seek."

With that, Hermione turned and walked out of the room. Sappho tested the bed by bouncing on it once or twice. Then she flipped back the covers to look inside. Not sure what she had expected to find, she smoothed them back into place and flopped down on the bed, facing down. Then she flipped over to look at the ceiling. The bed smelled sweet. *The straw must be fresh*, she thought. *And some herb or flower is mixed into it*. The leaves on the tree outside her window rustled and drew her attention outside again. She returned to the window and took another long look out into the trees and lawn below. Her window faced south, but she couldn't see the bay because the temple blocked her view. She noticed that the blue of the temple was darkening with the fading light, giving it a mysterious density like the sea at dusk. She stared at it for several minutes, feeling calmed by the scene from her little window. Some girls' voices in the corridor broke her reverie, and she washed her face and hands and set off to find Atthis and go to dinner.

Atthis was still on her bed when Sappho came to her room, though she had moved into a reclining position. She wasn't sleeping, though the fading light in her room made it difficult for Sappho to distinguish whether her friend's eyes were open or shut. Sappho noticed that Atthis's window faced north toward the wall that protected the temple complex, which made her room considerably darker at this time of day than Sappho's room. It had a gloomy feeling, but Sappho thought that the atmosphere of the room might well be the result of her friend's bleak outlook. She couldn't imagine what must have been bothering her friend. The house, the temple, the grounds, the priestesses – everything about this new place seemed like a pleasant dream to Sappho.

"We should go to dinner, Atthis," she suggested. She was choosing not to question her dispirited friend about her melancholy.

She knew Atthis was homesick. They had talked about the separation from home during the journey here. There was nothing to be done about it, as far as Sappho could tell, except to embrace the new life and new home they were being given and make the best of it. Sappho didn't think it would be hard to make a happy life here. Surely Atthis would come to realize that soon enough. "Have you washed yet?"

Atthis rose from her bed and washed her face and hands. With head drooping, she obediently followed Sappho to the courtyard. Hermione was there waiting for them as the other girls in the house were already seating themselves at the table and taking their portions of fish, rice, fruit, and water. Atthis and Sappho came to her directly and tried to ignore the stares and whispers of the girls who had noticed the newcomers. Sappho didn't feel like they were being rude or unkind, but she also wasn't sure how she should respond. Clearly, an introduction was in order, and she would allow Hermione to make it as they had discussed.

By the time the two newest pupils reached their tutor, all the other girls had hushed for the anticipated announcement. Sappho could sense the curiosity coming from the other girls, and she found the knowledge that she had aroused so much interest both odd and gratifying. She was not at all uncomfortable with the attention, and she wished that she knew some way to continue holding it. Part of her wanted to introduce herself or offer a song or some other entertainment, but she wisely refrained.

"I am sure you all will join me in welcoming two more young ladies to our house," Hermione began in a clear voice that filled the courtyard without overpowering those situated close to her. "Sappho and Atthis are sisters, coming to us from Mytiline. Their mother and stepmother once dwelt in this same house and studied as you do now. These girls seek the wisdom of Aphrodite, and we welcome them!" Cheering broke out, along with shouts of welcome. Sappho was taken aback, not expecting so hearty a greeting from girls who were total strangers to her. Several even waved for her and Atthis to come sit near them.

"I suggest you sit separately at this dinner," Hermione quietly advised them before they chose their seats. "The sooner you make friends with other girls, the sooner this place will feel like home to you." Sappho squeezed Atthis' hand and then silently encouraged her to take a seat at a table a little removed from the one she intended to join. As she sat down amongst the girls at her own table, she saw the girls near Atthis welcome her and begin asking questions. Sappho thought Atthis looked nervous, but a little relieved at not being an outsider at this first meal.

"What is your name?" the girl next to Sappho was asking. She had auburn hair and startlingly blue eyes.

"Sappho."

"I am Malva," the girl said. "I'm from Mytiline, too." She pointed at the other girls at the table and began naming each of them. Sappho couldn't keep track of all the names. There were Kallista, Melanthe, Eunice, and four or five other names. Sappho didn't think she could put the names with the faces if she had tried. Throughout their meal, they talked about where they were from and pointed out who their closest friends were. There was a constant buzz of conversation coming from their table, matched in intensity and volume by the girls at the other tables.

When the meal was over, one of the priestesses rang a bell that signaled the beginning of the clean up. Each of the girls grabbed her cup and plate and took them to the scullery. Then they each washed and dried the dishes and put them on the shelves that lined the wall. Finally, they came to claim and clean the serving dishes and wipe down the tables.

A priestess came to Sappho and Atthis, who had come together when the bell sounded. "On this one night," she explained, "you don't have to continue with the cleaning. You should go to your rooms and rest for a time. Think about what you hope to learn in the years ahead of you while you live in this house. The other girls will also be sent to rest for the ceremony that will officially welcome you into our home and mark you as one of us. When you hear this bell ring five times, that will be your signal to come back to the courtyard to begin the procession."

After these instructions, the two girls retired to their respective rooms to await the summons to their new lives.

Chapter 13

Sappho lay on the bed in her room staring at the flickering flame of the oil lamp that hung from her window. She had lit the lamp herself from the common lamp hanging in the hall. She feared that if she laid down in the total darkness of the deepening night she would fall asleep and fail to address the question she had been instructed to ponder.

"What do you hope to learn during your time in this house?" The question continuously repeated itself in her mind. Unfortunately, the answer didn't form itself as easily as the question. She had no idea what she wanted to learn. She didn't know what was available or possible. It hadn't been at her own request that she came here. She wasn't disappointed in her father's choice for her, but it had been *his* choice. What had he wanted her to gain by being here?

He had told her that she would learn the skills needed to make her an appealing wife. What did *that* mean? As a wife, she imagined that she would need to know how to make her husband happy and give him babies – specifically, boy babies. Certainly her father would intend for her to be her husband's *first* wife, which would give her more responsibility and power in running the household. So, her father would want her to learn to manage servants, give birth to children, and do whatever it was that men wanted from their women. But was that what she wanted for herself? She hadn't been asked to think about her family's purposes in sending her to the temple. The priestess had asked her about her own desires.

"What do you want to learn during your time in this house?"
How am I supposed to answer this? I want to learn. *I want to* know. *I*
just don't know what it is that I want to learn or know. My father wants
me to learn the wifely arts so he can make a good bargain out of me. Is that
all that there is *for me to learn here?*

She tried to quiet her mind, to push her father's face out of
the foreground. *What do you want to learn …?* She thought of her
earlier conversation with the *hiereia* regarding names and the truths
they revealed. She wondered if "Sappho" was her true name and how
and when she might know if it wasn't. She wondered what truths
about herself would be revealed to her as she learned her own names.
She wondered what other mysteries the temple could reveal to her –
answers to questions she hadn't known to ask. *That* was what she
wanted to learn.

She felt her thoughts weaving in and out of each other in a
labyrinthine spiral. She felt her mind spinning and wondered
whether her spirit moved or if it was the room around her that
shifted. She wondered if she had fallen asleep, and then she heard a
clear bell chiming five times in the courtyard.

She rose from her bed feeling as refreshed as if she had truly
slept all night long. She put her oil lamp near the doorway after
extinguishing the flame, making it more accessible for relighting
when she returned. As she stepped through her doorway into the
hall, she moved with the flow of the other girls into the open air of
the house's interior courtyard.

She saw Atthis in front of her, also clearly wondering what
she was supposed to do at this point, if anything. All the girls were

assembled together, facing five priestesses standing near the altar.

As if in response to Sappho's unasked question, a priestess garbed in yellow and white spoke. "We are here tonight to welcome into this *thiasos* Sappho and Atthis, daughters of Scamandronymus of Mytiline." Sappho noted that this proclamation, which had been met with cheers at dinner, was now accepted with silent reverence. Sappho had the impression that this woman was a figure of particular power in the eyes of the girls gathered around her. "Sappho and Atthis, please step forward."

The girls did as they were told, and Sappho felt a rush of excitement that she would come to associate with the beginning of ritual, though she would later learn to direct that nervous energy into something more focused and productive. They stood facing the woman who had called them forth. Arranged around and behind this woman, the four other priestesses carried a flaming brand, a basket with bread, a smoking incense burner, and a golden cup filled with water.

The priestess hung garlands of vines and fragrant blossoms around the girls' necks before calling to the rest of the assembly. "Musicians, play! Dance and sing, daughters of Aphrodite!" Then she turned to the other priestesses and to the two new maidens, "Let us laugh and lead the way!" And so the procession began.

The four priestesses walked at the front, dancing and singing and smiling as they walked. Sappho and Atthis were immediately behind them with the directing priestess just behind and between them. The remainder of the girls followed, with several of them playing a light, bouncy melody and rhythm that inspired the whole gathering to dance and have hearts as light as sunshine.

They walked into the heart of the village, past the courtyard they had seen earlier, past the many houses where several *hierodulei* waved and cheered and sang from the doorways. The night was dark, and Sappho had a hard time distinguishing the buildings on the other side of the houses of initiated priestesses. There seemed to be other buildings here, but she couldn't imagine what they were. They continued following the path to the western end of the complex until Sappho could see a grove of trees to the right, illuminated by the partial moon from above, and, to her surprise, a temple on the left, illuminated by the candles and lamps lit from within.

When they reached the doorway, the priestesses holding the bread, flame, water goblet, and incense took positions on either side of the opening. Hermione, who was holding the water goblet, stood near a large vessel of water and sprinkled all who entered after her with water from her cup, which she refilled from the vessel. When all the company were inside the walls of the temple, the four priestesses walked several times around the group and then arranged themselves around the altar that stood in front of a statue of Aphrodite.

Sappho was struck by the beauty and intimacy of the icon. She was entranced by the lifelike colors and features of the Goddess and her female lover in a tender and passionate embrace unlike any she had ever witnessed between two women before. She stood and stared at the statue for several moments before the priestess raised her hands and the music ended.

The priestess held her hands aloft for a moment as silence descended. She poured wine from a nearby cask onto the floor as she said, "Hear, Aphrodite Ourania, Queen of Heaven! Hear, Aphrodite Pandemos, Queen of Earth! Kyprian Goddess, crowned in sunshine and roses! With whatever name it pleases you best to be called, come to us from your bath in the sea. Come to us from your mountain grotto. Come to us from your apple grove." She then sprinkled chunks of frankincense onto the censer. "Always have the priestesses of your order been faithful servants to you, since the time Kinyras the king began your cult – so long ago in Kyprus. Always have you shown us your love and beauty, your protection. You have extended your blessing to the initiated and to the uninitiated members of your *thiasos* on Lesvos, for you are able." She placed one hand on the top of each girl's head. "Golden Lady, we bring before you two young ones who have been sent to us to study your ways. We ask that you extend your blessing over them, showing them your love and beauty from within themselves, from within the women around them, and from the world at large." She took a knife and cut a lock of each girl's hair, throwing both snips on the fire. "In so doing, we vow to teach the lessons you would have them learn, that they might always honor you."

At this, all the girls and women said, "Hail, Aphrodite!" The priestess then addressed Sappho and Atthis. "It is now time for you to profess your own intentions in coming here. In your own words, say what you hope to learn while you live in this place. Finish by making a vow to Kypris, something you will give or do for her in exchange for learning what you desire to know. Then, pour this honey on the ground as a libation and say, 'Hail, Aphrodite.'"

She handed the first container of honey to Atthis, who

looked positively stricken for a moment, before speaking in a timid voice. "I wish to learn what I must know to be the wife my father wishes to give to my husband." She faltered slightly when she referred to Scamandronymus as her father, though only Sappho would have known why. "I vow to give a part of my bridal gifts to the temple. Hail, Aphrodite." She poured the sticky, golden honey onto the floor at her feet.

The priestess gave a second dish of honey to Sappho, who felt a lump in her throat because she was still unsure exactly what to say. She felt even more uncertain after hearing Atthis say the very thing she had considered in her room. Perhaps this was the proper response after all. Would the girls think she was ungrateful to her father and to the temple if she didn't necessarily wish to be a good wife?

She cleared her mind again, took a deep breath, and opened her mouth to speak. She was surprised that the words came so fluidly. "In my time in this house, I wish to learn to ask the right questions."

The priestess was clearly surprised by Sappho's statement, though her delight was not so obvious to the young girl. "Why do you make this request, Sappho?"

"So I will know who I am," was her response.

"And what are you prepared to give for such deep knowledge?" There was a note of challenge in the priestess's voice. *There must be a challenge here*, the priestess thought. *This child asks for more than she can yet comprehend. Let her hear in my voice that such revelation comes with sacrifice.*

Sappho said the first thing that came into her mind, "I am prepared to give myself in service of Aphrodite."

The entire room bristled with alert attention that only a moment of deep ritual significance can bring. "This is no initiation, child," the priestess warned. "You are not of an age to give yourself, nor promise to give yourself, to anyone or anything. If you are indeed called into her service, you will make that vow some years from now."

Sappho felt a sting of tears, as of being rebuffed by an admired elder. She had spoken her heart and now felt foolish. The priestess saw the little girl's face fall and felt the cry that welled within her. She felt Aphrodite's touch on her shoulder and heard her voice whispering in her ear. She repeated the words she heard, "Darling child, dear one. Hear the words of the Goddess to whom you would give all: Your vow is noted with respect and admiration. You give freely of yourself. Do not despair that you are warned to walk more cautiously along the path that you would follow. You cannot give what you do not know. Make a vow that is within your power now to give."

The priestess looked gently at the girl, who felt placated. She took another breath to steady her voice and said, "I vow to sing the best song I can write in honor of Aphrodite when she tells me the time is right." She poured the thick honey on the floor. "Hail, Aphrodite!"

Chapter 14

Several months slipped past, like leaves caught in a swift stream, as Sappho and Atthis acclimated themselves to their new lives. Sappho formed friendships more easily than Atthis, but the older girl did find connections with a couple of the other pupils given time. She felt less homesick than when she had first arrived, but the thought of her brother's face in her mind brought a pang of loneliness that even Sappho couldn't beguile away.

Both girls were good students – Atthis because of her natural respect and obedience, Sappho due to her unquenchably inquisitive spirit. Atthis demonstrated nearly immediate competence in all of the more pragmatic studies, and Sappho had a gift for the artistic ones.

More months slid away, and soon it had been over a year since Scamandronymus's daughters had come to Hiera. In that time, the youngest girls, including Sappho and Atthis, had been taught the basics of reading and writing, a little about the history of Lesvos and the other islands in the northern part of the Aegean Sea, and they had all been encouraged to sing and dance whenever the mood came upon them – though they had received no formal training in movement or musicianship, as yet.

When the first anniversary of Scamandronymus's daughters at the temple arrived, the father, wife, two boys, and a servant came to visit and celebrate. Scamandronymus's family were kept overnight in one of the vacant rooms of the house closest to the *hiereia*. Guests were frequently housed here, and the families of the girls in the *thiasos* were always treated as honored guests of the temple.

The family spent the morning and afternoon together in the central courtyard. Sappho and Atthis were excused from thir chores for the day; however, they were still expected to attend lessons. Atthis had a particularly difficult time in focusing on the reading they were practicing. It was poetry, which she found very little interest in. She was a little young to understand the truths that were published in a poem, as well as a little too unimaginative. Sappho, of course, had shown an inclination toward poetry long ago, but even she was not fully ready to comprehend the beauty of the work she was deciphering that day. Moreover, she too was struggling to focus.

For their noon meal, Anassa had packed several items from home for their journey, and Sappho and Atthis brought a few other morsels from the kitchen in their house. The two girls sat with their brothers and Sappho's parents under the shade of a large tree on the grassy lawn. While they picked at cold chicken and licked soft cheese from their fingers, they enjoyed the whirring noise of the cicadas and the light breeze that played with the rose petals and the waxy green leaves of the bushes and trees.

The boys ate little before chasing each other and a few insects across the courtyard. Nilo seemed like such a big boy to his sister, who had watched him with great interest since the moment he came into her sight. He was sweet, but wary, as toddlers often are. He took some time in warming up to his sister, but he did warm. By mid-afternoon, his favorite game was running between Atthis and Anassa to collect kisses and cuddles and running to Sappho for a sound and noisy tickling.

The baby Kharaxus had changed considerably, of course. There was little for Sappho to recognize in her brother of the tiny infant she had left behind a year earlier. Only his name had remained unchanged. Sappho didn't see much change in herself over the course of the year, but she commented to Anassa about the passage of time that was evident in her young sibling.

Anassa laughed kindly at her. "You've changed, too, my dear. It's not just the boys who've grown."

Sappho was disbelieving. "I'm not much bigger than I was." She looked at the hem of her peplos for proof, but she found it shorter than she had noticed in a good long while.

Anasssa smiled again. "That peplos will serve you for a while yet, but it does seem to be shrinking." She winked. "Luckily, when a piece of fabric gets too short to wear as a peplos, you can drape or fold it differently, and it becomes something else. As long as it isn't threadbare, you'll always have your favorite garments."

"I've only had a few robes since we've been here," Sappho said, "but we haven't needed many. I suppose we aren't very hard on our clothes here."

"Nonetheless, we have brought new linen and wool for you and Atthis," Anassa said as she popped a green grape into her mouth and handed two others to the little boys. "Of course, you've grown in other ways. It's not just the hem of your skirt that you are quickly outgrowing."

"What do you mean, Anassa?" Sappho stealthily looked at her hands and feet and tried to gauge whether or not her shoulders felt broader within her dress.

Anassa looked at Atthis, who was romping in the grass with her brother, and chose her words carefully. Then she pointed two fingers to Sappho's brow. "Here. You've sharpened your mind already in the time you've been here," she said. Then she pointed at the child's heart, "Something here has grown, as well. Just as Kharaxus is now learning to walk and chase after Nilo, you are taking your first steps in search of something larger."

Sappho was getting used to the adults around her speaking in riddles. It was a common practice of the priestesses. Sometimes she fancied that she glimpsed the ideas they were trying to convey. At other times, she felt like the child she had the sense to know she was. In this particular instance, she knew that she had experienced some sort of change in her heart, mind, and soul, so she figured she knew what her stepmother meant.

Throughout the remainder of the afternoon, both Anassa and Scamandronymus slipped off to fulfill their private devotions to Aphrodite among the *hierodulei*. Anassa also enjoyed a few minutes' conversation with Hermione, who had just begun teaching in the *thiasos* when Anassa was a student. Anassa had always admired Hermione and had felt close to her as a pupil. They reminisced about their shared comedies from a few years prior and promised to visit again when the family returned to check on the girls.

The visit had ended the next morning with the parents departing with their sons on the journey back to Mytiline. Whatever financial arrangements had been made for the coming year of study, the girls hadn't been privy to them. And though nothing was substantially different in Atthis's daily dealing and duties, she seemed rejuvenated by the brief visit with her little brother and the promise of a return trip in a shorter lapse of time.

Sappho was glad for her friend's renewed contentment. An image from their recent reunion seemed to epitomize for her the source of that renewal. When Scamandronymus had been secluded with a *hierodule*, and Anassa had been dozing with Kharaxus in the shade, Nilo had climbed into his sister's lap and fallen asleep. Sappho watched her friend, who was as close as a sister by both law and spirit, as she cuddled the little boy, and she saw love so perfect and contentment so complete that they could sustain Atthis through the duty she felt bound to serve. That love and contentment brought a serenity to Atthis's face that made her beautiful to Sappho, and the little girl felt the first compelling urge to bring joy and peace to her friend's heart.

Chapter 15

The months sped by so quickly that they turned into years before Sappho had time to count them. She was surprised to find herself turning ten and then eleven years old before it seemed she had even had the time to turn around. She and Atthis were now among the older girls in the dormitory, though they were still not the eldest. By chance, Atthis's room had been reassigned so that she was now in the same hallway with Sappho, though her window overlooked the interior courtyard while Sappho was still afforded a view of the temple and the space often used for lessons under the myrtle tree.

The girls in the third level of training, the level at which Sappho and Atthis were currently studying, were seated on the benches below Sappho's room, protected from the sun by the accommodating branches of the tree. The breeze was crisp and cool, but the sun was still warm enough to scorch Sappho's fair skin, if given the opportunity. Hermione often encouraged her to wear a veil while she was outside, but girls of that age never recall such simple precautions at an appropriate time to do them any good.

Today's lesson was about the Muses, delivered by Rhodia, the oldest of the priestesses who taught in the *thiasos*. She was also the head of the school, the one who had led the welcoming ceremony a few years earlier. Every now and then, Sappho would look at Rhodia's face and be reminded of her own vow to Aphrodite. *The best song I can write,* would flash into her mind, and she would try to think of the deeds of Aphrodite that would best serve the verses she would compose. But today, like other days, she had to postpone any further thought on the matter. Today, she needed to focus on the topic at hand – the nine Muses, daughters of Zeus who lived just below the peak of Mount Olympos and sang the praises of their father while they inspired mortals to create great art.

Sappho had always heard of the nine daughters of Zeus and Mnemosyne, the Goddess who ruled memory. She was surprised to learn, however, that her people had once believed in just three Muses, and before that they only believed in one. This presented her with so many questions. How could they have been so wrong in their accounting of these Goddesses at any time? Weren't there always the same number? Did the people not see them all until later? Were they unprepared to understand the complexity of nine? Or did the Muses hide from them? Did the truth actually change? And if that happened, was it likely to change again? For that matter, what exactly was the truth? If two people believe two opposite things to be true, how are they to decide which is in fact *true*?

She caught her mind from spinning out on these tangents just in time to hear the names of the nine. She decided to come back to these questions later because she had to dedicate her attention to remembering the names and duties of each of the divine dealers of human creativity.

First, Rhodia described Kalliope. She was the most distinguished of all the Muses, and she was the eldest. She governed the qualities of eloquence as well as providing inspiration for epic poetry. She was the mother of the singer Orpheus, who Sappho remembered was torn apart by the frenzied women who followed

Dionysos. Kalliope was also the mediator in the argument between Aphrodite and Persephone, the queen of the underworld, and she came to an arrangement that didn't entirely please the Golden One. Rhodia showed the girls a vase with a picture of the Muses. Kalliope was the one holding a stylus and wax tablets.

Then there was Klio, holding a parchment scroll, who was the Muse of historical and heroic poetry and who gifted mortals with the Phoenician alphabet. She was followed by Erato with her lyre, the Muse who bestows inspiration for lyric poetry. Next came Euterpe, who also loved lyric poetry and music, especially flute playing. She was holding a double flute, the instrument she created that mortals loved so well. Polyhymnia was the Goddess of sacred hymns and dance, the most solemn-looking of the figures on the vase with her long cloak and her finger held to her mouth. Terpsichore was also an inspirer for dancing and was the patroness of the dramatic chorus. Rhodia explained that she was also the mother of the sirens, the beautiful, bird-bodied, singing seductresses who lured unwitting sailors onto the rocks to their peril. Melpomene and Thalia were the Muses for tragedy and comedy, respectively, and were shown holding the masks of the stage. Ourania, the last Muse to be discussed, was shown wearing a cloak spangled with stars and gazing toward the heavens, illustrating her rule over astronomy and astrology.

Sappho pictured each of them in turn, visualizing how they would look if standing before her in the flesh. She saw each with the implements of her art. There were so many related to poetry alone. And three Muses were related to drama, one each for comedy, tragedy, and the chorus. Some of the Muses had familiar names, but one in particular stood out to Sappho. Another girl in the class must have noticed the same connection, because she posed the question that was forming in Sappho's mind.

It was Eunice who spoke. "I thought Thalia was one of the *Kharites*, the Goddesses of grace and charm who followed Aphrodite. Is she a Muse as well?"

Rhodia smiled, pleased at her pupil's attentiveness to detail. "It is true that Thalia is the name of one of the Kharites. The other two, of course, are Aglaea and Euphrosyne, and they are also said to be the daughters of Zeus but of a different mother than the Muses. Naturally, you know that all names have a meaning. Even your own names lay bare the qualities that your parents would hope for you to have. Do you recall what the name *Thalia* means?"

"Good cheer," said another girl, Kallista.

"Well done." Rhodia continued to smile as she began to lay the maze that would eventually have the girls answering their own questions. "Why would good cheer be a quality that one would associate with grace and charm?"

The girls thought about their own experience and about the lessons from long ago in which they had first been introduced to the Kharites. Sappho ventured an answer by saying, "A pleasant nature puts people at ease. 'Good cheer' means to laugh and enjoy life and other people. To be charming, you must make those around you comfortable."

"And why would such qualities also be important in comedic plays?" Rhodia prodded the thought process along a bit.

"It's obvious isn't it?" said Kallista. "Comedy is all about laughter. You can't really laugh unless you have good cheer, or happiness."

"I understand that," Eunice said. "I see why 'Thalia' is a good name for both a Grace and a Muse. But what I want to know is whether or not they are the same figure? Are there two Thalias or one?"

Rhodia smiled again, this time somewhat enigmatically. "What do you think?"

Eunice was clearly frustrated. "I don't know."

"Do you need to know?" asked the teacher.

"Yes," said the exasperated girl. "Of course I need to know."

Melanthe spoke this time. "We should know the truth, shouldn't we? That way we will know the right way to make prayers and offerings to the Muses and the Graces without offending them."

"That point makes good sense," replied the older woman. "We certainly don't want to offend the Gods. We are given too many lessons in what happens to mortals when they irritate the Immortals." The girls all nodded, recalling all the stories in which some human was chastised for an offense to the Gods.

Sappho wasn't sure whether she should speak or not, but she decided to offer her thoughts on the matter. "If we call Thalia as a Muse and ask for her guidance in regards to a comedic play, would it offend her if we didn't mention that she is also a *Kharite*? Or if we call Thalia the *Kharite*, would she be offended not to be called 'Muse' as well? I don't think it really matters. We are calling a particular Goddess by the most appropriate name we know for a specific purpose. The name represents the truth of the divine being. Thalia the Muse and Thalia the Grace may be the same being, or they may be close cousins with the same name. But in either case, Thalia _is_."

The girl couldn't decide if she had explained herself well or not. Her fellows were all chewing on the idea, and her teacher just continued to smile her enigmatic smile until she gave an assignment. "Return to your rooms, or whatever place is best for you to think, and ponder the relationship between the _Kharites_ and the Muses. See if there are other connections you can find besides the one common name." With that, the girls were dismissed.

Chapter 16

Atthis was older than Sappho, but it was Sappho who first experienced the bleeding that marks a girl's transition into womanhood. She was twelve, and she had already noticed several changes in her growing body by the time of her menarche. Her breasts weren't large or rounded like the women of the temple, but there was more fullness under her *peplos* than there had been a year earlier. Her hips weren't yet voluptuous like the grown women, but there was a growing distinction between the size of her waist and that of her hips.

She'd noticed other differences, too. Some were less obvious and more confusing than the changing curves of her body. At times, she found herself wanting to stay longer in the presence of a friend or linger in an embrace that had begun in an offhand way. She had always been particularly close with Atthis, but now she was noticing her own compulsion to please her friend and her desire to be the one to comfort her when she was feeling low.

Once, on an occasion when Nilo had just returned to Mytiline with the family after a visit, Atthis was mourning his departure and Sappho was attempting to console her. Sappho had been stroking her friend's hair and her back – common things that she had done a thousand times before, since the time when they were very small children. With her hand on Atthis's hair where it fell onto the smooth skin between her shoulder blades, Sappho felt a shock of sensation that penetrated her body and landed in a knot just behind her navel. She was acutely aware of the warmth and softness of her friend's back, the silky texture of her hair; and the trembling that began in her own stomach and must have fluttered into her hand because Atthis seemed to have felt it, too. She pulled her hand away awkwardly and put it in her own lap where her other hand held it tightly, as if it were a prisoner. She had smiled weakly at her friend to hide her embarrassment and tried to act as if she had experienced nothing. But it was a full week before she could look Atthis in the eye without feeling her face warm.

With her first blood, she knew there would be other changes. She would move to a different hall in the dormitory, one where only the girls who had begun menstruating resided. She would begin her classes in the fourth level, as well. The transition from third to fourth was not based on age, but based on blood. The girls of this age were considered women, or nearly such, and were taught the secret skills of womanhood that are not shared with children. This meant that she and Atthis would be separated for a time, though perhaps not long since the other girl should have her own blood soon enough.

When she rose that morning and saw the thin brownish stain of dried blood on her bedclothes, she wasn't sure at first what was wrong. If it had been red, as she had expected, she would have realized immediately that her time had come. As it was, it took her a few minutes to make the connection. When Kallista came to see what delayed Sappho from joining the other girls in the morning chores, Sappho asked her peer to fetch one of the teachers so she could be taken to the other hall. She gathered her personal things together to take with her since she knew she would now stay in the new room until she left the *thiasos*. As she was preparing to go, Atthis came to her.

"I saw Kallista in the hall," Atthis began. "She tells me you are going."

Sappho couldn't read her friend's expression or the tone in her voice. She felt guilty, somehow, as if she were betraying her friend. Menarche was an important time in a girl's life. She was finally going to be considered a woman, though she didn't gain official status as such until she was married or initiated. Sappho had always thought Atthis would reach this critical stage first, and now she realized that Atthis had probably expected this as well. Sappho felt like she was taking something away from her friend, as if she had a choice as to when her blood would come. She also felt like she was deserting her, which was more painful to her than any of the dozen departures of their family in the last five years.

"It would seem so," was Sappho's response.

"Congratulations, Sappho," Atthis hugged her, though Sappho thought she remained somewhat aloof. "I hope I'll join you soon."

Through her irrational guilt, Sappho replied, "I am sure it can't be long now."

Atthis departed and Rhodia arrived to escort Sappho to her new quarters. Before they left, she tied a red sash to Sappho's waist. As they passed the courtyard along the upper level balcony, Sappho saw the girls below notice her and her sash. Though she was proud of her transition, she was sure her face must have been as red as the adornment at her waist.

The hallway for the girls in the fourth level of their training was on the first floor of the house. It was on the west side of the building, affording its outside rooms with a view of one of the houses of *hierodulei*. The hallway was near the main door of the house and was partitioned from the other sections of the building by red curtains that hung at both ends. When the young women who lived here were menstruating, the curtains were closed. At all other times, they were open.

Since women tend to fall into the same rhythms with the moon and with each other, the curtains were closed when Sappho arrived. The other inhabitants of this hall had already begun the cycle of bleeding, and Sappho was joining them mid-course. As Rhodia explained while showing Sappho to a vacant room, the first cycle is generally weak, and it can sometimes take a few months to fall into sync with the other women.

Sappho placed her belongings in her room, which she noticed was outfitted with a large quantity of straw, and then followed Rhodia to another room at the older woman's request. This room was larger than the individual sleeping rooms and also had a good deal of straw scattered about. Sappho also noticed basins of water and braziers of sweetly smoking incense. Three red-curtained windows allowed a breeze to pass through while maintaining the privacy of the room's occupants.

"This is the common room," Rhodia explained. "While you are menstruating, you will meet in this room for classes. In here and in your own room, make use of the straw. It is much easier to clean afterwards since it can be burned."

"Will I stay in this hallway the entire time?" Sappho asked.

"If you were in your father's home, the answer would be 'yes'," Rhodia replied. "You should expect the same in your husband's house as well. Men do not understand the mysteries that make our role as child-bearers possible. And since we so often revile those things we can't understand, most men prefer their bleeding women to be shut securely away in the *gyneaceum*. But most women also take comfort in their secrets and their mysteries, and we often enjoy the solitude that we can only find behind the red curtains. However, in this house, as in few others, women surround you. There are none here to ridicule you or call you unclean. When your flow slackens, and if you feel comfortable, there are ways you can dress yourself in linens so that you do not stain your clothes if you choose to leave this hall on some errand or other. The other women will show you."

Rhodia left Sappho in a sitting room to return to the other students. Since she had already been through menopause, she had no need of the red rooms and could be available for the classes and supervision that needed attention while the younger priestesses working in the *thiasos* were otherwise occupied.

Sappho returned to her room for a few minutes to organize her belongings a little more efficiently. She had spent six years in her other room, and she had grown more attached to it than she realized. She had lain on her bed for countless hours breathing the aroma of the tree outside her window and thinking about the Gods and Goddesses and all the mysteries that swirled around them. She had engaged in numerous conversations with friends while sitting on the floor or bed and giggling or crying about the fumbles and frustrations of the day. That room, though it looked remarkably like the new room, had felt like an old friend with a spirit and familiarity that gave it warmth.

The rooms were set up in exactly the same way. They had the same type of box bed filled with straw, the same storage box that doubled as a table, and the same oil lamp hanging from a wall bracket. There were a few differences, though. The lamp didn't hang in the window of this room due to the red curtain that already claimed that place, and straw filled the space between her bed and the wall.

As she was taking in the physical characteristics of the room, including the odd glow of the sun through the red fabric of her window, Eunice came into her room. "I heard Rhodia showing someone around," she said, "and I came to see who it was."

Sappho wasn't sure how to respond, so she just smiled and nodded.

"Isn't your sister older than you?" Eunice asked, and Sappho nodded again. "I thought she would be the first." More nodding.

"Are you okay? You seem quiet," the other girl asked. "Does your belly hurt?"

Sappho did a quick check. No, nothing actually hurt, though she felt an odd sort of sensation in her pelvis that made her want to sit down. She would have sat, too, but she didn't want to get blood on her *peplos*. "I just don't know what to do with myself," she admitted. "I don't want to stain all my clothes, but I can't stand for five days."

Eunice giggled. "I know exactly what you mean. It all takes

some getting used to. I moved to this hall five months ago, and I still have a hard time remembering what to do." She giggled again. "You end up washing your clothes a lot." Then the more experienced girl explained a few of the tricks. "If you pick one gown to wear all week, you can wash it every night before you go to sleep, and it will be dry by morning. It's good to have one that is red or at least dark brown. Pick one that you can pull up easily when you sit down. You'll always be sitting on the straw, but sometimes it can poke you. You'll want an old strip of fabric that you can put down first. Or you can also break up the straw a little bit to make it softer."

Sappho made mental notes of these instructions. "Rhodia said something about using a piece of cloth under my garments when the flow is lighter." Eunice nodded and said that most of them used that in the last day or two whether they left the hallway or not. Then, she showed her how to do it.

"Like I said," she reiterated, "you'll be washing cloth a lot. And after all is done, we'll change the straw."

With the help of her friends and the priestesses, Sappho learned other ways of keeping relatively clean and fresh. She was welcomed to the red rooms with a special ceremony at the beginning of the week, and they all bathed together at one of the springs in what felt like an ancient, informal ritual after burning the straw a few days later. They sat in the common room and talked of the mysteries of women and the cycles that bound them to each other, the pull of the sea and the waxing and waning of the moon.

Chapter 17

Anassa made two trips within a couple of months. At the first visit, which she made with the entire family, she learned of both girls' move into the next level of their studies and the menarche that had marked the transition for each. On her second visit, she returned with two servants, Kastor for protection and a woman for assistance, and gifts for her oldest daughters. Her youngest daughter, who was now two, was also with her.

She instructed the servants to attend to the young child while she entered the dormitory with the girls. Sappho and Atthis now had rooms next to each other. Since Atthis had begun her flux only a month after Sappho, she was given the next available room, which shared a wall with her friend. Sappho had been the first to greet her when she arrived, and she shared with her the advice that she had received from Eunice.

Anassa now met with both girls in Atthis's room, which felt incredibly small with three women occupying it. She placed two packages on the bed, which was springy from the fresh straw that had been placed there a week earlier. The girls opened the bundles to find identical items to welcome them to womanhood. They both had dark red wool for new clothes during menses. They also found several strips of soft, undyed linen. "For undergarments or whatever other needs you have." They received small bottles of olive oil mixed with rose, as well. But the most unusual gift was wrapped inside the folds of the red fabric.

"What is this?" Sappho asked as she held up the unfamiliar

133

object. It was made of a cylindrical piece of stone that had been polished until it was extraordinarily smooth. One end was grooved and the other was rounded.

"The time will come when the purpose of this object is made clear to you," Anassa smiled, somewhat self-consciously. "For now, I will say that it is a symbol of one half of all that creates and all that is created. It has a meaning and purpose that are both spiritual and physical." At the girls' quizzical expressions she could only say, "You will understand soon enough."

Chapter 18

Sappho had been shocked in the beginning at how directly her new lessons addressed the irrational and chaotic stirrings that she was feeling in her body. The priestesses who taught the girls at this final level were less likely to lecture than they were to start a discussion about some aspect of the physical body. Sappho found herself engaged in conversations about touch and dance and hygiene, all of which were initially embarrassing. The physical act of sexual intercourse was explained in great detail within the first month of Atthis's arrival, and it was referenced repeatedly thereafter.

She also noticed a lot more physical closeness between the young women in the last stages of their training. The oldest among them seemed especially comfortable with sitting in close proximity, touching each other's hair and shoulders, or squeezing a friend's hand. On more than one occasion in the first few months of her new education, Sappho had seen girls kissing and holding each other passionately in the limited privacy of their rooms. And once, when she was restless in her bed at night, she heard the whimpering sighs of two bodies desperate to find connection and release in each other's arms.

Sappho grew bolder as she realized how natural her desires were. She flirted with flirtation itself and experimented with the effect of an intense stare or a lingering touch. One girl who was probably close to fourteen was fond of flirting with Sappho, and Sappho enjoyed flirting back. But most of her attention was directed at Atthis.

Atthis had always had Sappho's heart, as a friend and a sister, and now Sappho knew that more than just her heart was moved by Atthis's presence. Sappho felt dizzy when she stood near Atthis in the dim light of the oil lamp at night. She could smell her skin and the rose oil as her body heated it. She longed to kiss Atthis as she had seen other girls do in those stolen glimpses of tender moments. She wanted to hear her friend whimper as someone else had done on that restless night.

Atthis did not object to Sappho's attention. She was more reserved than her friend, but she enjoyed the moments when they stood close to each other and the air seemed to crackle. She could feel her own body respond to Sappho's growing need to touch her lips, her shoulders, her hips. She could feel the pressure of their soft curves melting into each other as they embraced, and she knew that she wanted more.

The common room in the hallway they all shared was cleaned and aired after every menses cycle, and it was used as a private room for dancing and ritual that was exclusive to the girls in the upper level. They frequently danced with the other students in common festivities, but there was a freedom in the red room that couldn't exist with a larger number of girls. It was in these private dances that the girls first experienced the mind-numbing surrender of ecstatic dance. Some would play music on the double-flute or the lyre, many would drum a primal and frantic beat, and all would lose themselves in the whirling motion that seemed to rise up from the ground and engulf them.

Sappho reveled in the intensity of the dance, letting

everything leave her mind as her body took over. Then it, too, would lose control and she would tumble to the ground in a breathless, exhausted, contented heap. She liked to lie there and imagine that she was enfolded in Aphrodite's embrace, like the fortunate girl in the temple statue, and that the combination of Aphrodite's scent and kiss had brought her body and mind this sweet oblivion.

This type of dancing would usually happen in the evening, after a light dinner. On one such night, Sappho laid on her bed anticipating the night to come and trying to meditate on the need for this release, this catharsis. She had been fasting for the day, as she had been encouraged to do by Sanura, the teaching priestess who had been given to the temple by an Egyptian merchant. She felt weak and in a state of anxious arousal at the coming event.

When Atthis stepped into her doorway, she didn't notice for several seconds. She became conscious of being watched and turned her gaze to the door to see who was there. When she saw Atthis looking at her, she immediately rose, feeling very self-conscious for some reason that she couldn't have explained. Of course, she had been feeling rather self-conscious around Atthis for a while.

Sappho tried to smooth the wrinkles she had pressed into her robes while lying on them for so long. She also tried to readjust her hair, which she knew couldn't be in the neat little knot in which she had tied it earlier that day.

"Hello," she said somewhat nervously. "I didn't see you there."

Atthis smiled slyly. "Obviously."

Sappho felt her hair prickling at the flirtation she sensed in her friend. Atthis was usually very passive in their encounters, allowing Sappho to make whatever advances were made and basking in the attention. Sappho felt rather exhilarated by the role shift. She didn't quite know what to say next, though. "Do you …," she couldn't form what seemed like a coherent sentence. "Did you need to ask me something?"

Atthis clearly wasn't sure exactly what to say, either. "I came to … I mean, I thought that … I just wanted to …" She was flushing from embarrassment and frustration. She knew she must look very silly tripping over her tongue like this. She wanted something, but she couldn't exactly identify it. She certainly couldn't put a name to it. She wanted to be near Sappho. She wanted Sappho to look at her and make her smile. She wanted to feel the prickle of excitement when Sappho's hand brushed her own. But she couldn't just walk into her room and say, "I want to be with you." So instead, she just said, "I don't know … Never mind," and she turned to leave the room.

"Wait," Sappho called just as Atthis reached the hall. The other girl turned, and Sappho said, "We don't have long before we are supposed to be in the common room. I can't meditate anymore anyway."

"I'm sorry for bothering you," Atthis interrupted before Sappho could finish.

"No, it's fine," Sappho put in quickly. "I was having trouble before you came in. Honestly. Anyway, why don't you stay here until we have to leave?"

"Are you sure?" Atthis had already started to sit on the bed.

"I wouldn't have asked if I hadn't wanted you to stay," said Sappho, realizing that she had once again taken control of the situation. Whatever else was to happen, Sappho would have to initiate it.

The girls sat for a little while on Sappho's bed without looking at each other or speaking. Then Sappho asked, "Are you looking forward to the dancing tonight?"

Atthis sighed and reclined back all the way on the bed. "Yes, but I hate all the preparation for it. I can never focus long enough to meditate, and fasting makes me sick."

Sappho moved onto her side, facing Atthis. She was closer to her friend's outstretched body than she had estimated, and that knowledge sent a thrill through her belly and chest. As she spoke, she allowed her hand to rest in such a way that she touched Atthis' waist as she supported herself. "I love that dizzy feeling, though – the one you get just as the music and chanting begin."

"And then later, when you swoon on the floor," added Atthis. "That feels so amazing – like nothing else."

"I've felt something else like that," Sappho said as silkily as she knew how.

Atthis turned her face toward Sappho and searched for her friend's eyes in the gloom of the early evening light. "What?"

"This," said Sappho. "Being this close to you makes me feel like that."

Atthis didn't respond verbally, but Sappho could feel the shiver that coursed through her. They had never actually spoken words of longing or desire for each other, even though they had both felt it. Sappho held Atthis's gaze through the misty light and tried to read her expression. She felt pulled toward her, or maybe pushed. She was compelled. She eased a little closer so that their bodies touched, moved her hand to the other side of Atthis's waist so that she could lean part of her weight toward the other girl, and kissed her.

It was the first kiss of desire either of them had shared with anyone. It was the first kiss either had experienced that wasn't given with familial devotion. It was the first kiss that left them wanting nothing but another kiss or a closer touch.

Sappho felt like her body was on fire, and yet icy in the same instant. She thought her arms would give out. Her hands felt like they might be going numb. Her heart pounded in her ears.

She heard a noise in the corridor and jerked away from her first touch of intimacy. In the same instant, Atthis scrambled off the bed. She smoothed her skirts and hair as Sappho had done when surprised by Atthis's presence a few minutes before and muttered something about going to the common room. She was out the door before Sappho had a chance to say anything. Sappho had looked down at the bed below her for the brief moment that Atthis looked back. Both girls worried what the other one thought.

Sappho pulled herself from the spot where she had just touched Atthis then pulled the pins that held her hair in place. Her wavy curls spilled onto her shoulders, and she enjoyed their silky tickle along her back before shaking them out. She wanted her hair down while she danced. She also hoped it would hide the scarlet in her cheeks. She removed the belt that gird her *khiton* close to her body as she left the room, wanting nothing to keep her bound to the everyday world as she lost herself in the ecstasy of the dance.

Even as she entered the corridor she could hear the beat of the drum. It was a beat that got into her blood. It echoed her own heartbeat. Tonight, it reverberated in every part of her body that had been awakened by the moment's physical connection with Atthis. The drumbeat stirred her to further excitement, further anticipation, further hope of a future delight.

The smell of the incense reached her just before she entered the room. She could distinguish cedar wood, rose oil, and orris root. There were other scents she couldn't place, but the total effect was both sweet and biting. Her mind swam. The chanting began as she crossed the threshold. "Come, beautiful Goddess. Come, golden Kypris." Her voice fell into the pattern of the rhythm as her mind followed the melody played by the girl with the double-flute.

She felt the priestess acting as the *hydrophoros* sprinkle her with cleansing water, and she accepted the blessing the woman spoke. She felt the water begin poured over her hands and instinctively brought it to her brow and to her lips before raising both arms skyward and saying, "Hail, Aphrodite."

She continued chanting with the other girls, and tried to let everything leave her mind. She especially wanted to push the thought of the kiss away. No, she wanted to keep the kiss. She wanted the kiss to be the only thing she could recall. She wanted to rid herself of the sight of Atthis walking away from her. She wanted to be cleansed of the embarrassment of being so forward only to be rejected. Had she been rejected? She wasn't sure. As her body moved in beat with the drum and chant, she saw the scene playing out again in her mind.

She saw herself lying next to Atthis. She leaned toward the other girl. She could feel the softness of Atthis's mouth. She could smell the sweetness of her breath and warm rose oil as it pulsed from the place on her neck where she always applied it. She could feel the wetness of their mouths as they came together and the wetness that now grew between her own legs.

She was entirely transported to that moment, and the room spun around her as she was swept away again by the swirling passion that was now consuming her. She pulled away from the girl she was kissing and was mildly surprised to see a face other than Atthis's. The face she saw was young-looking, not much older than she herself, but something behind the eyes belied the wisdom and experience of this girl. She was not taller than Sappho in the flesh, but some power that shone through her dwarfed Sappho. Her lips curled in a seductive smile, and she was not at all timid about holding Sappho's gaze with an intensity that told her she could get burned by the passion there.

Sappho's heart tightened at the knowledge of who embraced her. She saw Aphrodite behind the girl's eyes. This other girl, this vessel of Aphrodite, reached out her hand to touch the place on Sappho's chest that felt like it might burst. Sappho was simultaneously calmed and exhilarated. The hand moved deftly to Sappho's breast, and the girl's breath caught at the pleasure of the touch.

Sappho wanted to speak, but her mouth was completely dry. The other girl spoke instead. "You are not yet ready for a true encounter with me. There is one who you must seek first. You are ready for each other. Do not be afraid to speak your love. It is the greatest treasure you can give to another. Give it freely and without regret."

Sappho wanted to respond, but her vision of the golden daughter of Zeus was replaced by a blur of gold and violet. When the room around her became solid again, she could see her peers in various stages of losing themselves in the dance. Their bodies moved of their own accord. Their hair swung free, their hips circled and sometimes their whole bodies spun in chaotic rhythm.

Atthis was near Sappho, where she sat on the floor. She watched her friend dance for a minute before feeling driven to the point of action. Then, when she could restrain herself no longer, she stood and traced the line of Atthis's shoulders with her hand as she stood behind her. Atthis turned and looked directly into Sappho's eyes. Never in such clear light had Sappho seen the girl she knew so well look at her with such smoke and fire behind her gaze.

They each took a step toward the other. They wrapped their arms around the neck and waist of the other. They met with equal desire and equal force in a kiss that ripped the breath from each of their bodies.

Sappho turned on her heel and lead Atthis by the hand out of the common room where the other girls and priestesses continued losing themselves in the swirling madness of ecstasy. When they came to the door of Sappho's small, unlit chamber, Atthis stopped stood facing Sappho in the doorway before curling her lips in a seductive smile and pulled her friend into the room.

Chapter 19

There was no self-consciousness between the girls as regarded their new-found intimacy. All the nervous fumbling that had preceeded their encounter was forgotten and replaced by an irrepressible desire to be in each other's company at all possible moments. They were the closest confidants and most energetic playmates, as they had been long ago when they were children in Scamandronymus's house.

Finding time to be together was not a difficult task, given the circumstances of their lives. Every lesson was shared, every chore, every meal. Their rooms shared a wall, and on many nights the girls shared a bed.

They played like children who had been given a new toy. In public, they giggled and sang and rollicked in the courtyard like any childhood playmates. In private, they giggled and sang and rollicked in the darkness of the bed as they discovered the secrets of their own and each other's bodies. The songs of the night were the whimpers and trembling sighs of pleasure that Sappho had heard on other evenings by different singers.

Sappho noticed other bonds of friendship and intimacy among her peers. As she experienced the first blossoming of love in her own body and mind, she could see its effects on those around her.

Of course, not everyone was so filial. Two other girls could barely be in the same room with each other without one being cruel and the other weeping. One particular girl would look disapprovingly each time she saw the lightest caress of the arm or the slightest brush of the lips. And yet there were others who were oblivious to or uninterested in the romantic energy that was swirling all around them. When she thought of these differences she could almost hear the priestess Sanura repeat one of her most well-worn adages. "There are many flowers in the garden."

Perhaps it was the season – spring always seemed to inspire rut and lust. Perhaps it was the age – girls just coming into their sexuality can barely control themselves for long. Whatever the case, the priestess's lessons turned their attention almost entirely to the concepts of sex and sensuality.

The philosophy in the *thiasos* had always been that an Aphrodisian wife brought a sense of love, joy, and pleasure to the relationship, the home, and the marriage bed. Aphrodite's influence was not only sexual. All acts of grace and beauty and charm were infused with her blessing. To this end, the students of the temple had spent years in refining their mental faculties so they could engage in stimulating conversation, their physical movements so they could walk and dance gracefully, their musical ability so they could entertain. They had discussed art and the various ways to present themselves and their homes in a fashion that was visually pleasing. They had tended to the roses in the gardens and paths that decorated the *demos*. They did all these things to lend Aphrodite's influence outside the bedchamber.

Aphrodite's influence was not *merely* sexual, but it would have been inaccurate and inappropriate to claim that it had no bearing on the sexual side of human nature. Furthermore, the temple would have been remiss in neglecting to teach not only *that* Aphrodite ruled the affairs of the bed, but also *how* she presided there. The *thiasos* would have been foolish not to instruct the girls in multiple techniques to enjoy and be enjoyed in their bridal beds.

It was at this time that the priestesses acknowledged the sexual relationships that were forming between the girls. Rhodia had been the first to give practical advice in the matter.

"It is fine that you find pleasure together," she had said. "Our bodies are made to enjoy each other's touch. Your mates will appreciate that you respond with satisfaction to their contact. You will be glad to know what feels best to you when you lie with your husbands. You will always be likely to have close relationships with the women of your house, for you may not be the only wife to your husband." She paused for a moment before saying, "This pleasure of touch is a gift of Aphrodite. It is wonderful and intense, but it is also common. It is available to everyone. This is why she is sometimes called *Pandemos*. It is special, and it is very powerful and it is available to all." Another pause, and with a tone of light warning she continued, "Do not mistake lust for love. Kypris gives both, and both are a delight, but they are not the same. Enjoy each for what it is." And with a more somber tone, "Your husbands may delight in your knowledge of pleasing them, but they will rage in suspecting you've been with another man. Make certain you come to your bridal bed with bloody proof of your virginity." The girls knew what she meant. They had already learned of the physical details of intercourse, and they knew that a woman usually hurt and bled the first time she was penetrated by something as large as a phallus. Many of them had also learned, through experience, that their own touch would cause no damage.

Other conversations focused on other aspects of their sensual development. They were led in meditations in which they visualized themselves as active participants in sexual encounters with a man. Through this method, they could have some amount of experience with the rough, strong hands and muscular, hairy bodies that prodded and penetrated and touched so differently from their soft, silky counterparts. The girls came to anticipate an actual sexual experience with the men who would be their husbands while still appreciating and holding dear the intimate caresses of their female friends.

They were also led in practical applications of sensual and therapeutic touch, which they practiced on each other. After the teachers described and demonstrated the various techniques, the girls would form pairs and attempt to do what they had been shown. Some exercises were conducted in the common room; however, the more intimate and personal maneuvers required private study. For these, the girls would either be released to their chambers with explicit instructions to practice, or, as was more typical, the theoretical details were explained and an unstated practice session was arranged after sundown.

The girls were also encouraged to discover the pleasures of self-touch. "One of Aphrodite's lessons is to love yourself," Hermione had said. The girls really didn't have to be told to love themselves in this manner. They would have done it anyway.

Sappho, for one, was reassured to know that she wasn't the

only one who enjoyed the feel of her own skin. There were times when she actually preferred some time to herself over an encounter with Atthis. It wasn't that she didn't enjoy Atthis's body. On the contrary, she relished the opportunity to touch and taste her friend's mouth, shoulders, breasts, navel, thighs. Nor was she disappointed in Atthis's touch. Indeed, her friend had learned quickly and could manipulate Sappho's body in such a way as to render her helpless. Instead, her reasons for wanting private sexual time stemmed, she felt, from a certain laziness or greed. Sometimes, she just didn't want to perform or have to focus on anyone's climactic pleasure but her own.

Not all of the personal sensual time was intended for the purely physical slaking of the body's desires. The girls had been taught how to raise and collect their energies into a climactic offering for the violet-crowned and golden Aphrodite. They were encouraged to perform this personal rite on a regular basis, however frequently seemed best to them.

Sappho had discovered that her meetings with Aphrodite in her dreams, or in the half-waking time that seemed like dreams, were clearer and more intense as she became more adept at giving her gift to the Goddess. These meetings began with Kypris at a distance and silent, and Sappho was unable to speak or move closer. But with time and focus, Aphrodite was nearer and clearer, with her beautiful smile of acceptance for Sappho's simple gift. Sappho couldn't form all the words her heart longed to say. "I yearn for your blessing, golden Lady. I seek your touch in my life." All that would come out was, "I yearn, and I seek." But the delectable daughter of heaven acknowledged her desires with a knowing nod and a gesture of approval.

Sappho's most intense encounter yet had come during the full moon in Aphrodite's month, according to the Lesvian calendar. Though most of the rituals she had attended were either in the dormitory's courtyard or in the common room shared by the girls in the fourth level, this one was in honor of a festival to the patroness of the temple and was held in the secluded sanctuary on the west end of the grounds.

As the girls followed the procession to the temple, Sappho's gaze was drawn to the sacred grove that lay in close proximity to it. Somewhere in her mind, Sappho noted that both places were sacred to Aphrodite, though one was a man-made reflection of the other. No matter their construction, both were consecrated and made holy by the hand of Aphrodite.

She saw the glint of the setting sun on the leaves and thought about the shine of the candlelight and lamplight on the pillars of the temple. She heard the whistle of wind through the branches and knew its echo in the breath blown through the double-flute. She felt the pulse of life in the earth and recognized it in the pounding of the drum. She smelled the fragrance of the apple blossoms opening in the grove and remembered the scent of incense wafting through the temple. She thought she imagined the form of Aphrodite embracing her within the depths of the apple grove, and she was reminded of the statue she saw on her first night in Hiera, the one she was about to behold again.

The usual ritual preparations took place inside the temple.

The celebrants were cleansed and unified as the hydrophorous priestess poured the water over their hands. The incense hung delicately in the air between them as the scent of the herbs and beat of the drum distinguished this time and place as separate from the world outside the temple door.

The *hiereia* herself led this ritual, and some other priestesses of the temple, many of whom they had never met, joined the students. Large golden mirrors had been hung on the walls, and smaller mirrors had been stacked on and beneath the tables. A glittering, smoky, golden reflection filled the room and caused the light of the countless flames to dance and play on every surface.

The *hiereia* poured water in controlled measures to the floor as she said, "Now rose the moon, full and argentine, while round stood the maidens at the shrine." She poured the clear, clean liquid into a large circle around the altar. "The gleaming stars all about the shining moon hide their bright faces, when full-orbed and splendid in the sky she floats, flooding the shadowed earth with clear silver light."

Sappho felt her mind cooled and stilled as the *hiereia* spoke the poetry as effortlessly as she had poured the first libation. She watched as the chorus of priestesses intoned the summons to the Kharites. "Come, rosy-armed Graces, virgin daughters of Zeus. Come now, gentle Graces, and fair-haired Muses." Sappho wasn't sure if the shimmers of reflection from the mirrors tricked her eyes, if the incense clouded her mind, or if, in fact, there were now more women in the room. She definitely had the sense that more people were suddenly in the temple.

When she refocused on the ritual, Timas was holding a jar filled with honey tipped so that a golden stream trickled onto the ground before her. She had already begun the invocation to Aphrodite when Sappho could center her attention enough to hear her words. "Come, *Akidalia*, from your bath, dressed in garments shot with innumerable hues, your shining ankles clad in fairest fashion." A priestess poured a small amount of wine on the altar fire, which sprang to immediate life. The *hiereia* threw more incense onto the fire. "So came the Goddess," she announced.

Sappho was stunned. As she looked from the *hiereia* to the statue behind her, she saw the most beautiful woman standing there. Sappho knew her from her dreams and visions. She had seen this immortal woman many times already. The image was not always the same, but she knew the Goddess's spirit. Her heart raced. This was no vision. This was no ethereal image formed in her mind. The woman facing the *hiereia* was corporeal.

Sappho checked the faces of the girls and women around her for signs of recognition. She needed evidence to prove whether or not she had gone mad. The reactions were difficult to gauge. Most of the priestesses saw her, and they all made gestures of respectful greeting when Aphrodite looked at them. The *hiereia* knelt at her feet, and Aphrodite touched her brow in blessing before Timas rose again. Sappho's breath caught when Aphrodite winked at her. Such a familiar gesture! From Aphrodite! She tried to get Atthis's attention, but her friend had a pleasant, far-away look that floated near where the Goddess stood. None of the girls from the thiasos seemed capable of focusing directly on Aphrodite. One of the priestesses smiled reassuringly at Sappho as she tried to assess the situation.

Timas had once again continued speaking, "Aphrodite brings love and shows us beauty." She was now making eye contact with the participants in the ritual, giving them instructions. "See now the beauty that sits within your spirit and shines out through your form and face." Timas indicated the mirrors, and the priestesses led by example. Each of the women gave the girls a small, golden mirror, a polished circle just big enough to descry one's face. Then, several of the priestesses moved to stand before the mirrors on the wall.

As she gazed into her mirror, Sappho heard music. Perhaps some of the celebrants were chanting and singing. Perhaps she was. Maybe the music drifted in through the open doors. Maybe it came from her mind. She didn't struggle to identify its source. It was beautiful and pleasant and light, and she continued looking at her own reflection.

She saw her face mirrored in the highly polished, golden disc. It was the face she knew from other reflections. It wasn't as beautiful as some of the faces belonging to some of the other girls, but the wit and life behind her eyes and the joy in her smile afforded her a charm that couldn't be induced by simple good looks and a simple mind. Her hair was unbound tonight and cascaded in chestnut waves around her face, onto her shoulders, and down her back.

Then, it seemed to her that the face in the mirror changed somewhat. It was the visage of a woman ten years older than her, but the features were similar. The twinkle in the eyes was still there, but it was tempered with something that Sappho couldn't define. Maybe it was wisdom. Maybe it was experience. The charismatic smile looked much the same, though it was a bit more sardonic. The hair was fuller, almost totally untamed.

Again, the image shifted, aged ten more years or so. Sappho saw herself from more of a distance, one at which she could view her entire body. There was something odd but familiar about her clothing. She was wearing a khiton of golden yellow and a white veil trimmed with gold. She held a jar filled with honey, which she poured in a controlled fashion onto the floor.

Then the face changed again. It was not her own. The face staring back at her from the mirror was the same as the one she had seen moments before when she faced the *heireia*. Her hair was a dark gold. Her eyes were as green as the sea, brightly lit by the sun. Atop her head rested a wreath of violets. Her gown was barely sheer, and the color was indefinable. At first glance, Sappho thought the gown was green, like the woman's eyes, like the sea at noon. Then, it looked like the azure sky, but it darkened like midnight descending. The dawn rose in the fabric, and it was gray, pale, red, orange, golden yellow all in succession. The changes were subtle, but constant.

A voice behind Sappho whispered softly, directly into her ear. It was the voice of the one who looked at Sappho through the mirror. She could feel her breath on her shoulder, feel a brushing against her hair. She could smell a light scent of salt and roses.

The voice said, "You once offered me yourself, not so long ago. You were young. You are still young, but now you are old enough to offer again." Sappho couldn't speak. She only nodded.

"Come to the grove tonight and give me your song."

Chapter 20

Sappho stole away from the dormitory well after everyone else had gone to bed. The ritual had ended and would be discussed the next morning, allowing everyone sufficient time to encounter the delectable Aphrodite in her dreams. As Sappho had re-dressed herself in dark robes with a dark veil wrapped around her hair and arms, she wondered about the encounter she was preparing to have with the golden Goddess in the silver moonlight.

The path was easy to see in the pale light of the changing orb. Sappho saw nobody else as she walked, a fact for which she was most grateful since she wasn't entirely certain how to explain herself. She was out of the *thiasos's* residence when she should have been asleep inside it; and, while such action wasn't expressly forbidden, she feared it wouldn't be met with approval. She planned on hiding in the shadows with her veil drawn around her if she saw any priestesses on her path. This was unnecessary, though she did hide a time or two as a precaution when her nerves got the better of her and she thought she heard a noise on the path.

She saw the grove ahead, its apple blossoms glowing in the pale, silver light. The late night had a chill that hadn't set in during the mirror ritual. Sappho was thankful she had worn the veil. It was a comfort to pull the fabric around her shoulders and arms to keep the chill at bay. She hoped she wouldn't be too cold, but somehow she figured that wouldn't be a problem tonight. She thought of Aphrodite, the heat of her breath on her neck and the way her body responded reassured her that she would certainly be kept warm enough. As long as she *thought* about Aphrodite, she would be as hot as if she stood near a bonfire.

The little twisted apple trees clustered together in the darkness, their white blossoms quivering in the breeze. There was an opening in the trees that revealed a walkway leading into the heart of the grove. Before she stepped onto the grove's path, she looked to the left, to the south where the temple sat. A little flame was flickering from an oil lamp on the altar, the fire of Hestia that was never extinguished within the temple. From somewhere inside, a priestess moved, disrupting the play of light and shadows on the wall.

Sappho took a few steps into the grove and turned her gaze toward its center, the place she had set as her goal. She thought she saw the glow of flames from within the midst of the trees and a figure moving there as well. Was Aphrodite there awaiting her? Was someone else using the grove for some tryst this night? With great curiosity and great trepidation, she wrapped herself more securely in her veil and moved as stealthily as she could manage toward the tiny flickers of flame.

She smelled a sweet perfume, as of incense, but she saw no smoke. She did, however, see the distinct figure of a woman just beyond the trees in front of her. She heard the singing of a delightful song, and as she watched and listened she was sure she watched Aphrodite. This time the Goddess had dark hair that was unbound and hanging to her waist in thick curls. She turned and faced Sappho through the trees. Sappho was shocked. Aphrodite looked like her!

She spoke directly to Sappho through the camouflage of

night and veil and tree. "This grove has always been a favorite of mine, so close to the hot springs that feed the baths. I have always been here, among the apple trees and the sweet, hot waters. When the men and women living nearby felt how sacred this grove was, merely because it had my favor, they began having rites here. They marked the entrance with stones and made a simple stone altar for me. They offered me their love, their sex, and their first fruits in this grove long before they built the temple. I gave my blessing to the temple and all else that was built on these grounds because of my love for this place and the devotion of the people who have come here so long."

As Aphrodite spoke, Sappho moved into the clearing at the heart of the grove. There was a thick carpet of grass and soft beds of moss. Wild roses grew here, shaded by the apple branches. Sappho saw twinkling lights from within those branches, but she couldn't comprehend their source. She saw no flame. The lights reminded her of stars, and she wondered if Aphrodite had taken some from heaven and bewitched them to hang here.

When she was in close proximity to the Goddess, she was even more stunned to see what she would have sworn was her own face. Aphrodite looked like *her*, except this was an ideal vision of herself imbued with all the grace and charm of immortal Kypria. This countenance, so much like her own, had no flaw, no scar, no harshness of any sort, and it almost glowed with the power of Olympos.

"May I ask a question?" Sappho inquired politely. Her insides fluttered at being this close to an immortal – a Goddess who had commanded her presence and a performance. Aphrodite nodded. "I know you may have any appearance you wish, but why would you choose mine? I'm no great beauty. There are several other girls of my own age in the *thiasos* who are far more fair than I. Why not look like them?"

"Perhaps at some other time, I shall. But do not discount your own beauty. Your face, your voice, your spirit are all pleasing to me," the Goddess said simply. "You are touched by my beauty and my love. You dishonor me by not recognizing my gifts to you."

"I wish to honor you," Sappho said sincerely.

"There are many ways you may honor me," said the Goddess. "There are countless ways to serve me."

"How would you best like for me to honor and serve you, Lady?" Sappho asked.

"Cultivate your beauty. Tend to it as you would tend to a rose garden," Aphrodite said. "This is the simplest task. See yourself as beautiful, and all who meet you will feel my mark upon you."

Aphrodite was silent, and Sappho feared for a moment that the Goddess wanted nothing more from her. "Is this all?" she asked.

"No," she smiled wryly. "You are likely, someday, to wish my requests of you were so simple. You may also serve me by honoring the love you find in others. You, Sappho, have a great capacity to love, and men and women alike will be drawn to you. Share your love and theirs, always honoring whatever vows you make."

"What vows will I make?" Sappho asked, desperately hoping that she would take the temple vows and become a priestess here. She had wanted that since the night she came to Hiera. She held her breath in anticipation of Aphrodite's response. She hoped to be called immediately into service, but she braced herself for rejection.

"Your vows are always made of your own accord," said the Goddess. "No mortal man or woman can force you to make a vow against your will, though they can take your like if you refuse. Such as this has and will always continue to happen. I am immortal, though, and I say you are mine. Vow or none, I will always come to you, and I will demand your service when it suits me."

Sappho fell to her knees before the Kyprian beauty and kissed the hem of her robes. "I am yours." She wept tears of joy. "What service would you ask of me tonight?"

"Your song," Aphrodite gently demanded as she lowered herself onto a mossy cushion.

"I have not written it all," Sappho admitted, ashamed and fearful of the Goddess's anger.

"You vowed to sing me the best song you could write whenever I should call for it," Aphrodite reminded her. "I call for it now."

"As you wish," said Sappho, and she picked up the lyre that was next to her on the ground, awaiting discovery. Sappho sat on the grass before Aphrodite and began to play the instrument. She'd pluck a pretty melody between the lines, while constantly looking into the eyes of the Goddess.

Shimmering-throned immortal Aphrodite,
Daughter of Zeus, Enchantress, I implore thee!

Thou hast come, leaving thy father's golden dominions…

With chariot yoked to thy fleet-winged coursers,
Fluttering swift pinions over earth's darkness,
And bringing thee through the Infinite, gliding
downwards from heaven.

I yearn and I seek your face and your favor.

By the time she ended, Sappho was exhilarated, titillated, enthralled. The presence of the Goddess of Love was having a bodily effect upon the girl. The power of the inspiration behind her impromptu song moved her as it moved through her. She felt as though she hadn't been at all responsible for the beauty and arousal of her lyrics. Instead, she felt as though she had channeled some other power and had merely given it voice as it flowed through her.

Aphrodite held her gaze throughout the song. She smiled sweetly as the girl made her offering, the fulfillment of her first vow. Aphrodite accepted this offering graciously, as if it had been the sweetest libation or most precious jewel the girl owned.

Aphrodite continued to compel Sappho's eyes. She leaned back on her bed of moss and soft grass for a moment. Then she sat forward and beckoned Sappho closer. The girl happily obeyed and came nearer to the Goddess, feeling the soft carpet under her knees.

"What gift are you willing to give me now?" enticed Aphrodite.

"Any that you wish," whispered Sappho.

160

Aphrodite swept a curling tendril away from Sappho's face. The girl thrilled at the touch of the Goddess. The reaction of arousal at the contact was far more intense than any she had felt with Atthis or as a result of her own hands. She couldn't have denied Aphrodite any request, and she wouldn't have wanted to. "Give me yourself," Aphrodite requested.

Sappho had a moment of clarity, as if Aphrodite had released her momentarily from a spell so that this choice would be entirely her own. With every part of her soul, she knew her response. "I am entirely yours, now and hereafter," she pledged.

"I will hold you to this vow," Aphrodite said as she pulled Sappho's face to her own and kissed her, tenderly at first but with growing intensity. Sappho was overwhelmed by the ecstasy of their embrace. She felt the world reel around her and the stars spin wildly out of control over her. She let herself sink into the delirium of a choice that has been made and the wild ardor of being taken by the Goddess.

She knew that she made love to Aphrodite – that every touch was an act of tenderness and devotion and lust that brought dizzying and explosive climax ever closer. She could feel and smell and taste the body of the Goddess. She drank her in and became intoxicated. She could hear her moans, gasps, sighs, and laughter – all the sounds of pleasure – and knew there was no sweeter music in the universe. She saw the face, the breasts, the curly hair between her alabaster thighs and knew that no statue could ever show the true beauty of Aphrodite. *Surely*, Sappho thought, *she is most beautiful as she is now – giving and receiving pleasure in the arms of one who is completely devoted to her.*

The two became a tangle of hair and legs and torsos, their hands and mouths continually searching for and finding each other. The pleasure, to Sappho, seemed as if it would last an eternity. She had no other thought in her mind but to enjoy and be enjoyed by Aphrodite, bordering on climax until the stars faded and fell from the heavens. Sappho felt as though she had the stamina to remain intermeshed with Kypris until her very life was ended. And when she knew orgasm was about to take her, it felt like a little death, indeed – such sweet release into oblivion, such cramping desire to sustain it, such remorse that all was ending.

Sappho sang again.

> *Then in my bosom my heart wildly flutters,*
> *And, when on thee I gaze never so little,*
> *Bereft am I of all power of utterance.*
> *My tongue is useless.*

> *There rushes at once through my flesh tingling fire,*
> *My eyes are deprived of all power of vision,*
> *My ears hear nothing but sounds of winds roaring.*
> *And all is blackness.*

> *Down courses in streams the sweat of emotion,*
> *A dread trembling o'erwhelms me, paler am I*
> *Than dried grass in autumn, and in my madness*
> *Dead I seem almost.*

They panted and smiled, stretched like cats on the mossy ground. They kissed and petted each other until they were content to be still, and Sappho felt the world around her become substantial again.

Aphrodite whispered in her ear, "You will be trained now as a priestess – my priestess." She reached her slender finger down to the secret places Sappho had just explored and touched the moisture there. Sappho wondered if they were going to find heaven together again. Aphrodite smiled as she made an invisible mark on Sappho's brow. "Now you are anointed by me."

Chapter 21

The *hiereia* was present for the debriefing of the past night's full moon ritual in the girls' house. She knew they had experienced other rituals as a part of their education and honor of Aphrodite. They had taken part in her festivals and also in celebrations on a smaller scale, generally in the courtyard of the *thiasos*. However, she also knew that the last evening's ritual was likely to be the most intense and meaningful they had yet experienced. She hoped this was the case, at any rate. She had planned it to be such.

Sappho was exhausted by the time the girls convened in the courtyard with Timas. Her mind was clear, and her body was more resilient than she would have supposed it to be, but she was tired nonetheless. Timas looked at her oddly, and Sappho thought she must have been obviously depleted to arouse such quizzical expressions from the *hiereia*.

The girls were each given the opportunity to share their experiences in the ritual, as well as any unusual points of insight they might have had during their encounters with their mirrors. Many of the girls expressed a sensation of really feeling Aphrodite's presence in the temple with them. Others said they heard her speaking to them as they gazed at their reflections. One or two said that they saw a vague form that they thought was the Goddess.

Sappho was hesitant in sharing her experience in the temple. She didn't want to seem boastful to her peers, none of whom had seen Aphrodite as clearly as she had. She certainly didn't want to share anything about her experience in the grove. She would be profaning something sacred, in her opinion, if she said aloud to a room full of girls what had befallen in the arms of Aphrodite.

When her turn came, she said, "When the Goddess was called, I saw her standing behind the altar."

"You had the impression of her standing there?" Timas queried. "Or did you see a physical presence?"

"I saw a physical presence," Sappho replied.

Timas was very intrigued. She continued questioning the girl. "What did she wear? What did she do?"

Sappho described the gown that changed colors like the rising and setting of the sun over water. "She blessed you as you knelt before her, and she smiled at many of the priestesses around the room," Sappho said.

"And did she make eye contact with you, or give you a gesture?" Timas asked.

"She did," Sappho hesitated. "She winked at me."

Timas smiled, a knowing kind of smile. "And when you looked in the mirror, did she speak to you?"

"She did," Sappho said. She didn't want to disclose Aphrodite's instructions to her at that point in the rite because such disclosure would lead to her experience in the grove. To her surprise, though, Timas didn't press the issue.

"Thank you for sharing this, my dear," Timas said to her. "If you will please remain after the others leave, I would like to continue this discussion later."

Sappho nodded assent and spent the remainder of the debriefing period in nervous anticipation of the conversation to follow. She would have to tell the *hiereia* what transpired, but she knew she would have to do that anyway. Aphrodite had told her she would be trained in the temple as a priestess. Certainly, the *hiereia* would need to know about that.

When the other students were dismissed to their regular classes or to their chores, Timas stood and beckoned Sappho to follow her. She led her past the rows of priestess homes and onto the path that led to the center of the grove where she had been just hours ago.

"You were here last night, were you not?" Timas asked with all the authority of the *hiereia*. Sappho was intimidated by the power behind the words. She didn't know if Timas was angry with her for sneaking out of the house, irritated that she hadn't confessed immediately and publicly, or pleased that Sappho had followed the instructions of the Goddess who bade her come.

"I was," Sappho replied. She would wait for a better gauge of Timas's mood before she volunteered information.

"I see Aphrodite's mark upon your brow," the priestess declared. "She has chosen you to be a priestess, Sappho, and you have agreed."

Sappho was stunned. How could Timas know? She could *see* Aphrodite's imprint? Was this, then, the way all priestesses were chosen? That seemed impossible, given the astronomical number of the *hierodulei*. Surely not all of them could have been students in the *thiasos* who were then called into illicit encounters with the immortal Aphrodite.

Timas could see Sappho's mind searching for answers that

she couldn't find just yet. *Let the girl struggle some*, she thought. *She doesn't need to know everything from the start. Let her always have respect for the training and intuition of those above her. She received her call in the same manner as I, and she may be called to more than simple priestesshood. She needs a sense of humility and awe for what lies ahead.*

Timas nodded resolutely and then proclaimed, "Then, we will begin to prepare you for the rites of initiation. You have received one initiation, directly at the hands of Aphrodite. Your encounter here marks and binds you as her servant. If you so decide, you will also take vows to this temple to serve her in the custom and fashion of the priestesses here at Hiera. Is this your will?"

Sappho had always wanted this, but now she thought of her father. What of his plans for her? Was she not to be married to bring honor, fortune, or reputation to his household? "It is what I wish," she said, but the uncertainty was evident in her voice.

"What keeps you from sounding sure?" Timas asked.

"What of my father and future marriage?" Sappho asked, though she wasn't sure Timas could speak for her parents.

"This should not be a concern," said Timas flatly. "He brought you here to train you for your future life. A connection with this temple only enhances his family's name. He will be glad of your call."

"Will you tell him, or will I?" Sappho asked. She was a little afraid of her father's reaction, despite Timas's assurances.

"When a woman marries, she is finally seen as an adult," Timas began. "It is the same when she initiates. You are bordering on adulthood, Sappho, and you must take responsibility for your choices. However, you do not have to face those choices alone. I will be present the next time your parents arrive, which will be soon. There will be details that your father and I must discuss."

Sappho wondered how Timas knew her parents were coming soon. Perhaps they sent word ahead of time. Perhaps parents were always encouraged to do that. Sappho hoped nothing was wrong. She had an uneasy feeling about the visit as she was dismissed from the *hiereia's* presence to return to her own class.

Over the course of the next week, Sappho thought about what had happened in the grove and about her discussion with Timas. She told Atthis what she knew, and poured out all of her excitement that her friend might share in her good fortune. She was surprised at Atthis's lack of enthusiasm and the grudging way in which her friend congratulated her. Sappho was stung by the apathy with which her dearest friend greeted this happiest of news. She decided not to speak of it for a time in order to allay the growing tension between them. Instead, the unspoken words formed a dark cloud between them that Sappho feared was brewing into a fierce storm.

When her parents arrived without the older boys, matters only seemed to worsen. Nilo and Kharaxus were now old enough to be in school, too. Their school was in Mytiline, as more options existed for educating male children, and so they had been left with Kastor, who normally took them to and from the school. Anassa brought her daughter and youngest son Eurygius, and she was clearly pregnant again. The girl, Zeta, was now nearly five years old. Sappho figured that she, too, would be sent to the temple in a couple of years.

The little children were well-behaved, and Anassa was in good spirits. She always seemed happiest when she was carrying a child. Scamandronymus seemed happy, too, almost exuberant, which was unusual for him. He was generally quite reserved around people he didn't know well, including his eldest daughters.

What made the visit unpleasant in the beginning was Atthis's obvious and nearly brooding disappointment in not seeing her brother, in conjunction with the growing tension between her and Sappho. For Sappho, though, misery came with the exchange of news between the parents and their daughters.

Timas was indeed present at the first part of the visit, as she had promised she would be. It was the *hiereia* that first brought up the topic of the girls' plans for the future. "As we are all aware, Scamandronymus, your daughters are nearing the end of their time in the *thiasos*. Indeed, they are both now old enough for marriage." Scamandronymus nodded, gravely, but he was clearly pleased and amenable to the conversation he anticipated. "Some circumstances have come to light recently that Sappho needs to address to you, as her father and guardian."

Scamandronymus stiffened a bit at these words, and Sappho was nervous about what to say. She had run the scenario in her head many times, but now all the words she practiced seemed to leave her. Her mouth was dry. She was afraid to look her father in the eye. She took a deep breath and decided to meet his eye like a grown woman. She was asking for his approval, his consent, in her decision. He would never agree to let her make this choice if she seemed too weak or too immature even to mention it.

"Father, I know that, ultimately, you will decide what path I am to take – whether I marry or take some other road," Sappho began, trying to keep her voice as even and clear as possible. "You have made good decisions on my behalf in the past, and I trust that you will in this case, as well." Her father looked placated by her words and ready to hear the rest of what she had to say. "Over a week ago, the Goddess Aphrodite told me that I am to be her priestess." She hurried through the next part for fear that he might interrupt her, and she wouldn't be able to finish her plea. "This is the greatest desire of my heart, and I pledged to obey her in whatever command she might give me. It is my hope, Father and dear Anassa, that you will support me by giving me – allowing me to give myself – fully to her service and the service of this temple."

Scamandronymus's reaction was surprising to Sappho. He smiled broadly and looked at his wife for her approval. Anassa was clearly in favor of the proposition. "Agreed!" he exclaimed. "A union with this temple pleases me very much," he said. Then he looked at Timas and said, "I suppose there are arrangements that you and I will need to make for her dowry."

"Dowry?" said Sappho.

"In a sense, a *hierdoulei* comes with a dowry" said Timas. "Your family will make certain provisions for your care, and you will take vows. Aphrodite will bless the union of the individual to the temple much like Hera would bless the union of the wife with her new family. In many ways, it is like a marriage. There are many benefits to both sides in the arrangement."

Anassa said, "Surely you know that some women are given to the temple as slaves. They are given by their families to be priestesses, *hierodulei*, as an offering to Aphrodite. Some families do this because they are poor and cannot provide a better marriage for their daughters. Other families, like ours, are in favor of this option because of the connections that are forged between the family and the temple and, of course, its patroness."

Atthis had bristled at this information. It had reminded her too forcefully of what the cook had told her so many years ago. Based on what Anassa had said, she thought this sort of thing didn't happen. Now, she wondered how much she had been lied to within the scope of subtle differentiation.

"It seems that both of my eldest daughters now have security and good connections in their futures," Scamandronymus said proudly. Atthis and Sappho both sat bolt upright at this announcement. Was Atthis also to be given to the temple? Sappho knew she wouldn't like that choice, but she might not hate it so much if it meant they could remain together. "Atthis, as my oldest daughter by law, and in keeping with custom, I have arranged for you to be married first. I have been entertaining suitors for you both for some time now. Sappho, I can stop my search on your behalf since your future has found you. Atthis, I am very pleased to announce to you that you will marry Andronikos, a man of both wealth and good name."

Sappho's euphoria at being allowed to initiate into the mysteries of Aphrodite's priestesshood faded and was forgotten at these words. Her spirit crashed. She felt like the wind had been knocked from her body. She was dizzy. She thought she would vomit. Atthis was going to be taken from her!

With barely any voice in her throat, Atthis asked, "When am I to wed, father?"

"We will return to Mytiline in two days, at which time we will begin the last preparations. You will spend several days with us, bidding farewell to your childhood, and then you will be taken to Andronikos's home to live with him as his first and most honored wife."

"I thank you for your gracious consideration of me," Atthis said respectfully, and Sappho was astonished at how dry her eyes were when she herself fought tears. "I am honored that you would arrange such a noble match for me. I will always be grateful for your kindness."

Sappho couldn't believe what she heard. How could Atthis accept their separation so calmly? How could she be grateful that they would never see each other again? How could she be honored to bid farewell to the childhood that they had shared? How could she be thankful to say goodbye forever to Sappho's bed?

When Scamandronymus and Anassa retired to their quarters, Atthis and Sappho both walked glumly back to the dormitory. Sappho was irritated that the luster had been dulled for her initiation. But then, Atthis had already done her best to take the gloss off of this gift through her dull reception of the news a week ago. Sappho knew it was irrational, but she let herself be angry with Atthis for the first time in her life. She told herself that she was angry because Atthis had shown no joy for Sappho's joy. She was angry because her friend was selfish. She would not let herself believe that her anger might have stemmed from the rejection she felt at Atthis's passive acceptance of her new life.

By the time they reached the entrances of their rooms, both girls were stewing in their private emotions. They didn't speak as they parted but just exchanged looks of frustration and hurt. They each walked into their own rooms, and each brooded on separate beds.

Sappho fed her anger, let it build to the point where she needed a confrontation. She had given so much to Atthis, been forgiving for far too long. She had always been concerned with Atthis's happiness over her own, and she wanted to remind her of that fact before she left.

Atthis was folding her clothes on the bed when Sappho entered. Her eyes were now dry, but Sappho could see the traces of tears on her cheeks. She felt some satisfaction at that fact, cruel though she knew it was.

"Are you never going to say one word of pleasure at my good fortune?" Sappho demanded, more scornfully than she had intended. Letting loose her wrath felt good, better than she had expected. Atthis just stared at her for a moment. "I have sought to please you since we were babes, and never have you given me the same. I want you to be happy for me!" Sappho knew she sounded childish, but she didn't care.

Very sarcastically, Atthis said, "Oh, please pardon me. I hope you will be most happy here. You will no doubt win yourself fame and good fortune, eclipsing all others who stand near you. I am just glad to be going far away so I will not have to stand in the dark shadow of the little *hiereia* for the rest of my days."

"How dare you call me names! 'Little *hiereia?*'" Sappho was incredulous. "When have I ever taken any glory or renown that was due to you? When have I ever made you feel little or small? I have pulled you up, Atthis. If it hadn't been for me, you wouldn't have come here. Remember that, Atthis! If I hadn't loved you so much, Anassa and my father probably would have exchanged you for a more useful slave than you would have been."

"Am I not a useful slave?" Atthis spat back at her. "Your dear father, who cares only for my well-being, I am sure, has sold me off to the highest bidder. Am I not a slave, then?"

"You are a daughter," Sappho said. "And soon you will be a wife – an *honored* wife."

"That's right," Atthis retorted, seeming happier about her words than she actually felt. "I will run his house, lie in his bed, bear his children. I am sure that I will find more pleasure in those things than I could ever have found in staying at this temple …" She cut her words short. She wanted to bite at Sappho's heart. She wanted her to hurt as she did, but she couldn't say the thing that she knew would cut deepest.

Sappho knew what Atthis did not say, and she felt a swelling of hatred that her friend could cut her so deeply. She felt rage and loathing that blistered and covered the raw pain of the rejection and scorn she felt at her friend's hands. "Say it," she seethed. "Say it!" They glared at each other, flushed and fearful. They sensed the precipice. Sappho pushed. "Say what you were going to say or remain a coward as you have always been."

"I would rather fly to Andronikos's bed than stay here another day with you," Atthis said and felt herself falling.

Sappho plunged into words she knew she could never take back. "Andronikos has a fair reward in you, Atthis. Your heart is stone, and you care for none but yourself. I thought you loved me, *dear friend*, but you forget me already. Or else you love another more than you love me. No, not your husband. You can't love what you don't know. I see now that you never knew me. No, you love yourself above all else." Sappho was sobbing openly above her rage. "I loved you, but to you the thought of me is hateful. Go! Fly to Andronikos!" Sappho wanted to say more, but she was incoherent.

She ran from the room, through the open doors of the dormitory and down the pathway to the grove. At whatever cost, she would not return to Mytiline with her family to the wedding, and she would not see Atthis again before she left.

Chapter 22

Resolutely and without yielding to any tenderness that remained in her heart for her friend, Sappho avoided all contact with Atthis and tried to push her out of her mind. Sappho said goodbye to her father and stepmother and declined the opportunity to return to Mytiline for the wedding on the basis that she had to prepare for her own transition into the mysteries of adult and temple life.

Anassa had seen the anguish that was evident in both girls at this rift, but she was powerless to change the circumstances. Both girls would have to lead their lives, and that usually involved a distinct separation from the things, and people, of childhood. Atthis had to turn her love and attention toward her husband and her new family, and Sappho had to give herself into the service of Aphrodite. As painful as their choices might be to the other, Anassa knew that life could be no other way.

Before she left, Anassa asked Sappho, "What gift will you give to your sister and friend upon her wedding day?"

Sappho wanted to retort, *What gift will she give me upon my initiation?*, but she held her irrational anger at bay. "She would want nothing from my hands. A gift from me would be a curse and not a blessing upon the bridal bed."

Anassa knew Sappho was reacting from a place of deep and chaotic emotion. *Does the girl even understand what she feels?* Unlikely. All energy and no control. Anassa hoped the training of a priestess would help Sappho comprehend the sources of her own emotions. Strong as those feelings were, she would have misery in her life if she couldn't see the wounds that caused her so much pain. Better than seeing them, she would need to begin healing them.

Anassa appealed to Sappho's sense of duty. "It is proper that you send a token of well wishes to your sister and friend for this occasion." Sappho didn't seem moved much by this plea. Anassa added, "If Atthis can recognize and obey her duty by accepting marriage to a stranger, how can you be so unruly and unkind as to wish her ill?"

Sappho didn't want to think of Atthis as dutiful and obedient because she might have had to see her friend's suffering. Sappho didn't want to see any speck of pain in Atthis because she didn't want to pity or forgive her. She needed her anger, her sense of betrayal and abandonment – however irrational – to keep her from weeping in despair.

"Say no more," she protested. She took a small golden ring from her little finger, one her father had given her years ago. "You may say this is from me, and …" Sappho searched for words that wouldn't bring tears to sting her eyes. "And that Andronikos must be a peer of the Gods to win so fair a reward."

Anassa seemed placated by the gesture, though still somewhat unsatisfied. Sappho wondered if Atthis would feel the barb that was embedded in her fair-sounding words.

On the morning of their departure, Scamandronymus and Anassa presented Sappho with a small cedar box. "This is our last gift to our daughter," said Scamandronymus, more sentimentally than Sappho was used to hearing him speak. "Accept this and our blessing." Sappho opened the chest to find a carefully folded length of rose-colored silk and a golden ring set with a blue stone. The piece of silk was not very large, given its expense and rarity. And she had never seen a stone like the one in the ring. It was polished and rounded in such a way that the sunlight cast a glowing star on its surface.

"These are magnificent," she said, touched by the thoughtfulness and apparent cost laid down by her parents to give her gifts so precious. "Where did you get them?"

"They were your mother's," said Scamandronymus. "When she carried you in her womb, she brought them here and entrusted them to Timas. She had a sense, before she had even seen your face, that you might one day serve here. These were originally gifts to her from her own parents, brought back from a country far to the east."

"They are treasures," said Sappho. "Thank you."

As they said their farewells, Scamandronymus placed Sappho's hand in that of the *hiereia's*, signifying her new status. When they had gone, Timas looked at Sappho and said, "It is time to prepare. You are no longer of your father's house, but neither are you of this one. You have been cast out and must remain on the periphery for a time."

Timas released Sappho's hand and led her to the southern side of the temple village, to an area that Sappho had not had much need to see in her time at the *thiasos*. A small building stood there, too small to merit the name "house." It was one room, suitable only for sleeping.

"You will remain here until we come for you – *if* we come," Timas instructed. "In the morning before dawn, enough food and water for the day will be left outside your door. There won't be much. You must fast. You are not to speak aloud, even to yourself. During this time, you must abstain from any sexual actions. You must take care not to be seen by any man or woman. Your purpose is to meditate on the significance of your choice to become a priestess, your place as a maiden in this temple, and your unique relationship to Aphrodite. Prepare yourself, now, for the ordeal of initiation."

Chapter 23

It became difficult to keep track of the days. The combination of fasting, intense meditation, trance and sleep caused Sappho to lose count somewhere around the third day. She would loosen her focus on the reality of the solid world she normally inhabited and journey to groves and fountains and grottoes, and she would return to find that an entire day had slipped past her without her having so much as a glimpse of the sunrise or sunset. She couldn't even be certain that only one day had passed.

In the darkest part of the night, some time after Sappho relinquished any desire to know how long she had been waiting and she no longer cared how much time she would continue her silent and solitary vigil, two heavily veiled priestesses entered her room and stood motionless on either side of the door. The room was so dim and the women so otherworldly that Sappho was unsure whether this was an encounter of vision or substance. She stood and faced the women but said nothing, as she had not yet been released from her imposed silence.

One of the priestesses stepped forward and pulled Sappho's hands in front of her body, tying them together with a rough cord. The binding was a little tight, though not unbearable. The rope was coarse, but Sappho found that by pulling her elbows together a bit, she could alleviate some of the agitation caused by the fibers rubbing her skin.

The other priestess then stepped forward and placed a very large, thick veil over Sappho's head, securing it in position with a band that came across her eyes and cinched at the nape of her neck.

The priestess who had tied her hands pulled Sappho forward by the lead in the binding. Sappho could see nothing through the veil, but she thought the other priestess fell into step behind her. At times as they walked, Sappho thought the little procession was either being watched or attended by other priestesses, but it was impossible to know for sure. Aside from being blind, she was slightly off-balance from the positioning of her arms straight in front of her, her wrists were being chafed a little by the rope, and her bare feet kept finding small, sharp rocks that jabbed painfully into her soles.

Sappho thought she was being led to either the private temple or the apple grove when they began, but she soon lost her bearings. The priestess guiding her didn't travel in the same direction for long, it seemed, and she rarely kept to the paths. Sappho could feel the abrupt changes in texture below her feet as she crossed bare dirt, dewy grass, hard flagstone, and jagged gravel. Before she had time to force her foggy mind to recognize some sort of pattern in the landscape she treaded, the guide changed direction.

Again, Sappho let go of all her ideas of control and allowed herself to be led freely through the village. She tried to ignore the growing pain in her wrists and feet. They were unimportant. It was more vital that she should keep her balance and keep the pace. She put her trust entirely in the hands of the one who guided her.

The procession halted and both of the priestesses left her standing in the blindness of veil and night. She was lost. She might have been taken outside the temple grounds through one of the gates. She might be left in this place for hours. She didn't know what to expect. She didn't know, nor did she struggle to solve the mystery. The answers would certainly come at the right time. She was beginning to understand that now. All she could control was herself. She must be ready for whatever this night held.

A voice called to her through the misty night air. "Who stands at this door?"

She knew she was supposed to answer, but no one had taught her the formal responses. She wasn't entirely certain how she should frame her answer. She hesitated before offering her reply, "Sappho, daughter of Kleis and Scamandronymus."

The voice belonged to Timas, but it sounded more rigid, cold, and distant than Sappho had heard it, even in the most formal of settings. Timas had clearly noticed Sappho's hesitation and said rather harshly, "Are you certain, girl? Be clear and strong or you waste my time. Tell me who you are."

"I am called Sappho," she said more forcefully.

"*Why* do you stand at this door?" Timas asked.

Sappho wanted to speak quickly, but she also wanted to be clear in her response. "I've come to this place to seek initiation into Aphrodite's priesthood." Sappho quailed a little. Was that the correct response? Timas was silent. Sappho wondered if she should say more. She chose silence for the moment. It felt safer.

"Sappho, why worship most happy Aphrodite?" Timas's tone seemed kinder, but Sappho recognized the challenge in the words.

"Because she has called me to serve her," said Sappho, "and I choose to answer the summons."

Silence dominated the night air again, until Timas finally

said, "You have been separate, but you wish to join. You have been led, but you must choose the path now. Your road has been easy in comparison with what will come. Blind and bound, come of your own accord to the place of your death and rebirth."

Sappho took a step forward and found a rock with the ball of her foot. She lost her balance and stumbled, her hands groping in front of her, searching for equilibrium. Her knee struck something hard as she fell forward. Her hands felt the smooth steps of the temple terrace. She pushed herself up and regained her balance, feeling for the stair under her foot. She took a step up and then felt for the next. Step up, search. Step up, search. She reached the top and nearly lost her balance when she sought another step. Standing uncertainly still, she turned a little as she tried to decide whether or not to continue walking. She took a tentative step forward, and then another. Was she going in the direction of the temple door? If she was faced the wrong way, would anyone stop her from falling off the terrace and down the steps? Or would she just be allowed to fall to injury and possible death because she was unfit to pass this first test?

"Stop," said Timas. "You have gone far enough. You may not enter the temple without being cleansed." Sappho stood motionless as the priestesses around her moved. She was startled to feel two sets of hands slide under her veil and up to her shoulders where they unclasped her garment. The *khiton* fell to the floor after her belt was unbound. She hoped her hands and head would be freed as well, but the attendants silently stepped away from her. Her arms and wrists were starting to ache from restriction, and she was becoming uncomfortably warm under the thick veil.

Sappho was nearly knocked over by the shock and concussive force of a large amount of water being poured over her. It felt as though the entire vessel of water that normally stood at the door of the temple had been dumped onto her. She shivered at the cold liquid on her bare skin, and the veil clung damply to her chest, back and arms. She had only enough time to remember that two vessels flanked the entrance when she felt a rush of cold water swirl past her feet and ankles before it cascaded down the steps.

"Lead her to the altar," commanded the *hiereia* from somewhere behind Sappho. As she was pulled by the rope, unsure what fate awaited her, uncomfortable and a little frightened, Sappho was forcibly reminded of the sacrifices she had witnessed as a part of the community rituals. The bound animal was lead into the midst of the crowd and made to stand before the altar. It, too, was dowsed with water. It was offered water to drink, and the bowing of its head to reach the water signaled its consent to be the sacrifice. Its throat was cut, spraying blood across the altar and into a bowl. She wondered if her purpose here was to be the sacrifice.

When her progress was stopped, she felt a press on her shoulder that indicated she should kneel. She did so, but she winced as she felt thorns piercing into knees and legs. She was left in this position for some time as the women around her watched in silence.

Sappho thought of those women. Did they know how much pain she was in? How the thorns dug further into her flesh if she shifted her weight? Did they know how badly her arms ached at the shoulders when she tried to protect her wrists? Or how the rope dug into her wrists when she tried to ease her shoulders? Did they know how close she felt to retching from the pain in her body and the dizzying, damp heat below her veil? She felt a surge of rage and defiance. Maybe they didn't know. Maybe they didn't care. Were they sadists, enjoying her misery?

Or are they recalling their own discomforts from their own initiations? In some strange way, the knowledge that all the women in the room had endured these, or similar, trials made her situation easier to bear. They had survived. It had been worth it to them to continue with the initiation. And, after all, didn't she have a choice? She could stand up if she wanted to. She could rip the veil away from her tear-streaked, sweaty face and bite the knot that bound her hands. She could scream and run from the temple like a crazed woman. She could throw herself at the *hiereia's* feet and beg pardon and release. Nobody held her here against her will. It was her own will that kept her knees on the thorny floor. Her own choice left the veil in place. And her will became a stony comfort – the knowledge that she was strong.

"Sappho, daughter of Kleis and Scamandronymus, called to serve most happy Aphrodite," Timas was now very close behind her, "what can you give to the temple and its Goddess?"

"I offer my loyalty, my obedience, my desire to learn and serve," Sappho replied. "All that I am and all that I possess, I give freely to Aphrodite and her temple."

Timas placed her hand on Sappho's head, and Sappho felt Timas's other hand near her throat. "*All?* Even your life?"

"Even my life," said Sappho.

"I have my knife at your throat," Timas said clearly and

slowly. "If I tell you that the Kyprian Goddess has need of a blood sacrifice this night, how will you respond?"

Sappho nodded her assent and felt the edge of the knife move under the veil. Its cold blade now touched her hot skin. She could feel the pulse of her life beating against the sharp metal. "I am the willing sacrifice," she said, and she leaned her head back to expose her throat. She pulled her eyes shut tightly as Timas moved her hand to the other side of her neck. Sappho pictured the slice that would spray her own blood across the white altar and onto the temple floor. The knife point pierced her skin and she felt the first drops of blood trickle down her collarbone when Timas's hand quickly jerked the knife away, up and over Sappho's head. The cut veil was thrown to the floor in front of her.

The dim flickers of flame licking the air above the oil lamps dazzled Sappho. Her eyes had been shielded too long. She focused her eyes upon Timas, who wiped the few drops of Sappho's blood onto the veil and then dropped the bloody garment onto the altar fire. "Your sacrifice has been accepted," she said, "and the words you chose will be your vow."

Timas pulled Sappho to her feet and pointed at the cut and bloody veil withering in the flames. "There is the blood of your death as a girl of Scamanrynomus's house. There is the blood of your birth as a priestess of Aphrodite, her dove" the *hiereia* said. "You will ever remain a virgin in this house, giving your body as Aphrodite instructs but being held by vows to no man. You are a maiden of the temple."

Some of the other priestesses stepped forward. One knelt at Sappho's feet and gently plucked the thorns from her knees. Sappho saw that they had been rose thorns. Roses on their thorny stems, rose petals, and individual thorns had been strewn in abundance at the base of the altar where she had bowed in supplication. The priestess at her feet applied a cool balm to her sore knees and shins, and she felt relief immediately.

Sweet maidens came forward with delicately woven garlands around their tender necks, and they bedecked Sappho with the same. Her ropes were cut, and salve was applied to her wrists. A woman rubbed her shoulders to ease the ache. *She must remember*, thought Sappho, *from her own trials*.

Music and drums started playing familiar rhythms, and the women began dancing and singing. Sappho felt the ecstatic trance of the dance overtaking her. She was so open to vision, and she felt the last phase of her initiatory experience coming upon her. In her vision, she danced with and for Aphrodite. The Goddess spoke words of guidance and personal mystery that Sappho knew she could never share with another person. Sappho awoke on the temple floor in the arms of another maiden.

As daylight broke over Hiera, Timas spoke. "Just now the golden-sandaled Dawn has called," she announced. "Sappho, new-made priestess in the house of Aphrodite, have you heard the Goddess's voice this night?"

Sappho thought of her vision. "I have."

Timas then asked, "And what did you hear?"

Sappho pondered the question. She didn't want to share the words Aphrodite had given her. She wasn't even sure she understood all of the experience yet. She weighed her words carefully and said,

"Far sweeter than the throbbing lyre, a voice more golden than gold, new found, the daughter of Ournaos whispered mysteries in my ears this night."

The *hiereia* eyed her with an evaluating expression. "Truly, you are called to her service. *Khaire*, and welcome!"

Chapter 24

The houses of the priestesses didn't differ much from those of the students in the *thiasos*. They held narrow rooms entered through a curtained doorway, ventilated by a single window, and furnished with a straw box-bed and a wooden storage box that doubled as a table. The rooms encircled the building and were topped by a second, identical floor of rooms. Each house had its own women's room on the first floor that the residents could use as a combination kitchen-dining-social room, its own red room, its own men's room for entertaining guests, and each had its own central courtyard with an altar.

With so many priestesses – about three thousand – living in the village, there were many jobs to be done in the service of Aphrodite. Sappho knew of the *hierodulei* and their primary duty, but she didn't realize that there were so many other paths to service until she was living among the women. She learned quickly that not every priestess currently served as a *hierodule*. All of them had or would perform this critical work at some point in their tenure as priestess. Some would always serve in this fashion, usually based on personal talent and temple need. However, many women were assigned other duties related to maintaining the temple grounds, managing the treasury, stocking the storeroom, preparing meals, teaching in the *thiasos*, receiving visitors to the sanctuaries, officiating festivals and mystery rites, and more.

The women were not segregated into separate dormitories based on their duties. They were mixed together so that each interacted with all the others and appreciated the roles that were fulfilled by her fellows. They learned from each other and shared experience so that all grew in their understandings of the temple and its numerous functions. Frequently, informal apprenticeships arose between priestesses who were masters of a particular art or trade within the temple and those whose natural tendencies drove them to pursue similar occupation.

Sappho found herself listening to and watching the other women a great deal of the time. She was so new to the priestesshood that she didn't feel she was in much of a position to question or advise on the topics of their conversations. She had a basic knowledge of all of the areas of expertise, but no intensive training or experience in any given one. She wasn't sure what she wanted to pursue first, so she watched and waited and did what work was given her to do.

The training of the newest priestesses seemed to favor this approach. Her first week as a priestess included a variety of work. She was given a day or two to recover from the ordeals of initiation – time to process what she had seen, heard, and experienced throughout the night. She tried to relive as much of it as possible, to suck the meaning out of every breath, every heartbeat; but she found that she was already starting to forget some of the details. They were there, below the surface of her memory, but she saw them dimly, as through a dusky mirror clouded by vapor. She knew that it might take years to fully remember and comprehend every part of her experience.

After this recovery time, she was asked by various priestesses to assist in their daily tasks. She happily agreed to whatever work was given her, though her body and mind were tired by the end of each day from the physical and mental rigor of the tasks. She helped one with tending the rosebushes lining their dormitory one morning, and carried offerings from the temple to the storehouse with another priestess that afternoon. Another day was spent in helping two women account for the inventory of goods in the storehouse, and yet another passed in assisting a chipper, motherly *melissa* with cooking in Timas's meals.

One of the women in each of the houses acted as an advisor to the other women. She offered them counsel and friendship in times of crisis and question. She also helped the younger priestesses in adjusting to their new roles in the temple. The woman who held this role in Sappho's house was an older priestess with kind eyes and a beaming smile. Her eyes and smile were both becoming heavily lined from the strength of the joy that filled her and creased her face in happiness. She wasn't an old woman, Sappho noticed when she was close to her, but she was not young anymore, either. She embraced Sappho with the same zeal that she had used to embrace life, and Sappho found herself warm and invigorated after a sincere hug and a few minutes conversation.

Her name was Agueda, and Sappho thought she was well-named. "Agueda," after all, meant "kind." Agueda approached Sappho by the end of her second day in the dormitory. Their conversation was brief, but the older priestess had let her know at this time that Sappho could ask any questions of her, and that she was welcome to come to her at day or night. Agueda also told

Sappho that she should use these first few weeks to acclimate herself to the schedule and needs of the temple. "Be available to the women around you," she advised. "Help them when they need help. Ask them about what they do. Offer to assist someone during the day if you've not already committed your time to another."

The second time they met and talked, Sappho had been living and working as a priestess for two or three weeks. Several women in her hall had intentionally included her in their conversations at mealtimes and greeted her as she passed. She had been recruited by some to help with their duties. To others, she had proffered her assistance so her hands wouldn't be idle. She'd even been given specific time to be idle – "to enjoy the breeze and the meadow and the bliss of being young," one priestess had said.

On these days, she strolled around the grounds and watched the comings and goings of Aphrodite's people. She saw priestesses of all ranks and responsibilities, their duties and positions noted in the colors or styles of their robes or the cords and veils that seemed like nothing more than accessories to outsiders. Most of the priestesses had been moving about on some errand or other, but some were worshipping the beauty of the day. Sappho had watched the men and women being escorted from their business in the *hierodulei's* rooms, noticing the changes in their bodies and expressions *after* their time with the priestesses. She had walked to the northern wall of the sacred village and watched a group of priestesses tending to several happy, laughing children. They were the priestesses' babes, the sons and daughters of Aphrodite.

Only a few of the women in Sappho's dormitory had

children. Generally, the *hierodulei* took special precautions to avoid pregnancy, but the contraceptives weren't fail-proof. Of course, sometimes the priestess intentionally left herself open to the fertility of the Goddess, as was necessary for certain rites. And, infrequently, the children were the products of marriage unions between a priestess and her mate, who was usually either a former devotee-lover or a political ally of the temple.

When she met with Agueda again, she learned more about the temple children. Agueda explained that many of the priestesses chose to bear and rear their children in the temple because of the motherly influence of Aphrodite. The Goddess had several children, and her devoted attention to Eros and Harmonia, especially, demonstrated her capacity to care for them. Typically, the children would be watched and cared for by the priestesses until they reached an appropriate age for schooling. At that time, the girls would usually go to school at the *thiasos* here in the temple of Aphrodite, while the boys were sent to schools established near the temples of Ares, Apollo, or Dionysos.

Many of the temple children would move through roles as priests and priestesses themselves as they grew. In the cults of most of the Olympians, service within the temple was not the constant and long-lasting commitment that it was for women in this particular temple. Usually, one served as the priestess of the rite or for a specific season, returning to household tasks when the civic and religious responsibilities concluded. Most of these children, therefore, would also learn trades or crafts or would marry with influential families on Lesvos. A few of the girls, however, would stay at this temple to serve as their mothers had done.

"You will learn to care for the children, of course," said Agueda. "It is one of the duties that all priestesses must perform for a time."

"I would like that, I think," reflected Sappho. "I believe I would enjoy playing with and teaching the little ones. In fact, I think I might like to teach the girls in the *thiasos* some day, as well."

Agueda eyed her shrewdly. "Yes, that may be an option for you. Some day." She raised her eyebrows and smiled. "You are far too young for that role yet. You will need to familiarize yourself with many aspects of study before you can teach others. In fact, you would need to be adept in the skills of a *hierodule* before you could teach in the *thiasos*. A wife, after all, fills much the same role for her husband."

Sappho considered this for a moment. She had wondered when she would begin this portion of her training. She knew it would come eventually. Truthfully, she looked forward to her sexual training and service with great anticipation. She'd heard some of the women in her house. She'd heard the men and women who'd come to worship with them. She was indescribably moved by the sounds of lust and ecstasy that issued from their rooms. She missed the nights with Atthis in the dormitory, and she grew more and more curious about the pleasures of intercourse with a man.

"And the training of a *hierodule* awaits us all, doesn't it?" she asked Agueda, already knowing the answer.

Agueda knew the game Sappho was beginning. It was somewhat typical. The girls were generally at the mercy of their newly developing sex drives when they initiated. They were, after all, at the age when their fathers would normally have married them to some man in order to protect their reputations. The common belief was that an unmarried fourteen-year-old girl was all too likely to fall to temptation and dishonor. The novice initiates generally wanted to begin the sexual discovery of the *hierodule*. They did not, however, wish to seem too eager. So they asked as many questions around the topic as they could generate in the hopes that someone else would suggest the young girl begin her training immediately.

It was an age-old dance, Agueda thought. But the girls dancing around the subject in this fashion were deemed too immature to begin. Only when they had the strength of will to ask for what they wanted would it be granted to them. Even then, many would still have to wait. Priestesses like Agueda were the gatekeepers for certain training and advancements, and Agueda had to be convinced of a novice's ability to handle the next steps before she would be permitted to take them.

"Yes, we all serve our turns," she said, smiling. She wasn't giving any extra information yet.

Sappho was pensive a moment. Then she asked, "When are priestesses most likely to begin this training?"

Agueda smiled. She enjoyed the dance. "It varies. Much depends on the priestess."

Sappho waited for more explanation, but none followed. "How is it decided?"

Ah, Agueda thought, *she is dancing ever closer*. "I will make the final decision."

"'Final'?" Sappho repeated. Agueda said nothing. Sappho was ready to burst with unanswered questions. If Agueda made the final decision, who made the preliminary ones? When would the process begin? What step would come next? How long would she serve as a *hierodule*? She suspected that Agueda knew what she was asking. The older woman was either being coy or stubborn. Sappho didn't want to press her. Perhaps she should save her questions for another day.

Agueda was watching her. She didn't seem in a particular hurry to change the topic or to leave just yet. Sappho decided to continue her questioning about her role within the temple, though she planned to avoid the topic of *hierodule* training for the time.

"For now," she began, "I am to watch, help, and learn all that I can about the temple and the priestesses. Is that right?"

"Yes," said Agueda.

"What happens next?" asked Sappho.

Agueda chose her words carefully. "Please clarify your question."

"Well," said Sappho, "how will I move from one level of service to the next?"

"Who says you will move?" Agueda asked.

Sappho was embarrassed. "Nobody," she said. "I just assumed –."

"Never make assumptions," Agueda instructed. "It is always better to ask a direct question and get a straightforward answer." *There*, she thought, *I've given you the key. Use it to open the door you are pounding your head against.*

196

Sappho was frustrated and felt off-center. She wanted to know what she would be doing next. More than that, she wanted to begin the *hierodule* training. It was clearly on her way to whatever future awaited her.

"When will I serve as hierodule?" she blurted.

"After you have been trained," Agueda said, unruffled by Sappho's obvious frustration.

"When will I be trained?" Sappho asked.

"Only after you ask to be," Agueda replied coolly.

"Haven't I already asked?" said Sappho, agitated. "I thought that is what we had been discussing."

"No, you haven't asked," responded the older woman. "We have been discussing the hypothetical training of some unknown woman."

Sappho took a shaking breath, "May I please begin the *hierodule* training?"

Chapter 25

It had been several weeks since Sappho had been told she would soon become a *hierodule*, but Agueda had said nothing since. Sappho's days had continued in much the same way as before her conversation with her advisor. She continued to aid the priestesses around her in their many tasks, but she found that she was spending several days with each priestess instead of working just one day with each before moving to the next.

Sappho preferred this method. She was getting to know the women better, and she had a better understanding of their work by spending more days doing it. She finally felt as though she were making true friendships with one or two of the women, and more of the ladies in her vicinity knew her well enough to greet her by name as she passed them on the way to some chore. Of course, even the women who didn't know her name were likely to greet her with the common name used among the priestesses. "*Khaire, Adelphe!*" Be happy, Dear One! Any priestess may be called *Adelphe* by her sisters.

All of the women were given a sufficient amount of time at their own leisure, as Sappho discovered. Some tasks were more complex, other more monotonous, but very few required unabated attention from their mistresses. The women gave themselves generous time for rest and play throughout the day, doing whatever they fancied. The women of the Kyprian valued leisure, laughter, love – and they knew they wouldn't be able to serve Aphrodite properly if they were overworked and anxious from the toil of their daily tasks. Theirs was not a Goddess who delighted in drudgery.

One of Sappho's more relaxed days – a rainy, thoughtful day, one best for staying indoors and dreaming – she lit incense and watched it fill her room with cryptic, swirling messages. She opened her mind as she had been taught before she was an initiated priestess. She enjoyed practicing this technique, and she thought she noticed some improvement in her ability to see, experience, and understand the connections around her as she meditated in this way. As she opened herself to the sweet smoke and the rain, she also felt herself opening to the activities in the room adjoining hers on one side.

One of the many *hierodulei* lived there, a beautiful girl named Daphne. Being such close neighbors had afforded Sappho several opportunities to meet and chat with Daphne. Sappho admired the young woman for her beauty, which was highlighted by the infectious smile she usually wore. Sappho had naturally had occasion to see Daphne in the nude, as many of the *hierodulei* did not adorn themselves with garments of any sort during the designated times when they greeted and served Aphrodite's devotees. Having seen Daphne before and after entertaining these guests, her bare skin aglow with the inner fire of passion, Sappho had spent a good many solitary evenings worshipping Aphrodite in the imagined form of her neighbor.

Daphne was clearly receiving visitors today, as Sappho could hear through the wall separating their rooms. Sappho listened to the proceedings of the *hierodule's* rite, its cadences already becoming familiar to her after other afternoons spent listening. A priestess had guided the man to the room, where he knocked twice on the door frame before pushing aside the curtain and entering. He pulled the curtain shut behind himself and stepped further into the room. He dropped a few coins into the small dish by the door – a customary gratuity to the priestess who offered her services. Sappho knew that he must have left another donation for the temple itself back at the main sanctuary.

There would be some talking, the words coming to Sappho indistinctly through the wall. Daphne would laugh gently in delighted anticipation of her suitor. She would intone an invocation to Aphrodite, parts of which made the fine hairs on Sappho's arms tingle. Today, Sappho felt a rush of warmth and moisture envelope the budding rose of her womanhood, and her body quivered as she sensed the Goddess assuming the body of the woman next door. The man sucked in his breath and said something else. A few moments passed before Sappho heard the first moans of pleasure coming from both occupants of the adjoining room.

She was entranced by the rhythmic swaying and creaking of the bed. She was captivated by the need and longing in their throaty cries. Her hands moved over her own body, and she offered her need, her desire, her primal lust to the *Kytherean* Lady.

She found that today she was not imagining Atthis, or any other woman, moving deftly between her legs. She was surprised that it was not Daphne she envisioned. In this moment, she yearned for a man. She imagined the feel of his muscles and hair under her hands. Was the hair coarse or soft? She imagined the bristle of his beard against her neck and shoulders. She longed for the pressure of his body's weight against her inner thighs. No touching she could contrive could possibly simulate what she imagined sex with a man would be like, and for a moment she was frustrated with her situation. Then, she made the conscious choice to accept this solitary form of love-making for what it was. And as she opened herself that much further to the pleasure in her mind and between her legs, she felt her thighs convulse as her body was rocked by the orgasm. She allowed the sensation to pass through her, feeling it only in the moment as it was given to Aphrodite.

Sappho lay on her bed in a blissful delirium for a long while and lost track of the events in the next room. Daphne and her gentleman were finished, by the sound of the shuffling Sappho could hear through the wall. The man was undoubtedly redressing himself. Sappho wondered what Daphne was doing. She heard the muffled sounds of voices – first hers, then his – followed by the footsteps that told Sappho the man was leaving. Her own curtain swayed in the doorway as he walked past.

After listening to most of the interaction between the *hierodule* and the devotee, Sappho was filled with questions about the process. Obviously, she already knew how sexual intercourse was supposed to work – she even knew several different positions that could increase the pleasure or shift the focus for one or both partners. But without having actually experienced it, she felt like she didn't have the whole story.

Most of her questions, however, revolved around the duties and demeanor of the priestess before and after sex. What words does she say? Are they scripted or divinely inspired? How does she invoke Aphrodite? What does she do when the man stands up to re-dress? Does she continue lying luxuriantly on the bed? Does she clean up?

Do they ever speak to each other as lovers? As acquaintances? Or do they always speak as the Goddess and her devoted worshipper?

Her mind filling with technical questions, Sappho didn't notice that Daphne had entered her room. Sappho had taken a strip of cloth and was beginning to clean her hands and the area between her legs when Daphne spoke.

"A *hierodule* should never wipe away the traces of love that remain on her body immediately after she has accepted the honor and devotion of her visitor," she said silkily, with a smile playing around her pretty mouth. She could see Sappho's discomfort. "Nor should a priestess of Aphrodite ever feel ashamed or embarrassed about her body or expressions of love." She gently pulled Sappho's knees and arms away from her body so she was exposed and reclining once again. Daphne continued speaking as she ran her hand over Sappho's skin. There was something both casual and intense in the *hierodule's* touch.

"A *hierodule's* body is a tool – a gift from Aphrodite," she said. "It arouses pleasure and delight in herself and others, men and women. Both the priestess and the Goddess are able to enjoy the sensations coursing through it. This body is powerful, pleasurable and pure.

"Our definition of purity differs somewhat from those beyond these walls. In other temples, those not consecrated to the Goddess of Love, a body wet and alive with the sweat and the semen of lovemaking is considered unclean. It must be washed before it can approach the altar. But that is not our way. To us, such a body is sanctified and pure – worthy of being the altar. Aphrodite teaches us that bodies clenched together in the ecstatic search for climax are seeking something primal and pure – a force depicted in the holy marriage. And what is left behind is no less pure than the rain that clings to the rose after a storm."

Daphne didn't seem to be trying to arouse Sappho or engage her in a sexual embrace of any sort. Her touch continued, moving over Sappho's arms, breast, belly, legs, and back again in an endless sweep of her body.

Sappho had regained some of her composure after the initial shock of Daphne's entrance into her room. Sappho asked, "So you don't wash up at all after... the act?"

"No, not exactly," said Daphne. "We don't rush to wipe and wash away the traces of our combined pleasure the moment the man moves away from us. Generally, we don't do it at all while he is in the room. Since we don't view it as dirty, we can take the time to dry off later. There is nothing half so graceless or uncharming to a man as a woman bent and twisted in trying to wipe off his seed before he has even had time to find his clothes." Daphne smiled. Sappho was dazzled by how seductive she could be. "Remember, we are the face and the body of Aphrodite for these worshippers. They need not see us bogged down in the mundane."

Sappho absorbed what she had been told, but frowned slightly as she said, "There is so much I don't know. I can see I have a lot to learn."

"This art is less complicated than you'd think," Daphne winked. "If you have a natural talent for it, it will come surprisingly easily. If you listen to the voice of Pandemos in your ear, pay attention to your suitor, and remember to enjoy yourself, you'll love this service more than any other."

"How will I learn?" asked Sappho. "I've never spoken to a man that wasn't my father, brother, or servant."

"I am your first teacher," Daphne said. "A man will be your next teacher – probably a priest. Every man and woman you encounter will teach you something about being a *hierodule*." She winked again, and with a gleam in her eye she said, "First, you'll watch."

Chapter 26

Sappho was unable to find words. She had no idea how to respond to Daphne's announcement that she would begin her training by watching the more experienced priestess perform her duties as *hierodule*. The idea was both shocking and titillating.

"What do you mean, 'watch?' I'll just sit there while you …?" Though she had started speaking, Sappho was clearly still at a loss for coherent speech.

"While I have sex," Daphne said, as though it were an ordinary matter of business. Again, Daphne evaluated the expression on Sappho's face. "I am surprised that you respond to this suggestion with such apparent discomfort and disbelief. Is the idea of sex distasteful to you?"

Sappho was getting more accustomed to Daphne's blunt and direct manner of speaking. She decided to respond in the same simple, honest, and direct way. "No." She paused, still a little embarrassed about the topic at hand. "I don't mean to sound like a prude. It's just that I've never experienced sex, and I have always thought of it as a very private matter – just between the two people who are doing it."

"I see," Daphne reflected for a moment. "It is personal and intimate, but it is not always a private act – especially in the lives of courtesans, prostitutes, and *hierodulei*. In the Temple of Aphrodite, you'd best acclimate yourself to the sights and sounds of lovemaking all around you. Not a day will pass in which you will not see, hear, or feel the raptures of physical, sexual bliss."

"Courtesans and prostitutes? Are the *hierodulei* whores?" Sappho said, this time with obvious distaste.

Daphne gave her a harder look, like a mother trying to be patient with a child who couldn't learn a simple rhyme. "We are not, but what great shame would it be if we were?"

"Such women are dishonored," insisted Sappho.

"Dishonored by whom?" asked Daphne. "There are courtesans who hold higher political and social roles in Greece than the esteemed wives of the men who employ them. Some courtesans – whores, as you call them – are honored above other women by occupying seats at the *symposia* with the men. No wife is given that honor. Men hear and heed what these women have to say, and these women are given freedom and privilege and respect far beyond that of the legitimate wives of the household."

"But they sell their bodies and are used by any with a coin," said Sappho.

Daphne made a noise of derision. "I say that a woman may make a living in offering her skills, just as a man might ply his trade in carpentry or smithing for a wage. I will not argue with you about the ethics of that profession. You have been raised in a temple largely dedicated to the physical expression of love. I would hope that you would not scorn those who embrace many of the same ideals that we support and teach, just because they do not feel the shelter of the home or the temple. However, I *will* tell you that the world's ideas of buying and selling have no place in the temple, and so the *hierodulei* do not see themselves in the same way as the marketplace prostitutes."

Sappho listened to Daphne's passionate words, and felt confused. She knew very little of prostitution – only what she had overheard in her father's house and in the *thiasos*. "I'm sorry to have offended you, *Adelphe*. Please forgive my ignorance."

Daphne's expression softened. "This is a bias that is deep-rooted, and I am defensive against its thorns. You will learn many truths about the world as you serve the Gods. One, I hope, will be to care less for the world's opinion of you as you seek to fulfill your service."

Daphne said nothing else for several moments, allowing Sappho time to absorb this first lesson. After a brief time, Sappho resumed the original topic. "So," she began, "I am to watch you. What should I do? What am I to expect?"

"I will explain to those who come to my room that you are an apprentice, of sorts," Daphne explained. "At first, you will do nothing but watch. You will stand when they enter and sit on a cushion for the remainder of the time. As you become more familiar with the proceedings, you will help with certain tasks – undressing and redressing the devoted one, applying oils to my skin before I invoke Aphrodite, and so on."

Again, Sappho looked slightly embarrassed as she began to ask the next question. "Will I ever … well … be involved in these devotions?"

This line of conversation, however shocking, was also clearly arousing Sappho. Daphne could see that the girl's nipples had hardened again and that her hand had mindlessly moved to a place where it could apply subtle pressure.

Daphne smiled seductively once again. Sappho wanted to kiss her, to touch her, to lie back into the bed with her. "There are ways in which you may be involved," she began, a flicker of arousal and anticipation playing at the corners of her mouth. "However, you will not fully enter the *hierodule's* role in my bed." Sappho responded with a quizzical look. "In other words, you will not lose your intactness there. There are some things that you may not do until the right situation has been arranged for you." Sappho looked a little disappointed. "Not to worry, *Adelphe*, there are plenty of things you can do to heighten the pleasure for the Goddess, the devotee, and both of us if you so choose."

"How long does this phase of my training last?" Sappho inquired.

"That is for Agueda to decide," was Daphne's response.

"When do we begin?" Sappho asked.

"The next time a suitor comes to call. Maybe today."

Chapter 27

Daphne spent the next couple of hours briefing Sappho on what she would be seeing from the priestess's perspective. There was a certain liturgy to the proceedings given that they were, after all, part of the sacred worship of the divine. A *hierodule* was no common streetwalker who had her skirts lifted in a cluttered alley near the marketplace. Nor was she a wife who must obediently surrender to her husband in the darkened hours of the night. The *hierodule* guided the encounter. She set the pace. She said the words of invocation and blessing.

Daphne had taken Sappho into her own chamber. "I need to be in this place today, in case anyone else should come to see me," she explained. She showed Sappho a large cushion on which she could sit while Daphne laid with the man. She also indicated the shelves on which she kept the oils, perfumes, and incenses that were required. Sappho saw the bowl by the door in which a few coins were already collected.

The experienced priestess laid her young charge on the bed and detailed the experience of calling Aphrodite to possess her body. Her hands continued to explore Sappho's body as she described what would happen. More and more of Daphne's attention turned to the girl's form, and Sappho detected an increase in her instructor's intensity as she spoke. Daphne was arousing herself with her words – and arousing Sappho, in turn. Sappho could feel her body responding to the trained touch of the woman caressing her. She touched Daphne in return. They kissed and tightened their embrace.

Sappho was feeling herself swept away with the eroticism of the act she knew she would soon witness. She felt intoxicated by the honeyed words of the other priestess.

Someone knocked in the doorway. A priestess spoke from behind the curtain. "Daphne, one comes to you."

"I am prepared," she responded, moving away from Sappho with a smile. She stood and pulled her hair back, smoothing it away from her face. When she turned away, Sappho noticed how silky and luxurious Daphne's dark hair looked as it hung far down her ivory back. "Today," Daphne said, "you will only watch. Sit down there and be comfortable."

Daphne took an oil bottle from the shelf and poured some of its contents onto her hands. With this, she gently massaged the mound and opening between her thighs. She rubbed and then pinched each of her blushing nipples. She opened a different bottle, and Sappho noticed that a distinct and beautiful fragrance filled the room as the other priestess applied a little of it to the soft hollows alongside her throat, elbows, and knees. She pulled a sheer piece of white fabric around her body and draped it into a careless wrap. Sappho shot her a quizzical look and said, "I thought the *hierodulei* didn't clothe during their receiving days."

"That is only partially true," Daphne said. With her sly grin she said, "Men like the anticipation of uncovering a woman. I like for my body to be shrouded until Aphrodite takes full possession of it."

They heard two sets of footsteps approaching – one heavy and one light, and Daphne signaled Sappho to sit down. Sappho also covered herself with a soft garment pulled loosely about her form as she knelt on the pillow that gave her a view of the proceedings. The priestess who brought the man to Daphne's chamber tapped lightly on the doorframe. Daphne said, "You may enter," and the curtain was swept aside long enough for a short, muscular, balding man to pass through.

He looked furtively at Daphne, made a gesture of greeting and reverence like those used to honor the statues of the Gods when passing by, and knelt briefly just inside the doorway. When he stood, he saw the little bowl of coins on the table and added the few that he had in his hand. He looked again at Daphne. Sappho knew that he had not yet seen her.

"I extend the greetings of Aphrodite to you," Daphne said. "Tell me, why have you come?"

The man blinked and stared for a moment. Had he not been expecting a challenge? Had he not visited the temple priestesses before today? Perhaps he had only lain with the marketplace whores who pocketed the money in the darkened alley and spread their legs in welcome of their customer. He recovered well. "I have come to show my reverence for the golden Kypris and receive her blessings," he said. Sappho thought perhaps he had been dazzled by Daphne's beauty, or else the Goddess was close to her already and he was bemused.

He looked down and away from Daphne, and his eyes met Sappho's. He looked surprised, even somewhat fearful to see another woman in the room. Daphne had noticed his recognition of her new charge and answered the unasked question behind his eyes. "She learns." The man seemed less comforted than he would have liked, but he resolutely turned his gaze back to Daphne. She said, "I will call the Golden One to you."

Daphne held her arms out from her body, the palms facing up. Her feet were together, and Sappho thought she could detect a certain flexion in Daphne's thighs and buttocks. Sappho could feel the sexual tension and flood of sensation that Daphne was coiling in her preparation to call the Goddess. Sappho looked at the man and could see his erection creating an odd angle beneath his clothing. She felt a thrill of satisfaction at how easily and quickly Daphne had aroused him.

Daphne spoke the words of invocation, and they were as sweet as poetry to Sappho. She felt herself swept away in the tide of lust and longing that was now surging through the room and through all three of their bodies. Sappho saw the moment that Aphrodite took on the body of her priestess. Daphne's stance changed, though the difference was subtle. Her gaze changed. The man seemed to have noticed, too. He fell to his knees in supplication.

When Daphne spoke, her voice had also altered. It was sweeter and more melodious, though it had been beautiful before. "I see your reverence for me. Rise and pay me true worship."

As he stood, the sheer garment covering the priestess fell. Both he and Sappho drew in their breath. Sappho had seen Daphne's naked body already. She had looked at it for the last several hours. She had touched it, and still she was not prepared for the splendor of her form when inhabited by the immortal light and beauty of the Goddess.

The man trembled as Daphne extended her hands and unclasped his garments. They, too, fell to the floor, where the *hierodule* deftly swept them aside with her foot. She ran her hands up his chest and neck and gently pulled him to her with a kiss. His hands, shaking at first, found her body. As he caressed her, he found new strength and force. His hands began to roam – first both to her waist, then one on her breast, then the other pulled her closer to him at her bottom. She gave a little moan and laugh of delight, meeting his lustful gaze directly. One of his arms was around her waist, and the other hand moved slowly between her thighs. Sappho could almost feel the sensation in her own body, and she let her hand find its way to the same place as she relaxed into the pillow.

A golden light surrounded Daphne as she gave a soft, throaty laugh and pulled her suitor toward the bed. Sappho saw a hint of purple in the air atop priestess's head and thought vaguely of the description "violet-crowned Kytherea" – yet another name for Aphrodite.

Daphne pushed the man onto his back and pressed her full length against him as she continued to kiss his mouth and neck. The *hierodule* slowly began moving her attention down his frame as the sweet touch of her mouth found his shoulders and chest. Sappho saw that Daphne's soft hands played and lingered at the well-muscled chest before moving lower to the man's stomach. He quivered as if tickled by her touch on his belly, and Sappho could both see and feel the tense energy circling and winding around the bed. Interestingly, she could see strands of that energy coming from her own body, and she knew that she was part of the magic being created. This tension that she felt was delicious. She felt like she wanted to release and extend it simultaneously.

The embrace on the bed changed slightly. Daphne leaned forward sensuously to kiss the man again, her breasts and body shifting points of contact upward once more. Then she quickly moved even lower, her long hair skimming the man's torso and falling into a curtain around her new endeavor below his waist. Sappho couldn't see clearly with her physical eyes what was happening, but she had a perfect picture in her mind, and her body spasmed slightly in response to this new pleasure.

Though the man was clearly responding with utmost delight to the manipulations of the priestess, she once more shifted her attention. She looked up at his face as she slid her body once more up to equal stature. She placed one knee on each side of his hips and hovered momentarily before taking his erection into herself. Sappho found that she was breathless. She had a perfectly clear view of the encounter. She found herself both shocked and enthralled by the penetration. The controlled rhythm of the joining was hypnotic and exciting in a way that Sappho had never imagined it to be. She felt a dull echo of what she imagined the sensation to be, and she desperately wished that she was the *hierodule* and Daphne was watching.

Just as Sappho thought she might go mad at the prolonged, perfectly controlled pace of the priestess, the suitor, too, seemed unable to abate his wild and spasmodic lust. In a single swift motion, he pulled Daphne to him at the waist and flipped them both over.

Sappho could see her legs and arms pulling him down to her as the pace of their lovemaking was quickened.

Still vaguely aware of the energy twisting and writhing about the bed, Sappho dimly noted that its pulsing was now as frantic and fast as the physical actions of the intertwined couple. She, too, was keeping in time with the thrusts of the man until she could see that he had suddenly tightened his entire body, suspended and motionless above the woman who pulled her body ever closer to his and began shuddering with a riot of pleasure. Sappho, too, found release, and she saw that the energy they had all raised filled the room and then sped away as they all relaxed. They were each covered in a soft golden glow, though Daphne, who was still filled with the spirit of Aphrodite, shone the brightest.

As their eyes refocused on the room around them and their breath regained its smooth and stable pace, Daphne spoke. "It is time for the Goddess to be gone and the priestess to return," she said in a voice that sounded like honey to Sappho. "I accept your devotion and bestow my blessings upon you." With this, she touched his forehead, his heart, and his genitalia. He thanked her and stood, still looking down at her naked and dewy body. She exhaled deeply and Sappho could see the departure of the brilliant gold and violet light. Daphne opened her eyes, and this time Daphne was behind them.

She stood and helped the man regain his clothes. He thanked her again, made a small bow and backed out of the doorway. She stretched out once more on her bed and shot a playful look at Sappho. "That was example number one," Daphne said. "What do you think?"

Chapter 28

After several weeks of observing Daphne in her primal and primary role, Sappho had seen a great many variations to the act of love that she first witnessed. Daphne generally spoke similar words of opening and closing for the encounter, but what happened between those extremities differed with each person who came through the door.

Some were gentle and sweet, others were timid and nervous, and some were rough and demanding. Sappho was unsure how she felt about some of the rough handling. She was frightened that Daphne would be injured until the experienced priestess explained, "I always have control of the situation." She paused and smiled. "Actually, Aphrodite always has control of the situation. If she did not approve, she could easily overwhelm the mortal man. Also, don't forget," she added in a tone that reminded Sappho of being in a lesson, "one of her favorite lovers was Ares. He's no lamb in the bed, I can assure you."

"But, doesn't it hurt you?" Sappho asked cautiously.

"Usually not," Daphne replied in a very factual way. "My body is more forgiving of the wear of Kypris. I don't feel much of the soreness or fatigue that you would think I would have after some of my more *athletic* encounters. Also, there is a very fine line between pain and pleasure. Sometimes the hurt feels the best."

Some of the devotees were there entirely for themselves, while others were truly trying to give pleasure to Daphne, and Aphrodite through her. Most were men, but some were women.

216

Once, a husband and his *pallake* came to worship together in Daphne's room.

The more she saw, the more she felt driven to participate. Eventually, her hands began to indulge in the erotic sensations, then her mouth. She desperately desired to replace Daphne in the role of *hierodule* – to take Daphne's place in the bed. But part of her vows at her initiation had been to follow the instructions of the *hiereia*, and she had not yet been given approval for full sexual encounters.

Daphne tried to comfort her during breakfast on one of their retreat days while the women of the house secluded themselves during menstruation. "It won't be long now. The virgin-making of a priestess is a significant event – one that requires some planning. But I suspect yours is approaching soon."

Sappho was confused. "What do you mean by 'virgin-making'? Am I not to lose my virginity by serving this way?"

"Temple maidens are always virgins," Daphne explained. "We may have sexual intercourse, but that sex is given to a higher power than our husbands' simple lustful desires. There are many ways to understand a single word, Sappho. 'Virgin' in this sense means simply that we are unmarried. You will never be ruled by a husband's will."

"Priestesses may not marry," stated Sappho, breaking a grainy piece of bread and beginning to eat.

"Actually, that's not entirely true," Daphne corrected her. "Several priestesses have been married, even *hierodulei*. It just isn't the normal choice for a maiden of the temple. Most husbands don't like to know that they are not the ultimate authority in their wives' decision-making. She has more power than him, and her oaths bind her more strongly than her own will." Daphne ate a piece of fruit as she talked, sucking the juice delicately from its fleshy pulp. "Still, some priestesses choose a life outside these walls, when they have served long enough to make such a choice."

"How long is that?" Sappho asked curiously. She had not thought this lifestyle was even a possibility.

"That time is different for each woman," Daphne began, "but it involves elevation to a certain level within the mysteries of Aphrodite. It also requires the permission of the *hiereia*."

"Oh," said Sappho.

"Why?" asked Daphne beadily. "Is there a man you love?"

Sappho laughed outright. "No. I don't even know any men but the ones who have come to you."

Daphne grinned. "True, but when you are seeing men on your own, you might find that you do fall in love with one. Maybe more."

"Really?" Sappho asked, a bit incredulously. "I've seen very little opportunity for falling in love."

Daphne considered her answer for a moment before saying, somewhat reflectively, "There is, sometimes, the opportunity for more conversation between the woman and the man after the Goddess has finished with her devoted follower."

Sappho watched her mentor and friend for a moment. Daphne seemed to have fallen into a memory that she enjoyed, but that somehow gave her pain. Sappho wasn't sure if she should ask her question. Then, "Have you fallen in love that way?"

"Yes," said Daphne. "Twice." She didn't seem interested in giving more details of the experiences. She briskly shifted the focus. "It is far more likely that *they* will fall in love with *you*. Sex and love are so easily confused, and so intimately joined. Ours is a Goddess of both, and these loves are a blessing – though sometimes a mixed one. Every *hierodule* in the temple has a story of a man or woman who fell desperately in love with her. It is sometimes harder on us than on them at the point when they feel rejected by us, if that point comes."

Sappho felt a twinge as an unbidden image of Atthis flashed in her mind. She certainly knew how that rejection felt from the petitioner's side. She had a hard time believing, though, that Atthis might have felt worse about their parting than her.

The conversation drifted onto other, more daily, matters as the women took solace in their communal time of separation. Sappho had been amazed to learn, when she first came to the house, that each of the priestess-homes had been assigned a time at which the women within were scheduled to bleed every month. But she found it less difficult than she had imagined to alter her courses to fit a different moon time than she had observed in the *thiasos*.

The dormitory houses were divided into four groups, each designated as a house of a particular moon phase. She had bled before during the full moon, and she was grateful now to have been placed in a third-quarter house. This meant that she had only had to shift her cycle back by one week. At first she hadn't seen the necessity of it, but then the reality of thousands of women bleeding at the same time struck her in a most unceremonious way. The disposal of the discarded straw alone would be an enormous task, and all of the functions of the temple would have to cease for a week of every month.

Near the end of their sequestration, Sappho overheard Daphne speaking to another priestess in semi-hushed tones. Sappho had turned to leave them in privacy when she heard her name whispered and thought she had been summoned. As she came closer to the doorway, she realized they had not seen her and called for her to join their discussion. Instead, she was the topic of discussion.

"No, I don't think she realizes," Daphne was saying. "Timas hasn't shared anything with her about her initiation. I don't know much myself. I only know that Timas said she was chosen for him because of the place she will eventually fill within the temple." The other priestess asked what place that was. "I don't know, but it must be very important. He's rising to power quickly, I've heard. He's very well-respected in Lesvos and in the islands near us."

"He has been to see me before," said the other woman, "but that was long ago. I was very young, then, and he wasn't so influential."

"Well, he's influential now," said Daphne. "And it seems he likes the younger priestesses best. He's using his growing persuasion and has requested to participate in a virgin-making, and it seems it will be Sappho's."

Chapter 29

When their seclusion ended, the women of Sappho's dormitory took part in a cleansing ritual in the temple baths. Prehistoric hot springs dotted the landscape across Lesvos, but ones in Hiera were particularly abundant and sacred. Once a year, Sappho was told, they would re-enact Aphrodite's bath with great splendor and pomp. The story was one she already knew.

Diomedes's spear had pierced the Goddess's beautiful flesh on a battlefield outside Troy. She had fled to Zeus and Dione, sometimes accounted as her parents, to seek sympathy. Zeus had soothed her by reassuring her that she had no place on the fields of war. Fighting was not her skill. He advised her to go to her bath and take comfort in the splendors of beauty, love, and adoration. She went to the waters of Kyprus, where she had been born amongst the foam, and cleansed herself of the soil of war. The Hours dressed her there, in a fine, sheer cloth that only they could weave. And thus, she set about her own place in the world, far away from the grime, pain, and strife of battle.

The annual ritual echoed the plot of the story and served, magically and practically, to clean the icons and sanctuaries quite thoroughly each summer. The rooms would be scrubbed, fumigated, and decorated with bouquets and swags of flowers. The statues would be bathed, anointed, and adorned with crowns and garlands of flowers and gold.

The monthly practice, Sappho thought, of ritually bathing and donning fresh robes was a reminder of the importance of cleanliness and purity. She loved the feel of the bathing water and the look of the crisp blue and white tiled pool that had been built to hold the steaming waters that bubbled up from the earth. The sweet oils and soft robes were refreshing and elegant against her fair skin. The chants and music of the priestesses as they bathed lingered in her ears and lifted her spirits after the days of confinement.

Sappho had spent much of this most recent seclusion in a state of nervous tension and contemplation. After the patch of conversation she'd caught between Daphne and her friend, her mind was continually trying to make sense of what she'd overheard.

The fact that she was going to lose her virginity, her intactness, soon and begin her service as a *hierodule* was the simplest to understand and accept. She was eager for – though admittedly somewhat frightened by – this impending physical reality, but she had little doubt as to what awaited her. She'd seen the act of love enough times – and with enough variations – to guess fairly accurately about what would happen once she and the chosen man were left to their business.

She was curious and apprehensive, however, about the amount of mystery and ceremony that would accompany this encounter. The knowledge that hers was some sort of special ceremony with a prestigious devotee struck a resounding chord of fear in her heart. Daphne's comment that the *hiereia*, Timas, had some foreknowledge of Sappho's future place in the temple simultaneously stimulated and sickened her. The implication that hers would be a place of power within the temple was the most fear-inducing and unbelievable aspect of the ordeal.

She knew she would not shun or abandon her destiny or her call to service, but she didn't see how she could ever become what Timas had suggested. She certainly could not be what Timas was.

And what of this man who had been chosen for her? Or was it she who had been chosen for him? This was a man of political power in Lesvos, according to Daphne. And he wanted to lie with a temple maiden in the rite that would make her a Holy Virgin. Was this desire fully aroused from his devotion to Aphrodite, or was it a more physical appetite for young flesh? Sappho supposed it must not matter much or Timas wouldn't allow it. Besides, from what she'd seen of the worship paid to Kypris through Daphne, all such devotion was a mixture of physical and spiritual need.

As she washed herself in the bath, she tried to wash herself free of her continual speculations. *I will know what there is to know in time*, she reminded herself. She closed her eyes and dipped under the water. When she stood up again, she looked down toward her feet. Her eyes shifted their focus to that of the water's surface where she expected to see a ripplingly distorted image of her own face. She blinked hard several times to clear her sight, though, because a face unlike her own shone up from the mirrored waves. A voice in her ear whispered, *Prepare*, and she looked to see who had spoken. The women nearest to her were paying her no attention, and she instinctively knew that none of them had given her the instruction. Her gaze wondered across the pool to the place where Timas stood, watching her. Sappho had not realized the *hiereia* was present at this cleansing, and indeed, she was fully clothed and seemed only to be watching – watching just Sappho. The high priestess nodded, as if satisfied with the encounter, and walked away, leaving Sappho to ready herself as she'd been told.

Chapter 30

Two nights later, she found herself drawing the man into a room that had been erected in the main temple. Long draperies of heavily embroidered fabric had been hung from poles around an area that included the statue of the Goddess and a lavishly decorated bed. A few priestesses were in attendance at the rite and served Sappho by helping her and her partner to prepare. Timas was among them.

Before the man had been brought into the temple, Sappho had been anointed with oils upon her brow, along her neck and breastbone, and at her wrists. Two women with very steady hands had drawn elaborate designs all over her body with a henna mixture. Another had dusted her with a strong but pleasant smelling powder that made her body shimmer with a golden luster. She had been given golden jewelry to wear around her neck, wrists, and ankles. Timas had draped a rich red fabric around her, and it fell in long, elegant folds to the floor. Sappho felt like more of an empress than a priestess.

Timas had pulled a golden veil over Sappho's head and shoulders before she had emerged from the little room to greet her suitor and thus begin the sacred marriage. When she walked into the dimly lit and heavily perfumed sanctuary, she could barely distinguish the man's features. She knew he could judge nothing of her except her height. She could see that he was also richly adorned, and she wondered vaguely whether he wore his own clothes and gold or if he had been further embellished by the other maidens.

She had spoken the customary greeting, as had he, and then

she had led him into the inner chamber. She turned to face him, and he knelt at her feet. He was clearly nervous. Sappho was thankful for the layers of fabric that covered her. If not for them, he would have seen how much she trembled. She was afraid of the million mistakes she might make. She was worried about the pain that she knew she must feel at first. Her stomach was a ball of snakes writhing within her. She didn't want to seem like a frightened child, but she felt like one. Was this how all brides felt on their wedding nights? And yet, she couldn't help but noticing that he had a certain power of his own that made her body react to him.

As she looked at the man kneeling before her, she noted that he was fairly average in build and looks, not that she had much experience in judging either of these qualities in a man. Still, to her, he was not as blindingly handsome as Adonis, nor as physically imposing as Ares. *Will he think I am not as beautiful as Aphrodite?* She wiped the thought from her mind. In a few moments, she would *become* Aphrodite, and all this man would be capable of seeing was the most beautiful of Goddesses shining before him in this little velveted room.

He took something from the folds of his garment. "A gift, holy one, for the priestess who bears Aphrodite's visage for me," he said as he held the prize aloft. Sappho reached for it and was surprised by its weight. It was a small ball of some sort, wrapped in green cloth. As she pulled aside the cloth, she saw a glint of gold, and then, when the cloth fell away, she saw a finely crafted golden apple. Inscribed upon it was the word *kallisti*, "for the fairest." Sappho was stunned by the costly gift. She was more surprised, perhaps, because he had not yet seen her face and could not have known whether she was fair or plain.

She set the gift aside and said, "I most graciously accept your gift, as does the lady whom I represent." Without any further discussion, she lifted her arms in invocation and spoke the words that would call Aphrodite into her body. Her mind seemed to withdraw from its normal vantage point, and she felt dizzy. She could still see and hear what was happening in the room, but she was no longer in control of it. She seemed to be viewing the encounter from above, or to the side, or maybe even from behind herself. She couldn't describe where she was, but her spirit was certainly not where it had been moments before. She felt disconnected from her body, and yet she could feel every pressure, every tickle, every thrill of her flesh.

She watched as she removed her own veil, and she saw the look of open awe in the man's face. He bowed even lower before her, prostrating himself on the ground at her feet. She waited for him to look at her face once more. She felt the beauty that Aphrodite shone down upon her face. She unfastened a single clasp and her robes slid silkily down her body. The effect was like the reddest wine pouring down an alabaster statue. Her skin was exceedingly creamy and soft beneath that fabric. Her shape was incredibly inviting. The man at her feet rose, and Sappho could see the erection that strained against his clothes. She saw her hands unfasten them, and she noticed his body more carefully as his garments fell away, too. Perhaps it was because she was no longer looking with the eyes of the flesh, but she saw even more about this man that was attractive and powerful than she could have dreamed was present in him. He was vital and strong.

She could see in his face that he was clever and cunning, and she felt her body respond to his open desire for her.

Her mind reeled and spun as her body was directed by the Goddess. She knew that she was on the cushioned bed with the man, but she was so overwhelmed by the sensations that she felt as if she no longer had any connection with the normal pattern of time or space. She felt his hands and the weight of his body. She felt the initial sting of the penetration and the way in which she eventually opened up to his thrusts. She seemed to hear music coming from within her own body that met and melded with the chanting and playing of the priestesses outside the thickly veiled room. Parts of poetry filled her mind, and she was entirely overcome by the erotic feelings that welled within her. She felt that her body was a vessel that was at once filled by the spiritual presence of Aphrodite and the physical presence of her lover. Both were mingling within her, and somehow she was present, too. She saw, with great clarity, the holiness of the temple maidens who had the ability to combine the sacred and the profane, the spiritual and the physical, the male and the female at one time within one extraordinary vessel. The knowledge of this power, in addition to the overwhelming feelings of lust and love that were swirling within her, made her feel as though she were overflowing with energy. When she finally felt him burst inside her, she sent all of the force in a mighty column toward the statue of the Goddess that had watched the whole scene.

After a moment of leveling their breathing during which Sappho steadied her legs, she stood and spoke the words of thanksgiving and release. She was once again entirely present in her own body. She noticed the blood between her legs and wondered for a moment if she should clean it off. Remembering Daphne's advice on the matter, and noticing that no cloth had been provided, she quickly forgot it. Now, she only wondered what to do next.

The man addressed her thoughts directly. "Will you lie next to me for a moment before we return to our normal places?"

Sappho wondered for a moment whether or not she should. She didn't really know him well enough to feel personal affection and closeness with him. And yet, she had just given him her physical virginity. She was aware that this act alone would create a bond between them. Already, she felt as if she knew him a little, remembering the vision of him she had seen through Aphrodite. He held his hand out to her, and she decided to take it. He pulled her onto the bed, and then he encircled her within his somewhat wiry arms.

"May I ask your given name, my *hierodule*?" he asked.

"I am called Sappho," she said. "And what is your name?"

"Pittakos," he said. "Have you heard of me?" Sappho shook her head. The only knowledge she had of him was vague at best. She thought it trivial to mention what she had overheard Daphne say. He said no more for a while, but stroked her hair and face and looked upon her as one looks at a rare jewel. He beheld her with a mixture of respect and longing, and Sappho wondered if he desired her again.

"This was your first time," he said softly. The priestesses were still singing in the temple, but their song had changed. It was now a low, sweet tune. Sappho was reminded of a lullaby she knew as a child. "I wonder, dear one, what does it feel like to you?" Sappho sat silently for a moment. She felt comfortable with this man, though she barely knew him. She inhaled deeply, feeling a deep satisfaction as the breath expanded her body and reminded her of all the glorious senses that were now awakened within her.

The poetry that she had heard in her mind moments before came back to her and mixed with the melody of the priestesses just beyond the curtain. She thought, *Now Love, the ineluctable, with bitter sweetness fills me, overwhelms me, and shakes my being. Now like a mountain wind the oaks o'erwhelming, Eros shakes my soul.* Pittakos was still watching her, waiting for her response. She said, "I am … filled. My soul is turned to sweetest nectar, and poetry will drip from my honeyed lips."

Chapter 31

When Sappho was summoned the following morning to Timas's cloister, she was only mildly surprised. Timas, though she hadn't spoken directly to the young priestess in several weeks, had been more present in Sappho's thought and vision. Her special message at the baths and her presence at the previous night's sacred marriage left an impression of promise with the younger woman – a promise for continued contact.

Sappho was once again draped in the simple linens of a priestess. The royal red silk, which she'd been given as a token of her new rank and position, had been carefully folded and stored in the wooden box in her small room. The gossamer, golden veil lay there, as well, accompanied by Pittakos's apple. The only adornment Sappho bore on her person as a vestige of the previous night was a golden comb inset with three dark garnets which she used to hold her otherwise unbound tresses in place.

Her sandaled feet skipped lightly over the smooth flagstone paths and stairs that led through the sacred precinct. She felt buoyant as she savored the congratulations of the other temple women as she had left the dormitory house in response to Timas's summons. The maidens honored her with their kisses and their words. Daphne had placed a thin golden bangle around Sappho's wrists in token of her "marriage." She flicked it, now, ever so subtly as she approached the *hiereia's* dwelling.

Timas remained seated as Sappho entered the room, led by a young man who attended the *hiereia*. She was reviewing the contents of a small wax tablet – a message, Sappho guessed, regarding temple affairs. When she finished, she raised her eyes to Sappho and smiled – a kind smile, but strong. Sappho was again aware of Timas's authority. The younger priestess knelt and made a gesture of deference to the *hiereia*.

"Sappho, my dear one," her voice was comforting but crisp, "come sit with me. We have much to discuss." The young priestess obeyed, sitting on the floor at Timas's feet. "No, sit here with me. Share the cushion. That's better. I'd like to talk with you about … your role – as priestess."

A moment of fear seized Sappho's guts. She felt icy and damp. *Have I done something wrong?* She thought. *Am I to be stripped of my initiation?* The wave of panic passed, and Sappho reprimanded herself. How childish to dwell in constant fear of reprisals. Whatever Timas was about to reveal wasn't likely to be a horrific punishment for some unknown misdeed. She cleared her mind, hoped her face had remained unshadowed, and awaited Timas's instruction.

"I do not know, as yet, where your eventual position in this temple will be," Timas began, "but I've always suspected you will be something more than a *hierodule*."

No surprises, yet, Sappho thought. She knew every temple maiden must serve in this manner for a time, but she had never thought she would remain there. She saw this level of service as a metaphor for one's understanding of Aphrodite. It began with sexual desire and carnal pleasure, but it led into many deeper layers of love, beauty, and passion. Of course, the sexual pleasure was always present, and one never entirely abandoned her sexual worship. None would want to.

"You have many tests and trials to pass, young one," Timas continued, "and your role may be ever-changing. I see you in a high place within this temple, Sappho, but you must learn and see so much before that can happen." Sappho nodded. She had no doubts that she was still a novice.

"The form of your service as a *hierodule* will be somewhat different than most," the older priestess explained. "The man to whom you were joined last night in the *hieros gamos* is no common man. He is a powerful and ambitious man. He has a great deal of influence on Lesvos, and in other places, as well." Sappho nodded again. She knew some of this, although she'd only overheard it as gossip between other women.

"He has requested that, for now, you serve as *hierodule* only to him." Timas spoke these words somewhat carefully. She was trying to gauge Sappho's reaction to them. "Indeed, he wishes something different for you than *hierodule*. You shared a form of marriage with him last night, one that he wishes to extend into his personal and public life. Pittakos wishes you to be a wife to him."

Sappho's eyes widened and then narrowed shrewdly. "Lady, I mean no insult or disrespect, but I never wished to marry in legal truth with any man. I gave my vows to this temple, to serve Aphrodite, and to be no man's property."

Timas reached her hand out to Sappho's. "I know this. I speak not of marriage as you are accustomed. You know, I presume, of two types of wives – the honored wife and the concubine. A man might have only one, or he may have multiples of each, if his purse is deep enough. Both of these wives are, as you said, his property. I do not ask you to be this type of wife."

The older woman caressed Sappho's brow, trying to smooth the crease of confusion that had wrinkled itself there. "There is another type of marriage that is more common among men of great wealth or political stature. I'm surprised your father didn't have one, though you might never have seen her, even if he did. This type of wife is given much honor and a good deal more liberty than the other two. You wouldn't be required to live in Pittakos's home, if you chose otherwise. You would be included in the *symposia* and other discussions that are generally reserved only for men. You could dissolve the union whenever you chose."

Sappho considered what she was hearing. "What, then, would be required of me?"

"Pittakos will be traveling for some time," Timas again took on the business-like air of a teacher. She sensed that Sappho no longer needed to be placated. "He wants a beautiful, educated, well-spoken, and poised companion to accompany him. You are trained as a priestess of Aphrodite, which means you are ... skilled ... in ways that will benefit him privately as well as publicly. Yet you are young and relatively inexperienced, which is a quality he finds appealing."

"Does he not have a wife who could fill these same needs?" Sappho asked.

"He has two wives, in fact," Timas said. "Neither will do. One is with child and cannot travel. The other is a concubine – a slave who warms his bed at night and assists his other wife during the day. He wants a mistress – an unparalleled mistress, one of

234

Aphrodite's women. He wants you."

Sappho flushed. She felt flattered at being pursued, desired.

"There are great benefits to you, as well," Timas pressed. Sappho gathered that the *hiereia* wasn't making the type of offer that a young priestess of no rank could easily push aside. She felt certain that the older woman's patience had a limit, and she didn't want to test it. "You will be educated to the political and cultural life that exists outside this temple. You will have the opportunity to visit other temples of Aphrodite and to take part in the feasts and festivals of other Gods and Goddesses. Your life in this place has been sheltered. Your focus has been only upon the face of Aphrodite. With Pittakos, you will see and learn so much more, and your appreciation of the one we adore will deepen and sharpen in ways you cannot imagine now."

Sappho looked intently at a piece of ribbon that curled on the floor. Timas's words swirled through her mind – not allowing her to catch onto any of them for close inspection. She wanted to think through this proposal logically, but she felt the weight of Timas's stare. The *hiereia* was awaiting her answer. She couldn't latch onto any reason to refuse. In fact, the offer of broad travel with an intriguing and powerful man seemed like the adventure she'd always hoped would find her.

"What say you, Sappho?" Timas pressed. "Do you consent to being Pittakos's mistress throughout his travels?"

Sappho thought another moment, closed her eyes hard, opened them and said, "I consent."

Chapter 32

Among the first of the preparations for the new *hierodule's* change in duties and degree was the drafting and signing of the contract between the mistress and her patron. This document would establish and ensure her rights as his chosen consort. It was not unlike the marriage contract signed between the husband and the bride's father. The roll of papyrus indicated what goods Sappho would bring to the union, what Pittakos would provide to the temple in her absence, and what special rights she was to receive beyond that of a typical bride. Sappho signed for her own part in the agreements, however; and Timas, as an official of the temple, served as witness and trustee. The contract did not go into the details of the expected duties of the mistress as that would have been too crude – and obvious.

Sappho knew she was not expected to run Pittakos's household. For the brief time that they would be staying on Lesvos, she was free, in fact, to live under a separate roof, if she chose. She was under no obligation to live in the women's quarters already shared by his wife and concubine. She didn't have to take orders from or be subservient to either of these women, as would have been expected had the marriage been of another type.

She would not have the opportunity to work at the loom while they traveled, though she did plan to embroider and embellish some fabrics that she'd been given as a gift from the temple. Furthermore, it would be largely unnecessary, she was told, for Sappho to tend to many of the daily headaches of housekeeping as they traveled. Though they would be staying in certain locations for extended periods of time, Pittakos employed another woman as a general housekeeper, and she was capable of tending to all of the basics of cooking and cleaning that would be required.

In essence, Sappho came to understand that she was expected to bring the love, beauty, and grace of her patroness into Pittakos's world. He wanted the touch of Aphrodite in his daily life, and Sappho was to be the vehicle for Kypriana's influence. He desired her accompaniment in the sitting room, the garden, the bath, the bed. In exchange for her exquisite and tender favors, he would show her cities of renown, introduce her to men of influence and let her educate herself in the temples of the Olympians.

As Sappho packed her few belongings, she reflected that she'd had little means, need, or desire to accumulate trinkets and possessions. She had a few lengths of fabric for garments and wraps, including the red and gold she'd recently worn before Pittakos. She had a golden comb, a few other modest hair pinnings, and a single gold bangle for adornments. A statuette of Aphrodite, a mirror, and the phallic stone she'd received as a gift rounded out her list of personal possessions. She smirked to think that of what little she had collected, one item was still unused. It wouldn't have been permitted until a few days ago, and there hadn't been time or need since then.

While Sappho was finishing with packing away her small collection of herbs and oils, taking great pains to make sure they didn't spill and stain her *peplos* fabric, Daphne entered the room. Sappho's most recent mentor wore a smile that seemed to radiate joy, hope, and promise. Mischievousness lurked behind that smile, as well, Sappho thought, as did some small, distant sadness. Sappho was suddenly struck by the realization that she'd made one real friend in the temple, and she wasn't sure how much time would pass before she saw her again.

Before panic about the mystery of her new situation or mistiness at the tug of foreseen separation had a chance to settle upon Sappho, Daphne had given her a quick embrace and then pulled her into the hallway by her hand. The women ran through the courtyard and into the open sunshine of the garden outside their house, giggling with the playfulness of children caught up in the mirth of Daphne's secret game. Sappho followed, willing to go anywhere or do anything with the person she knew she would soon miss.

A small group of women from their house sat under the shade of the bay laurels on the cool grass. Some of them rose when Sappho and Daphne drew near, flushed and glowing from their silly flight. Their laughter was infectious, and all the women smiled with genuine joy at the good fortune and fellowship they shared.

"Daphne tells us you leave tomorrow," one of them, a Phoenician beauty with dancing eyes and delicate hands, began to say. "She tells us, too, of the honor shown to you by Pittakos and the *hiereia*." There was an excited murmur among the women.

Another woman stepped forward, willowy and fair. "We've come to bid you a safe journey and return, little sister."

"And to shower you with the blessings of Aphrodite." It was Daphne who spoke this time. "You may have already experienced the sacred marriage, and so you are joined to this man in a certain way

238

already. But before you go to take the place of a wife, the women of your home may show you love and blessing."

Tears sparkled in Sappho's eyes like dew drops on the rich petals of morning glories. All through the weeks in which she'd been living and working alongside these priestesses, she had felt their kindness, but hadn't truly felt herself to be a member of their tribe. In these last few moments, though, that slight but persistent feeling of otherness was completely swept aside in the warmth of this tender and familial display. The women surrounding her were her sisters, and Sappho saw the intensity and beauty of this new reality. She had no words but only smiled at each of them in turn.

The women sat together for long hours as the sun's chariot was drawn across the feathery blue dome that engulfed them. Some of the priestesses had gifts for Sappho, little treasures from their personal stores of possessions. One gave her a pleasant blue and white length of cotton, perfect for a *peplos* in the hot summer. Another gave her a gauzy yellow cotton, the *himation* which she could drape for dramatic effect or modesty but which was a necessary part of a lady's wardrobe. The Phoenician woman gave her two gold bracelets and a string of little bells to wear on her ankle. Many women had advice, and all had kisses and kindness and comfort to bestow.

When they went to the evening meal, Sappho felt her stomach too tender to take much food. She sat for a while among the women, enjoying the chatter and business of living for a long while before she made her final farewells and returned to her room. As she added her new things to the box she would take, Daphne came to her a second time.

"I'm sure there's no good reason for it," she blushed, "but I wanted to give you my gift privately." Daphne stood closer to Sappho, and both women could feel the pleasant tension mounting between them. Sappho wondered if they would make love. Part of her hoped for it, but another, stronger part hoped that was not the gift Daphne intended. She wasn't at all sure that she could lie in her friend's arms tonight and have the will to go to her husband's tomorrow.

Daphne pulled a small package out of the fold of her *peplos* and handed it to Sappho. "It's papyrus, nothing more," she said. "No linens, no gold. Not those things from me. Not today." Sappho beamed. She knew it was a superb gift. A treasure. "I've listened to your poetry, Sappho. I've heard the beauty of the lyric that you speak. The words you breathe deserve to be recorded so they may last forever."

Sappho blushed. "You make too much of my small skill. It is not as rare as all that."

Daphne raised an eyebrow. "So you say. Just honor me with this: every now and then, write your poems down that you may share them with me when you return." Sappho knew, when she saw the paper, that she would.

At length, Daphne left and Sappho had nothing more to prepare. She knew she would be leaving with the sun's arrival, but she didn't have the patience to lie in bed and try to sleep. Her stomach was uneasy, and her mind raced. She flitted from one topic to the next, from emotion to emotion, in random patterns that left her tired, confused and wakeful. Hope and adventure enticed her. Duty and honor reminded her of her commitments to the temple and Aphrodite. Fondness for friends and worry of the unknown taught her trepidation for the new life that would begin with the dawn.

An hour or two before she had to rise, she finally drifted to sleep.

Chapter 33

Errita, one of the priestess who, jointly with the boy, attended the *hiereia*, had been sent on an errand to summon Sappho to the outer temple. When she drew back the curtain of the *hierodule's* room, she found her charge kneeling below her window, darkened with the pre-dawn stillness. An oil lamp, clay with the image of Hestia sculpted near the small spout of flame, sat beside her, the tiny light her only companion. She held a mirror in her hand, and she gazed placidly at her own reflection. Errita didn't want to interrupt the young woman in the midst of her meditation, but she had been sent for a purpose that she had no authority to postpone.

"With your blessing, *Adelphe*," she said, using the common title between priestesses, "the *hiereia* awaits your arrival in the public temple." Sappho's eyes focused and shifted to the woman standing in her doorway. She noticed, as always, the grace and quiet strength with which the priestesses bore themselves. This woman was no exception – refined and confident, compassionate. How Sappho could guess all these characteristics based on a single sentence and her presence in the doorway, she was unsure. *It must be the touch of Aphrodite upon her*, she thought. *Do I, too, give the same impression? Am I so obviously marked as a "Woman of the Golden One?"*

She stood and began gathering her few things. Errita came to help her. The box, containing all of her possessions, had been outfitted with two leather handles and a clasp, making it suitable for travel. Sappho checked the clasp, and, being reassured that it was

242

closed, lifted one of the handles. She hoped she seemed composed. She felt flighty, frightened, and very insecure. She wanted to check and readjust her *peplos*, her veil, her hair pinnings. She wanted to hold her hands out to test whether or not they were shaking. She knew, though, that any of those actions would have made her nervousness obvious and, therefore, more intense. She snuffed the flame from her little lamp, consciously steadied her breathing, and found her balance before grasping one of the box's handles and lifting the weight.

The summoner grabbed the other handle, and together they carried the box through the curtained doorway and down the deserted and quiet hall. Sappho knew that in an hour or so, the women of her house would rouse and prepare for the day, and it seemed strange to her that she would not be among them.

She felt awkward carrying the box. It was not heavy, since she didn't have much to pack inside; but it was unwieldy. She thought of her father and Anassa's wedding ceremony and the festive *pompe* parade that brought Anassa to her new home. She suppressed a little laugh at the idea that her wedding *pompe* included just two women wrestling an ungainly box through the early morning silence of a sleeping temple-village. *How had Atthis's wedding been?* she wondered. The unbidden image of her friend being borne in the bridal cart surrounded by dancers and musicians and cheering neighbors made Sappho shiver. She didn't want to think of it now, as she was going to meet her own life as a married woman.

Sappho was grateful to see the *hiereia's* male attendant awaiting the women out in the courtyard. He swiftly lifted the box out of Sappho's hands. Errita and the boy walked side by side with the box between them. The bride walked silently and smoothly behind them. She was thankful for this last opportunity to gather her composure and stealthily check her appearance before stepping into the temple. She draped her *himation* across the back half of her head and wrapped it around her arms and shoulders. She wasn't sure if the air had a chill or if the shiver she felt was a product of her nerves, but the opaque veil would help fight either. Just ahead, the temple had the soft glow of lamps and candlelight, and she knew incense would swirl around the temple's visitors even at this odd hour. Her mind reached ahead of her, trying to picture those who awaited her there and the manner in which they would greet her.

Just beyond the light of the entrance, the *hiereia's* male attendant took the full weight of the box, and Errita stepped forward to announce the arrival of the bride. She spoke when she was the only member of the small procession who stood fully in the light. "Honorable *Hiereia Aphrodites*, worthy Pittakos, I present the *hetaera* of Pittakos. I present the priestess Sappho."

Sappho thought she could sense Pittakos holding his breath, but she couldn't see him yet. As Errita stepped aside, Sappho emerged into the light, her head held high, her breath steady, her eyes matching Pittakos's startlingly intense stare. He took several steps toward her, and she did the same, meeting him just in front of the large icon of Aphrodite. Though Sappho didn't break their eye contact to look up at the statue, she did allow the faintest traces of slyness to enter her smile when she said, "I meet you again, Pittakos, a handful of days after our first encounter and under the same auspicious gaze." She lowered her eyes just long enough to bow her head slightly and say, "I greet you with honor and joy." When she looked back up and reconnected with his stare, she could feel the energy flowing freely between them along an invisible track. She didn't have much experience with men, but she doubted that many of them approached their desire with such open directness and intensity. *This is why he is powerful*, she thought. *Most men would falter under the strength of his will.* In the years that followed, Sappho would learn how accurate this early assessment was.

Pittakos flicked his eyes up at the statue and smiled at it before looking back at his *hetaera*. "I've already felt her blessing in your embrace, and I crave the continued presence of both love and persuasion as I sense them in your spirit." Now he bowed and said, "I greet you, Sappho, with honor and joy." He looked up, and again the young woman felt the pulsing strength of the bond between them.

"You have already been joined in the sacred marriage, the sexual union of male to female," Timas spoke as she stepped forward. "You have also been joined in legal contract. The ties that bind you together are already strong. It is time to tie one more knot into this union before you depart." The *hiereia* placed her hand just behind Pittakos's right shoulder. "Pittakos, if you join yourself to this woman, take her right hand in your right hand." Without looking away, he held her hand. Timas turned to Sappho and placed her other hand behind Sappho's left shoulder. "Sappho, if you would join yourself to this man, take his left hand in your left hand." Sappho reached over their right hands to join their left hands. As they connected, she could feel the tingle of energy as it swept a path around the track of their entwined arms. Timas placed one of her hands above this knot and the other below it. "You come to this union willingly and with honor. May you live together in the same manner. Take from this temple the blessings of Aphrodite."

Pittakos squeezed Sappho's hands, making her smile. They released each other, and Sappho felt the disruption of the energy that had been flowing between them. She felt momentarily dazed and wasn't sure what she should do next. Pittakos was in full control of his wits, though, and had already begun instructing Timas's boy to deliver Sappho's box to a servant who was waiting with the horses. He strapped her possessions to one of the animals – the only one who didn't already bear bags for the journey back to Mytilene.

Sappho turned to Timas. She seemed at a loss for words to frame a farewell. Timas eased the situation by saying, "You will return to this place, and I will welcome you back in this very temple." The statement was so concrete that it left no room for doubt or lonesomeness.

"Until then," she said, "say prayers to the Kyprian for me." With that, Sappho turned and left the temple grounds for the first time in years. More years would pass before she would make her return.

Chapter 34

The small party stopped a few hours after dawn, and Sappho was amused at the dialogue that passed between man and mistress during that time. Pittakos had taken a keen interest in hearing of Sappho's family in Mytilene, a family he knew mainly by reputation and not through any close ties of friendship.

"Your sister, I believe, is married to Andronikos," he said. "Is that so?"

Sappho paused a moment to formulate her answer. She wondered if she ought to go into the specific details of her family's composition. Atthis wasn't exactly her sister, but she didn't suppose Pittakos would care about the details in that respect. He was speaking in general terms and probably would have only put stock in the legal relationship anyway. In this sense, Atthis was her sister.

She vaguely remembered hearing the name Andronikos when Atthis left the temple. "Yes, that is true," she replied. "I did not attend their wedding, though, due to my …," she struggled for an appropriate explanation. *Due to my obstinacy and injured pride,* was the complete thought that came to her, but she couldn't very well say that. She didn't want to lie about the temple, either, by indicating that they wouldn't have permitted her to go. She compromised by saying, "… due to my devotion to the work of the temple. For this reason, I have not met my brother-in-law."

The phrase "brother-in-law" bubbled through her lips unpleasantly, like a sour belch on the fringes of a stomach sickness. She didn't like to think of Atthis and her husband at all, much less to think of him as family. The idea of such a close association with him agitated her and made his theft of Atthis that much more abominable.

Luckily, Pittakos moved on to more pleasant topics after sensing some of the melancholy behind Sappho's words. He chose not to press the matter now, when he was still getting to know her. He couldn't comprehend any obvious reason for the hint of sorrow as Sappho had spoken of her sister's marriage. Indeed, Sappho had brushed it quickly behind a curtain of composure, and a less observant man wouldn't have noticed it at all. Pittakos, though, was a very observant man. He caught the details in every conversation, every political maneuver, every military tactic. He was shrewd, and he had the sensitivity to know when and how best to press forward to achieve his goals. He knew Sappho was young and probably still a little delicate because of that youth. He would not win her absolute trust by displaying blatant insensitivity to the hurt he knew she wanted to hide. He let her think she had hidden it, in fact, and moved deftly to new ground, so she would continue being open to him.

The conversation had continued pleasantly through the early part of their ride, with Pittakos gently probing for details about Sappho's life. He cared less about the details themselves than he did about the ways in which she offered them up. He wanted her to see him as a compassionate and attentive lover. With a young woman like Sappho, he knew he needed to win her trust. That trust, he knew, was the key to having the power to influence those around him. That trust, in fact, was the cornerstone of his prowess in the political affairs of Lesvos.

The man was not young by any account. He had one son who was already grown to manhood. This son had married last year and had, to his credit, already made Pittakos a grandfather. However, Pittakos was not a doddering old patriarch, either, by any estimation. He was mature and seasoned, but vigorous in both mind and body. He was nearly as strong as he had been twenty years ago, when his grown son had been an infant. His hair was still thick and rippled with waves, but now traces of silver crested the black locks. His eyes, uncannily blue and clear, had all the more piercing intensity from his years of experience.

Ambition influenced every public move and many of the private decisions he made. To say Pittakos was ruled by a lust for power would be shallow and short-sighted. He was not blinded by his ambition. If asked, he would be more likely to say that his attraction to political power helped him see situations more clearly. It forced him to look further on in time for the consequences of every action and reaction.

Though his tactics and motivations may have seemed manipulative, if anyone had been in the position to see these inner workings, Pittakos found a great aptitude to win admirers due to the fact that he showed a genuine concern for the comfort and well-being of those around him. He did not demonstrate the callow ruthlessness of so many other powerful men, and he did not rush to sate his own vanity and pride.

It was with this seeming altruism that he listened to Sappho recount the childhood memories of playing knucklebones with

Atthis or tricking some servant or other out of sweetmeats before the evening meal. Sappho enjoyed dusting off these half-forgotten memories and sharing them with another person. She hadn't thought of Atthis in purely pleasant terms in several months, and her memories of their innocent childhood games were like little treasures hidden under neglected souvenirs of some other life.

By the first time they stopped to rest, though, Sappho found it ironic that as she was leaving one phase of her life behind, she hadn't fully embraced the new adventures that awaited her. Instead, she had regressed into dwelling on thoughts of a life so far past that she could never hope to reclaim it.

With a resolve to turn her face toward the years ahead, she said, "Enough of the past for now. I'm standing on the edge of a journey that is just beginning, and I want to know what awaits me. If I may be bold enough to inquire, I should like to know where we are going and for what purpose."

Her consort chuckled at her directness. "A natural thing to wonder. You asked two simple questions, and for now I will give you two simple answers. We are going to visit friends, some old and some unknown, in several locations. We shall see them in the hopes of strengthening those ties of friendship."

Sappho contemplated his response for a moment and then said with a wry smile, "I suppose if I want to be treated like a child or a simpleton, I could continue asking 'simple' questions." Pittakos looked a bit startled to hear her cut so candidly through the vague answer he had given. "I will have to be more coy and complex next time if I want you to take me seriously." She was clearly not offended, and Pittakos thought he sensed a flirtatious tone underlying her words. He caught the edge of a challenge in her voice. *Ah, there is more life in this girl,* he thought, and he felt the first stirrings of arousal for her since he'd taken her from the temple.

"Are you aware of the trouble the islands of the Aegean have with Persia?" he asked.

"I've heard mention of it," she said. "Our education in political and military entanglements was quite limited, though."

"Really?" Pittakos said, obviously surprised.

"Well, yes," Sappho explained. "Aphrodite's sphere of influence is the heart and bed and home, not the battlefield."

"And yet she is so closely connected to Ares," he countered. "They are practically inseparable. Love and War are intricately intertwined."

"True," she replied, "but the Goddess of Laughter isn't usually credited with great warrior skill."

"Not usually," Pittakos said, "and yet you may be exposed to ways of seeing Aphrodite in the next few months that may broaden your understanding of her."

Sappho grinned. "I hope so." *That is the main reason I agreed to come,* she thought.

"So you know we are ill at peace with the Persians, but you know little of the reasons for it. Is that so?" he asked.

"Yes," she said. "That would be a fair way to say it."

"Well, in essence, we Greeks have pushed rather far into their territory from time to time, and they are currently pushing back," Pittakos explained. "They are angry with us for certain grievances. Justified or not, they wish to retaliate. Furthermore, they may see an opportunity to benefit materially by taking the wealth of our more prosperous city-states for themselves. There are murmurings of invasion, though there haven't been many attacks yet. None of their efforts have been unified, and they haven't done any serious damage."

"If the threat of unrest is upon us," Sappho began, "why do you wish to travel at this time? Wouldn't it be more prudent to stay on Lesvos and prepare our military forces here? Aren't there provisions to be seen to at home?"

"A council has already begun the preparations for defense," Pittakos said, inwardly glad that Sappho was showing some aptitude for engaging in this conversation. With young girls, one never really knew what to expect. "We go to recall the bonds made by old allies, and to forge some new ones that look promising."

"Is there danger in traveling at such a time?"

"The war is not directly upon us yet," he clarified. "If we band together, in fact, it is my hope that we can avoid the war altogether. Traveling now is only slightly more risky than doing so a few years ago would have been." He smiled reassuringly. "There are always dangers. We can't keep to ourselves for fear that there may be a snake in the road before we reach our destination."

Sappho nodded, "I see your point." She thought for a few moments. "Where, then, do you plan to seek the allies of whom you spoke?"

"I will begin as near to my own home as I might," he explained. "I've mentioned the council, and it is with them I must speak first. We will have our meal this night at the home of one of those council members. You will join me there, my dear, as my *hetaera*."

"Is this a council or a *symposium*?" she asked, knowing her role would be determined based on his response.

"It is a *symposium*, not an official meeting," he clarified. "It is only as formal as *symposia* are – food, drink, conversation, dancing girls." He gave her a wink.

The position of the *hetaera* was more complicated than it might have seemed to a casual observer. Other wives, in fact, often underestimated the skill, charm, and education required to fulfill the *hetaera's* duties. A *hetaera* must be beautiful and pleasant – attributes which could come naturally to both rocks and women and required no particular finesse on the part of either. She must also be graceful and elegant while maintaining a playful wit. She had to be adept at making each man in the room feel comfortable and possibly even curious about her without continually making herself the center of attention. She must be confident and self-assured when she in fact became the center of attention, as she was when called upon to dance and sing or play music for the guests. She must be an adequate performer in each of those arts. This was her public role in the presence of her companion. Her private duties included the range of skills needed to arouse and satiate his physical, emotional, and intellectual desires. No small job, but Sappho felt equal to her duties.

She knew, of course, that she was to be more than a dancing girl tonight, though only another *hetaera* might appreciate the distinction. Still, dancing would be required of her, and she felt a fluttering of spiders' legs in her belly at the thought of performing a dance in front of men she didn't know. She had only danced with other women, as an equal participant. How would it feel to be watched? *I will invoke the Muses,* she thought. *And the Graces will bless my every step and undulation.* The thought gave her comfort, and she knew she would be fine.

"And where shall we go after the council?" she asked.

"First, back to my home," he said. "My wife and housekeeper have overseen the preparations for our journey, and everything should be nearly ready. We will depart within the week upon by ship. From there we will visit Lydia, Samos, Kyprus, Kythera, Athens, Sparta, and a few other locations of interest. It will be a long journey, and we will live in some places for a more substantial period of time than others." He looked at her, reading her once more. "I hope you will be able to endure such a long time away from your home and temple."

"I doubt very much that I will have any problem with either endurance of a long and possibly difficult voyage or with homesickness," she said, assuredly. "My calling is in this business for now, and my own training will fill this time with rich reward."

Pittakos found himself wanting this woman's approval and affection in a way he had never wanted of another woman before. "I hope you may find such reward in sharing my company along the way," he confessed.

Sappho sensed the need in his voice. "In that, my husband, I'm sure I will discover the richest treasure of all," the *hetaera* spoke.

Chapter 35

The wife of the council member was diligent in her preparations for the evening's *symposium*. The men's room, where they would dine and drink, was in immaculate order. The couches were arranged around the room, clean and inviting, lining the walls. Each couch had new mats, covered with a hearty and soft rug, and set on one end with a cushion. A table stood between the foot of each couch and the head of the next. The carpet that covered the stone floor had recently been beaten free of dust and crumbs and washed clean of old wine. A bowl of rose petals sat by the door, to be strewn on the floor as the guests entered. A cleansing herb burned in the censer hanging high in the center of the room, to be replaced soon by a more aromatic one.

When she had become the wife of this husband, the young woman had become the highest ranking woman in the home. Her husband's father lived with them, but his wife had died the previous year, and the old man was beyond marriage, he said. The son and his wife now had the responsibility of running the home and filling it with children. The ancient patron would take his deserved role as grandfather and advisor, relaxing as he chose and giving his opinions in an air of well-earned respect.

Of course, he was more involved in the daily workings of the household than the young wife might have preferred since he had given up other occupations, and she often felt she had been wed to two husbands. Luckily, in her opinion, she only had conjugal obligations to one. As unpleasant as her experience with the younger man had been, she shuddered to think what the doddering and feeble hands might do to her unreceptive body. The one, she knew to be domineering and overpowering, insensible to her physical and emotional needs. The other, she imagined to be impotent and weak, incapable of sensing even his own diminishing desires.

Both men, though, had allowed her to apply the sense of style she had cultivated in her earliest youth to the decorative touches around the home. She had paid a fair amount of attention to the men's room, where her husband's guests would spend their time, and to the women's quarters, where she would spend the majority of her own time.

The men's room she had adorned in deep, sophisticated wine colors with accents of gold. It was a rich and luxurious effect, highlighting her new family's old wealth and status. This color scheme had the added benefit of feeling welcoming and warm. It also suited the sense of mystery and sensuality that would seem the perfect accent to the music and dancing of the women who entertained the guests in this room.

Most wives did not approve very highly of the class of woman called "*hetaera.*" This wife, however, knew the benefits of having her husband's attention elsewhere. Some of the *hetaerae* were accommodating enough to keep her husband thoroughly occupied in his sleeping chamber after the *symposium* had concluded. Sometimes a more common prostitute could serve the same purpose, though her husband rarely brought one home. Still, visiting one in the marketplace generally slaked his desire enough that he didn't feel inclined to tax her with his lust.

This young wife was also glad to welcome her husband's friends' mistresses because they would often spend some time with her in the *gyneceaum*. She was hospitable enough to invite them there, which the other women appreciated. They were rarely welcomed by legitimate wives, who treated them with disdain and jealousy. Being made to feel a welcome guest among other women was a treat for a *hetaera*, one that she frequently repaid with devoted friendship.

As friends, the female guests and their hostess would talk and dance in their own way, away from the boasting and political plotting of the men. It was a few brief moments out of the whole evening, but the young woman welcomed the change in the otherwise monotonous routine of her world.

She checked on the preparations for the meal. A lamb was roasting over the fire, giving off a sumptuous smell. She instructed a servant boy to set out a number of platters and fill them with cheese, olives, grapes, and apples. Another servant she sent after bread. She mixed a savory sauce for the meat and thought she should have the jars of wine taken to the men's dining room. On second thought, though, she decided to have all the food and drink brought before the guests when they had already arrived – a procession intended to impress the guests with their host's abundance.

She gave the final instructions to the servants and returned to the *gyneceaum* to make herself presentable. The men, she knew, wouldn't see her for long, but she still wanted to represent her husband and home well in the few moments when she would be expected to greet them modestly. She chose a fresh *peplos* made of a green the color of sage. It was trimmed in a design of violets and honeysuckle by her own hand. She arranged her hair and fastened it in place with a braided cord. A few tendrils fell loosely around the back of her neck. Drops of pearls dangled from her ears, and she put on a necklace of small coral beads. She chose a dark blue veil that she draped over the back of her head and let rest on her shoulders. Finally, she checked her reflection in a small golden mirror. For a moment, she saw the image of herself, hair unbound in a perfumed and glowing temple. A tear, a solitary testimony to her loneliness, welled in her eye. She blinked it back, hoping it wouldn't spoil her complexion. She applied make-up around her eyes and mouth, and, upon hearing the first of the guests arrive in the courtyard, she went downstairs to be a proper hostess.

Chapter 36

Pittakos had paid every little attention to Sappho, making her feel beautiful and precious to him and, at the same time, a little awkward. She accepted his attention with grace and charm, and tried to resolve the slight sensation of discomfort from having her every move viewed by another person. She knew he didn't intend it as scrutiny, and so she began working internally on accepting this lavish attention as a sign of his growing affection for her. She was glad that his attention would be somewhat divided once they were among the other guests, and the talk would turn to politics and other issues.

The walk through this quarter of the city had been pleasant for her, though. She hadn't recalled much of Mytiline, though she had been born and raised in it. Certainly, she had never had the freedom to walk the streets as a child, though, and she had rarely left her own home after dark. She was captivated by the beauty of the homes, their walls washed white and shining like pearl against the indigo sky at dusk. The smell of jasmine and other night-blooming flowers filled the air, and she felt keenly aware of all her senses. They were reminding her of her childhood – that same indigo sky as seen through latticed windows or over the walls from her place in the courtyard. She heard music from behind some of the walls of the homes they passed and remembered dancing in her father's house with Tessa and the women.

They were not the first guests to arrive at the designated home. Two other men approached the door just ahead of them. One, an old man with grisly gray hair that stuck out in clumps around his

balding head, greeted Pittakos and said he was glad the younger man
was attending. The old fellow gave Sappho a look of interest but said
nothing. She assumed he could see little of her in the dark with her
veil drawn about her. She was flattered by the curiosity, though, and
thought to herself that he would soon be able to look at her to his
heart's content as it was customary for the *hetaerae* to dance for the
guests.

Pittakos and Sappho stood back from the host and his wife
as they were greeting the men, and Sappho found herself looking to
Pittakos for reassurance. She had never been in this type of social
situation before, and she was now wondering if she would make her
or her husband look foolish. He smiled calmly at her, unaware of the
panic she felt – unaware of the sudden knot in her stomach or the
tingle that made her suddenly think she needed to relieve herself.
The smile he gave her told her that she was beautiful and charming
and everything he had hoped to present to the other men tonight.
She felt encouraged, and she decided to pick up the role, like an
actor donning his mask, and play the part that Pittakos saw in her.

She turned as Pittakos addressed himself to the council
member. The man was young and handsome – very handsome,
Sappho thought. He wasn't looking at her, and so she was able to
evaluate him momentarily without seeming brash. He had a very
chiseled jaw and very light hair. His skin was bronzed from the sun,
and his body seemed quite toned beneath his robe and tunic.

He was speaking to Pittakos, welcoming him to his home.
His words were fluid and polite. Pittakos replied formally and
appropriately. "I am honored to be a guest in your home this

evening, Andronikos." The name gripped Sappho's heart. She looked at the man again. Desperation seized her. Eyes wide, she looked to the man's wife, standing at his side. Atthis was openly staring at Sappho, tears and fear already welling in her eyes. Sappho looked down, hoping the gesture would seem humble and proper to the men. "I, too, am honored, brother-in-law, to be a guest in your home. I greet you and my sister, Atthis, with joy and tribute."

Andronikos replied to them both, but he looked at Pittakos. "We are pleased to have you, and more pleased to know that the great Pittakos is so linked to our family. We are brothers now, Pittakos, of a sort, through the kinship of our wives." With these words, he offered Pittakos a more familial embrace and bowed deferentially to Sappho.

Sappho looked again to Atthis who still gazed directly back at her. A tear made a track down her face, and clung to the lower edge of her cheek. Andronikos seemed shocked by this reaction. "Are you not pleased to see your sister? Embrace her and welcome her to our home." Atthis offered Sappho an awkward hug – not knowing whether to cling or push her away. At a total loss, Andronikos suggested, "Perhaps you should both retire for a while to the women's quarters and compose yourselves of this overwhelming joy."

The two women moved like shadows, neither feeling like they had any substance to offer or share with the other as they proceeded to the women's room.

Chapter 37

Andronikos seemed largely unruffled by the encounter between Sappho and Atthis. He didn't say anything about it, and Pittakos got the impression that Atthis's husband wouldn't have known her well enough to know whether she cried for joy, sorrow, or a thorn in her foot. Pittakos, however, had met Sappho days ago, known her for a few hours, and he was sure she was unhappy about seeing her sister again. He didn't presume to know why she should feel this way, but she was clearly caught off balance at the sight of that familiar face.

He now feared he had done something terribly wrong. He had wanted to surprise her with a thoughtful reunion. He had wanted his first evening with her to be a little victory toward winning her affection. Pittakos had imagined that Sappho would have been overcome by her delight at seeing her sister. He hoped she would see that he was caring and compassionate. But now, it seemed, he had made a grave mistake. She looked horrified while leaving to go to Atthis's quarters, and he wasn't sure how he could fix this error.

There was no graceful or courteous way for him to leave the *symposium*. Now that he was here, he would have to stay and talk … and drink. That was the custom, and very little could extricate him from his social and political duties. More than that, he was well aware of the new family alliance that he now shared with Andronikos and his house. It was critical that he maximize that influence, and tonight would go a long way to lay that foundation.

Sappho was his *hetaera*, though, and Andronikos and the

other men would expect to see her dance and hear her sing. Pittakos was not at all sure how he could persuade her to be jovial and alluring when she was so emotionally upset. He certainly couldn't ask her outright to perform those tasks, at least not if he wanted to establish himself as a compassionate lover. Perhaps a solution would present itself. Perhaps if he waited long enough to call her down to the men's room, she would feel more composed and would want to dance, knowing that it was expected by the men and the other *hetaerae*. Or, perhaps those other mistresses would duly entertain the men, and Sappho could be left at peace with her turmoil.

Pittakos cringed. Riding out the storm hardly seemed like the best approach. He began thinking of lies he could tell and still save face. One of Andronikos's servants could be employed to take the ill wife of a guest back to her own home where she would be more comfortable. Surely that was a plausible excuse for her reaction. With the way the color had drained from her face, no one would doubt that she was overly tired from the journey to Mytiline that same day. She had seemed weak as she walked away, like she could barely journey another few feet to the women's rooms. Sending her home to rest would leave Pittakos free to talk with the men about the matters for which he'd come without seeming callous and insensitive to her needs.

Of course, Sappho had been at Pittakos's home only long enough to wash and change her clothing. She hadn't met his wives or the servants properly, and that might be an uncomfortable first meeting. She would have to introduce herself, and Pittakos wasn't sure how either wife would react to her presence. He had every intention of arranging separate living arrangements for Sappho while they stayed in Mytiline. They weren't to be here long, in fact, and Pittakos had hoped that she would share his own bed on the first few nights.

I'll wait a few moments, he thought, *long enough to play through the options. The right solution is embedded here in the puzzle somewhere. I'll wait for it to reveal itself.* And so he lounged on the couch and took his first sip of wine.

Chapter 38

Sappho stood in Atthis's doorway in stunned silence. She didn't have any words to speak. She felt every emotion all at once. She wanted to hug and kiss, kick and curse, laugh and cry. She felt dizzied by the swirl of feeling that coursed through her veins. A hot coolness crept across her skin, beginning from the back of her neck. She felt very much like she might vomit. Only keeping her mouth shut prevented a tide of love and rage from rising out of her like bile.

Atthis was even less composed than Sappho. She was like a fluttering bit of wilted foliage, limp and utterly without meaning or purpose. She couldn't sit or stand. She cried steadily and avoided Sappho's gaze. To her, Sappho seemed like cold stone – rigid, senseless to Atthis's grief. Where could she begin? She knew Sappho saw her as a betrayer, a deserter. Atthis had done her duty, had married a man she'd never seen because it was the will of the man who had cared for her as a father. She wanted to be angry with Sappho for begrudging her this act of duty.

Neither woman wanted to speak first, but neither of them could stand the silence of their sorrow when they shared this space. "Your *husband* looks well," Sappho said the word with a harshness even she had not known she felt. "You must be well-pleased with your match."

Atthis's eyes moved slowly from the floor to the place where they met Sappho's. As they did, they filled with resolution and anger. She was not happy in this match, or in any. She felt sold. She had been given to Sappho as a child, a living doll for Scamandronymus's daughter. Now she had been bartered to Andronikos in exchange for his family's connections. Sappho, whether she knew it or not, had profited twice now from the fact that her father owned an extra daughter. And where Sappho had been able to escape the slavery of marriage by clinging to the temple, Atthis was left no choice but to go to the man who paid the price for her. And now Sappho wanted to rebuke her for making the best of an unavoidable situation. She wanted to pour vinegar on the scratch.

"Let's not have this tired argument, Sappho," she said scornfully. "I'll not be made to beg your forgiveness for doing a beggar's duty to her patron. I took the husband I was given, as I had few other choices."

"You had other choices, Atthis," Sappho said. "I was one of your other choices. You could have stayed with me at the temple."

Atthis almost snorted, "Yes, and I see that you are not now at the temple. Where would that have left me? Do you think your – what should I call him – *devotee* would have wanted me as well? Do you expect me always to be your tag-along, or may I not have a life of my own?"

The truth in the words stung Sappho more sharply than any injustice could have done. "I loved you once, Atthis, long ago. I doubt you ever loved me."

"You think no one can feel with the same intensity as you," Atthis cried at her. "You think you are the only woman in the world who has lost the one she loved. You seem to think that if I don't show my love in the same way as you, that I must not feel it as keenly. I am not going to be torn down by you, Sappho. You must have accounted my love as a meaningless gift to have never seen it for what it was."

"And mine must have been worthless for you to drop it so quickly in favor of another," Sappho said, still holding back the tears.

Atthis looked back down to the floor and took a shuddering breath. "You do not know me. I wish you hadn't come."

Sappho turned to leave the room, paused at the door and whispered, "I wish you had not gone."

Chapter 39

The moon was full and vibrant, a shining queen in her inky palace, attended by countless sparkling maidens – the stars above Andronikos's courtyard. Sappho strolled in the cool evening air hoping to cool the blood that coursed through her veins. She took deep breaths, wanting to purge her lungs of the harsh words she said and purge her mind of the harsher words she thought. She could hear the laughter and the music of the men's conversation. She could hear the metal clink of little instruments that told her that inside the smoky chamber, women danced and men drank wine. She was supposed to be in that room, dancing for Atthis's husband.

A spiteful idea sprung up inside her heart. She knew, without doubt, that she could incite Andronikos to lust and longing for her. She could dance and sing for him, and he would want her. She could ply him with the charms of the Golden One, and he would prefer her body in his bed and regret that Atthis was the one to fill it. It was a vengeful, ugly thought, but it bolstered her for a moment. Knowing she could do this, she also knew that she wouldn't. There was no need to doubt that she could kill Atthis with a thousand cuts, but doing so wouldn't mend the slices she felt in her own enamel. And in that moment, she knew that Atthis wasn't the one who put them there.

The little madness of the moment was passing. Sappho felt tired but relieved of her weariness. She took deep breaths of the cool air, this time to inhale the sweet perfumes of the garden and find energy and succor in their scents. She fidgeted with her garments –

everything felt like it had been twisted and tightened around her – and went to the door of the room.

The men's dining room was exactly as she had pictured it and yet different. It was, indeed, filled with the smoke of incense. It was a luxurious room, more so than she would have guessed after having seen the women's room. Atthis had done well in decorating for her husband. She made a favorable impression for him. The women were dancing, and the men were watching – just as she had expected. And when she entered, all eyes turned to her.

She felt self-conscious, but she put on the air of one in complete command of the situation. "I apologize for my tardiness, gentlemen," she said, purring sweetly to them. "My dear Pittakos," she looked at his sparkling eyes, and then looked with a playful humbleness at the floor, "I hope I may still join you this evening."

He knew she was putting on an act. He could see the twinge of pain behind her eyes, but he didn't see a way to gracefully remove them from the room now that she had entered it. She seemed to bring an extra perfume with her – a light honey scent that mixed intoxicatingly with the wine. The men were already captivated by her, already imagining how she would dance and delight them. Now that she was here, he couldn't take her home before she satisfied their collective needs. He suspected she knew this already, and there was only one answer he could give. "If that is your wish, my dear, I would be most graced by your presence."

Andronikos made a gesture of welcoming Sappho into the room. She could feel the pull of his eyes. "We would all be graced by you, lady. Come and join us." He offered her a cup of wine, which she drank immediately. She was glad of its coolness in her throat and of the warmth it brought to her belly. Andronikos ushered her and her drink to Pittakos's couch. She sat next to him, and for a moment she felt the weight of the role she new she had to play tonight.

Pittakos sat up and moved closer to his new bride. The dancer on the floor was hypnotic, and Sappho was grateful that for the moment all the men watched this other woman. She, too, watched the jubilant, expressive girl as she bounced and shook and circled to the music. Two men had flutes, and the two other women in the room also carried instruments. While the girl danced, Sappho watched the curves of her body and looked for the form of Aphrodite. She felt the strength and the sexuality that emanated from the young woman, and she began to feel those qualities within herself.

She knew Pittakos was watching her, and it added steel to her strength. She pulled in a breath, added a sparkle to her eye, and turned her head slightly to look at him. He leaned closer to her, and she felt his presence brushing her own. The energy in both was tangible. He looked at her with tender concern and asked, "Do you want to return to my home, Sappho? We could make excuses and leave." She was surprised by his comment. She didn't know she had been so obvious in her distress earlier, and she felt like she was hiding the remnants of it very well now.

"Do you wish to leave, my husband?" Sappho asked. "Are you anxious to celebrate our union in private?" She fixed him with a stare of utmost intensity, and Pittakos felt the fire of her eyes. Whatever had troubled her earlier, she seemed determined to hide it now. He certainly couldn't leave the *symposia* this early just to make love to his mistress, though that was now the only thought in his mind. If she felt equal to the challenge of staying and enjoying the drinking and dancing and dialogue, he knew he ought to stay and make the most of the situation. There would be time enough for enjoying the luxury of her bed.

The girl had moved closer to Sappho and Pittakos and was now dancing exclusively for them, it seemed. She had laughing eyes and a playful mouth, and her hands moved as if brushing the surface of water. Her whole being seemed to shiver and skip with the delight of the music. The perfect isolation of her upper body from her lower was impressive to Sappho, who knew the skill and practice it took to move this way. The way she undulated as she gazed at the floor just beyond her own hip was an invitation to Sappho to come join the dance. When the music ended, Sappho knew she would take the floor.

As if reading her mind, Andronikos spoke as soon as the music had stopped. "Pittakos, you seem enchanted by your charming companion, and I can see many reasons why." He smiled at her, and she thought he might be trying to get more of her attention than was immediately apparent. "Will your lady dance for us?"

Pittakos smiled at Sappho, a half smile full of intelligence, and Sappho thought that he too saw the flirtation their host was trying to make to her. "That is for her to say, Andronikos, my friend."

"Kinsmen," Andronikos corrected as he winked. He shifted the question to Sappho directly, "Will you dance for us, lady?"

Sappho had the feeling that she was making strides already to win the thoughts of Atthis's husband, though she had not even tried to do so. If it was going to be this easy, and he was going to beg her into his attention and obsession, then she would do little to deny herself this little twist of the dagger.

She stood and walked to the center of the floor. She knelt and put her hands on the floor in front of her. It was a sign of her servitude to Aphrodite, and it also served as a cue for the musicians to play slower music. A drummer began the rhythm, and it echoed the light but eternal pounding of the heartbeat. Sappho moved to the slow beat, swaying and leaning from her place on the ground. The men watched her body as it arched far back along the floor, not quite touching, her hair skimming the rugs before she pulled herself, snakelike, back to an upright position. Her muscles were taut beneath her light gown. Her body was strong – very strong to move in all the ways that she commanded it. And yet it was soft and supple, her skin as sleek as silk where her shoulders and thighs peeked out of the folds of her peplos.

Sappho rose to her feet as if pulled by an invisible hand. There was no bobble or hesitation in the fluidity of her movements. Nobody breathed while she danced before them. The drummer picked up the tempo a bit, and the flute players joined in – still a pulse, but faster now. Sappho felt her own excitement rising, her pulse quicken with the beat of the drum. She pulled her veil at its edges so that it came away from her shoulders. She played with the fabric as she danced, using it as a mock shield between her sinuous dance and the eyes of her audience. She danced with it as though it were a partner, responding to her cues and following her lead.

The veil swirled about her as the music rose to a fever pitch. She flung the fabric to the ground and let her body be completely taken over by the pulse and pitch of the song. The breathless attention of the on-lookers fueled the delight she felt as she danced for them, for herself, and for Aphrodite. When the music ended, slowly as it had begun, she was standing in the far corner of the room with her veil once again pulled demurely over her shoulders and hair, casting a moldering glance at her little audience from beneath her dark lashes.

She stood there for a moment, collecting and centering herself back into the Sappho she had been before the dance, until finally she stepped forward from the shadows of the corner. The room erupted with the cheering of the men, and the women clanked their various instruments in honor of the *hetaera*. She bowed a little and moved back to her seat.

Andronikos signaled a servant to carry wine to both Sappho and Pittakos in gratitude for the gift of her dance. Sappho drank the wine and felt it go to her head almost immediately. She was already drunk from the dance. She let the wine sooth her and carry her to a place of calm comfort she hadn't felt since they had arrived at this home.

Conversation and song filled the evening, and Sappho observed and participated in both. When her eyes grew too heavy to stay open any longer, though, her husband made his move to depart.

"Andronikos, you have been a most gracious host," he said. "But my lady and I must retire to my house. We thank you for this night's hospitality."

"Of course, my friend," replied Andronikos. "And now that we are like brothers under the law, you know that the hospitality of my home is always welcome to you and your fair mistress."

Pittakos was flattered, though not entirely comfortable with the man's open admiration of Sappho. He knew he had chosen this woman to breed just this reaction in the hearts of his cohorts, but he had not expected any flare of his own jealousy. He checked himself and knew that Andronikos was harmless. No man could pose a threat to the relationship he had with this woman, due primarily to the nature of their relationship. Sappho was contracted to serve Aphrodite through her union with Pittakos for the time. The longing other men felt for her would not be quenched by Sappho, Pittakos was sure of it. That longing, though, could be used to his own advantage in many ways, and he knew that it was a good thing that young Andronikos felt so warmly toward her.

Pittakos responded to the host by saying, "I thank you, brother. I trust, then, that Sappho may attend me at the meeting in a few days."

Sappho, too, caught the spark in Andronikos's eyes as he said, "Certainly. You need not ask."

Chapter 40

The full moon still rode high in the sky, but was clearly sliding into the west when Sappho and Pittakos arrived back at Pittakos's home. Sappho had been there just long enough that day to refresh herself and prepare for the evening's gathering. She was too weary to notice much more about the house upon this second viewing. It seemed to be a well-furnished home, but not substantially different from her father's or Andronikos's.

The house was dark, and all but one servant had retired for the night. He groggily bolted the door after his master and the *hetaera*, and then shuffled off to bed. Sappho looked around and felt very cheerless. She was in a darkened house with a man to whom she was barely acquainted, but nevertheless bound, preparing for a voyage, and regretting the past.

Her mind was forlornly affixed on Atthis and their quarrel. Her last few encounters with Atthis had been unpleasant. Sappho knew that she had spoken so many words in anger that she didn't fully feel, but her stubbornness didn't allow her to apologize and make amends. Instead, she stuffed down the guilt of having hurt a loved one and focused on the hurt she felt at Atthis's words and deeds. Sappho didn't feel fully justified in her rage, and that hurt her all the more. She had been preoccupied with this circle of pain during the entire trip back to Pittakos's home, and now she was left feeling weak and worn with the awareness that she would likely have more duties to perform this evening.

Pittakos sensed her distance and gently guided her to the

room they would share. He didn't want to enter into an emotional conversation in the courtyard, so he talked about the practical matters at hand. "We will be here for five nights before we begin our tour of embassy to our allies. During that time, I would most prefer that you share my room, if such arrangements are to your liking. You may, of course, have separate quarters, if you desire them."

Somewhere in this house there was a women's dwelling that contained two wives with more seniority than the priestess. "What of your wives? Will they not be angry with you for barring them from your company? You will be leaving them for a long time, and they may resent being ignored in favor of a newer companion."

"Very well, my dear," Pittakos agreed. "You may have a point. I will arrange tomorrow for you to be installed in a small house nearby. Tonight, though, I fear no other options are available but for you to share my bed."

She smiled beguilingly, putting on the mask of an actor to cover her own disinterest at the moment. "This is my first night as your covenanted *hetaera*. It would be unthinkable to spend the night anywhere else." She slipped her arm around his torso and gently tugged at the fabric of his khiton with her other hand. "Will you show me the way to your chamber?"

He felt a pleasant shiver at her touch. "Will you show me the way to your heart?" His eyes held hers for a moment, and she wondered whether he was serious or not. He let her wonder by remaining absolutely silent as he led her to the upper floor and a room with a wooden door.

The room felt cool to Sappho, as if it had deflected the day's heat. An oil lamp burned where it hung from a bracket on the wall, giving a tiny glow to the chamber. It held no surprises, just a bed and a chair and a few other furnishings. The bed looked like a welcome retreat to Sappho. She wanted to lie down on the soft cushion, bury her face in the blankets, curl into a ball, and stay there until mid-morning. It seemed a little less comforting when she thought that she still had some tasks to perform with Pittakos in that bed. Her energy was depleted, and she wasn't sure that she would be a very good representative of Aphrodite tonight.

Pittakos had already begun disrobing, but he watched Sappho closely as he did so. He noticed the way she stared at the bed, and he couldn't miss the apprehension on her face. "Are you as frightened as any new bride, my dear one?" he asked her.

"I am a new bride," she said, more shakily than she had intended.

He crossed the few steps that separated them and Sappho was impressed by his physical presence. Only once before had a naked man stood so close to her, bending all his focus on her. But that time, she had not been Sappho. She had been Aphrodite, more than equal to any man who approached her as lover. Now, she could smell his scent and feel the tension in his muscles. She could discern that he was tall and broad. He did not intimidate her, but she was impressed.

With two easy movements, he had the fasteners of her *khiton* unhooked. The garment fell to the floor in a soft crumple. Her knees wanted to buckle and drop her body to the floor, as well. He touched her shoulder and ran his hand up the bare curve to her neck.

Cradling the back of her head, he pulled her toward him and bent down into the kiss. It was gentle, exceedingly soft and wet to Sappho. She melted into it and leaned her body against his. She felt the warmth of his muscular chest against her bare breasts. How she could be this aroused and yet utterly exhausted, she did not know. She wondered if she ought to invoke Aphrodite, if that was expected on a regular basis – if it was appropriate this time.

He pulled the pins from her hair, and the curls that had been suspended dropped to her shoulders. She suspected they were a tangled mess, sticking out at unlikely angles after having been bound for so long. She looked into Pittakos's eyes, and thought that her own must look red and weary – watery betrayers of her true condition. Pittakos led her by the hand to the bed and laid her down on it. He reclined himself next to her, pressing his naked torso against her side, and then covered them both with the lightest blanket.

Sappho waited for a moment, looking up at the ceiling and expecting him to readjust his weight – to reposition himself above her. But he stayed where he was, his head propped on his hand, watching her. She turned her head to look at him, unable to conceal the questioning in her eyes. Not really trying to conceal it, in fact. She held the question in her eyes for a moment, but when he offered no answers, she finally spoke. "What would you desire of me tonight, Pittakos?"

His eyes were very blue, she thought – like the sky above the sea in summer. His eyes could pierce her flesh, she feared, and read all the secrets she had hidden. It was a warm blue gaze with which he had fixed her, and she wondered if she might volunteer all the hurts that she felt if he kept looking at her.

"I've told you already what I want from you, my dear," he said. "However, I do not expect you to let me into you heart tonight. You barely know me."

Sappho knew this was true. She was surprised by his response, and she knew that she really did not know him at all. "Do you not want some delicate pleasure in my arms this evening?"

"I do, in fact," he said. "I want your lovely arms to encircle me as I fall asleep. And I want my strong arms to hold you close as you fall asleep. In this delicate embrace, I will find all the pleasure I need until morning."

Since directness suited her, and she was too tired to play coy bedroom games much longer, she asked, "I expected that you would want to make love when we retired to this room. Is there some reason you do not wish it? Have I done something to displease you?" Sappho hadn't expected to feel rejected by not having to fulfill the courtesan's duties.

Pittakos chose his words carefully before saying, "Your day has been long and full of transitions. You have had a number of firsts since we met in this morning's darkness at the temple. Your meeting with your sister was clearly not the pleasant reunion I had thought it would be for you. I do not wish to add another taxing encounter into your life today."

"Why do you assume that making love to you would be taxing for me?" she asked. "I'm a trained priestess of Aphrodite, and I take great joy in the acts of love."

"I appreciate your willingness to fulfill your obligations, my dear," he said, "but I don't want merely to be a duty to you. I don't presume that you would tell me of the unpleasantness you experienced with Andronikos's wife, but I have noted its marks upon you all evening. There was pain in your dance, beautiful and captivating as it was. How callous a lover would I be to thrust my way into your body when your heart so clearly needs to be healed?"

Sappho was stunned. She had thought she had hidden her grief over Atthis quite well. How had this man, a relative stranger, seen the damage of their fight? She felt like he saw the damage of years upon her soul. Tears streamed down her face. She covered the tears with her hands, and Pittakos pulled them down. She nuzzled closer to him and cried on his chest while he stroked her hair. She didn't notice when she fell asleep.

Chapter 41

Sunlight streamed in the window and Sappho stretched. She felt like she had slept for days. She didn't open her eyes for a minute until she realized that her bedding felt different. For a moment, her mind reeled and she was turned around in time. She was a little girl in the big, empty *gyneaceum* of her father's house; she was older, and it was her first morning in the dormitory of the *thiasos*. For a few seconds, her brain seemed incapable of latching onto where she was. Then she breathed more deeply to steady herself and the room came into clearer focus. She remembered coming into it the previous night with Pittakos. She remembered their arrangement, and she remembered how she had fallen asleep, crying in his embrace.

Pittakos didn't seem to be in the room now, a fact for which she was a little grateful. She wanted a moment to collect herself, suddenly feeling foolish for having shown so much selfish weakness on their first night together. She should have been focusing on him, and instead he spent the night comforting her. "I wonder if he even spent the whole night in this room," she said quietly to herself, thinking that he might have slipped off to visit his wife or concubine for affection after she had fallen asleep.

A servant had apparently brought her box of belongings to her room while she slept. She spotted it in the corner by a larger, more permanent looking chest made of dark polished wood. Sappho recognized that it had been decorated with a scene of the abduction of Helen. She laughed to think that a chest belonging to a priestess of Aphrodite sat next to a chest depicting a priestess of Aphrodite.

Also in the room were a table with a basin of water and a mirror, two chairs, and the bed on which she was sitting. She stood up and walked to her chest, noticing that the robes and pins she had worn the previous night had been neatly folded and placed on top of it. Laying the fabric on the floor to be washed later, she opened the box and looked at its contents. She was surprised at how comforting it was to have a few familiar possessions in an entirely alien new life. She chose a fresh garment and returned to the bed with the fabric and pins.

She had just begun to straighten the blankets when she heard the door creak open. Sappho pulled the garment quickly around herself out of modesty, not knowing who might be coming into the room. It would not be appropriate for one of Pittakos's male servants to see her nude. "You startled me," she said when she recognized that it was Pittakos himself. "I thought you might be a servant coming to rouse me."

"My servants always knock before entering this room," Pittakos said, smiling at the way she still covered herself. "Besides, I would only send another woman in here, knowing that you are in the room alone."

Sappho felt a little silly about continuing to clutch the garment. Little by little, she let it drop, tossing it neatly to the floor by the wall but maintaining eye contact with Pittakos. She had a playfully sultry look as she asked, "Did you come to rouse me, then?"

He shut the door and began walking to her. "You seem to be in higher spirits this morning than you were last night. I did indeed come to see if you were stirring." He was standing much closer to her now, but there was still more than an arm's length between them. Sappho took one step to close that gap.

"Thank you for being so gentle and understanding with me last night, Pittakos," she said softly. "It was very kind of you."

"I need no thanks," he said. "You had done as much for me last night as any man could have hoped. It was a gift to hold you while you slept."

"I am sorry I was so distraught," Sappho said. "Atthis and I were close for so many years, but we had a terrible falling out when she left the temple. Right or wrong, I haven't forgiven her, and we fought again last night. I hope I did not spoil the evening for you. I tried to keep that unpleasantness far away from your business."

"Then I think you did a wonderful job," Pittakos said. "I had no idea that you had grievances with your sister –"

"She isn't my sister," Sappho interrupted. She stepped back from him a little as she began to explain. "Her mother was a servant in my father's house. Atthis was my playmate. We were as close as sisters, and when her mother died my father all but adopted her. He sent us both to the temple for training."

"I see," said Pittakos, inferring some of what Sappho did not say about her closeness with Atthis. "I am sorry, at any rate, to have vexed you with so taxing an encounter. Had I known, I would have handled the situation differently." He looked a little remorseful. "I had actually hoped to please you." He let drop a box with which he had been playing. It thudded softly on the broad couch that had been Sappho's bed.

Sappho looked for a moment at the box, which was prettily

woven, and then looked back at Pittakos. He seemed disappointed in his failed attempt, and Sappho thought for a moment of making light of the hurt and anger she had experienced last night in order to ease Pittakos's hurt this morning. *No, I will not,* she thought. *To do so would be a lie, and I don't want to build this relationship based on untruthful communication.* "I cannot pretend that I was pleased last night at my visit with Atthis, but I do not blame you in any way. The gesture was sweet and thoughtful, and I am amazed that you would take the time to think of me in this way."

Remembering that she had not taken him into an intimate embrace last night, she felt the slightest stirrings of desire rising up within her now. She walked forward again and pressed her naked body against the soft linen of his tunic, she added, "I think you may find me much easier to please this morning."

Chapter 42

By midday, Sappho was sitting with her few things in a very small house along the same roadway as Pittakos's own home. It was abutted against another larger home and was the property of a friend of her consort. She was sent with a very young servant boy to the temporary dwelling. He would assist her with some of the dealings of daily life that she would encounter in the few days that she stayed in Mytiline. Going to the market, for instance, would be one of his daily tasks, as women rarely went there to conduct the business of buying or selling goods for the household. He would also fetch her water from the well, though this task normally did fall to the women of the house. Hers was a small house, though, and she wouldn't be living in it long, so Pittakos saw no need for her to adapt to the paths of this particular city just yet.

The boy brought Sappho an earthen cooking stove for baking bread and a pan and oils for cooking the vegetables he had purchased for her in the *agora*. There was a small supply of tinder and fuel for her cooking fires that had been left by the previous resident, and the servant brought enough that evening to stead her through the end of the week. Sappho thought that the pitcher of water he had provided would last her for at least two days, and by the time she ate her evening meal, she felt a little awkward at not having more tasks for her young servant to occupy himself. He seemed relieved to be sent back to Pittakos's house with the promise that Sappho would bar her door tightly from the inside and allow nobody to enter until he returned to her in the morning.

Alone in her only room, she sat on the cot and stared at the indigo sky of Mytiline's evening as it darkened in her tiny courtyard. She could hear the sounds of a woman and child in a similar apartment on the other side of her back wall. She wondered what circumstances had brought them into such close, and yet faceless, contact with each other. Her life seemed very strange to her in these solitary moments, having returned to the city of her childhood, confronting a deep hurt, and embarking on a voyage that she imagined might resemble Odysseus's epic journey to return to his wife and son after the Trojan War.

"At least he knew what he hoped to find at the end of his journey," she said to the table. "I might feel better in my travels if they were filled with such determination as he had."

And where do you hope to find your reason to make these travels? The question came from within her head, and sounded like her own voice, but it surprised her all the same. "Odysseus found his reasons to fight his way back home in the joys of his former life. I've only just started my former life, and now I've left it already."

What do you think you have left behind? "Everything I've known. I've left the temple and my training, the women who would have been my sisters."

Are there not temples in the places of diplomacy throughout the seas? Pittakos seeks treaties and alliances, but may you not worship and learn at the feet of the Sacred in any city to which he brings you? And have you not learned that the priestesses of Aphrodite grace the temples to her throughout these islands? Those women are your sisters, too.

"Yes, I see how my training continues. Every moment of

solitude brings the lessons of stillness and the contemplation of the poet. Every moment of tenderness teaches the skills of the courtesan and the sacred lover. Every step in this journey brings me closer to whatever destination has already been placed at the end of my road."

She crossed the room and lit the oil lamp that hung in the bracket above her cot. Opening the chest on the floor, she gently removed the papyrus, ink, and stylus that she had placed at the bottom for safe-keeping. Then she paused as the light flickered a little brighter to the side of her vision. "No. My road does not end in a destination, a final place to sit in complacency until death claims me in my old age. I do not seek the end of the travels, as my life will always be a journey, and the prizes I find will be won all along the way."

The morning found her playing with words on the dirt floor of her room until she was happy with every syllable and cadence. When satisfied, she busied herself transcribing them onto the precious paper, sending the boy away to busy himself with other chores while poetry filled her mind. She slept through the heat of the day, intoxicated with the wine of the words scratched in her book, and awoke in the late afternoon to knocking at the outer door.

"There is nothing I need, child," she said as clearly as she could, though she felt like cotton was in her mouth. How long had it been since she had taken a drink of water. "You may return to the house, as I am well-provisioned for the night."

"Shall I come back in the morning, then?" said a voice that didn't belong to the young boy who had attended her.

"Pittakos?" she asked.

"May I dine with you tonight, my dear one?"

Sappho unbolted the door and welcomed him into the humble quarters. She tried to smooth out her hair and clothes while he was looking in another direction, but she was sure that she looked disheveled all the same. She had slept little, eaten nothing, and felt unfocused as Pittakos grinned at her.

He had food in his hands, Sappho noticed, and she smiled, too. "I'm glad you brought the fare with you, as I am afraid I have little to offer."

"Oh, I doubt that," he said slyly. She blushed and felt the flutters of his flirtation as they tickled inside her chest. She made the mistress's eyes at him, and she saw the breath catch in his chest as she marked him with her look. She said nothing, but only smiled, refusing to release him from the heat they were building.

After a moment she said, "May I take this food out of your hands?"

"Only if you replace it with more a tempting offering," he said, bold in his obvious desire for her.

"As a devotee of the Kyprian, it is you who should bring offerings and gifts to her worship," she said as she pulled his hands down and placed him in a kneeling position at her feet. "And yet," she said as she sat down in front of him on the cot, "I offer myself to you in her service. May you find sustenance in my bed that no dinner could ever provide."

Chapter 43

Pittakos did not ask Sappho to accompany him to the home of Andronikos and Atthis on his next visit. He mentioned to her that he was going, and he discussed briefly what he had hoped to accomplish. Namely, he was collecting gifts and advice to use during his embassy to other regions in order to secure their friendship. He had already managed to stockpile a relative horde of such items, and they would be loaded into the cargo hold of his ship for the journey. A portion of the goods would be used to buy the necessary travel needs of their small household during their stays in each city.

While Pittakos made the final preparations in the last day or two before departure, Sappho remained in her abode. Her mind seemed to be thinking in strings of poetry, and she wanted to write down as much of it as she thought would be worth recording. Of course, paper was a somewhat precious commodity for a young woman of modest finances. She did not yet own enough of her own goods to sell or trade in the marketplace for her paper and ink, though she was sure that with time she would be gifted with trinkets suitable for trade.

For now, though, she knew she had to conserve the medium, and she would not waste it by scratching out words or lines as she crafted the perfect phrases to convey her feeling. The dirt on the floor once again became her drawing board as she scribbled in the dust. When the words were just right, she transcribed them onto her paper and read them again and again.

She also sang through much of the day, finding the lines of

melody that would best accompany her words. She longed for a lyre, since it was the most appropriate instrument to accompany the style of poetry she made. As she crafted the words, she paused here and there, imagining the gentle notes that could punctuate her emotion, the chords that would give color to the images she conjured.

Somehow, she would have to get a lyre in the next few weeks. Perhaps Pittakos would buy one for her if she asked. After all, as a *hetaera*, she was charged with the entertainment of Pittakos's colleagues, and she was a trained musician. In the temple, she had access to community instruments of all varieties, and she had never had need of her own. Away from the temple, she would need at least a few simple ones to make music and tell stories during the *symposia*.

The night before their departure from Mytiline, Pittakos brought Sappho a gift when he came to worship the violet-crowned queen of Kyprus. Kneeling at Sappho's feet, he presented her with two tablets made of wax and wood. She was familiar with these reusable tablets, of course, but had not owned one. She hadn't owned much of anything, and everything she had needed had been easily available to her at the temple. As a schoolgirl in the *thiasos*, she had used tablets just like this to practice writing and making calculations. The wood provided a solid base while the wax was a soft medium for carving words, symbols, numbers, even pictures. When you made a mistake or were finished with the writing, you simply rubbed the wax to soften and smooth it into a blank surface again.

"I noticed that you were using the floor," Pittakos admitted to her. "This is a cleaner and much more portable tool, I think."

Sappho thanked him and added the tablets and carving

stylus to her growing collection of treasures. She wanted to giggle at the thought that, at this rate, she was going to need a much larger chest for her possessions before a month was done.

As if reading her thoughts, a gift for which Pittakos seemed readily apt, he whispered, "I intend to shower you with gifts, honor, and high praise, my golden girl. You are Aphrodite to me in every way, and I want you to feel the luxury of lavish love."

When her consort returned again to his own home for the evening, Sappho remained in her room, once more anticipating the dawn and the sweeping changes of venue it would bring. With the sun's light, she would sail off of the island on which she had always stood and make her way to the first foreign soil she had ever touched.

Chapter 44

As Pittakos had already made several visits to the cities on the island of Lesvos, Sappho's first diplomatic excursions were scheduled to begin a little further from home. In essence, the couple would make a large, though slightly squashed and misshapen, circle throughout the Aegean Sea and its neighboring lands. Among the cities that they would visit, Pittakos had mentioned several on the islands of Samos, Miletus, and Khios, as well as cities in Lydia and Phrygia, which would require some travel by land. Sappho was both excited and anxious to learn that they would travel as far as Kyprus and Phoenicia before heading south for a stay in Egypt. Krete and Athens would be among their last destinations before returning to Lesvos, proving to be a long voyage, indeed, for a girl who had never even seen the eastern shores of her own island.

The beginning of the voyage would start slowly, though, which was a comfort to her. It wouldn't take long at all to reach the city on the neighboring island of Khios. For a warship, she had been told, the time would have been even shorter. Warships had two or three decks for fifty oarsmen each, and they were made both narrow and light. They carried only the men and their provisions, and had enough remaining space for respectable war treasures. Merchant ships operated under a completely opposite principle, though. They were wider, deeper, and carried fewer men and much more cargo.

The ship that would carry Pittakos and Sappho to so many ports was a merchant vessel. Sappho counted four oarsmen and only four other people besides them on board. Pittakos, another man with whom he seemed quite familiar, Sappho, and the housekeeper Larissa comprised the entire passenger list. The other man was named Eustis, and he had spent his life on the seas surrounding the islands. Sappho quickly came to understand that he and Pittakos had been partners for several years, with Eustis sailing the merchant vessel bearing the cargos funded by Pittakos. The hold of this ship was nearly full with a number of goods that Pittakos would be trading at the various ports in which they stopped.

"Our ship will always be loaded," Pittakos had explained as he showed her part of their cargo. "We leave from Lesvos with a good number of pots and other vessels. Further east, especially, they admire our pottery, and we're able to trade them for items that are harder to come by at home."

Sappho had seen these types of crockery and jugs her entire life and had never thought of them being a valuable commodity for commerce. To see so many assembled in one place, though, was an impressive sight. The black paint gleamed in the sunlight and shadows that extended between the prow and the stern of the boat. The men were covering part of the hold with large canvases, Sappho guessed to minimize the exposure of the cargo to the sun, wind, and sea spray. She looked for a few minutes at the red designs that shone from the black containers and saw scenes of heroes in battle and portraits of Gods and Goddesses in familiar poses. They reminded her of her childhood and the evenings when Tessa would entertain the girls while preparing dinner by telling them the stories that had been painted on the pots in her father's house. Wherever her eyes fell, she saw figures whose stories she knew.

In showing Sappho and Larissa to the small quarters they would occupy while at sea, Pittakos also pointed out some of the other items he had loaded for trade. There were grains and olives and wine in containers, and there were also a few rolls of finely embroidered and dyed linens and wools. There were a few provisions, Pittakos indicated, that were intended for their personal use as they journeyed, and a section of the stock would be traded for the things they needed from day to day.

The women would sleep and spend most of their waking time under a pitched awning near the prow of the ship. It was equipped in such a way that they would be afforded some small measure of privacy, but the measure was very small indeed. Most of their activities would take place in view of the men on board. Sappho comforted herself with the fact that the men would undoubtedly be too busy to pay much attention to either her or Larissa.

Pittakos was involved in sailing the ship as much as the other men. He told Sappho that merchant boats like this one were made to hold a great deal of cargo and still be operable by only a few men. Even on warships, it was expected that everyone on board give their energy and attention to either the rowing or the rigging. It was unusual for women to be aboard a craft like this one, though, it wasn't absolutely unheard of. Occasionally, a servant or *hetaera* would accompany her master on a voyage, and much more frequently were slaves transported across the waves, bound for new masters in foreign lands. The accommodations, however, were not ideal for any passenger who wasn't a sailor.

Sappho and Larissa had little to do but sit. They could

choose the relative shade of the hold or the fresh breezes of the open prow, which had a small platform on which they could sit and watch the water, but their occupation was the same no matter which seat they chose. Stillness and thought, watchfulness and napping, but always staying out of the way was the goal.

Larissa had accompanied Pittakos a few times before, though always for briefer travels. She had experienced the rocking, roiling boat on the waves enough to know what would be most comfortable for her. It was for this reason that the older woman chose to lie down in the shade of the cargo hold as they made way. Sappho was curious, though, about the working of the ship, the smell of the sea, and the feel of the sun. She sat, for several hours, on the platform and watched the commotion dissipate to a steady rhythm of old maritime practice before returning to the cool, protected enclosure.

There was a pallet made up for the women to share, upon which Larissa was already lying. She was curled and lying on her side, but she opened her eyes at the sound of Sappho's approach. She offered a weak smile and made an effort to sit up, but Sappho stopped her.

"There is no need to rise," she said. "I've come to rest here with you."

Larissa didn't speak but offered another weak but thankful smile and closed her eyes again. Sappho sat next to the woman and thought that perhaps lying on the perpetually moving floor was adding to poor Larissa's seasickness. She continued to sit in silence for several more minutes, consciously attuning herself to the motion of the waves so that she felt her body to be part of the sea, and not as some foreign object that was at odds with the water all around her. In a short time, she felt steadied and centered.

"Larissa?" Sappho tested to see if the housekeeper was awake. When the older woman groaned a little in response, Sappho said, "I know we've only just met today, and you may not normally trust a relative stranger with your health …," another little groan, "…but my priestess training has involved a little of the healer's arts. I was wondering if you would allow me to try something that might relieve your nausea."

"I'll try anything," was the muffled reply. "Just don't make me move."

"You can lie exactly as you are," Sappho said as she repositioned herself on the mat. She placed one hand on Larissa's abdomen just below her ribs and the other hand on her upper back. The sick woman's stomach knotted even more at the touch before gradually relaxing. Sappho breathed very calmly and steadily while focusing on her own body's comfort with the movement of the water. She poured that flexibility and absence of resistance into her companion's body. Sappho focused on her own rhythmic and cleaning breath and saw the foundation of breath enter Larissa as she fell into the same pattern of inhalation. When Larissa's body no longer shook with the tension of fighting vainly to still herself, Sappho's hands moved tenderly and determinedly to several energy centers in succession. At each place on Larissa's now exhausted body, Sappho sent her the stability of centeredness and pulled out the illness of anxiety.

When she finished, Sappho knew her companion was asleep. Larissa's breath and body were relaxed now, and she slept easily as her body recovered from its fight with the sea. Sappho reclined on the straw mat and blankets and let herself be rocked to sleep by the waves as she stared across the shaded place at the red-outlined image of Jason on board the Argo as it encountered the sea-monster, Scylla. She vaguely hoped that they wouldn't encounter any such creatures on their voyage as she drifted to sleep on her bed within the waves.

Chapter 45

If Larissa had been distant upon their first meeting, Sappho would never know for sure whether it was because she was ambivalent about sharing time and space with the *hetaera* or whether she was simply uneasy about the voyage. Whichever was true, and Sappho conceded to herself that they were not mutually exclusive, Pittakos's faithful housekeeper was admiring and devoted to Sappho after her seasickness passed.

"I just don't comprehend it," she said several times. "The sea has always made my stomach churn, and now it's still and calm. It's like you taught it to walk on the water! I've never felt so comfortable except when I've got both feet on solid stone."

Sappho tried to explain that she had really only reminded Larissa's body to relax into the motion, but Larissa didn't feel inclined to learn details of the theory. She'd simply cluck a little and repeat, "I've never felt this good on the water before. You're a talented healer, Sappho." The *hetaera* didn't have the heart to tell her that she was really only a mediocre healer and that her gifts were bestowed elsewhere.

They hadn't been on the ship too long before arriving at the island of Khios. By sunset, they had navigated to the southwest corner of the island and had partially beached the boat in the bay. The crew, minus Eustis and one other man, stayed with the boat, pitching small tents for shelter on the beach. The others, Sappho and Larissa included, carried a few items into the town and the house they would occupy during their stay.

The house was not nearly as large as Pittakos's usual home on Lesvos, but it was larger than the room Sappho had occupied for the few nights she stayed in Mytiline. The domicile had, of course, the ubiquitous courtyard, but it also had three other chambers to be used as the residents saw fit. Since they would only be in Khios for one week, there was no need to have separate dining quarters for entertaining male guests. Pittakos had already secured invitations to other men's homes for that time and could use one of the rooms as a common area that was protected from the sun. The other two rooms were to be men's and women's sleeping chambers, with the *hetaera* having her choice as to which one she occupied on any given night.

As the housekeeper, Larissa had the duty of making sure the rooms were properly furnished and clean and that the meals were appropriately provisioned and prepared. The household arrived at the dwelling so late in the day that she and Sappho made dinner together out of whatever rations they had carried with them ashore. Larissa began making a list immediately of the items that would need to be purchased at the market the following morning. Sappho made a request here and there, but Larissa clearly knew what she was doing and didn't need much assistance.

The house came equipped with some furniture already in place. The common room had a few couches and tables, a large rug, empty oil lamps, and what Sappho thought was a very nice mural depicting the story of Dionysos with a group of pirates who tried to use him in a ransom scheme.

The other two rooms were more coarsely outfitted with only a couple of tables, chairs, and beds between them. Larissa said there was little point in buying or hiring the furniture when they would only be staying the week. She and the two men from the ship could sleep as easily on the straw mats as anywhere else, and Sappho and Pittakos could claim the nicer beds.

Though she wasn't required to do so, Sappho spent the next day, their first full day on a new island, helping Larissa clean and bake bread. Since the house wasn't overloaded with furnishings, they could take their time to do the job well and still have time for talking. Sappho was glad she had decided to help the older woman, both with the housework and with the sickness of the previous day, as she was turning out to be a personable and informative companion.

Larissa had been in Pittakos's employ since his mother had died. She had been a much younger woman then, and she had started as a more general servant. It was his father who had hired her, actually, since he was still taking command of the household at that time. Pittakos had been married a year or two by that time, and his wife had borne him a healthy and strong son.

"Oh, how he loved that woman!" Larissa remembered fondly. "She, too, was trained at your temple, though she was never a priestess. Still, she had a grace that surpassed even her beauty, which was no small treasure on its own."

Larissa didn't know the story of how their marriage had come to pass, whether it had been entirely arranged out of social and financial alliances or if it had been spurred on by a romance that had already bloomed between the young couple. Whatever the case, though, Larissa said there was more affection between them than would usually be seen between spouses.

"The sun and moon rose and set in each others' eyes," she added with a laugh, "and usually in each others' arms, as well. She was pregnant again within a year of when I came to the house." All went normally with that confinement, as well, and a daughter was born. With the third child, though, there were serious problems, and the baby was lost. Larissa's eyes went dull and clouded as she recalled, "My first mistress was lost, too, poor dear, though death didn't take her at the same time as the babe."

Larissa sat quietly for a moment as she paused from her work to recount the sad events that happened twenty years ago. Sappho saw the hint of tears glittering in Larissa's eyes. "There was no spark left in her when that child died. She couldn't find any joy with the other children, not even with her husband. That was the hardest blow for Pittakos, when the sun and moon left her eyes. He was in mourning for her before she even left this world, I think."

Sappho felt herself instinctively draw a deep, shuddering breath at the same time that she felt a sting of tears in the corners of her eyes. She was a little surprised to find that she'd started to cry, mainly because she hadn't expected the upwelling of emotion that she clearly felt on Pittakos's behalf. *"I care about him already,"* she thought. With that self-knowledge, she smiled inwardly and continued the cleaning as Larissa recounted tales from her home of the last two decades.

Chapter 46

Pittakos tended to his business through the day, which primarily involved loading and unloading those portions of the cargo that were being traded at Khios or arranging the trade of those goods in the *agora*. Midway through their stay, he asked Sappho to join him on a trip to the marketplace. She was excited to go, as she had not had the chance before.

Women of affluent houses didn't do business of any kind in the market. Indeed, they were rarely seen outside the walls of their own homes. As a child in her father's house, the servants had been sent to the market, and Tessa had taken only Atthis, and rarely at that.

The temple precinct of Hiera was as a small town unto itself, and there was rarely need for the priestesses to travel to larger towns for provisions. In these rare cases, though, male priests and servants often accompanied them.

Sappho dressed in a light green *peplos* and pulled her *himation* over her head and shoulders to protect them from the sun. She wore her sandals and the bracelets she had been given. It was simple attire, but appropriate to her station and destination. Pittakos smiled in approval when he saw her fully bedecked for their outing.

As they walked to the *agora*, Sappho took in all the sights and sounds and smells of Khios as she and Pittakos talked. The city of Khios didn't look so different from Mytiline. It wasn't as hilly, and it was situated around a harbor. The houses were of a similar style and construction, but the accents she heard and the whiffs of food she smelled were different enough to notice.

"There will be a *symposium* tonight, my dear," Pittakos informed her. "I would like for you to join me."

"Of course, Pittakos," was her reply. "It was for these parties that you asked me to accompany you."

Pittakos might have flushed a little when he said, "It wasn't only for the *symposia* that I wanted a *hetaera*." Sappho winked at him as he hastily added, "Though that is probably the primary reason."

They walked for a while in silence that sparkled with their growing intimate knowledge of each other. Pittakos said, "I have been so glad of your company. You're an interesting woman, and I have enjoyed getting to know you better."

"In many respects, I'm just coming to know myself," Sappho said. "I hope I seem as interesting a companion to you as time continues."

"Of that, my dear one," Pittakos said, "I have no doubt."

There were so many sensations to take in when they reached the noisy marketplace. Sappho felt herself walk a little more slowly as she looked at the large, open rectangle of the *agora*. There were long colonnades draped with canvases to provide shade for the many vendors and services. Sappho saw animals of every variety for sale, along with fruits and vegetables, wine, milk, and other foods. A large fountain with several spouts stood at the nearest end of the *agora*. Women were there filling large water jugs to carry back to their homes for the day's washing and cooking. Sappho was inwardly thankful, watching them balance the jugs on their heads or shoulders, that she had lived in homes that had their own wells.

In addition to the raw foods that were available, Sappho could see and smell several vendors who were cooking little meals for sale among those doing their business in the semi-chaos of the market. "We'll eat something here later," Pittakos told her, and Sappho felt her stomach churn with the beginnings of a hunger she hadn't known was growing yet.

She walked with Pittakos and saw men getting their beards trimmed, a child being examined by a physician, and several small clusters of men discussing politics and philosophy. Sappho saw craftsmen displaying the tools of their trades and working on small projects that could be sold or carried back to their homes for storage. Sappho had been particularly impressed with the work of one carpenter whose furniture was both sturdy and ornately carved. The man knocked the furniture together as a much younger man, probably his son, carved and polished the wood. In another stall, she saw chairs that unfolded to reveal a rope and canvas seat that was then covered with a cushion. "If we were on Lesvos, I might want a chair like that for my little room in the temple," she said admiringly.

"If we were in Lesvos, I'd give you a chair like this," Pittakos said, making Sappho blush.

"I wasn't trying to ask for it," Sappho felt embarrassed. She didn't want to seem greedy and materialistic to Pittakos. She hadn't agreed to be his *hetaera* for material gain.

"No, I didn't think so," he winked at her.

Sappho thought she'd have to be careful about the objects for which she expressed appreciation or admiration. Pittakos was likely to buy them for her without thinking twice, and Sappho didn't want to abuse his generosity.

When they came to a merchant who sold instruments, both this theory and her resolve were tested. She picked up a lyre and felt longing course though her hands. The merchant, eager to make a sale, offered her a seat and suggested that she try the strings. She plucked the strings in random order, and before she had thought about it, she was making a melody line. It reminded her of the poetry she had just been writing, and so she superimposed her words over and between the music. She drifted into a kind of trance as she spoke a poem about the beautiful Helen.

> *She whose gentle footfall and radiant face*
> *Hold the power to charm more than a vision*
> *Of chariots and the mail-clad battalions*
>   *Of Lydia's army.*
>
> *So must we learn in world made as this one*
> *Man can never attain his greatest desire,*
> *But must pray for what good fortune Fate holdeth,*
>   *Never unmindful.*

When she finished the recitation, she tried to refocus her eyes. Her sight landed on the shocked face of the merchant, and she worried that she may have said or done something inappropriate. She looked for Pittakos, for reassurance, and instead saw the awed and appreciative faces of some other men and women in the market who had moved closer to hear the words of her poem and the strains of her music. As she looked at them, and they at her, they broke into applause and murmurs of praise. Sappho awkwardly handed the lyre back to the merchant and drew her *himation* up around herself again as she tried to find Pittakos among the crowd.

He was standing to the back and side of the crowd that was now dispersing. The merchant was following her with the instrument in his outstretched hands. "My lady," he said, "this tool belongs only in your hands. You command words so artfully, and this little lyre is honored to sing by your side. I, too, would be honored, as its maker."

Sappho smiled at him and then looked down at her hands. She didn't know how to say that she had no money. She didn't want, after having recognized the breadth of Pittakos's generosity, to imply that she wished him to buy her yet another gift. But she couldn't think of any excuse that wouldn't be an insult to the merchant who had clearly been moved by her impromptu performance.

Before she had even followed these thoughts out to their gloomy conclusion, she saw Pittakos give the man some silver in exchange for the lyre. He beamed happily as the merchant gave the instrument to its new mistress and said, "Such a fine set of strings belongs in the hands of one who can make it sing so beautifully."

She was overwhelmed by the gesture and touched the strings again, reverently. Lovingly.

"You have clearly been trained to play," said the merchant. "Do you also play other instruments? It is rare to find a musician who sings with just one voice."

Sappho nodded. "I can play several," she said, adding modestly, "though none so well as this. I've thought I'd like to learn to play the barmos, but I've not had long enough access to one to get a satisfactory comfort with it."

The merchant winked and ducked back into his wares, finally emerging with the instrument she named. It was also a stringed instrument, though it had more strings and was shaped differently.

This is the last of these that I've made in a long while. I've had difficulty in unloading them," he said candidly. "It's well-made, I assure you."

"Oh, I don't question its quality," she said promptly, "but we've already purchased one instrument today."

He smiled again and said, "I have a bargain in mind." Then, somewhat conspiratorially, he explained, "I'll give you this barmos as a gift, if you'll give me the gift of one more song."

Chapter 47

Pittakos was very pleased with the *symposium*. He had been able to conduct some well aimed business dealings with a fellow merchant or two and had also been able to discuss the politics of the moment with all of the most influential men he could access. Pittakos was a man of great savvy, and he had plans of his own creation that he was nearly ready to execute on his home island when he returned. The support of the men here would make those plans run much more smoothly once he felt inclined to put them into action.

He was also more than pleased with the performance of his talented companion. Sappho was radiant in her modest, but growing, collection of robes and adornments, and she was proving with each song, each poem, each dance the charming and artistic spirit that resided within her. He was more attracted to her with each passing encounter, and he knew that her attractiveness was not unnoticed by his peers. She did her part to soften the men with wine and song while he made bold business and political bargains.

Of course, the evenings were largely dedicated to conversations on such a wide variety of topics that Pittakos couldn't spend long in making deals without seeming rude. So he planted the seeds of thought to suit his own goals, and then carried on as any gracious guest would do. He discussed science and philosophy. He had points to debate about theatre and trade with various other city-states. He clapped and sang and danced with Sappho and the other entertainers. He got drunk on strong wine and nearly had to be carried home by his beautiful and small escort.

When she got him back to their temporary dwelling, she needed the help of the men inside to get him to his bed. She giggled as he grabbed her and pulled her with him onto the floor, landing on a few cushions that tumbled down with them.

"You were perfect tonight, my beautiful girl," he said to her.

"I am not so beautiful as all that," she said, critically. "In all truth, I am a little plain. Your affection for me must shade me with a beauty I would otherwise not possess."

"The Kypriot touches you, and so all I see is beauty in your features, " he said, before admitting, "though one not blessed by her may not seem so beautiful as you, even if she had the same face."

He looked at her intensely, and she allowed herself to be appraised before saying, "You are drunk, darling. You should rest before tomorrow's tasks rise up before you with the sun."

"At least one task is rising for us both with the moon," he said as he rolled over and pinned her underneath his strong torso. Her breath deepened in the way she had trained it to do, relaxing her body and heightening her pleasure. She felt the moisture as it flooded her most sensitive areas and dampened her thighs. His hand moved between her knees, pushing the soft, crinkly fabric of her robe out of the way as it slid up her delicate thigh. She giggled again as the sensation tickled her, and then she relaxed further into the moment. She arched her back to him so that her nipples would rub against his chest through the fabric of her garment. He pulled the pin from the left shoulder of her robe, loosening the drape of the cotton and exposing her breasts. He cupped one of them in his large, slightly roughened hand and lowered his mouth to kiss the creamy flesh.

She moaned and arched further, throwing her head back to push her breast closer to his mouth. Her pelvis tilted back and sought the hardness of his groin, finding instead the solid mass of his thigh as he knelt between her legs. She pushed against him and hooked one of her slim calves across his lower back. Pittakos pulled away slightly and appraised the situation, a nearly fanatic glow in his eyes.

When Sappho realized that he held his body away from her and wasn't making an immediate move to return his mouth or his pelvis to the places she most wanted them, she moaned a little and opened her eyes. With a playfulness around her mouth and eyes she asked, "What do you desire of me, Pittakos? Shall I beg you, tonight, to pleasure me?"

He looked wild and fierce for a moment before he grabbed her slim body and flipped her over onto her belly in one smooth movement. Sappho felt the cushion under her hips, pushing her rear into the air, while her upper body rested on the floor. Her nipples hardened further at the change in texture from soft, wet, warm mouth to hard floor. The soft fibers of the carpet below her teased her increasingly sensitive breasts.

Pittakos leaned against her and applied the pressure of his weight against the length of her torso. She could feel his legs supporting him as they pressed against her own. She curved her back and pushed against him, aware that his hardness was pushing into her tender thigh a few inches below where she most wanted it. He leaned to one side and rolled her with him a little, bringing her right hip up slightly from the cushion. His hand stroked the skin from her throat to her breast to her belly, passing over cloth for a moment before it touched her hip, squeezed the flesh there and then sought the same thigh into which his manhood had just been pressed.

Sappho felt a sharp intake of breath and a sensation like fire that shot through her midsection. She could feel him moving closer to her moist sanctuary, and she wanted desperately to press herself onto and around him, making him enter her. She didn't move as the fingers that had been inching toward the same spot found their mark, twining themselves in the damp, dusky curls of her most private places. Her body released even more pleasurable wetness as he nearly simultaneously entered her from behind. Sappho's mind went blank as she encouraged her breathing to relax and her body to pulse, knowing that this was the key to drinking from the goblet of this pleasure for as long as possible. She knew that her body could sustain this ecstatic wave of drenching orgasm for hours and that both she and her lover would be nearly blind with joy when the sun rose into their room. With each squeeze and each moan and each thrust, they pleased each other until exhaustion claimed them both and they slept in a sacred embrace until mid-morning.

Chapter 48

Sappho awoke the next morning with pain in her head unlike any discomfort she had ever felt. Her eyes felt bloody and bulging. Her stomach swam as if it were at sea. The clear morning sunlight that streamed into the room pierced her skull like a spear, leaving her dazed and weak. She struggled to her feet and found that she was walking with her head bowed down. Her hair was still tied up from the night before, and the tension of the ribbons and the fastenings pulled on her scalp. She tugged the adornments loose and set her hair free, grateful that the cascade of her dark tresses provided a curtain against the torturous light.

Sitting back on her couch, she wondered if she drank too much wine. She had made that mistake before and had paid the price of sickness, but this didn't feel the same. Today, she felt like her head would feel better if a kind butcher would carve it in two. Let the servants throw the shrieking, throbbing side of her brow to the dogs of the city, so long as it didn't trouble her any more.

The wine had, indeed, flowed last night, she remembered fuzzily, but she hadn't drunk very much of it. She normally mixed her wine with a good portion of water so that she was clearer in her mind and body through the evening's discussions and dances. No, this wasn't wine sickness.

Her stomach heaved, and Sappho's entire body clenched in response. Her neck hurt. It was so hard to hold her head up right now. The fabric of her couch was cool, and she was lying down on it again before she realized she had made the decision to do so. She pulled the blankets around her and covered her head, blocking out all light.

When Larissa came to rouse her, she was curled into a tight ball. She muffled her sobs because she had found that even those small noises brought waves of nausea that she feared she couldn't navigate. Larissa left and came back with a pitcher of cool water, a rag, and an empty bowl. Though she didn't have much of a fever, the woman washed her face with the cold, wet cloth, pausing for long moments over the temple and eye on the right side of Sappho's head. The bowl stayed empty, though Sappho had feared at every wave of pain that she would fill it with the contents of her roiling stomach.

Sappho slept throughout the morning, and at mid-day Larissa brought small portions of bread, fruit, and a mild cheese. The priestess was hungry, and though she feared that her stomach would rebel, she ate all that had been offered before sleeping again.

When Sappho woke again that day, the lightening strikes of pain had largely passed. A dull mist replaced the sharp throbs, and Sappho felt extraordinarily weak. Night had fallen, and she knew that she was drained from her body's fight with itself. She also recognized that she had eaten very little. Her mouth and throat were parched with thirst, and she poured herself a drink of water from the jug that still sat by her bed.

She sat in the darkness of her room for a long time, allowing her eyes to drink in the ebony night, the way her body had taken in the cooling water. The darkness was such a relief after the searing pain of the day. Sappho opened her window and admitted the tender breeze into her room. She sat on the bed and felt the soothing touch of wind and night on her face. For a moment, she considered making a trip to the storeroom to find something suitable to eat. In the end, though, she decided that she would benefit most from an uninterrupted rest and a hearty breakfast in the morning's fresh start.

Chapter 49

Aphrodite, the Kyprian, was said to have risen out of the foam off the coast of Kyprus. Kythera claimed its waters as her birthplace, too, but Kyprus felt like the enchanted and beguiling home of the Goddess in Saphho's mind. Sappho felt born anew as she bathed in the waters outside of the temple at Paphos.

Among the highlights of her journey with Pittakos were the many opportunities to study at other temples of Aphrodite and to participate in rituals and devotions with the acolytes, priests, and priestesses who cared for each of the Goddess's sacred places. With time, she became something of an expert on the Golden One's worship. After all, most priestesses never left the temple in which they served.

"In fact," she shared with a group of eager and engaging women while at Paphos, "many of the temples are quite small and only one to two priestesses attend the Goddess within them."

"You must be fibbing!" one incredulous novice exclaimed.

"No, she isn't," the Paphian *hiereia* said. "Most of the temples house the icon and an altar and little else. We in Kyprus have a large dwelling place for priestesses, and many come to worship with us. Our festivals are part of our civic foundations. But we have one of the largest temples to Aphrodite in existence."

"Have you been in temples larger than this?" the novice asked Sappho.

Sappho thought about the places she had seen so far. She smiled. "Yes, but only a handful. Korinth is larger. Your grounds house two-hundred maidens. The Korinthian temple is home to one-thousand. However, they don't all live in a temple precinct as you do. They live in cloisters near the *agora* that are akin to brothels." One of the women voiced her awe at the number of women with a little sigh before Sappho added, "And my own home temple on Lesvos holds three times that many."

A virtual uproar escaped the shocked women at that. "That's not a temple! It's a city."

Laughing, Sappho said, "You don't know how truthful that is. We have to operate much like a city. But the most amazing place of worship I've seen is an actual city in honor of our lady. Aphrodisias in Lydia is an entire city built in honor of the starry queen."

She talked with her audience for hours about the city's marketplace and amphitheatre, about the temple that stood at the center of the beautiful city. Aphrodite's name was inscribed on nearly every building, she told them. She also relayed the plans she's heard for the city's continued developed – a larger temple to replace the one that stood in the holy precinct, the expansion of the ampitheatre, the addition of an *odeon* for concerts and lectures. While she talked of Aphrodisias and the other temples she had seen, she transported them with her through the sparkling waters of the Mediterranean to stand under the sun at each shrine. Through her lyrical words and the music of her voice, they smelled the hyacinth on the warm breezes and heard the rhythmic tinkling of the brass cymbals the women played to accompany their dances.

"Our violet-crowned Lady has blessed you, dear one," the

hiereia told her privately. "She has given you the opportunity to see more of the world than many of her highest priestesses ever have the chance to see. You must be high in her favor. We will hear your name again, I think."

The festival Sappho joined while she lingered on Kyprus was one of the major holidays of the residents of that island. She joined the procession with the other virgins of the temple, leading the throng of garlanded celebrants to the countryside outside of the city. She played her finger cymbals as they danced their way to the place of ritual.

Once there, Sappho was swept away in the graceful, and yet playful, dancing that took place around the altar. The temple maidens and the young women of the village continued their dance while the men, boys, and matrons clapped out the beat and sang along with the tune that the musicians played.

Sappho noticed, even as she continued her own part in the dance, how beautifully the women moved around the altar and how that place of offering was strewn with flowers in fullest bloom. She made note of the way their gentle footfalls bent the delicate blades of grass, and she felt the tingling inspiration of poetry as it touched her mind.

"…the women, tender-footed, dance in measure round the fair altar, crushing the fine bloom of the grass." She would have to finish it later when she had the time to think of the rest.

The *hiereia* stepped forward and began speaking the words of ritual. The woman was petite, delicate, and more golden-haired than most. She wore gold at her throat, wrists, and ears. In the summer sunshine, she looked kissed by the golden skies, and again Sappho heard the voice of inspiration. *"The hand-maiden of Aphrodite, shining like gold..."* Yes, this ritual was touched by Aphrodite herself, and Sappho knew that she would compose several verses tonight in the privacy of her own room.

Returning her focus to the rite, Sappho heard the *hiereia* say, "Come hither, foam-born Kyprian Goddess, come, and in golden goblets pour richest nectar all mixed in ethereal perfection, thus to delight us." As she spoke the words, the gilded priestess poured a thick and gleaming quantity of honey into a cup of rich, red wine. She lifted the vessel high into the air before bringing it down to pour the contents upon the altar. The sticky honey and sweet wine mixed with the flowers and dripped down the sides of the altar into the grass.

"Aphrodite has many mysteries," the *hiereia* began. "She teaches us the love of a mother for a child, the love of a friend for a friend, and the love between a lover and beloved. We rejoice in her pleasures." The *hiereia* continued her short speech, which included high praise for the act of love-making, and a rather graphic description as well, before concluding with a feast of phallus-shaped cakes and sweet wine.

When, at last, Sappho had a moment to herself in the evening, she wrote many verses to capture the beauty of the ritual. Of Aphrodite's blessing on the whole assemblage, she wrote:

> *Her shining ankles clad in fairest fashion*
> *In broidered leather from the realm of Lydia,*
> *So came the Goddess.*

Chapter 50

When the slender merchant bark returned to Lesvos, laden with new wares and new political alliances, Sappho had counted two years of living in foreign quarters, visiting temples and shrines of Aphrodite, learning from priestesses in Lydia and Korinth and Kyprus. She had engaged and entertained merchants and aristocrats and dignitaries throughout the Aegean and in the lands of Ilium and Aegyptos. She had continued to suffer the blinding, nauseating headaches every few weeks, but she had largely been able to accompany Pittakos when he needed her. She had won distinction for herself abroad as a *hetaera* of particular grace and charm, a rival of Praxiteles's model, Phryne, in skill, if not in beauty.

She was not unlovely; indeed, she had grown into her unique looks in a way that enchanted and beguiled the guests at each *symposium*. Her eyes were captivating, and she knew well how to hold a glance. Her figure was strong and supple and slight, and she danced her soul in the dim light of the men's chamber when the wine flowed and the music played. But her honeyed voice, her lyrical gift, was her greatest treasure. She wrote and recited and sang her work with the magic of a weaver at the loom, bringing together the threads of ebony and ochre, scarlet and gold – each beautiful in itself, but shocking in the pattern and pace at which they created a picture greater than the threads or the weaver or the loom.

It was, with some small bit of fame and notoriety then, that the daughter of Lesvos returned to her home. Word of her skill as a poet preceded her in certain circles. Some number of the merchant class and emergent aristocracy had heard of the poetry and charm of Pittakos's young companion through friends and relatives on nearby islands and cities. Pittakos and his bright *hetaera* were invited to many dinner and drinking parties upon their return. It's true then, that Sappho was able to insinuate her consort into many homes – and gain him an audience and opportunity to share his philosophical and political views with many men who might otherwise have remained distant acquaintances or polite strangers. One could say that, in the years preceding Pittakos's rule as the "benevolent tyrant," Sappho opened the doors for Pittakos's politics. She was the gatekeeper of his revolution.

Of course, what Sappho heard and learned during her years abroad with her loving patron, she spoke of to no one else. Who was there to tell? She was kept exclusively by Pittakos, with no other clients, per the contract he made with her at the temple. Whatever secrets he had, she felt duty bound to keep. He was her husband and employer, her friend and her lover. He was a mentor and guide to her in many ways, opening her up so willingly to the innumerable delights of her body entwined with a man's.

She had no other lovers, either. He never requested that she perform sexual favors for any of the men at the *symposia*. This was a common enough practice, to lend one's courtesan to the host or to another powerful guest or an old friend. Pittakos, however, guarded her somewhat jealously, and a certain amount of titillating expectation arose regarding the treasures Sappho kept only for her master. This veiled sexuality added dramatically to her mystery and power during that time. It also affirmed Pittakos's personal virility, to an extent, while casting him as one who protected what was his.

Returning to Mytiline, the ship carried fine fabrics, exotic oils, beautifully carved furniture of all sorts, and many other valuable goods; but Sappho carried within herself commodities far more valuable than the trinkets and wares of a merchant ship. One such commodity was the experience she gained in the Aphrodisian arts. Between Pittakos, the priestesses of the many temples, and the various evenings spent honing her charm and grace, she was truly an embodiment of the violet-crowned Kytherian queen. She was an impassioned lover, a silky seductress, or a playful paramour as the moment needed. She learned and perfected techniques both in and out of the bedroom that made men feel needed and desired and strong. These skills, this experience, and her knowledge of her own body (which she explored avidly in her solitude) would bring (and keep) her clients and lovers for many years to come.

The other great commodity which she carried was the great bond of affection that she forged with Pittakos himself, and, by extension, the knowledge she gained of Lesvian politics and Pittakos's planned political maneuvers. Though she wouldn't betray him with this knowledge, it did place her and the temple of which she was an emissary in a very protected place during the storm to come. Pittakos loved and needed Sappho, and she knew it. He admired her talents, and he was dependent on the feeling of power he gained in being needed and desired by her. Other women, lesser women in wisdom and sexuality and talent, could need him, and he cared little. But to be so desired and coveted by a woman with the freedom to choose any man, as Sappho would soon have, was an example of his personal power that he couldn't duplicate without her.

This was part of Sappho's art, to give herself so completely in lust and sweat and satisfaction, to allow herself to be contented and dependent on her lover. Pittakos provided for and petted and pampered her. She hadn't given herself to anyone like this since Atthis, and she hadn't yet learned that this art was a double-edged blade – one that would cut her again and again. It would lend heat to her passion and poetry, and it would eventually break her.

Chapter 51

"I'd like for you to continue to stay with me." The declaration from Pittakos came without prelude as they ate their morning meal. Sappho had counted two months in Mytiline since their ship unloaded its wares. She felt the pull of the temple growing stronger each day, though there had been no mention of that sanctuary from either Pittakos or herself.

She faltered a little with her response. "W-what … in what capacity would you have me stay?" Did she sound ungracious? Oh, please let him understand. "Are we to continue traveling, Pittakos?"

His grin reminded Sappho somehow of a cat, and in that moment she felt like a pretty pet bird, barely safe behind the bars of her cage. "No, we won't travel any more across the sea, but you have been a valuable partner, Sappho," Pittakos began. "You have helped me through the nights and days of politics and pleasure, and I don't yet want to disrupt the partnership we have built these last two years and more." He paused and pretended not to watch her as he deliberated on his next few words. Finally, he said, "I'd like for you to be my *hetaera* indefinitely. Permanently, to be more precise."

Sappho did not pretend to look away from Pittakos's face as she carefully considered her reply. She cared deeply for this man, and she didn't want to hurt him. She knew that he could offer her opportunities that might never be available to her at the temple. He would adore her and treasure her, and she would undoubtedly become the most celebrated courtesan of her time. Too bad these were not the goals to which she aspired.

"My love, I am a priestess, and my place is in the temple," she began gently. "I have valued our time beyond any comparison I could hope to make. I love you, and I never wish to lose you. Please don't think I'm rejecting you or your offer." She made sure his eyes were locked with hers so that he could feel the emotion behind her words. Her hand caressed his brow and came to rest on his forearm. "We have always known, though, that I would return at the end of this journey to my place in Aphrodite's temple. It is still my intention to continue with my work there, having thanked you for the many lessons of love that you have imparted to me."

Pittakos's shoulders sagged almost imperceptibly, though he didn't allow any other show of emotion to escape his control. Sappho felt that little slump like a blow to the gut. Her hands were still on his skin, and she knew she had just felt the impact of her rejection through his body. Tenderly, she sent a warm swell of compassion through her palms, hoping that it would find the places in his body that needed the sweetness of her touch the most.

A moment passed in silence, and Pittakos seemed as if he were carved from marble. Then he filled his lungs with a breath that wasn't quite a sigh, squared his shoulders, stood, and spoke. "In another two months, then, I will escort you back to your temple. Until then, I will enjoy you every moment I can so that I may leave your side without regret."

Sappho rose and wrapped her arms around this man. One hand caressed the nape of his neck, gently playing with the greying curls. The fingers of the other hand traced the groove of his spine down to the small of his back, where she grabbed the fabric of his tunic and pulled him closer with a gentle pressure. After nuzzling his chin and kissing his cheeks and ears, she said, "I hope you will not leave me without a backward glance. We have shared so much together, and I cannot fathom a lifetime bereft of your presence." She stopped speaking and looked in his eyes for a moment. "I belong to Aphrodite, it is true. But it is also true that Aphrodite has given me to you, in part, and I will always be partially yours."

"It may be a curse, Sappho, that I am so enthralled by you," Pittakos said with a mixture of hope and pain behind his pale blue eyes. "A man like me shouldn't be caught by any woman as I have been captured by you, and yet I see no hint that you have tried to enslave me. Beware, dear one, for I may do whatever you ask of me. You are my Aphrodite."

Chapter 52

She hadn't realized that she had missed the temple so much during her journey until she was facing it again. As she and Pittakos had climbed the hills, and the buildings and women started to come into view, it was all Sappho could do to restrain herself against her impulse to run headlong toward the place that had been her home and her sanctuary.

Pittakos had been withdrawn, though, and she imagined that he was struggling with this return. She wanted to be kind to him, after all the kindnesses he had lavished upon her during their time together. More than that, though, she cared for him, and his pain and anxiety had an impact on her. She was glad to be home and to return to her work within the temple, but she would miss the relationship that she had developed with this man. She would long for their conversations, and she knew she would yearn for his touch upon her body. She had come to know herself better through him, and that, in Sappho's mind, was the most precious gift he had given her.

In actuality, she returned to Hiera with a veritable treasure trove of trinkets and remembrances that Pittakos had showered upon her during their years together. Small, carved ivory and wooden boxes held hairpins and *fibulae* and earrings. A larger box held fabrics that he had purchased for her to use as *peploi*, veils, and even blankets. She now owned two pairs of sandals; one tooled and fine-looking for making an impression, while the other was plain and functional. And, of course, she had the wax tablets and stylus, the

326

paper, and the lyre and barmos she had won on Khios. Added to what she had taken with her when she left the temple, she now returned with nearly three times as much property and little idea where she would store it.

Pittakos had showered her with gifts, and she appreciated the sentiment behind each one. In truth, Pittakos enjoyed buying her the little presents because she was always so grateful for them. Every pin, every ring, no matter how simple or ordinary, was received with such pleasure and adoration that he became a bit insatiable in his desire to please his young courtesan. He kept a few on hand so that he could present her with a new prize every few days. Even as they approached the temple gate and the impending farewells, he had a gift tucked away in his bags for her.

He knew he couldn't be separated from Sappho for too long. His errands would take him all over the island, but he somehow felt that Hiera and his *hetaera* would be home to him as much as Mytiline and his wife. Within two or three months' time, he would return here to visit with his beloved and pay tribute to Aphrodite.

He had been silent and sullen, though, as they approached the outer wall and gate. Having sent word ahead of their arrival, Timas, he knew, would be waiting for them. The contract between him and Sappho would be ended, as each had fulfilled their duties, and he would forever lose any legal right that he had to the young woman.

Sappho couldn't endure the pained silence any longer. Just shy of the gate, she stopped. "Turn to me, dear one. Turn your face, and unveil for me in your eyes, their grace."

Pittakos stopped walking and turned his eyes toward her. His shoulders sagged for a moment and then regained their strength and poise. "You are beautiful to me in every way," he began. "The fool in me that is still a young man would like nothing more than to turn with you away from this place and run toward a destiny other than what we have."

Compassion and homesickness for a life that could never have been welled in Sappho's eyes as she looked at her lover. She said nothing as she took his hand and looked on him in love. Her feet still pointed toward the temple, and she knew that neither of them would forsake the duties and destinies that had already been laid out. Sappho couldn't know the details of the life that still lay very much ahead of her, but she knew that she would always be Aphrodite's maiden, and her world lay on the other side of the temple wall.

Knowing Sappho's heart as he did, and accepting his own plans and ambitions as he had done long ago, Pittakos finally added, "It's time to return you to your home, my love." Then, a bit imploringly he asked, "Has our time together been enough to earn me a special room in your heart?"

"And in my mind and in my bed. I will always love you, Pittakos."

The remainder of the time they had together was steeped in formality, and Sappho watched her lover become again the man of power and composure that she had seen so many times. However, she saw the paleness of his cheeks that she knew no other would recognize, and she felt the steadying breaths he took when he thought he was unseen. She could see that he was struggling with his need for her, a need that would outlive the contracts and legal bonds that they had made. She knew his need frightened and frustrated him. To himself he seemed a thing much whiter than an egg, and far more fragile. Before he left Hiera, Sappho saw his shell thicken and darken into the armor he needed to face the world.

Chapter 53

Two years abroad after a barely budding start as a priestess left Sappho needing to reorient herself to temple life. She had gotten accustomed to setting her own schedules and running her own household so completely that the workings of the great temple complex seemed overwhelming and strange. She also missed Larissa terribly, and she regretted that she hadn't gotten to spend more time saying goodbye to the older woman who had become her only female companion during her time with Pittakos.

Timas was somewhat sensitive to the young woman's heartsickness and displacement. She allowed her some freedom from temple duties for a week or so following her return so that Sappho could acclimate herself once again to the rhythms of the temple. However, the *hiereia* already had an assignment in mind for the younger woman, and she wasn't going to allow her to wallow in her malaise to the point where it overtook her.

Indeed, Timas insisted that Sappho join her daily for the mid-day meal, at which point she would induce Sappho to tell another tale of her adventures among the world's priestesses. These visits were both a joy and a strain for Sappho. She enjoyed relating the stories she had collected over the last two years, including some stories that were told to her by other women, just as she had done while she was still in the process of traveling. But she sometimes grew nervous under Timas's sharp eye. She suspected that the *hiereia* was evaluating her against some standard that was unknown to

Sappho, and she wondered whether or not she measured up.

The *hiereia*, Sappho figured, must have once been a handsome woman. She was certainly not beautiful now, at least not in the way that the world normally saw beauty. She was no longer young, and the years of service showed on her face and in her body. Her jowls were a little loose, and her eyebrows were thin and gray. Her hair remained a vibrant red, but Sappho knew that the color must have come from the dyes that the priestesses often used to accentuate their looks. Middle age had added thickness to the high priestess, and a long past injury had taken away her youthful flexibility. Timas rarely danced, and when she did dance as a part of ritual, she paid the price for several days.

Despite the inevitable aging, though, that enumerated her years, Timas had a quality that drew people to her. Sappho secretly doubted that the *hiereia* was ever considered to be a beauty, and yet she was sure that the woman's assured and powerful presence and her sometimes sultry and seductive expression held her lovers in a special thralldom.

Sappho wanted the high priestess's approval, and she feared her criticism. Sappho didn't anticipate any particular rebuke, since she'd done nothing wrong; but she continued to fear the imagined lash of her elder's chastisement. An unwitting defense, then, was Sappho's need for approval, which Timas noticed and regarded as sweet and endearing, if also as immature as a puppy.

Timas didn't regard herself as a woman particularly worthy of another's fear, but she recognized that Sappho needed to discover that on her own. The younger priestess didn't see herself as an equal to the *hiereia*; and in many ways, Timas conceded, she was not. Sappho's feet had walked this path only a short while, whereas Timas could see that she herself was growing weary from the long miles she had journeyed in service of Aphrodite. The *hiereia* wasn't ready to abandon the trip yet, but she knew that she would take her rest soon enough.

Perhaps Sappho's steps will trace some of my own, she thought. *Indeed, her young feet may wander further than I will have been able.*

Chapter 54

Sappho's living quarters were much like the ones she occupied before she left Hiera with Pittakos. She had a slender couch for sleeping and sitting, a box in which she could store her personal belongings, an oil lamp, and a supply of oil and a curtain to cover her doorway for a sufficient measure of privacy. This room, though, felt very different to her. One of its previous occupants had painted a beautiful fresco of Aphrodite and Adonis on one of the long walls, and Sappho had her own personal treasures to add to the space – mementos of her travels and her time abroad. Fore the first time since she came to the temple, she felt like her personal dwelling reflected something of her personality.

Her new residence was adjacent to the smaller temple used by the priestesses, close to Timas's dwelling. In the time immediately following Sappho's return to the village, she was given the freedom to acclimate herself to temple life once more. She spent time visiting her friend and mentor, Daphne, and the women from that dormitory. One of the women, Frona, was pregnant, and another, Kastalia, had a small child who had been born during Sappho's absence. Kastalia watched her babe toddle and then cuddled her while the women talked.

"Just two more moons," groaned Frona. "I'm scared of the birthing, but I will be grateful for the relief when this child comes." She fanned herself in the shimmering haze under the acacia trees.

Sappho considered the toddling child and the pregnant girl for a few minutes before asking, "Does having a child affect your service to the temple?"

"In what way?" Kastalia asked.

"Well," Sappho thought more deeply about what she was asking, "will you still be available for sexual service and offerings?"

"Not during the pregnancy," Frona answered. "We are safer if we don't engage in intercourse with so many partners while we carry our babes. Too many women lost their children—"

"—or their lives," interjected Kastalia.

"—before the injunction," Frona finished.

"What about after the baby comes?" Sappho asked.

"After the healing, once the bleeding has stopped and the mother feels whole and strong, the women closest to her will usually conduct a cleansing rite," said Kastalia. "Then she is free to serve again in any way she may."

"I have made arrangements to be a nursemaid to other infants while I care for my own," Frona said.

"And, when I was healed and ready, I returned to the sexual service that gives me such joy."

"Are you not concerned that you'll get pregnant again right away?" asked Sappho.

"Only a little. We use several herbs to prevent pregnancy just after birth."

Sappho had more questions, but they were so jumbled up in her mind that she didn't feel she could ask them properly. They could wait, she decided.

In the following days, she accompanied Frona to the areas where the young, nursing mothers played surrogate mother to several temple children. Sappho was surprised, though, that there weren't more.

"Remember, Sappho," began Frona, "that not all of the temple's women engage in sexual acts on a regular basis. And most of those who are temple 'prostitutes,' as we are known, choose pregnancy and childbirth when the timing suits us."

Sappho sat contemplating the planning of these pregnancies, more questions rising to the surface, as a small girl toddled up to her with a ring of flowers. The child sat on the floor in front of the priestess and sang a song that she improvised in that moment. Sappho abandoned her ponderings regarding the gargantuan scale of the temple's influence and intertwined mechanics and lost herself for a while in the joy of watching this child play.

She couldn't have been more than three years old, with loose curls that tumbled around her face and grazed her shoulders. Her garment skimmed her round knees, leaving her legs free from tangles when she ran and danced. Her eyes were brown and bright, and the girl's expression was at once serious and joyful. Sappho was transfixed by the tiny singer, watching her pet and pick at the garland of wildflowers as she earnestly composed her lyrics. They were largely nonsensical, Sappho noted. Something about a butterfly and another bit about a bee. Then the child sang a few words about her mother before rushing on to images of the nearby cliffs and finally ending with another look at the bee.

At the end of her melody, the little girl placed the chaplet on Sappho's head and looked merrily into the priestess's clear blue eyes. Sappho instinctively made a gesture of blessing at the sweet offering so clearly made through her to the violet-crowned Kyprian. In fact, she had noted a wild violet or two in the flowery coronet and felt certain that it was she who received the blessing.

"What is your name?" she asked the little girl, who proceeded to climb into Sappho's lap while clasping chubby arms around the priestess's neck.

"Adara."

"Who is your mother?"

The girl pointed to a woman nursing an infant and playing a guessing game with an older child. She was unknown to Sappho, who then asked, "What is her name?"

"Adesia."

"Well, Adara, daughter of Adesia, you sing as sweetly as a dove coos. I hope you'll keep singing your beautiful songs."

Taking this as an invitation to sing immediately, Adara began another ballad that incorporated everything most important to her in that moment. It was a story song that followed no plot, but it kept Sappho's attention as it skimmed over the room they occupied and the garden beyond the door. Adara worked her own name and that of her mother into her song, probably, Sappho guessed, because she had just been asked them, so they took a momentary significance to her.

The priestess stayed and played with Adara for quite a long time, sometimes taking a turn at singing her own songs for the girl, sometimes engaging her in a game of "find me." Near the end of Sappho's visit, Adara crawled into her lap again and fell asleep while Sappho hummed a child's tune to her.

She sat rocking and humming to the girl, completely immersed in the scent and touch of the moment, the feel of the child's sweet weight on her lap, and the absolute contentment that filled her as she found stillness in the moment. She wasn't going anywhere in the foreseeable future, and if she wanted to spend hours playing with Adara, she was free to do so. In fact, she wasn't sure yet what her next duties in the temple would be, and she certainly had no idea when they would be assigned. She was free, now and indefinitely, to enjoy her leisure in any form it took. Later, she might explore more adult pleasures, but for now, she was content to sit in a room aglow with the westering sun and be a resting place for a three-year-old child.

"You're a natural mother," Adesia said quietly in Sappho's ear as she seated herself next to her. "My daughter is a friendly girl, but this is still very unusual for her."

The women sat and talked together while Adara slept, covering topics from training in the girls' *thiasos* to early life at home to Sappho's recent excursion through the Aegean Sea. They talked and laughed together until Adara stretched and yawned herself awake. Once she'd gone through the ritual of re-waking in its entirety, she bounded off Sappho's lap to find playmates her own age.

Sappho and Adesia continued talking for quite a while before Sappho excused herself to go in search of Daphne. She found her friend still full of the Goddess and highly aroused, having just seen a devotee. Daphne was glowing from her crown to her toes, and her eyes smoldered with an intensity from which Sappho could not turn.

"My friend, my sister, my lover," Daphne purred as she embraced Sappho. "Let me welcome you home with all honors due to you." She kissed Sappho in a completely unhurried manner, showering the younger priestess with affection and attention. Sappho, too, felt the power of Aphrodite filling her, as wine fills the clay jars, and she embraced Daphne with the passion and wholeness of the Goddess reuniting with herself.

When the women came fully back to themselves, giggling and panting on the floor in a tangle of hair and limbs, the sun was nearly set, and an orange glow reflected off the room's walls.

"You need a picture on your wall, my love," Sappho said at length.

"Yes, several of the rooms I've seen are adorned, and I would very much like some sort of decoration in here," Daphne agreed.

"Who do you know with any skill for frescoes or mosaics?" Sappho's query was partially to herself, although she had to admit that she knew so few people that she wasn't likely to land on an answer.

"Maris was always gifted at depicting scenes of importance when we were in school together," offered Daphne. "I wonder if she would be willing to come help me. I have an idea of what I would like, but I have never attempted something like this."

Over the next several days, Sappho repeated this day's schedule – helping Adesia with the young children and then going to visit Daphne until dinner. Maris came to help Daphne with her mural, and Sappho assisted the process as well as she could, usually by fetching materials for the other women or singing to keep them entertained while they worked.

Sappho's voice was clear, strong, and melodious; and her lyrics were sometimes heartbreaking, sometimes uplifting – always conveying a palpable emotion into which her sisters submerged themselves completely and willingly. Indeed, Sappho's fame grew within these few evenings such that as the sun lowered each night, scores of women gathered in Daphne's house to hear the provocative poet and songstress.

Having heard no other commands from Timas, nor any of her agents throughout the temple, Sappho continued to order her days as she chose, with this simple routine forming the basic pattern of her daily schedule. She was satisfied and content with her daytime role with the youngest children, and she was gratified and inspired by the response she received from her music and poetry. These performances continued even after the mural, a fresco of Daphne's namesake hiding under a bay laurel tree, was finished. The informal evening concerts took place in the common room and, on warmer nights, out under the acacia trees.

On one such balmy evening, Sappho sat with her lyre and shared a poem that was spoken in the voice of Psyche to her mother-in-law, Aphrodite. The audience, swept away in Psyche's desperation and loneliness as she begged to be returned to her husband, felt with great detail the heartache, hope, and yearning of Psyche's love as she attempted to complete near-impossible tasks given to her by Aphrodite.

The little crowd eventually dispersed, and Sappho walked

back to her own quarters. As she passed near the smaller sanctuary, she saw a small flicker of light from within the marble structure. Knowing that it was from Hestia's flame, the fire that was never extinguished in either hearth or temple, Sappho wasn't particularly surprised or curious at seeing the jumping little light. She did, however, acknowledge a tug, a calling into that most sacred space. Having recognized the summons, however subtle, she could not ignore it.

She knew that a priestess would be on hand to care for the flame throughout the night. The temple was never empty. A living embodiment of Aphrodite was always present within this building and in the larger sanctuary. The woman, though, was not readily visible, and Sappho had the sensation of being alone with the Goddess. She approached the statue of Aphrodite and the maiden and threw some myrrh resin on the fire as an offering.

"Violet-crowned Kytherian, most golden and adored Chryseis, lovely Aphrodite, hear me!" She sprinkled more incense on the coals. "Come to me from your bath off the pebbled shore of Paphos, from your place among your peers on high Olympos, or from any place that you love and bless." She waited for a moment, her face uplifted and palms outstretched. "I am your child and servant, having offered my body and voice for your pleasure and praise. You have blessed me with great love and tender lovers. I have felt your touch in the grove, and you have accepted my song. I ask now, Kypris, that you continue to bless me and guide me in your service. I wish to please you, though I don't know what form my service will take. I beg you, Kypris, to look on my work with favor.

All that I do is in your bright honor."

"Rightly asked, dear one," said a voice behind the praying priestess. Sappho turned to see the high priestess watching her from a short distance away. "The long road of your service will take many turns during your life, and there will be times when you find yourself resolutely walking in a direction from which you had once run. Best not ask the Gods to make the pathway easy or filled with the scenery you think you like; but instead, learn to love the path as it is and ask for help in walking it with grace," Timas said, her eyes on Sappho throughout her speech.

Sappho blushed at first, knowing that the temple's highest priestess had heard her prayer, but she met the other woman's eyes and heard the truth of her words. She walked away from the icon after an appropriate genuflection and came closer to Timas. "Have you decided, then, what work you'll have me do now that I am returned?"

"You'll keep doing the work that you have begun, for now," Timas said. "Adesia needs the help with our littlest residents, and you seem to work well together. You seem to have found your next spot quite naturally on your own."

"Yes, *hiereia*," said Sappho. "I serve at your pleasure."

Timas looked at her judiciously, "You'll find, in time, that's not entirely true. Most frequently, you serve at and for your own pleasure – and that of the Goddess."

Sappho took in her words, but she knew she lacked the experience to appreciate them fully.

"I heard you tonight as you sang," Timas announced. "You

really do have an exceptional gift."

Sappho blushed again. Timas quickly added, "You'll learn, I imagine, toaccept that particular compliment with great grace. Someday, you won't be as surprised when people notice your talent." Sappho's blush deepened, imperceptible to the eye but with a burning heat to the touch.

"Not yet, though," Timas added. "For now, you will have that modest humility that only accentuates the freshness of your youth. And that is just as it should be."

Sappho wished to seem the sophisticated, graceful, and mature priestess; and she willed herself to move closer to that image even now. Her cheeks cooled only slightly.

"Actually," Timas said after a minute's reflection, "when you come see me at the midday meal tomorrow, we'll discuss several possibilities of your service together. I want just a little more time to consider the options before we make any lasting choices."

With that, Sappho left the *temenos* and *hiereia*, and Timas began her evening devotions.

Chapter 55

Timas tended the herbs in her personal garden, which grew in unadorned pottery on each side of her dwelling's entrance. Stooping and squatting always left her stiff, but she wasn't going to call on an attendant to take care of something so routine and undemanding. *I might groan like an old woman when I stand up*, she thought wryly, *but I'm not going to call for a young set of legs and back if mine still work well enough.* She vaguely wondered how many more years she had before she would be confined to a chair or her couch. Behind that thought was the inevitable, though distant, nag of the day when she would cross Styx, and Cheiron, that greedy ferryman, would be the last to help her move from one place to the next.

The day was nearing its zenith, and Timas's young charge would be arriving soon for lunch. *No doubt*, Timas mused, *Sappho will be hungrier for information than she is for any food I might offer.* Given this assumption, she decided they would eat very lightly while they talked.

The *hiereia's* joints creaked only a little as she stood, with a few freshly cut herbs in hand, and moved to her small, private larder to gather the noon's victuals. Cheese, a few olives, some bead, a little oil, wine, and the herbs she'd chosen would sustain them very well. Timas poured the oil in a dish and the wine in a cup, both of which the women would share. She cut the wine with the customary amount of water and then crushed the herbs so they could release their aromas and flavors into the oil. With all things sitting on the little table, she sat herself down on her couch and waited for her visitor.

In just a few moments, Sappho arrived at the open door and was beckoned inside by the *hiereia*. She received the high priestess's blessing and welcome and then took her place on the other settee.

"How have you been spending your mornings?" Timas asked without preamble. "I know you go to Adesia when you leave here."

"I've been cloistering myself in meditation and prayer until I come here."

"Very good," Timas replied. "Beginning tomorrow, though, I want you to come attend me until we've eaten."

Sappho's head swam a little. She knew it was an honor to be kept this close to the *hiereia*. All of the highest-ranking priestesses had served the temple's *hiereia* in their times. That service lasted varying lengths, but every woman with authority here had been brought into the bosom of her high priestess.

Sappho ruminated on the political implications of this move as Timas said, "I remember your mother as a student in the *thiasos*." Her attention snapped back to the present conversation.

"Really?" Sappho breathed. Why did Timas's simple declaration create a knot in Sappho's gut? "I never knew her. She died when I was born."

"I didn't know her well, either, but I did see her very often. I was just helping with the younger students' work when she was at an age to be married to your father," Timas explained. "Now, I knew your father much more closely for a period of years. I no longer serve as a *hierodule*, but I knew him in the years I did. I remember very clearly when he brought you here for your education."

This was all a surprising revelation to the young woman. She would never have presumed that the *hiereia* knew her family or had paid her much attention before she was marked for priesthood. "I suppose that you know or have known more people than I can imagine," Sappho concluded.

Timas chuckled. "Yes, I suppose I have. Service as a *hierodule* certainly exposed me to a number of men and a few women. Of course, I know great many more women on this island from my years as a tutor in the *thiasos*. Indeed, I can safely say that I know at least one woman in every family on Lesvos and in a great many homes throughout the Aegean."

"I hadn't realized that you taught," Sappho said.

"Oh yes!" Timas exclaimed, though the way she said it sounded, to Sappho's ears, like the older woman expected that everyone should have known. "I loved my years in the *thiasos*, and I make a habit of lecturing on a few points even now."

"Why did you stop? Is the *hiereia* not permitted to teach as one of her primary functions?"

"There's no prohibition, but my other duties eventually got in the way of my time with the students. My service was needed in other capacities."

Both women sat and thought about teaching for a few moments, Sappho considering its prospects in her future; Timas recalling the glories of her past.

"Hero of Hiera, that swift runner, I taught," she said, drifting through memories of students both celebrated and obscure. Then, returning from her brief reverie, Timas said, "I wonder who you will have the opportunity to teach when you begin at the *thiasos*." The older woman's eyes twinkled as she waited for Sappho to absorb this new pronouncement.

"So... I will be allowed to teach?" Sappho asked, hesitant only because she was afraid she might have misunderstood and had based the growing flutter of joy on a shadow.

"Actually, no, Sappho, I'm not 'allowing' this," Timas spoke carefully. "I'm asking you to share your skill and experience within the *thiasos*. I know that you enjoy spending time with Adesia and the children in her care, but I feel like your particular skills are going to be best utilized with our students. You can still visit the children, of course, but your duties are going to take you elsewhere."

"So," Sappho recapped, "I'll be with you in the mornings and at the *thiasos* in the afternoons?"

"Yes, that is an accurate summary. Be aware, though, that you are still the only *hierodule* who will be with Pittakos. If he arrives here for devotion, you will be called away from your other duties to act as priestess to him."

"Yes, that makes sense," said Sappho. She realized at the mention of his name that she missed her only male lover. She hadn't seen him for two weeks, after having spent upwards of two years with him. She pushed Pittakos from her mind and returned her focus to this moment.

"And you may be assigned, by me of course, to be Aphrodite's representative to a few other persons," Timas clarified. "I will determine when and with whom this will occur. You will not be a general *hierodule*, though sexual service will be a part of your overall experience."

There was a quickening below Sappho's heart, and a tingle even lower still, at the flashing image of embracing another lover. She had assumed that she would eventually learn the touches of other men, but she'd had no idea when that would come. She said nothing in response but nodded girlishly.

"One final thought," Timas added. "Your poetry is so much a part of you, and it is becoming a growingly important part of this place. Know that you have the blessings of your temple and *hiereia* in composing and sharing that aspect of your work."

The women continued to discuss Sappho's new tasks in detail, and Timas informed Kallista that Sappho would be joining her and the other tutors the following day. Timas also explained that Sappho would be Timas's attendant, companion, and pupil for as long as she came to work with the *hiereia* in the mornings, and Sappho came to understand that she was one of four such pupils.

When Sappho left the *hiereia's* quarters to tell Adesia of her new schedule, she felt the changing tides in her blood that signaled a significant transition. She was becoming the woman that she would be throughout her adult years.

Chapter 56

Sappho spent the first days of her teaching career in silent observation of the pupils and other tutors. She was introduced to the girls and young women by Kallista, but she said little of herself at that time or for days following. She watched the interactions between the students and the priestesses in order to get a feel for personalities and relationships. She allowed herself the time to re-acclimate to the culture and speed that dominated this portion of the temple's campus. It was a girlish innocence that pervaded here, an eager and inquisitive energy.

She also needed the few days of low interaction in order to move beyond her own persistent memories of this section of the sacred village. Everywhere she looked, she seemed to see Atthis. She saw her friend at nine years old, sitting solemnly under the acacia trees during a lesson; at twelve in the common room, laughing and talking with their peers; at fourteen, gazing sweetly into Sappho's eyes in a remote spot behind the buildings. For the first two or three days, as she re-tread paths she hadn't walked since Atthis left, she was confronted with these shades and found that she had to make peace with them in order to free herself from this haunting.

The first weeks and months of her new life were uneventful, aside from the piercing pain and seclusion she endured during her headaches.

These months of new service were personally very exciting, though. Her mornings with Timas revealed that she was being groomed for a probable future within the temple's leadership. The

348

other women whom Timas engaged as companions and assistants were also being made ready for a life of leadership. What Sappho didn't know, and wouldn't until much later, is that Timas intended that her successor be chosen from the group of four women who now held positions close to her.

Sappho's morning duties included preparing the *hiereia's* breakfast and lunch, meals that she and another attendant, Eugenia, enjoyed with their high priestess unless the temple was hosting a notable visitor. In these instances, the subordinate priestesses ate in the nearby courtyard and returned to clear the table.

Sappho received a valuable political and social education at Timas's elbows. The attendants were present for most visits and discussions with the area's luminaries. It was on one of these visits that Sappho met Alkaeus.

He had come to the grounds before, and he worshipped Aphrodite through several of her priestesses. Young as he was, he was slightly older than Sappho, and he clearly sprang from aristocratic stock. His features were soft, but there was a sharpness to his eyes. His body looked strong and lean, graced with the lightness of youth. His *khiton* was of a fine cloth, and two ornate *fibulae* held the folds of fabric together at the shoulders.

On this occasion, he'd been invited to enjoy some wine and sunshine with the *hiereia*. He would then be guided by a priestess to a room for private devotion.

"I hear very impressive reports about your talents," said Timas.

Without blushing or betraying any sense of false modesty, he replied, "I'm glad to know that my work is meeting with some approval." He had an air of cocky grace that managed not to cross the line into arrogance.

"I hope you'll share your skill with us," Timas said, somewhat pointedly.

"Certainly." There was a long pause as Alkaeus seemed to wait for Timas's next comment or request. Timas cocked an eyebrow at him. "Oh! You mean now." He threw a quick wink in Sappho's direction, and she felt herself blush at the young man's flirtatious inclusion of her in the conversation.

"Well, to do lyric poetry any justice at all, I'm afraid I need a lyre." He offered his empty hands as evidence. "I'll do my best without my accompaniment since I left my own instrument at home."

"I'm certain that Sappho, here, would loan you hers," she turned to look at her attendant. "For a special recitation, my dear?"

Since Sappho brought her lyre with her every morning in case the *hiereia* wanted a poem, she was able to retrieve it quickly from its hiding place. She offered it to Alkaeus, whose hand brushed hers as he took the instrument, before moving back to her usual location.

Before plucking the strings a few times to test their tone, Alkaeus looked appreciatively at the instrument's sounding board. "Your companion is quite lovely," he said to Sappho. "The enamel depiction of the Hesperides and the dragon Ladon guarding the apple trees is very well done."

"Thank you," said Sappho, quite recovered from her earlier

350

flush. "It was a gift."

Alkaeus looked at her for a moment, then at Timas. He smiled quickly at Eugenia for good measure. "I offer this, too, as a gift."

Behold! the tender autumn flower
Is purpling on the hill,
The roses wither on the bower,
And vanished is the dill.
The morning air is keen and bright,
The afternoon is full of light,
And Hesper ushers in the night
With breezes damp and chill.

The purple harvest of the vine
Is bleeding in the press,
And Bacchus comes to taste the wine
And all our labors bless.
Then bring a golden bowl immense,
And mix enough to drown your sense,
And care not if you soon commence
Your secrets to confess.

For wine a mirror is, to show
The image that is fair,
The friend of lightsome mirth, the foe
Of shadow-haunting care.

So fill your Teian goblet up,
And scatter jewels from the cup,
And drink until the last hiccough
Shall drown your latest woe.

As he sang, spoke, and plucked the strings in various cadences, Sappho was both awed and inspired by him. She'd heard many poets during her education and throughout her travels, but this young man's words and voice did what few others had managed to do. It brought forth in her a poetic response. She felt, in that moment, as if she was a part of his creative process, and she knew that he was enticing hers.

When he had finished, he returned her lyre, and he offered a trade of seats. Sappho took his spot and laid out the poetic musings of her heart. It had been an act of spontaneous intervention by the Erato, the Muse who governs lyric poetry and expressions of love. Sappho's eyes slid to Timas, hoping she hadn't overstepped her boundaries. The older woman smiled, winked, and said, "Sappho, dear one, take this young man, please, and accept his devotion of our beloved Kytheria."

Alkaeus followed her from the room, across the small courtyard, into her own tiny bedchamber, and into a dizzying world of bliss.

Chapter 57

Alkaeus didn't normally spend so much time in Hiera, preferring the relative bustle of Mytiline to the quiet sobriety of the temple community. However, in the weeks following his introductions to the young priestess-poet, he couldn't find the will to leave. He was fascinated by her, more so than he'd yet been drawn to any of the other priestesses at the temple. The other women may have been beautiful, charming, and engaging – and they always were – but they were never moer than graciously receptive audiences to the gifts of his spirit. As much as any poet's soul reveled in a warm audience, it resonated when in contact with similar souls. Sappho was the first woman he'd known who was unequivocally possessed of the poet's gift.

His offering to Aphrodite had always been two-fold – his physical adoration and his poetic votive. For the first time since he had first offered poetry to the Kypriot, she now gave her blessings back to him in kind. His spirit soared, and he felt as if he had fallen in love with the Goddess herself, sharing with her through her servant.

He created new poems almost daily, and he didn't allow two days to lapse without having visited Sappho. In some ways, Alkaeus felt exposed by his sudden desire to be close to the priestess, and the Goddess behind her. He was a staunchly independent young man, and he was irked by his immediate need to spend time with his poetess. This self-consternation didn't stop him from coming to see her, but it did give him ample opportunity to chastise himself in private. This self-castigation made its way into his poetry, but he was kind enough to spare Sappho this minor insecurity during the weeks when he was initially getting to know her.

For her part, Sappho had never dreamed of meeting a man so much like herself. She had met and conversed with dozens of poets during her travels with Pittakos, but their styles were so divergent from her own that she could respect their craft without truly feeling a sense of kinship with them. They were largely too interested in the epic pursuits of great heroes, whereas Sappho dwelt in a more personal, emotional realm. They respected each other, but Sappho and these poets shared little with each other beyond the general art-form.

Sappho shared with Alkaeus a poem that she wrote in affectionate ribbing of their fellows.

> *A troop of horse, the serried ranks of marchers,*
> *A noble fleet, some think these of all on earth*
> *Most beautiful.*

Alkaeus came to visit Sappho in the late mornings, near the end of her day's service with Timas. After their first encounter, Alkaeus brought Sappho lunch, having heard her stomach rumble in protest of the missed meal. The young lovers would then nibble their morsels before Sappho excused herself to go to her students at the *thiasos*.

Sappho definitely saw the sleek young man as her lover, aware though she was that their love affair was secondary to

Alkaeus's relationship with the Goddess. She was also aware, though, no matter what their official association may have been, that Sappho the woman yearned for him every bit as much as Sappho the priestess welcomed him. She discovered very quickly that she adored Alkaeus with every fiber of her being. She felt giddy every time his face appeared in her mind, and she bordered on melancholy on those days when he restrained himself from coming to see her.

Daphne, with whom the young priestess spent most of her evenings, commented one night on Sappho's clearly infatuated behavior.

"That enigmatic grin is your constant companion these days," she said. "Of course, I doubt the mystery is all that hard to discern. I've worn that smile, too. What is the boy's name?"

"Why don't you assume it's a woman who makes me smile?"

"Two simple reasons," Daphne said. "The first is that the woman would have come from this temple, and if she made you smile like that, you' be with her instead of me right now."

Feigning injury, Sappho said, "And you don't believe I love you enough to smile like this?"

Her friend fixed her with a sultry stare that made Sappho blush down to her neck and chest. When she winked and smiled, Sappho laughed at herself for the easy rise in color her friend had been able to inspire.

"Oh, you love me, and I know I can make you smile," Daphne said easily, "but I didn't give you that persistent smirk."

"So, it's a 'smirk,' now, is it?"

"The second reason I know it's a boy," Daphne said loudly,

in order to regain control of the conversation's focus, "is that your poetry's subject has taken a turn away from the ungrateful woman in favor of a handsome and adoring young man."

"I suppose you have me figured out pretty well, then," Sappho sounded mildly impressed.

"I do," she said. "And I saw you with him today." Daphne burst out laughing.

Sappho gaped for a moment before laughing loudly and nudging Daphne playfully. "Oh yes, my dear, I see your powers of deduction are beyond rival."

Still giggling, Daphne said, "He's a pretty one, Sappho. Do you think you'll share him?"

"Not with you," Sappho said playfully. "Besides, I don't think I'm ready to share him. And, anyway, you might break him."

Daphne chortled. "Only the way a horse is broken. I'll make him easier for you to ride." Their sides were starting to ache with mirth.

"I'd say I 'ride' him quite well enough as it is. He's here at least three times in a week."

"Have you drugged him, little priestess, so that he is never sated?"

"Only drugged him with my words," Sappho said.

"Oh, now we have it! Our little Muse has held her captive in thrall, bound hand and foot by a web of golden words."

"And like Ares caught in the golden net with Aphrodite, my Alkaeus would not have me set him free," Sappho boasted in fun.

They sat for a moment and allowed their laughter to ebb. At

length, Sappho said, "Oh, Daphne, no man has ever made me feel like this."

Daphne choked back a laugh, not wanting to insult her young friend. "My dear, how many lovers have you had? Have you served as *hierodule* to many men?"

Again, Sappho blushed. She was beginning to dislike the betraying color that rose in her flesh. "Only two."

"Pittakos, and now Alkaeus?"

"Yes."

"I'm not saying that you don't love your young man – and deeply. I'm just saying that you may be surprised at how often a woman can love a man as you do now." Daphne paused. "I take it you did not feel this way for Pittakos."

Guilt that she didn't know she had suddenly stabbed at Sappho's chest. "Oh, Daphne! I do love him, but it has never felt like this. He is a kind and devoted man, and I have certainly found pleasure in his arms. But he never stole my breath away the way Alkaeus does. With Pittakos, I felt warm and content, and I was happy to give him the love he so obviously deserved. But Alkaeus …."

"Your Alkaeus puts a fire between your legs as well as a warmth in your heart?"

Sappho nudged her friend a little for her crassness but followed the feeble gesture with, "Yes. The fire he gives me fills my whole body. And it tingles," she breathed. "In fact, I tingle when I think of him."

"Lucky girl," Daphne said. "It's a delicious feeling. Enjoy

every moment."

Sitting in silence again, Sappho wondered if she'd done Pittakos a disservice by not having these feelings for him. She had watched him closely enough to be reasonably certain she made him tingle. *Would he be hurt if he knew my reactions were milder?* In that moment, she resolved that he should never know this little fact. She was a priestess, she had been his *hetaera*, and she gave him all that she could. She would always do so, and the intensity of her personal feelings was no reflection of the affection of the Goddess whom she served.

The women talked until late that evening, Sappho telling Daphne all about her poet. When they parted company and Sappho headed home, though, the image of an unhappy Pittakos, saddened by a love unrequited, swam before her eyes. She tried to banish the specter with logic. *I do love him, but love takes many forms.* But the phantom's sad eyes haunted her that night, even in her dreams.

Chapter 58

Afternoons at the *thiasos* were as engaging and gratifying for Sappho as late mornings with Alkaeus. She felt invigorated by the girls' energy. She was also surprised at how much she had to share in terms of instruction and advice. Sappho hadn't realized she'd gained much experience in the few years since she had been a student, but she was pleased to discover that she could contribute in a meaningful way.

Just as when she was a student, most lectures and discussions were held outside in the *pnyx*, an open-air auditorium of stone nearly enclosed by short wall. The retaining wall held several carved, stone seats within its boundary, as well as an altar and an orator's stand. The teaching priestesses brought a chair with them if they needed to sit, but they usually just stood at the orator's post or paced while they spoke. Because her lessons so frequently involved her lyre, though, Sappho almost always brought a small, collapsible stool and her instrument.

Topics ranged from womanly secrets of beauty and grace to issues of history, religion, politics, and science. As in her instructive years, the young women were taught rhetoric, the most valuable art of discourse. They were taught to listen to the conversation happening around them and to engage in it appropriately. In the company of men, so they were told, the topics would veer toward the political and scientific, while conversations with women would generally focus on more domestic issues.

"Be prepared to discuss anything, though," warned Sappho.

"Rules are so often broken, and you may find yourself discussing the politics of the day in the women's quarters and sharing domestic affairs, in more detail than you thought he'd want, with an attentive husband. The greatest key to conversation is the act of listening. Listen more than you speak, and the world will praise you for your wit."

Sometimes the discussions were as lazy and carefree as the young girls, and sometimes they spiked in frenzied debate. Sappho noted how greedily they absorbed information about hair coloring and fashions, and they were particularly interested in the lore Sappho might provide in regards to foreign beauty. A hint of the exotic or mysterious captured their interests like little else, although they would never dare to espouse any look that was too foreign for fear of being treated like an outsider.

Sappho told them of Scythian wood. "It's a resin that our women, even here at the temple, use to lighten their hair to a golden color, like honey."

"Only prostitutes and *hierodulei* dye their hair yellow, though," said Dica.

"True, so most of you won't be in need of that resin, though you may like some of the others for adding richness to your dark strands," Sappho explained. "The marketplace and brothel prostitutes on Lesvos frequently dye their hair yellow or red, but in some places they use blue dyes in their hair."

A ripple of astonishment shot through the group as the girls gasped and giggled at the thought of such shocking and deviant hair color. Golden and auburn shades at least occurred naturally, even if their dyed facsimiles looked a little too rich or intense to be real.

"That can't be considered beautiful," Dica stated a bit scornfully.

"It is surprising to see, I must concede," Sappho said, "but some women were it gracefully." She reflected for a moment before continuing. "It's not likely that many of you will ever have the opportunity to know any of the women who work in the brothels or scrape a wage as a prostitute hovering in the alleyways near the *agora*. Some, though very few, have chosen their livelihoods and have a dignity and grace not unlike our temple maidens. Many, if not most, are the most forgotten, abused, and degraded beings I have yet seen. They do not stand in for the Goddess, as we do here, and they are entirely ignorant of their once sacred heritage. These poor women are the forgotten, unfortunate, used, and broken vessels of someone else's profit. The beauty many are born with is ripped away from them, sometimes even in childhood. Do not judge these women harshly, my pupils. Aphrodite pities them."

After a short but thoughtful silence from the group, Kallista added, "Let's also remember, Sappho, that prostitutes call on our most adored Goddess to bestow favors and offer them protections in their work."

"True," said Sappho. "And at the end of a courtesan's career, she is often known to make an offering of her mirror in Aphrodite's temple in thanks for the Goddess's blessings of beauty and love throughout her life."

"I want to be beautiful," said Dica, wistfully.

"And you don't think you are?" asked Kallista.

The girl shrugged. "I'm plain. Not fair like Milesia or graceful like Anactoria."

The other girls, her friends, all pushed and poked her in playful chiding. They were mollified by her praise of them but uncomfortable by her own insecurities, and so they handled both with the same girlish response – giggles and absolute denial.

Sappho made a quick mental note never to giggle again. Laughter is fine, but giggling is clearly a mark of young girls. She smiled to herself and offered more helpful advice to Dica. "She should be fair who is fair of face. And she will be fair whose soul has grace. Your beauty shines from within you, dear Dica."

That evening, Sappho and Kallista instructed the girls regarding ritual preparation as a part of an on-going discussion they were having about participating in civic and temple rites. They had already covered issues of cleanliness both in body and garment, and they would soon be talking about *miasmos*, or a pervasive wrongness of being that prevented ritual participation due to conditions like madness, childbirth, and menstruation. But that conversation was so complicated that the priestesses chose not to broach it yet. Better give themselves the whole afternoon, especially since certain taboos didn't apply in this temple the way they did elsewhere. Instead, they decided to address adornments in ritual.

"Set garlands upon your lovely hair," Sappho said. "Weave sprigs of dill with your delicate hands; for those who wear fair blossoms may surely stand first, even in the presence of Goddesses."

"And they look without favor," added Kallista, "on those who do not wear garlands."

Chapter 59

Alkaeus had gone back to Mytiline for the last two months, and Sappho had been nearly sick with loneliness for him. Actually, she had been quite literally sick on a couple of occasions, and she was irritated with herself for this lack of control. She was sure that Timas had noticed – and disapproved – as well, by the way the cunning, sharp-eyed older woman looked at her and made knowing nods at Eugenia.

"Don't treat me like a heartsick schoolgirl," Sappho grumbled under her breath as she truculently tidied up a room the other two women had just vacated. "I just got used to my routine, and now it's been upset again. Once I re-adjust, I'll be fine."

A messenger arrived, spoke briefly and quietly with Timas, and then left. Timas then turned her attention to Sappho and said, "You are dismissed for the remainder of the morning. Go attend to the devotee in your chambers. And feel better, my dear."

Conflicted, because she felt that Timas was judging her low spirits but she was simultaneously thrilled that Alkaeus had come to see her again, she left the high priestess's presence with only a cursory salute and farewell. Her stomach was a jumbled mess as she practically skipped the short distance to her room, holding the skirts of her *peplos* so that they didn't entangle her feet and trip her. Before pushing the curtain aside, she smoothed her *peplos* again and attempted to wipe some of the sweat from her brow. Funny, she hadn't realized she was so warm.

She knew she was glowing as she swished the curtain aside,

and Pittakos turned to smile back at her. Cold beads erupted again on her forehead, but she cried, "Pittakos!" as she rushed to him. He embraced her warmly while she wondered, in a panic, *Did my smile falter? Did he notice?*

Pittakos's release came a little sooner than Sappho expected, and again she found herself fretting as to whether or not the man could read her every thought and emotion. *Compose yourself*, she said in silent self-reproof. *You are a priestess, embodiment of Aphrodite.* She felt her body calming in submission to her will.

"I've surprised you," he said.

"Well, yes. Timas didn't tell me you were here."

"So you always smile like that when coming into your private space?" His smile still looked friendly, and his voice matched, but something about his body seemed strange and distant to Sappho. She had the feeling that she was formally meeting Pittakos the politician for the first time in their long acquaintance.

"No, I knew a devotee awaited …," again she felt cold sweat on her brow and neck, but she corralled her thoughts and emotions to surrender again to her station. "It's been over a year, my Pittakos. I've missed you. I'm surprised and very, very pleased to see you here." She smoothed his hair and felt that she had done her best to sooth his ego.

Somewhat mollified, he allowed himself to be touched and loved by her. This was, after all, what he wanted. He craved her touch, her attention, her interest, her passion. He knew he couldn't claim those commodities as his alone, and he was certain now that she shared them with other men. *At least one other man*, he thought

364

bitterly, and then pushed the distasteful idea from him as he recognized his insecurity and the discomfort it caused him.

"I've come to honor the Kyprian and you, her priestess," he said solemnly. With this utterance, the formal ritual began. Sappho invoked Aphrodite, brought the Goddess fully into her own human form, and accepted the gifts that Pittakos brought to the temple. Sappho felt her own cherishing of the man mix with the affection and adoration of the Lady as she took him into her arms and lay with him in her bed.

At the end of the rite, Pittakos looked contented as Aphrodite left the body of her servant. They lay together, smiling and caressing each other's hair, faces, and arms. Sappho studied her lover and thought she saw something creeping back into his manner, into his eyes. It was a distance mixed, she thought, with a desperate desire for closeness. She felt both a push and a pull in Pittakos that she wasn't sure how to satisfy. All she knew was to give of herself, as much as she had, and so she held him close and kissed his brow.

He leaned up on an elbow and said, "I brought a gift just for you, my love."

"You've always been so generous, Pittakos. Thank you."

"You've always been so appreciative," he said. "You're thanking me, and you haven't even seen the gift."

"I hardly see how that matters," she said. "That you gave me a gift at all is worthy of thanks and blessing." With that, she kissed him on the forehead in sweet benediction, and he tugged a bag up from the floor near the bed.

"Make good use of this, my sweet girl," he said as he handed her a small sheaf of paper.

She squealed in delight and threw her arms around his neck. "Oh, you thoughtful, delightful, darling man! I'm nearly out of the paper you gave me before, and I've been hording it. Gold itself wouldn't have been more welcome to me."

"I knew you would like it, love," he said. "And I hope I may always be a patron of my favorite poet."

She cocked an eyebrow at him. "Are there any others contending for those laurels?"

He looked very solemn for a moment, a disquieting change from the playfulness they had just been sharing. "No. In fact, one whelp of a lyrical idiot in Mytiline is starting to cause me a great deal of grief."

Cold sweat again. "Oh?"

"An aristocrat. Young and arrogant. Spoiled." Pittakos was building a wall around himself with these words, barricading himself into his anger and dislike for a person Sappho suspected she both knew and loved. "He criticizes and satirizes me at every opportunity. He's doing his best to undermine my reputation in the city. Detestable Alkaeus."

Sappho sat silently, torn between the real sympathy she felt for one lover and the artistic camaraderie and passion she shared with another lover. She hoped Pittakos saw the sympathy in her eyes and felt it in her touch.

"Of course," he continued, "he says only beautiful things about you."

In addition to the cold sweat, Sappho felt a fist squeeze her belly. She searched for words that might be appropriate, but she couldn't find any. She couldn't find any words at all, and she hoped that the sympathy she was still sending him through her eyes and body might be enough to soften the wall he was still building.

Pittakos had stopped looking at Sappho. He wasn't sure what else he could accomplish by sitting here, and he was starting to feel an admittedly irrational anger with her that she could associate with a man that was becoming his political enemy. Before he allowed himself to indulge in that anger, he simply stood up and started dressing.

"I'm so glad that you came to see me," Sappho said earnestly. Part of her felt like she was pleading with him about something, but she wasn't sure she could have identified what that was. "I hope I'll see you again soon."

"Yes. I'm sure we'll celebrate the Kytherean again before another year has passed." He gave a thin smile and sounded upbeat but superficial. Sappho could practically see his wall now, and she wondered if he would let her back in the next time they saw each other. Or would she just stand outside and tap on it, instead?

She kissed him goodbye, and then prepared for her afternoon duties. She was hungry, and it was midday. As she walked through the courtyard to the nearest pantry and well, Eugenia stepped out of Timas's quarters.

"The *hiereia* says that if you would like to join us for lunch, you are welcome."

"Did you see Pittakos leave, then?"

Eugenia nodded.

The *hiereia* wanted to eat under the acacia trees, so the women lounged with the food on a piece of cloth between them. They shared a jug of water. Sappho picked at her food. Her stomach was still tense, from the morning's conversation with Pittakos, she assumed.

She felt shaky, and she decided to just lie down in the grass and cover her eyes with her arms.

"Not feeling well, dear one?" Timas asked. She clearly already knew the answer. Sappho nodded minutely. "You know, if you eat a little snack every couple of hours, it might help," Timas suggested. "Pregnant women should never let themselves get too hungry. By then, it's too late."

Chapter 60

Her mind scrolled back quickly through recent weeks. Because she wasn't living in the same dormitory situation as most of the women, and because she had been so busy with her duties and emotionally-consumed with missing Alkaeus, she simply hadn't noticed that two months had slipped by without any menstrual blood. It seemed ridiculous now, not to have noticed. She also hadn't noticed that she was once again sitting upright and that all of the color had drained from her face.

"Though I assume you didn't plan this conception," Timas said archly, "you can take as much joy in it as any wife with marital security. The temple cares for its own, as you've already seen."

"What do I tell Alkaeus? What will be his role in this child's life?" Sappho wondered.

"That choice is yours, as are most choices, really," Timas said. "You may want to wait until you see him again before you decide what to say. After all, you may be well gone with child by then, or your babe may already be here. Meeting your child may make your decision for you as to what involvement you want the father to take. Besides that, you never know how his life circumstances may have changed by the next time you meet. He may have taken a wife and made another child by then."

Though she knew the woman spoke truth, Sappho wondered how her high priestess could be so cruel to slap her with the image of Alkaeus in a happy family that didn't include Sappho in almost the same moment that she pointed out that Sappho was bearing his child. His first child. Her first child. Tears sprang to her eyes.

Timas sounded gentler now. "Why don't you take a few bites of this food back to your room and lie down for the afternoon, Sappho? You've been walking the edge between tears and nausea all morning. I'll let Kallista know that you'll join her when you feel better."

Sappho nodded mutely, stood, and started dragging herself back toward her room.

"The food, dear. Take some," Timas urged.

"I'm not hungry," Sappho mumbled without turning around.

As soon as Sappho reached her room, she wretched in the utilitarian pot that she kept by the door. She set it outside the door and hoped that a breeze wouldn't bring the smell back in. She was feeling weak from today's lack of food, weaker still from the shock of her body's newest inhabitant, and she wanted to lie down. Her little room felt cool compared to the courtyard she had just left, and she welcomed the soft touch of her light fabric, which she used as a blanket. The room undulated around her, and she felt sick again, but she willed the moment to pass.

She lay there, imaging the fresh smell of the cypress grove when Eugenia came to her. She brought in Sappho's pot, the one she'd left by the door, rinsed and scrubbed clean, along with a fresh jug of water and an apple. She also pulled a little bundle of herbs out of her *peplos* and set them on top of the box near Sappho's bed.

"Steep these in boiling water when the sickness comes on you," she said. "Timas swears by them, and she's been using this infusion herself a lot lately."

Sappho was alarmed. "Is she ill? Surely she isn't pregnant?"

Eugenia smiled but couldn't quite bring herself to laugh. Timas was past safe child-bearing age, and she would certainly have put an end to any pregnancy that threatened her life in that way. The *hiereia* had been tired lately, Eugenia had seen that. The once robust appetite had weakened, as well, and this herb drink had soothed the high priestess's disquieted stomach more and more frequently. Whatever was causing her discomfort, though, she kept it to herself. Eugenia didn't know with anything other than pure intuition whether the venerable woman was sick or simply suffering from malaise.

"I'm no more privy to the status of the *hiereia's* womb than are you," Eugenia said with an attempt at a grin, "but I don't believe so. She's the right age to undergo that transition away from childbearing completely."

"Oh," Sappho leaned back on her cushions, "I'm sure that's all that's wrong, then." She was feeling very tired and queasy again. She wanted to shut her eyes against the seasickness that had invaded her room.

Eugenia left her, making sure that the water and the utility pot were near enough that Sappho could reach them at need. With concern for the sick young priestess on her mind, and dread for the ailing older priestess in her gut, she returned to sit like a ghost in the shade of a cypress tree, waiting for one of them to need her again.

Chapter 61

She could never have known how much her own pregnancy was like her mother's. She couldn't have guessed that this would be her only pregnancy nor that its solitary nature would not be by choice. As she wretched and rested her way through the months of gestation, she knew only that she felt terribly alone.

She wrote a poem during one of her long nights that she kept near her all the time. She read its words by candlelight when she couldn't sleep.

The sinking moon has left the sky,
The Pleiades have also gone.
Midnight comes and goes, the hours fly
And on my couch alone I lie.

Surrounded by lovers, friends, pupils, and still I feel lonely, she thought in despair. *Alkaeus has no idea that I'm suffering, nor does he know that I bear his child.* She wept to herself in her isolation, and yet she never sent the message that would have told him what she yearned for him to know.

Timas languished, too, and Sappho was forced to keep her distance. The physician who treated her couldn't be sure that the disease that was ravaging the high priestess wouldn't take some toll on a young woman in Sappho's delicate and receptive condition. Sappho sank further into her private gloom at being removed from Timas this way. The older woman had been a friend, a mother, and a teacher to Sappho, and she was feeling the bite of her own recent impatience with this figure that had loomed so large over her for the last couple of years.

Sappho sat in a chair that had been brought near the cliffs for her by Daphne. She liked to sit here when she felt melancholy and watch the waves as they tried to make their progress in from the sea. Futile effort, she thought glumly. She studied the cliff walls that cupped the bay and watched the sea birds soaring high and low on invisible currents. Daphne combed Sappho's long, dark hair and twisted it into a knotted design as she absent-mindedly sang a lullaby.

Eugenia appeared beside Sappho, her tawny hair working its way loose of the bun in the high wind atop the cliff. She carried a rolled and sealed slip of paper in her hand and, Sappho thought, the weight of a dying woman on her shoulders. Eugenia knelt next to Sappho and said, "From her. She asked me to bring this to you right away." Eugenia's eyes welled with tears, but they did not let the water spill down her cheeks. "I'm going to the apple grove tonight, and I will stay there until morning." Her voice caught in her throat, "I hope she lasts that long." Kissing Sappho on the cheek, she turned and hurried away, the wind in her face. Sappho was sure that the woman wept now, her tears carried on the wind to the saltwater of the sea below.

Sappho turned her attention to the letter in her hands. She broke the seal of green wax embossed with the head of Aphrodite. Unrolling the letter, she read Timas's perfectly formed characters marching in measured height in straight regiments across the page.

Sappho of Mytiline,

As one of the women under consideration to fulfill my post when I am no longer able, you are afforded the privilege and right to know directly from me about my decision. I had once believed you to be the likeliest candidate to serve as hiereia *at the Temple of Aphrodite at Hiera. As this illness has taken me, though, I see more clearly that you will go another way. Your path has changed, perhaps, and this act of service will not be yours, as I once foresaw. I hope that, if you saw this future for yourself as well, you will forgive me before we meet again in Hades's kingdom. Surely, we will not see each other again before Cheiron brings you to me there.*

Timas

Numb in every way, Sappho let the paper slip from her hand and watched as the wind carried it out to fly with the gulls before dipping down below the line of the cliff.

Chapter 62

Timas saw the dawn of the next morning and then left the world of living women to journey with her ferryman across Styx. Sappho saw that same watery dawn through eyes that were puffy and swollen from a weeping vigil through the long night. When the mourning cry went up from Timas's little house, sounded by the other three attendants, Sappho joined them in the wailing and left her own confinement to be with her peers.

She heard other women picking up the cry, and some part of Sappho noticed that the grief they all knew was coming had spread like fire in a wind through the temple village. The sound rose and fell and groaned on behind her as she entered the cottage.

Eugenia was sitting on the floor, rocking herself back and forth with a sharpened knife in her hand that she was using to hack away at her long hair. The other two women were passing incense over and around the *hiereia's* hollow-seeming body as tears and sobs freely passed their lips and eyes.

Whether the others noticed Sappho's arrival or not, she didn't know. They didn't acknowledge it, in any case.

Sappho went to the small hearth that held Hestia's ever-burning flame, a pitcher of water lifted from the table along the way. "Hestia, virgin Goddess given honor in every home and temple, hear me now, though my mind is numb and my tongue is nearly dumb with grief. The spirit of life has left this dwelling place, and so must the flame while the mourning period lasts." She poured the water over the fire and coals, heard the hiss and spit as the two elements battled, and water drowned the spirit of the hearth. Little coils of smoke rose off of the ruins of the fire and filled the house with its acrid ghost.

Dropping the pitcher on the floor, where the clay vessel broke at her feet, Sappho turned and stumbled through her tears to where Eugenia sat on the floor. She stooped down onto all fours before crawling into a seated position next to her friend.

The knife hung limply in Eugenia's hand, and the strands of her hair hung lank around her face in uneven bands. Clumps of her shorn locks lay around her on the floor.

Sappho took the knife from Eugenia, who at first resisted until she saw that Sappho was tugging her hair free from its loose restraint. Sappho's glossy curls joined Eugenia's straight hanks on the floor, and the knife passed from hand to hand as each attendant sacrificed her hair in grief and sorrow. They took damp ashes from the drowned fire and rubbed them onto their tear-streaked faces, down their fair arms, and onto their heads.

The doorway and courtyard beyond were crowded with temple maidens singing dirges and letting escape low moans of pain. The priestesses of higher rank and office came through the crowd outside to join the four women closest to the *hiereia*. The ritualized shearing and sullying continued among the highest ranks of women, and Sappho found comfort in the old tradition of wearing one's grief so prominently. She found her mind slipping away from the motion around her, and she moved through the remainder of the day in a trance.

She was aware that someone took her back to her room and

made her eat something, and then she was sleeping again. It was a troubled sleep, long but dark. She stood on a rocky and barren river bank, looking across the water into a land of caves and hollows. She was searching the craggy bank on the opposite side for someone who she was sure was there, just beyond her sight, hiding perhaps. In the way dreams do, she'd forgotten for whom she searched, only that she wanted to find this person. Was it her mother? Yes, it must have been. They had just been talking, after all, and her mother had walked away mid-thought and ducked into one of the caves. Except, Sappho suddenly recalled with shocking lucidity, that she didn't know what her mother's face looked like. How could that be, if they were just talking? *No*, she thought, *she died at my birth*. And with this, she woke.

Timas's body had been washed, and on the day following her death, she was ritually prepared for the funeral rites. She was anointed with oils and dressed in fine linens. Her jewels were set onto her neck, wrists, fingers, ankles, and ears, and garlands were woven for her. The women placed Timas's body upon a litter and bore her from her home, through the temple grounds, to a place near where Sappho had sat two days ago and watched seabirds flying high above the cliffs. Cypress wood, fragrant and ready for flame, made the pyre upon which Timas's shell was placed.

The late afternoon deepened into evening as the solemn procession made its way to the pyre. All the women in attendance wore rough cloth and had dirtied their arms, heads, and faces in mourning. Eugenia, Sappho noticed, made the offerings to Hades and Persephone, king and queen of the underworld, keepers of the dead. Several women came forward to offer a prayer, and without realizing she had done it, Sappho found herself standing before the crowd, her arms raised to signal that she, too, would speak.

"The mother of my flesh died when I came into this life, but I have been blessed with a host of women who have been as family to me," she began. "Here lies one, my many sisters, who was as a mother to us all. Like you, I feel lost without her. And so, like a child after its mother, I flutter." She stopped to breathe, to think. She hadn't planned to speak, and she was feeling herself unwind a bit in front of everyone.

> *Here lies the dust of Timas who, unwed,*
> *Passed the dark portals of Persephone.*
> *With sharpened metal, when her spirit fled,*
> *Her mourning friends each shore her fair-tressed head.*

The gift of verse was the last and only thing Sappho could offer. Other prayers were spoken, and eventually the wood was drenched in oil and set ablaze. Drums beat and double-flutes played haunting melodies as the women cried, yelled, danced, feasted, and drank in honor of the dead high priestess. Sappho watched the colors of Timas's fire against the indigo of the sky, noted the indifference of the surf and stone to human pain, marveled at the texture of hope and heartache in the sounds around her, and wondered if her simple poetry would ever be enough to capture, even for an instant, what it is to live and feel and be a part of the world.

Chapter 63

The cleansing naturally followed the funeral. The *miasmos* of death had to be washed from the bodies of the living and swept from the dwelling of the deceased so that it couldn't pollute the vibrant energy of those it had briefly touched. The women washed away the ashes, donned clean clothes again, and ritually re-lit the fire in the now-empty home.

Of course, Timas had named her successor before dying, and Eugenia was now in seclusion and awaiting the trials that would consecrate and elevate her to the office of *hiereia*. Sappho wondered, in her own semi-seclusion, what her friend and comrade pondered as she meditated in preparation of this initiation.

Sappho would normally have been involved in the rite, but her condition was perilous after the stress of Timas's parting. An initiation was a rigorous experience for everyone involved, and she would be risking too much to join it this time.

She understood, with that logical part of her brain, that she couldn't attend. However, her heart broke and sent the taste of bitterest bile into her mouth at this forced exclusion. The bitterness, she knew, came because she knew that she had once been chosen for the role that Eugenia was about to claim. Now, not only would she not be *hiereia*, she would not be present for the making of the *hiereia*. That event was not likely to come around again in her lifetime.

"And Eugenia is my friend," she said to herself through angry tears in the room only she occupied. "I want to show her my love and support, and I can't do that from here."

During the evening leading into the initiation of the *hiereia*, a messenger brought Sappho a letter from home. Anassa, her father's wife, had no way of knowing that Sappho was enduring a long and anguished confinement. Sappho didn't keep regular contact with her family in Mytiline, and nobody outside of the temple complex even knew she was pregnant. So Anassa's announcement that Sappho's father would soon die and her request that Sappho join the family for the mourning process wasn't an extraordinary request from Anassa's perspective.

For Sappho, of course, it brought up a world of fears. Could she safely make the journey? Would she arrive before her father left? They had never been terribly close, but she realized that she loved the man. Her impending loss of him left a hole in her heart – near the one left by Timas, she thought.

She found, too, that the prospect of leaving Hiera for Mytiline held some hope for her. She'd been so separated, so isolated these last few months, that she didn't feel herself to be a part of the temple life any more. Maybe she'd never truly been a part of it.

Alkaeus was in Mytiline, and Pittakos, too. She knew others there, as well, people she'd met through Pittakos, some women she knew at the temple who had returned to their home city.

She could have her baby at home, in the same room where she had been born. Her eyes welled with tears that quickly spilled down her cheeks and onto her *peplos*.

"I'm not just going to say farewell to my father," she spoke again to the empty room. "I'm leaving this place and going home."

Chapter 64

Her farewells were kept brief. Now that she had made the choice to leave Hiera and the temple behind, she felt done with it. There was no point in dragging out the last moments, making them as painful as possible. No, it was much better to turn her face in the direction she was headed and start going there quickly.

Besides all that, she had an ailing father waiting in Mytiline, and she wanted to see him on this side of that dark river one last time. Not until she was faced with losing him had she realized that she was frightened of being cut off from her family, and Scamandronymus was truly the only person walking this world who was wholly her family. No one else shared that blood bond that rooted her to other people.

Her hand rested on her belly, the swell under her *peplos* a new comfort. *One other person shares my blood*, she thought. *One person who is coming into the world, just as my father leaves it.*

Though she didn't linger over her farewells, she did make certain that she had the permission and goodwill of the new *hiereia* before she left.

"My father is dying, and I am called to our family home in Mytiline," she said tearfully, not at all certain where the emotional instability was coming from.

Eugenia looked exhausted. "Will you be returning to your duties here at the temple?"

Sappho was gripped by how directly her friend and new high priestess had seen into the truth of Sappho's murky request. "I don't know," she said quietly. "I don't believe so. Something has changed for me, and I am not sure what it is. Some turning in my path, and I can't see far down this new road. I know that I still serve Aphrodite, but I don't think I am meant to be here."

"I know you've been ill," Eugenia said tenderly. "I'm not sure it's safe for you to travel."

"I know," Sappho agreed, "but I must. My father's wife needs me, I think, and it's better that I make the journey now than attempt it later. I'm not sure how much longer my father will live, either. Better that I go soon."

Eugenia was pinning what remained of her hair up while they talked, trying to get ready for her first day as *hiereia*. "I will not force you to stay, Sappho. I will only remind you that you remain a priestess of Aphrodite, attached to this temple. You are not an entirely 'freewoman,' though you'll probably find yourself more free than most of the married women on Lesvos."

Sappho nodded.

"You know that from your travels, don't you? Well, one thing I can do to make your life immeasurably easier is to sign a warrant stating that you are given permission to enter into your own contracts. That way, you won't have to scurry back here if you choose to marry or be a courtesan again."

"Thank you, my dear Eugenia," Sappho hugged her so abruptly that she knocked loose a few uncooperative tendrils of her friend's hair. They smiled at each other – the watery smiles that shine through tears and leave-takings.

When Sappho left Hiera that morning with her escort, she

took with her every possession she held dear, packed safely into the boxes she'd used on her previous journey, and she took more freedom than she'd ever known. She left behind an offering she'd made in the apple grove and the women who had been her friends and lovers since childhood.

Chapter 65

Sappho hadn't returned to her father's home since the day she'd left as a child going to the temple for schooling. When she arrived on the section of road where her childhood memories still lived, she felt like she was a six-year-old waif, a pretend-priestess playing an elaborate game. The rolling, fluttery thing in her belly reminded her that she was not six, not a child in any way.

She could hear the voices of the home behind the arched gate that was the entryway off the street. Servants were working near the doorway, and she could distinguish the voices of two young boys. Sappho tried to find her own voice to announce her presence outside the gate, but a lump rose in her throat instead. Helpfully, the man who accompanied her knocked in her place and loudly said, "Grace and blessings upon this place."

The sounds behind the gate changed as someone was nominated to answer the call, followed closely by two small and curious boys. The door opened and Sappho saw a face she recognized and wondered if the man would know her for the child she had been. His eyes widened and then righted themselves. He looked frightened to Sappho, which wasn't at all the reaction she had expected.

"I am Sappho, priestess of Aphrodite Kypria and daughter of Scamandronymus," she said as confidently as she could manage, assuming the man didn't know who she was or why she was there. "My father's wife has summoned me home during his time of illness."

The fear ebbed out of the man's features to be replaced with astonishment. "Forgive me, child. Old Kastor wasn't told you'd be returning to us. I thought, indeed, we were being visited by your sweet mother's ghost. You look very much as I remember her."

Sappho smiled and raised her hand in blessing, and she saw the man's eyes catch sight of the temple marking on her palm. This, more than her words of introduction, seemed to reassure him that she was not a specter released from the halls of Persephone.

He ushered her into the courtyard and to a stool that offered Sappho a perch while she waited for Anassa to be notified of her arrival. Her traveling companion unloaded her boxes from the small wagon while they waited. All the while, two very round sets of blue eyes followed every movement the two of them made.

The youngest was ready to burst with curiosity and enthusiasm. He rushed over to her and asked loudly, "Who are you?" Sappho gauged his years at about five. His brother, still watching her with the large eyes from a cautious distance, looked to be a bout seven.

"I'm Scamandronymus's daughter, Sappho," she said simply to the smallest boy. Then she added, winking at the older one, "I think that makes me your sister."

The boys laughed and ran all over the courtyard, clearly showing off for this amazing stranger who was also family, and then ran to the stairs with shrieks of, "Mother! Mother!" as Anassa descended.

Sappho crossed the courtyard almost as excitedly as her little brothers, wrapping her stepmother in a warm embrace that was flanked by the two little guardsmen who clutched Anassa's *peplos*.

Aware of two swollen bellies between the hug, the women parted and looked down to each other's navels before gazing once more into eyes now moist with laughter and tears.

With the confused children still clutching Anassa's robes, the women went to sit in the shade and say their hellos properly. "Eurygius, Larichus," Anassa said, "this is your sister, Sappho, the priestess we've told you about so many times."

"We know," said Eurygius, the oldest of the two. He was a very serious little thing.

"Oh, do you?" Anassa gave an expression of mock surprise, making her eyes even larger and rounder. "Such smart boys. Prophets of Apollo, no doubt! Well, my little soothsayers, why don't you go play for a little while and let us talk?" The boys reluctantly dragged themselves the first few steps away and then scampered out of sight.

"Before we get too engaged in visiting, I'd like to let my escort get a little more comfortable," Sappho said. He stood and looked grateful. "Can someone help him take these things to wherever you'd like me to stay and then show him to a good meal and a nice bed?"

Anassa had Sappho's belongings deposited in the women's room where a bed already stood available for her. Sappho's escort was shown to food and furniture, and Sappho didn't see him again until he departed the following day. Sappho spent that first hour in her father's house outwardly settling in and telling Anassa about her short day's journey to the city. Inwardly, she was preparing to see her father, though she knew one could never truly prepare to behold and embrace a dying parent.

Chapter 66

If she'd seen him anywhere other than in his own home, Sappho wouldn't have known who this man was. His once robust frame now sagged and hung with loose skin and swaying flesh that no longer seemed interested in clinging to his bones. His skin was sallow, and his eyes were darkened purple like the color of eggplants. The coarse, curly chestnut hair and beard that haloed his face had turned a limp, grayish yellow in places. Life, that vital essence that had once coursed through Scamandronymus, was ebbing away.

He was standing when she entered the room. He was actually attempting to shuffle his feet along the floor and move his old bones from the bed where he felt captive. A servant had his arm, and Sappho noticed how her father's spine curved and stooped so that he was no longer the giant bear of a man she remembered from even a few years ago.

When he saw her, he smiled and winked and started scuffling his bare feet across the floor in her direction. "I wondered if you'd come," he whispered conspiratorially. "I'm not quite ready to go, but I'm glad you're here all the same." He looked at her long and lovingly. A thin tear streaked out of his eye. "You look just like I remember you, my Kleis."

Sappho felt a little pain just behind her heart, and a lump rose in her throat. She didn't particularly care that her father didn't know her as his daughter, but it struck her as sad that he was ready enough to have the accompaniment of her long-dead mother in preparation for the river-crossing to come. *To whom is he married in*

Hades's realm? she wondered. *My mother? Damara, who also died trying to give him children? Or Anassa, the bearer of sons and the longest wife?* The knot in her throat threatened to choke her, and the tears spilled unhindered down her cheeks, *All, and none,* she decided. *He'll be free to love with no oath or bond of commitment.*

She stepped closer to him, his frail face still alight, and said, "Father." The whisper of that single word poured confusion into Scamandronymus's joy, and he blinked hard for several seconds while Sappho came closer still and kissed his hollow cheek. A blush crept over his face and she feared she'd embarrassed him in his bewilderment, so she started to talk. She wanted to clear his mind as quickly as possible and spare him any humiliation at her hands.

"Anassa wrote to me and told me your were ill," she said. "Though I remain a priestess of Aphrodite, bound to her temple," she displayed her palm as further clarification, "I have been given the freedom to live where I choose and enter into contracts on my own volition. With your consent, Father, I'd like to stay with you in our family home for the foreseeable future." She didn't know how long she would really want to live in this place, but she couldn't bring herself to say "until you die."

During her speech, Scamandronymus had recovered his senses a bit and knew Sappho for who she was. He was astounded at how much she resembled her mother, and he found that he was curious about her pregnancy but wasn't sure if there was a polite way to ask a priestess about such feminine details. Luckily, he was an old, dying man, and people in such circumstances were afforded great leniency in the area of manners. He decided he'd just blurt it out at some point soon and pretend that it was a perfectly ordinary thing to ask.

As for whether or not his daughter could live in his house, his mind didn't hesitate for a moment. He had been delighted and honored when she had become a priestess, and it would be an honor for the home for her to occupy it once more. Furthermore, his mind was still keen where business was concerned, and he sensed an opportunity for her to help his family, the wife and young sons he was leaving behind. The oldest boy, who was with his tutor now, wasn't quite ready to support the women and children and household as a grown man, but Sappho might be able to help Anassa bridge that gap. Anassa, too, was a very capable woman, but Sappho had freedoms that Anassa did not.

Scamandronymus returned to his bed and crouched on the uppermost end of it, his bare calves dangling over the edge. They looked ashen to Sappho and no thicker than twigs. He was smiling at her again, but this was not the look a lover gives his beloved after a long separation. This was a look of pride and of hope.

Sappho sat next to him and recounted her journey, again, from Hiera to Mytiline. She thought to herself that she had a good many stories to tell him as she sat by his bedside in the days or weeks to come. *How long do we have left, Father?* she asked silently.

Chapter 67

The oldest of Sappho's brothers, Kharaxus, was thirteen years old when she'd returned to Mytiline. At first, she wondered if this age was as difficult for boys as it was for girls. She didn't have to wonder long. The struggle between childhood and adulthood was a war that was evident in the young man.

He had the usual ungainliness of adolescence, but Sappho could see that he favored their father's bulk and would quickly grow into an imposing man. He had quick eyes and a sharp tongue, and Sappho felt relatively certain that he was dealing badly with their father's decay. This was likely the first death to have touched him so closely, and the young are notoriously poor managers of infirmity in others. He was angry with their father for dying, and he was angrier with himself for being so selfish.

He had been forewarned of his sister's possible arrival in his home, and he had known a little more of her than his baby brothers. His mother had spoken of Sappho on occasion, and even Scamandronymus had mentioned her recently once or twice. The most recent conversation about his somewhat mysterious sister had come a few months ago when Father had heard a poet make reference to her. His health was already beginning to fail, but his eyes had sparkled with pride as he recounted how his daughter's poetic ability had been lauded so openly.

Kharaxus was wary, though. After all, he had spent thirteen years as the eldest in his father's house. He was still the oldest son, and he was close to manhood. What did this priestess want from their father at the end of his life? And what would Kharaxus lose if she got it?

The little ones loved her, of course. She couldn't chase after them, but she could sit and sing in the courtyard or the women's quarters while they played nearby. She was their morning lark and their evening nightingale, and the sweet bird sang for both sons and father.

When Kharaxus was not at lessons or haunting the marketplace with a gaggle of his peers, he was usually watching Sappho. Watching and listening. He was generally discreet in his observances of her, lingering in a shadowed corner or doorway. At other times, he openly stared at her from across the room. He always refused her invitations to join her in whatever she was doing.

"Anassa," she said after about two weeks of this, "I don't believe my oldest little brother cares for me overmuch." The women were combing out their hair and preparing for bed.

Anassa's ebony waves tumbled down her back and draped silkily over her shoulders. She shrugged. "He's an unhappy thing right now, my Kharaxus. He doesn't like anyone that I can see. Since Scamandronymus became ill, Kharaxus has grown increasingly sullen and withdrawn. I imagine that he's frightened. He'll be the head of this household soon enough."

Sappho's eyebrows drew together in a knot, and the hand holding the brush dropped to her lap. "You can't mean that he'll actually take on those responsibilities when Father dies, do you? As bright and strong as I'm sure he is, he can't be ready for that."

"No," Anassa said gently, "not that soon, but it can't be too many years later. He's close enough to manhood now, and this will push him closer. You'll see, Sappho. He'll take it on even if we try to protect him from it. I think it's best to help him do what he must do, however hard it may be."

Chapter 68

Sappho hadn't informed Alkaeus of her return to Mytiline, and she hadn't ventured from her father's house in the two months that she had now been in residence. It was a shock, therefore, when she was summoned to greet him in the courtyard.

The months she'd spent in Mytiline had been easier on her body than those first months of pregnancy at the temple had been. She still had days when the headaches, fatigue, and nausea crumpled her in her own bed, but the need to care for her father had moved her from her room the way that nothing in Hiera had done.

Of course, some days found her weeping inconsolably or staring at the wall in distant, blank melancholy. She was unable to explain her despair in these times, surrounded by the family who loved her, except that she grieved already for the father she knew must leave and fretted for the child who would soon arrive.

Anassa found that Sappho's youngest brothers brought her step-daughter the greatest cheer on these dark days.

"Poets are melancholy in their very nature," Anassa explained to Kastor. "Sappho has always ridden a high tide of emotion. We'll let her cry it out for a while, and then the little ones will bring her flowers, song, and sunshine. Let her have the tears she seems to need, but then bring her back to laughter. This is what seems to work best."

She wasn't feeling ill in any way today, but she was self-conscious as she approached her beloved. She felt swollen, engorged. Her belly filled the folds of her *peplos*, and her feet were uncomfortable in sandals. She walked barefoot through the house and flexed fingers that felt stiff. She longed to see Alkaeus, but she dreaded having him see her.

What would his reaction be? Horror? Repulsion? Pity? Fear? Shock? As silly as it sounded, Sappho felt like even mild surprise might break her heart right now. Ridiculous, of course. The man should be expected to be surprised. When he saw her six months ago, she hadn't known she was already carrying his child. She'd shown no signs then, and he would be expecting a slender maiden now, not a swollen sow.

She took a breath and squeezed her hands into fists just outside the door. She let out the air, let loose her hands, and walked in, as ready as she would ever be for his reaction. She was the one expressing astonishment as he crossed the room in two strides, a sunny smile overtaking his dark handsomeness, and put his hands on her belly.

"I'm certain this is the worst sort of presumption and impropriety. I know I'm impious and will likely pay a terrible penance," he began quickly, "but please tell me this babe is mine."

Sappho didn't speak at all. She flung her arms around him and squeezed him to the point that her arms shook with the tension. She choked on her laughter and felt the tickle of tears.

"Yes, my love, she is ours," she said, thick with unnamable emotion.

"'She'?" he held Sappho back so he could see her face and arched an eyebrow.

Sappho hadn't even realized she'd identified the baby as a

girl until then. "Yes," she nodded. "She."

He grinned mischievously. "My love is a poet and an oracle. What good fortune."

Chapter 69

As Alkaeus came to call on Sappho in the weeks ahead, he expressed a strong desire to meet her father. He was clearly uncomfortable to be in a man's house and not pay proper respect to the man himself. Sappho insisted, though, that the proper and respectful act would be to allow him his privacy in his final days.

As Sappho's pregnancy drew to an end, so did her father's life. She was certain that he wouldn't survive to meet his first grandchild, little kicker that she was. No, Scamandronymus was struggling to see the sunrise each morning and the sunset each night. He no longer left the bed to prowl the room, however slowly. He couldn't hold his bowels, and most of the time he was completely unaware of time, place, and person. He routinely mistook Sappho for her mother, and on occasion he believed her to be his own mother. Sappho now found herself praying to Persephone to welcome him to the kingdom across the river and spare him the agony of another day in this world.

She knew she was right to spare her father's dignity by denying Alkaeus an introduction, and she also protected his image by not describing his deteriorating state to the man she loved. Alkaeus had never met Scamandronymus, and she didn't want the younger man to think of him only as a feeble and incontinent old man.

Truthfully, Alkaeus didn't appear in her courtyard more than three times before the night little Kleis was born, but on one of those occasions he managed to win the respect of Kharaxus, a feat Sappho was growing more certain that she might never accomplish.

It happened on Alkaeus's second visit. Kharaxus was home, then, and Sappho introduced Alkaeus to her stepmother and half-brothers. After politely and charmingly accepting the introduction, Alkaeus addressed Kharaxus directly. "May I have the courtesy of a private word with you, sir?"

Kharaxus blushed to the roots of his hair but nodded and turned to lead Alkaeus to the men's quarters. Sappho tried to catch her lover's eye, and she expected him to wink in his normal playful style. But he kept his focus on her brother, and she looked questioningly at Anassa. Her stepmother shrugged and watched them leave, then turned her attention back to the younger boys who wanted to be in on the secret, too.

When Kharaxus returned, leading Alkaeus back into the room, he looked both slightly baffled and somewhat inflated. Again, Sappho tried to signal Alkaeus with her eyes that she wanted to know what was said, but he pretended not to notice. She was starting to get irritated, but she decided to let it go. Perhaps he would share some portion of the conversation when they had a private moment.

Actually, he flatly refused. "For my part," he said, "that is a matter only between Kharaxus and myself. If he chooses to tell you, it will be a matter of his own judgment."

She dropped the subject. If he was going to be difficult, she decided, she would either find some other way or forget it entirely.

The answer came soon enough, though. That night, as she and Anassa prepared for bed, Anassa asked about Sappho's feelings for her handsome poet.

"My sweet mother, Aphrodite's spell has taken all sense and

reason from me," she said. "Yearning for that dear, beloved youth, I can't see the pattern of my tapestry."

Anassa smiled. "I can see why he is telling all of Mytiline that you are the tenth Muse. Between his obvious adoration and your talent, he is a man smitten."

"Does his affection for me seem so apparent to you?" Sappho asked, feeling a bit insecure.

"Do you know what that conversation with Kharaxus was about?" Anassa asked, grinning.

"Obviously not. Alkaeus wouldn't give me even the smallest hint."

"Well," Anassa began, thinking of how best to phrase what had happened. "Alkaeus honored your brother as the head of this household by asking for his permission and blessing to come visit you here."

Sappho leaned back in her chair and nodded. Alkaeus used charm and tradition in his favor to win her brother's respect and loyalty. It was a bond that would remain intact between the two young men for the rest of their lives. It's a pity that Pittakos couldn't have been similarly swayed by Sappho's charming poet.

Chapter 70

It had been a year of death for Sappho, but it had also been a year of life. Change was sweeping through her world, and there were days when she sobbed until her eyes were swollen shut, her head throbbing with the pain of another of her blinding headaches.

On these days, she'd lie in her darkened room, a rag soaked in cool water thrown over her eyes. She'd question her choice to leave the temple, sometimes convincing herself to return when the babe came, when her father passed, when she'd spoken with Alkaeus, when she'd paid a visit to Pittakos.

On the darkest of these horrible days, though, she knew what she deemed to be a horrible truth. She wouldn't return to service at the temple. Not now. She convinced herself that she didn't belong. She had fouled up her station there, and it was time to do something new. Mytiline held all the future she would have, and she couldn't imagine yet what that would be.

Sappho hated her despondency. *This isn't the person I am*, she thought. *I'm happy.* And then she would cry even more.

Anassa was a link to sanity for Sappho on these miserable days. She brought the young woman infusions made from lavender or milk thistle and shared her own mood swings.

"My body and mind worked in awful tandem when I carried Kharaxus," Anassa said. "Unlike you, who gets so sad, I flew into rages a time or two. I thought I might have to murder your father once. Luckily, Tessa was still with us, and she was as good as a nursemaid to me during those times. The lavender helps, doesn't it?"

Sappho nodded, her eyes leaking a little at the thought of Tessa. How many mothers had Sappho lost in this lifetime? And now she was on the edge of losing her only father.

"My sadness came," Anassa offered, "after Kharaxus arrived. It was better with Eurygius. When Larichus came, I was too exhausted to feel anything." She smiled a little thinly. "I imagine it'll be the same with this little one. With so much happening, and the boys still so young, I doubt I'll have much time to despair."

Sappho felt guilty now for wallowing in her own emotional muck. Of course, the added emotion did nothing to ease her depression.

"I've been wondering," Sappho began, tentatively, "if it might be a wise choice for us to bring in a woman as a nurse to help with the children. With two infants, and the boys so young, and father, we might need the extra help."

"I've considered it, too," Anassa said. "I'll need to consult Kharaxus since it is a financial matter, but I think he will consent."

The following day, Anassa told Sappho that she had spoken to both Scamandronymus and Kharaxus. Scamandronymus, who was having a mentally clear day, agreed with his son that the expense was small to keep the women and children of the house healthy and well-provided for. So it came to be that within three days, the midwife Anassa favored had recommended a suitable young woman to act as nurse and helper to the women of Scamandronymus's house. She would take up residence when the first of them delivered, which should be any day, in Sappho's case.

Chapter 71

The first pains of labor, and the hours that surrounded them, were very clear to Sappho. What began as the common urge to relieve herself turned into the monthly cramping of menstruation and eventually became the worst pain she'd ever known. She was quite certain that women couldn't be reasonably expected to survive this pain, and only the strongest women had managed it successfully.

Her own mother had died in childbirth, and hadn't everyone said she looked just like her? Now Sappho was in the same room, in the same pain, certain she was dying the same death. Before the dimness set in, she thought she saw her mother standing with Aphrodite, their arms wrapped around each other's waists, smiling at her from beyond the circle of women struggling with her in the bloody and smelly straw to bring her baby out of her body.

Though she never lost consciousness to the point of immobility or incoherence, there were segments of the birth that Sappho couldn't recall after she'd rested and regained some strength. She knew that at points she was on her feet and walking, supported between two sturdy women who were sweating with the effort of this childbirth. At times, she was aware of the circling of her pelvis. She laughed once at this, thinking that this same dance had been used to very different effect in a gathering of men during a *symposium*.

She was spared the memory of the worst portion of pain. Her body was crippled and torn with it, and the stench of soured blood, stool, and acrid urine as it escaped her body filled the chamber. She vomited from pain, pressure, and the odors of childbirth. Her hair was matted to her head, neck, and back, and sweat flowed freely down her body.

When her daughter emerged, coated in film and blood and something that looked like curdled milk, she was the iconic image of infant vitality. Her lungs wailed their first high scream, and her arms and legs kicked with the unsettling freedom of life outside the womb. Sappho, though, was damaged beyond repair.

Reah, was given the babe for her first feeding as Sappho finally collapsed under the exhaustion. As she was cleaned and tended, Anassa wept quietly.

"Please don't let her die here," she said to the midwife. "It would be too bitter."

The midwife looked grim but nodded and continued her care of the broken woman. "She'll live, I think," she said toothlessly. "But the girl's ruined for more babies. She'll never bear a man a son, as you have."

Anassa's laugh escaped her. "I don't think that will matter too much to her." She was so relieved that she didn't notice the midwife's skeptical look as Anassa turned to find a seat.

Sappho slept for two days, and Anassa and Reah held the baby to her breast to suckle to make sure her milk came in properly. Reah would help, but Anassa knew Sappho would want those moments with her little girl.

Anassa slipped quietly into and out of her fourth labor, giving the midwife barely enough time to arrive to wrap the little girl in clean linens and present her to her mother.

She was holding her own little Iantha when Sappho roused

from her sleep. Anassa was nursing her own daughter and singing a lullaby when Sappho's eyes fluttered open.

"You're too good to me, Anassa, taking my child to breast while I sleep," she said. "What a long day it's been."

"Longer than you know," said her stepmother, winking. "Your daughter lies there, in the cradle on your right. This is my own daughter, Iantha, two days younger than her niece."

Sappho lifted the sleeping bundle lying next to her. Her chest was filled with a sensation that she had never experienced. It was love commingled with pride, joy, hope, and fear. Her eyes filled with tears, and for a moment she had no words. Only for a moment.

"I thought I died, my daughter," she whispered to the infant who slept in her arms. "I thought I was dying and leaving you. I was broken-hearted to think that I'd never know my child. And I never knew my mother. Mine would have been a life bereft of the most important women." She kissed her babe's tender, fuzzy head. Sappho giggled through her tears as she looked at the soft curls that seemed silver-blonde, thick through the middle of the baby's head like a rooster's comb.

Wrapped in the enchantment of her first conscious moments of motherhood, Sappho sang her daughter the first of many songs written for her.

> *A fair daughter have I, Kleis by name.*
> *Like a golden flower she seems to me.*
> *Far more than all Lydia, her do I love,*
> *Or Lesvos shining in the sea.*

Chapter 72

Scamandronymus met his youngest daughter and his granddaughter, though he was too weak to hold either of them. The women brought the babies into the sick man's room, and he smiled at all of his girls. They sat in chairs, cooing the shortened versions of their birthing stories into the faces of their daughters as Scamandronymus rested after the initial excitement of their entrance.

Later, they returned with Kharaxus at Scamandronymus's summons. Reah watched the infants, and the little boys played happily in the courtyard, very much unaware of the transitions into and out of life that were happening all around them.

"I have so few days left, I think," he said simply. He was very clear in his mind right now, which was why he wanted to speak with them. "That I held on to see those babies is an accomplishment I didn't think I could manage. I want to establish a few of my wishes before I go.

"The three of you will make joint financial decisions until Kharaxus reaches manhood," he continued. He was already getting tired, and his speech was slurring. "From the moment of his initiation, though, he will be the absolute head of this household and the controlling force behind all my assets."

Kharaxus nodded somberly and tried not to look to his mother for support. Sappho instinctively put a steadying hand on the small of his back. She felt him stiffen momentarily and then relax.

Scamandronymus was fading. "All the documents are in that chest," he said, wagging a weak finger vaguely to the right. "Take

404

care of your family. Your mother, brothers, and sisters all depend on you, Kharaxus. Be both strong and fair." He simply couldn't talk any longer. Sleep was overtaking him, and his eyes were slipping out of focus.

Anassa chose to sit with him for a while, and Sappho and Kharaxus left together after squeezing his hands. In the courtyard, Sappho risked reaching out and touching her brother again. He turned and looked at her, but he didn't seem as tense as he had when she'd touched him a few moments earlier.

"If I can help you, Kharaxus, in any way," she said tenderly, "please ask me. I don't know if Father told you, but I am free to enter into contracts on my own accord. I don't have to stay in this house, if my presence becomes burdensome to you or the family. I'm at liberty to make other arrangements for myself."

Kharaxus was silent for several moments, and Sappho reflected that he was more contemplative than she'd been at thirteen. "I am no soothsayer, and I don't know what will change in our years ahead. You may be the one who wants to leave, sister. But I like having you here, I think, and I know my mother and brothers do. You are my family, and you are included in my responsibility."

"Family is a shared responsibility, my brother," she said. "I will do all in my power to help you bear the burden you've been given." She looked at him as though appraising him, scrunched her nose and said, "Of course, your shoulders and back look like they'll be quite strong enough, if you ask me." She smiled and winked, and Kharaxus chuckled.

One of the babies cried from the upstairs rooms. Sappho

prepared to go up, but then stopped and turned again to her tall, lanky little brother. "I hate to impose upon you, Kharaxus, but I wonder if you might do me a favor?"

"I might." This time Kharaxus winked, and the rare humor from him caught Sappho a little off her guard.

"Well, I'd like to get word to Alkaeus about the baby, but – "

"That favor has already been done," he said seriously, more like himself. "When I was out today, I paid him a little visit with the news. He said to expect him here tomorrow."

Unfortunately, "tomorrow" was the day that Sappho's breasts swelled with milk for the first time. They were each the size of Kleis's head, and they felt as hard as stones. Sappho cried in pain as Anassa and Reah tried to help.

"Feed the babe as much as she'll take," said Anassa.

"But she isn't hungry. She's sleeping right now," Sappho protested.

"Well, wake her," said Reah. "We'll strip her down so that she's a little cool. No, don't look so worried. Your body will keep her warm enough. But she'll wake up, cry a little, and you can comfort her with milk."

Warily, Sappho let Reah help her into this position. When Kleis woke, though, she didn't just cry a little. She screamed so hard that her whole head turned red. Her thin voice shook with fury, and she beat her uncoordinated fists against Sappho's left breast while her tiny feet flailed against the right one. She refused to suck and only screamed harder when Sappho tried to encourage her.

Reah eventually took Kleis away from a tearful Sappho and

bundled the little girl in soft cloths, hoping to calm her. Kleis continued her angry wail for three hours, finally consenting to nurse when her rage had exhausted itself.

Anassa was having no difficulty feeding Iantha, and she managed to find time to show Sappho how to make some milk leak out of the hardened flesh so that she enjoyed some minor relief. She also had Zoe, the woman who helped in the kitchen, prepare an infusion that helped calm Sappho tremendously. She even had a remedy to help Sappho sit without too much pain, and the younger mother was grateful for Anassa's experience.

When Alkaeus arrived, Sappho felt weary but presentable. Reah carried a sleeping Kleis so that Sappho needn't put any unnecessary pressure against her tender breasts. She kissed Alkaeus's cheek, but she cried out when he hugged her. Sitting quickly on a cushioned chair that was brought for her, she said, "It's been an ordeal, my love. My body is battered, and I need the gentlest touch right now."

He'd brought gifts. Some were for Sappho, and some were for Kleis. Both of his ladies received a golden bangle, fine cloth, oils, and honey.

"She can't eat honey, silly man," Sappho said.

"Then you eat it. Share it with the household. Nobody who cares for my loves should be without a little sweetness."

"We thank you," she said, kissing him again.

He caught her hand and looked at her with an intensity that would've caused her knees to buckle if she'd been standing. "You have spoiled me for other *hierodule*," he said. "Indeed, I'm practically ruined on all women."

Something was bubbling to the surface in Sappho's mind, and she was about to speak, but Alkaeus pushed on, "When you can, if you can, I would like for you to be both *hierodule* and *hetaera* to me. I would love to offer some financial support to you and the babe, and this is the best way I know."

"Kleis," she said. "Her name is Kleis, like my mother."

He took the wriggling thing from Reah and looked into her face, now awake and dazzled by the brighter light of the courtyard. "Hello, daughter Kleis."

"I would gladly enter this agreement with you, Alkaeus," Sappho said. "Tomorrow, come back with the proper officiant, and we will arrange the documents."

Chapter 73

Scamandronymus died one spring afternoon while he slept. His rattling chest stopped its long struggle, and his body melted into eternal relaxation. Kharaxus and Kastor were both with him, and they both muttered prayers to the Gods and guardians of death to watch over him in his new home.

The door was marked and the fire extinguished so that all were aware of a death in the home. The family felt a mixture of grief and relief that comes after the long struggle that inevitably ends with a funeral.

Scamandronymus's funeral rites were well-enough attended, but there were not hundreds of women wailing and singing their good-byes. No maidens cut their curls for her father, though every member of the household wore rough cloth and rubbed ashes on their heads and arms.

Kharaxus bought a bull for sacrifice, and Sappho felt it was a touching and appropriate tribute. The feast it provided for the funeral guests was also auspicious for the boy's future as patriarch of the family.

The cleansing after the funeral closely coincided with Sappho's and Anassa's cleansing rite after their bleeding stopped from childbirth, so that the entire household seemed renewed and alive. The fire was rekindled, and Sappho felt that her own life sparked and flashed anew in the hearth.

She was shaking off the dreariness of the winter and the death that had surrounded her. She celebrated the lives of Kleis and

Iantha, the vitality of Eurygius and Larichus, and the strength that was emerging in Kharaxus. She felt like she was a clear, golden mirror, reflecting back the life, joy, and strength around her.

Her body was healing from the trauma of Kleis's delivery, and her heart was healing from the weariness that she had suffered during the long months in isolation. She wrote the springtime into being. Honeyed verses dripped from her pen. She sang the new life around her with the reflected and refracted light and brilliance of a prism.

Kharaxus was prone to brood in dark melancholy, but Sappho's spirit was infectious. Some weeks after their father's death, he watched her in the courtyard, singing and dancing a silly trot for the babies and boys, who laughed delightedly.

"Sister, you are the messenger of spring," he said, "the sweet-voiced nightingale."

She flapped her "wings," a bright cloth she used to guard her fair skin from the sun, and chased him in pretended flight. Her smaller avian fellows took up the attack and nearly pulled Kharaxus down onto the tiled floor in their excitement.

"Enough, my little nestlings," she said above Kharaxus's protests. "Eurygius, Larichus, go get something to drink and bring me a cup, too."

She and Kharaxus sat for a moment, catching their breath and enjoying the pleasantness of the moment before Kharaxus turned to her and said, "A poetic contest is happening soon in the amphitheatre, and I think you should enter."

Sappho blushed, touched by her brother's thoughtfulness

and by his conviction. She was unsure, though. "I've never sung that way – prepared and practiced, for a competition. What if I should fail miserably?"

"You won't," he said confidently, as the young always do. "Alkaeus will be there. And all of Mytiline is clamoring to hear your lyric ability, after the praise he has given you."

That didn't help. "I'll consider it," she conceded.

When she next saw Alkaeus, he goaded her into agreeing, and before she had time to change her mind, the entire household made arrangements to be there with her.

The day arrived, damp and dreary, and the huge amphitheatre was crowded with a breathing, swarming, pressing mass of people. So it seemed to Sappho, in any case. Wine flowed in honor of Dionysos, God of the vine, and most of the poets were a little drunk, as was the audience. Alkaeus took a healthy share of wine, which didn't surprise Sappho. She was coming to know him as a Bacchante. Sappho would've had a cup or two of strong wine, but Kleis wouldn't tolerate the intoxication she got through her mother's milk. Sappho had already learned that through unpleasant experience.

"It's a shame, too," Anassa had told her. "A little wine for me helped both Kharaxus and me relax when he was fussy as an infant. It seems, though, that Kleis is a mean little drunk." She'd giggled, and Sappho had stuck with her lavender infusions for relaxation.

No herb or wine could help her today, and she looked panicked. Anassa was frightened for her, not knowing if Sappho would bolt or freeze under the pressure of so many eyes.

"You have sung often enough for us, Sappho," she began. "Did you also sing at the temple?"

"Yes, for my friends, and later at the *hiereia's* request."

"And when you traveled, did you sing in front of strangers?" Anassa pushed gently.

Sappho nodded.

"This is no different," Anassa declared. "Your family is with you, your friends. These people will be friends to you once they hear you. Be still. Find calm, and you will be fine."

Sappho looked largely unconvinced, but she didn't want to disappoint her loved ones. She decided to lose herself for a while in the poetry of other speakers, and she found herself smiling and thinking about an afternoon of lyric delights with Alkaeus back in Hiera.

Just as she was thinking of him, she heard Alkaeus saying her name from the *orchestra*. "Sappho of Mytiline, priestess of Aphrodite, come take this place that I leave for you and grace us with your song."

She walked forward, greeting him with a gesture of blessing, and turned to face her audience. She was stunned by their silent anticipation and overwhelmed by their number.

She turned again and moved to the altar on her right. Taking some myrrh from a pouch, she sprinkled it on the coals and said in a voice that carried over the crowd, "Hither now, ye Muses, leaving your golden arbors to lend enchantment to my song. May I win this prize, O golden-crowned Aphrodite!"

The audience around her grew quiet to the point of

reverence. She stood before them and found the faces of Anassa, Kharaxus, Reah, Kastor, and Zoe. She smiled widely, and her eyes twinkled. However nervous she was moments ago, and might still be, nobody could tell. The composure of the priestess had descended, and she seemed at perfect ease. "This will I now sing skillfully, to please my friends."

She placed herself lightly upon the chair reserved for the poets and singers of the day. She lifted her lyre between both hands and said, "Come, oh come, divinest shell, and in my ear, all your secrets tell." Then she tucked the instrument neatly into position and began plucking out a melody. With it, she said the words she had written for the day, which were built on her first improvised poem for Alkaeus.

A troop of horse, the serried ranks of marchers,
A noble fleet – some think these, of all on earth,
Most beautiful. For me, nothing else considered,
　　Is my beloved.

Understanding this should be most simple,
For gazing long on mortal perfection
And knowing well what life could give her,
　　Paris chose fair Helen.

He, the betrayer of Ilium's honor.
Then, she thought neither of adored child or parent,
But yielded to love and, forced by her passion,

Dared life in exile.

How quickly is the will of that woman bent
To whom things near and dear seem worthless.
So might you fail, my friend,
*   If my beloved were with you.*

Her gentle footfall and radiant face
Hold the power to charm more than a vision
Of chariots and the armored battalions
*   Of Lydia's army.*

But we must learn, in a world made as this one,
Man can never attain his greatest desire,
But must pray for the good fortune Fate offers,
*   Ever grateful.*

The respectful silence endured while Sappho came out of the mists that seemed to have enshrouded her mind while she performed. When she stood, though, signaling the end of her recitation, the crowd erupted into stomps and cheers and shouts of praise.

Alkaeus approached her again and said loudly, "I did not lie, citizens of Mytiline! One of our daughters is surely the tenth Muse."

The crowd cheered again, but Sappho held up her hands and said, playfully, "If I am a Muse, then so are all poets. Here is Melpomene," she said, pointing to a dour-faced man with a huge belly, "inspirer of tragedy, come among us. And over there," she pointed to a tall, balding man, his shiny head reflecting the sun, "Urania, in whose radiant brow we see all the stars of heaven." The crowd roared with laughter at her antics. "And you, Alkaeus, are Thalia, youngest, cheerful, inspirer of comedy."

Though other singers followed her, she was the darling of the day. She wore the laurel wreath atop her head that night as she walked home with her family, and she was sure she'd never worn a lovelier adornment.

Chapter 74

"It was an unexpected delight to hear you sing in Mytiline's amphitheatre," he said. "I've always adored your poetic gift. Of course, I'd had no indication that you were away from the temple. I wish you'd sent a message so that I might have welcomed you properly." Pittakos didn't sound or look like a man who was dealing with an emotional wound, but Sappho recognized that he was acting like one. She recognized his invisible barriers, too, from their last interaction. His words were clipped and formal.

She had been stung by his initial appearance in her courtyard. A guilt she was starting to associate with him crept over her skin and stole her voice for the first few moments of his mild chastisement. But this spring had brought her a renewed strength, and she did her best to reject the guilt he was trying to give her.

"I do apologize, my love," she began diplomatically, "but I came home quickly due to family need. My father died not long ago after a withering illness." She was pleased to see that he looked appropriately shameful for his attempt to make her feel guilty. "And, of course, I had my own recovery to facilitate," she added, not sure, once it was said, that she should have opened the door just yet to a conversation about Kleis. Still, she felt that, in the end, it was better not to look like she had anything to hide.

"You were ill?" he asked, concerned.

"Quite," she said simply. "Though childbearing isn't so hard on most women, it bedded me from near the start, and it nearly killed me to see it through to the end."

"Childbearing?" he said. "You're a mother now?"

She nodded. "My daughter sleeps with her little aunt right now, two days her junior. The girls were born just before my father died."

Pittakos hesitated and then dared the question that had just arisen to gnaw on him, "And the father of your babe? Are you at liberty to discuss who that might be?"

"Temple custom dictates that the child is only mine," she said delicately. She knew this was the dangerous part of the conversation.

Pittakos's eyes narrowed, and then he smiled. "How many weeks old is your babe?"

She told him. His smile grew, and a light reached his eyes that she hadn't seen there in a long time. *He thinks Kleis is his.*

He bounced twice on the balls of his feet. "May I see her? Your daughter? I have cared for you so long that it is only natural that I should care for your baby."

Sappho smiled and nodded. "Certainly. I'll go get her. Make yourself comfortable in the men's chamber."

Would you care about my baby if you knew she was fathered by Alkaeus? She couldn't tell him that directly. It wouldn't be appropriate, nor would it be kind. Most importantly, it was unnecessary. Total disclosure on this topic wasn't expected of a temple maiden, and she was protected by those years of custom. The only thing she needed to do was make sure that Alkaeus and her family respected that custom so that Pittakos didn't feel deceived by her.

Kleis was sleeping peacefully and soundly, and she nestled into her mother's bosom when lifted from her bed. She had fattened up a bit from the skinny, long thing that she had been as a newborn. "Life in the world is treating you well, my girl," Sappho whispered as she kissed Kleis's forehead. She was always kissing her daughter's head. It was a compulsion she'd developed these last few weeks.

Her smiling lips still close to the head of her daughter, she entered the room where Pittakos waited. *He looks nervous,* she thought.

He walked over to her and looked down at the slumbering babe. "What is her name?"

"Kleis," she said. "It was my mother's name."

Sappho wouldn't say that Pittakos was crying, but his eyes did look a little wetter and brighter than they normally did. Sappho felt a stab of guilt, but then reminded herself that his own assumptions were to blame. Furthermore, she couldn't be sure that he even thought the child was his. Maybe the emotion she sensed in him was his struggle with the idea that this was Alkaeus's daughter. *Either way,* Sappho thought, *the assumptions he's making are his own doing, as is the emotional price he's forcing himself to pay.*

"Will you return to the temple or stay in Mytiline?" he asked her.

"I plan to stay here," she said, and she explained the legal situation in which she found herself.

"Very good," he said, smiling. "I'm glad to know you will be close. I've... missed you, Sappho."

"I've missed you, too," she said, sincerely. She leaned in to kiss him, and Kleis stirred in her arms.

"She's waking. I should leave and let you tend to the duties of motherhood," he said, seeming a little nervous about the infant who was now looking at him with her clear eyes. "One question before I go. Will you still serve as *hierodule* for my devotions to Aphrodite?"

"It would be both an honor and a pleasure," she said.

"Do I...," he searched for the right phrase, "do I visit you here in this house?" He looked very skeptical and uncomfortable with that idea.

"Oh," Sappho's brow furrowed, and she bit her lip. "I hadn't considered that. I'm not sure. Let me figure that out, and we'll discuss it soon."

"I'll think on it, too," he said with a nod and a serious expression, more grave than Sappho thought was necessary.

Chapter 75

"Father owned a small house that has sat empty for quite a while, from all I can tell by the records," Kharaxus said after Sappho explained the situation. "I can see no immediate need for it. If you can use it, you should."

Sappho was touched by her little brother's generosity and openness with her. "So that we are clear, Kharaxus, let me say that at the temple, the gifts given to Aphrodite were property of the temple. They were used to feed and clothe and care for all of the women and men in the complex. I intend the same here. Gifts given to the Godddess through me will be used for the benefit of this family. That way I will be able to compensate for the care you extend to Kleis and me."

He nodded, and they hugged. Sappho had essentially made her third contract since leaving the temple, and she felt empowered about finally making these choices for herself.

"Should we go see the house?" Kharaxus suggested. "It may be crumbling and inhabitable."

They went that afternoon. The house was indeed small, and it was a fair walk along winding and hilly roads from the family home. The houses that surrounded it were equally small, but they were in better repair than the unused dwelling of Scamandronymus's. Luckily, it was not crumbling, though cobwebs and twiggy nests gave ample evidence that spiders, birds, and other likely small inhabitants had taken up residence in the absence of humans.

A couple of dusty and mouse-eaten chairs and cushions

remained as gifts from the previous tenants, along with some broken pottery that Sappho suspected of hiding more living creatures.

Kharaxus's nose crinkled at the tickle of dust and the acrid scent of something he didn't want to identify. "Maybe not," he said apologetically.

Sappho was holding her veil over her nose and mouth with little effect. She walked around the little rooms – there were only two – looking them over critically. Then she stepped into the small courtyard that separated the two. A small fire pit had been built here, and it still stood in decent shape.

"Yes, actually," she said. "This will work perfectly. It needs some cleaning, and a few pieces of furniture on which to sit safely, but that is about all it needs." She looked at the place where the fire should be. "It needs the spirit rekindled, but I suppose we all need that from time to time."

Chapter 76

Sappho's little house didn't take long to clean, not with the help of Anassa, Reah, and Kastor. The four adults were easily able to sort out the mess, even with Eurygius and Larichus making new messes of their own while they worked. The following day, Kastor and Kharaxus led a mule and cart loaded with a few bits of furniture and household goods from the family home to Sappho's retreat.

They fumigated both rooms and even the courtyard with incense, and Sappho led them in a procession of holy objects through the rooms to bless them. She carried fire on a torch lit from Scamandronymus's house. Anassa bore a water bowl. Reach carried a basket holding bread and barley, while Kharaxus held the winnowing fan. The little *pompe* sang cheerfully a song of blessing as they moved around and through the house. The simple rite ended with Sappho lighting the fire in the cooking pit and offering the first of her votive offerings to the house's guardians. She and the other women made a meal of some of the provisions they brought, and they all enjoyed the food and company in the shade of the sitting room.

"Sister," Kharaxus said to her confidentially before leaving, "I know that you've chosen to sleep here tonight, but I don't like the idea of you being here alone."

"I'll bar the door and be as safe as a clam," she assured him. Of course, he didn't look at all assured. "Why don't you send Reah to sleep here with me after the evening meal? Anassa will be able to handle what is left of putting the boys to bed and getting Iantha settled in. And you'll rest easier knowing your big sister has company."

After everyone left, and Sappho was alone with Kleis, she started wondering how best to let Alkaeus and Pittakos know where to find her. As they had worked on cleaning and furnishing the little abode, she had noticed two young boys playing in the street. She could hear them outside her walls even now. She pulled two coins from a bag that she'd brought with her and went to meet them.

The youths were younger than Kharaxus but older than her younger brothers by several years. They were certainly old enough for the tasks she had for them. Making sure her *himation* covered her well enough from the sun and immodesty, she strode up to them.

"For a silver coin each, would you be willing to do a task for me?" she asked them. Their eyes widened and they nodded. "Do either of you know Alkaeus the poet or Pittakos the merchant?"

The boy with straight hair and skewed mouth shook his head no, but the curly haired boy said, "Alkaeus, I've heard him in the *agora*. Know his face."

Sappho pressed the coin into his palm. "Go to the market and find him. Find where he lives, if you have to. Then tell him that Sappho lives in this house," she said, pointing, "and give him directions to find it." She turned to the freckled boy. "And I need you to do the same for Pittakos."

The boys sprinted toward the market and Sappho returned to her little house. She actually hadn't decided, yet, whether or not she would take up residency here full-time, but this would be an ideal place to meet her lovers and devotees with some discretion, and she was pleased with the arrangements. "We could live here, couldn't we?" she said to Kleis as she bounced her in the mother's universal, swaying dance. "Yes, we certainly could."

Alkaeus appeared in her doorway near dinner time, and his arms were laden with gifts for the new household. He brought food for the larder, wine, pottery, cushions, and a blanket for the baby. He brought so many things that the boy Sappho had hired as a messenger had been paid again by Alkaeus to serve as a porter.

"Anytime you need my help, my lady," he said deferentially, "I live right there." He pointed to a house across the road. "I'm Fotis."

She smiled, and she knew that she was dazzling him in that moment. "Thank you, Fotis, you've been most helpful." She gestured a blessing over him with her marked hand, and he ran home clutching his new prosperity.

She hoped the other boy didn't arrive with Pittakos in tow while Alkaeus was still here. She'd have to think of a way to keep suitors discreet in their visits. These two paths, especially, would be troublesome to cross. Perhaps she'd be sending messages through Fotis and his friend on a regular basis.

Alkaeus joined Sappho and Kleis for a simple dinner followed by a beautifully harmonized lullaby to soothe the infant to sleep. They had time to enjoy each other's company, and for Alkaeus to pay his deepest respects to Aphrodite, before Reah arrived for her overnight stay.

The poet bade both women farewell and whistled as he walked through the evening streets, completely unaware that

Pittakos, seething with suppressed rage, watched him as he disappeared behind the hill.

Chapter 77

Pittakos didn't arrive for a week, and Sappho was starting to question whether Fotis's friend had even delivered the message. She'd seen the boy again, and he had insisted that he'd completed his task, but something about him struck her as haughty and insolent. She was starting to suspect that he'd taken the money and enjoyed a leisurely stroll instead.

When Pittakos arrived, she knew she'd been wrong about the boy's actions this time, but she wasn't anymore sure about his character.

The merchant, who no longer saw trading wares as his primary role in society, intentionally delayed his first visit to Sappho's new home. He had felt the power of his anger at the sight of a man he was beginning to regard as a personal enemy. Alkaeus was a threat to him on several levels, now, and he knew he needed to deal with him. He was fairly certain that he knew how and when he could rid himself of this young pest, but he needed a bit more patience.

He was less sure how he would handle Sappho and the anguish that her involvement with Alkaeus was causing him. That was the main reason that he'd avoided this visit for the last week. Fearful of saying or doing something for which he'd later be embarrassed, he kept himself free from saying anything at all.

These issues were clearing, though, and he wanted to make a bold gesture in order to regain some control in the relationship. He began by presenting her with a very large and very ornate amber ring.

"A woman as beautiful and compelling as you should have some more impressive jewels."

She was speechless. She hugged and thanked him, and she cried happily as she put it on her finger.

"You should also have more suitable living quarters," he said, looking around.

Sappho's spine prickled, and her eyes narrowed almost imperceptibly before she recovered what she felt was an acceptable facade of grace. "I'm actually quite pleased with my lodgings, Pittakos," she said as politely as she could. "Do you have other arrangements in mind?"

"I do," he said. "I would like for you to stay in the house I provided for you when you came with me to Mytiline last. You could stay there as long as you like, of course, and it would be a gift from me to you."

It was hard for Sappho to keep from laughing in his face as she said, "But, Pittakos, that house and this one are almost twins in design and space. The only real difference is that you own the other."

He said nothing.

She smiled airily despite her irritation at Pittakos's attempt to manipulate and control her. "I'm actually quite fond of this place," she said. "I own it, in a sense. My family does. My brother suggested it for me, and it was a family effort to make it livable again. I do hope you'll be happy to come visit me here," she said hopefully.

"Yes, of course." He was being diplomatic, and Sappho

knew it. "I hope you'll forgive any offense I may have inadvertently offered. I want the very best for you, and I'm selfish enough to want you as near to me as may be."

She twined her arms around his neck. "This little home will be like the temple to me, my love," she cooed. "And I will gladly entertain you and worship with you in this place." She thought for a moment and then added, "Will you do me the favor, though, of sending a messenger in advance of your visits? I plan to exercise my new liberties and visit the marketplace, my brother, and friends – as I make them – quite freely. I'd hate for you to trek across Mytiline to find me not at home."

After he agreed, keeping his jealous suspicions silent, they embraced in honor of Aphrodite. Pittakos fell asleep after release, snuggled into the warmth of Sappho's body and smelling the sweetness of her hair.

Chapter 78

A month went by with Sappho neither seeing nor receiving a message from either man. Kleis was growing more aware of her world, and Sappho sang to her unceasingly. She had decided to take up residence permanently in the house, an independent woman, but she made the walk back to her family's home every few days to visit with Anassa and the boys.

Reach continued her nightly ritual of coming to sleep at Sappho's quarters, and the women were becoming very close friends. Sappho entertained Reah with tales from the temple and the sea, and she shared her poetry with the pretty young nurse. She even encouraged Reah to try writing poetry of her own, which the girl did with some small amount of natural skill. They shared their poems in the indigo light of evening as they lay in bed together, Kleis softly sleeping nearby.

> *Dark-eyed Sleep, child of night,*
> *Burdens lovers' tired eyes*
> *Delivering them to Morpheus*
> *While all night long, Sleep holds them.*

The women enjoyed sharing their poems with each other this way, and they found that even poor poetry gave them ways to bond with one another. They would laugh over clumsy phrases and try to gallop their way through unruly meter.

"I have a friend who would enjoy this," Reah said one night

as the women unfolded new poems before each other. "She has a beautiful way of seeing the world, and she speaks as delicately as a daisy."

"Maybe we could have her join us sometime," Sappho offered.

Reah laughed and patted the cushions on the bed with a sturdy hand. "It would be a little crowded, I think."

"I was thinking of more suitable hours for company and conversation," Sappho said, mocking an attitude of exasperation. Then her eyes lit up. "Oh, Reah! I have an idea!"

"What?" Reah asked cautiously. She was feeling a tingle in the pit of her belly, and she wasn't sure if it was excitement or worry.

Sappho's own excitement was growing, though. She was now sitting upright in the bed and pulling her hair away from her face in a loose knot behind her neck. She always felt like she could think more clearly when her hair was out of the way.

"We could have our own *symposium*," she said. "It can be just women, friends and sisters from Mytiline. We can share poems, food, stories, wine, maybe."

Reah looked a little scandalized.

"Well, maybe not the wine," Sappho conceded, "although, I have no quarrel with it."

Reah somewhat recovered, said, "Women wouldn't want their husbands or fathers thinking they'd been carousing at the taverns."

"Let's plan one," Sappho blurted. "Is nine days too soon? That is the fourth day after the new moon, Aphrodite's day, an auspicious start to our festivities."

Sappho barely slept that night, and she spent the next few days arranging for food and inviting the few women she knew. She kept Fotis busy sending messages. His friend, whose name she forgot from disuse, was also employed to send a few messages, but he wasn't as swift or industrious as his playmate.

She utilized them both as porters when she went to the market, though, and both boys then learned a little of their neighbor's growing fame. As she was inspecting some nuts that she planned to use in a sweet dish she was making, a woman approached her.

"You're our 'Muse,' aren't you? Or so you claim," the woman said loudly.

Quietly, and as restrained as she could manage, Sappho replied, "I've never claimed any place on mighty Olympos, nor on any of the high places that surround it. I am a poet and priestess, nothing more."

The woman eyed Sappho greedily, taking in every detail. She was fat and stiff-backed, and her face was puckered into a perpetual mask of suspicion and disdain.

"'Nothing more,' you say? That bauble on your finger is a pretty piece for a priestess. Perhaps, it's more apt to say that it is a pretty price for a prostitute."

"Eranna!" some other woman scolded from nearby. "Leave her to buy her food in peace." Sappho noted that neither woman spoke delicately, as educated women were prone to do. Their hands were rough, and there was a general coarseness about both of them that suggested a life of hard physical labor and few intellectual pursuits. Of course, these characteristics didn't seem to work against the woman who had come to her defense, but they certainly cast the one called Errana in a more unfavorable shade.

"I'll say what I want, when I want, to who I want." Errana said forcefully. "I'm not going to worry myself about some glorified whore's feelings." She spat on the ground at Sappho's feet.

Sappho stepped back from the glob in the dirt and stepped neatly around it. The boys moved to let her through freely. They were clearly shocked and shaken by the interaction happening in front of them.

"You are an ignorant woman," Sappho hissed, her anger clearly rising as a scarlet flush appeared on her neck and cheeks.

"And you are a heated harlot, more fond of children than Gello, that old ghost who carries them away in the night," the fat woman said hatefully. "These two following at your skirts are very eager to please you. To get them to do your bidding so happily, do you please them in turn?"

Sappho's blood was pounding a heavy rhythm in her ears. She'd never felt rage so completely, and she was practically snarling when she said, "Again, I say you are ignorant, and foolish as well. When your time comes to pass the gates of Hades's kingdom, you'll lie dead forever, and no remembrance will be made for you now or hereafter, for you have never had any of the roses of Pieria, the Muses' tokens of learning and wisdom. No, indeed, for you shall be doomed to wander in the houses of Hades, eternally disregarded, flitting among the insubstantial shades."

432

The woman's pinched face blinked in shock that Sappho would respond with such force. "You try to shame me with your fine language and pretty words?"

Sappho sighed. "You are nothing to me." She shook her head and offered up a sad laugh. "One more scornful than you, Errana, I have never found. And I hope not to."

She turned her attention away from the unpleasant distraction in the pink *peplos* and purchased the nuts where she'd nearly forgotten about her reason for being in the *agora*.

Still angry when she came home, she wrote a furious poem about the encounter, smiling about the reaction she imagined Reah would have when she heard it.

Chapter 79

The women's *symposium* was an unparalleled success by the reckoning of all who attended. They had been in such need of an outlet that this communal outpouring of poetry, dance, music, and conversation felt as sanctified and holy as any ritual that Sappho had attended.

Most of the women present were young, unmarried girls who were barely older than the students Sappho had recently left. One or two, she was sure, were the same age. In fact, Anactoria was among them, a girl Sappho remembered well from the *thiasos*. Anactoria had been one of her favorite pupils.

"Reah is my cousin," she said brightly. "When she told me about the *symposium*, I knew I had to come. I missed you after you stopped instructing us." She shrugged. "I returned to Mytiline shortly after that." Her eyes brightened as joy shone through her. "Dica and Milesia are coming back soon, too, I think. Dica is to be married this summer."

Sappho marveled that almost a year had gone by since she'd seen her pupils. Anactoria's delight was infectious, and Sappho was glad for the chance to know her as a peer. Of course, Anactoria wasn't the only young woman from her past to surprise her that day.

Atthis had been invited by her husband's sister, and Sappho was obliged to be civil amidst the gaggle of women.

"Hello, Atthis," she said courteously. "How have you been these many years?"

Andronikos's little sister practically squealed with delight.

"Atthis, you deceiver, you didn't tell me you knew Sappho!"

"Didn't she?" Sappho said innocently enough, but she felt the barb of her pointed phrase pierce Atthis's heart. "Well, it was a lifetime ago, but we were as sisters then." Turning her attention fully to Atthis, she said, "The uncountable hours that have passed between us seem to have been kind to you Atthis. You look well. How is Andronikos?"

"Seeming isn't always truth, Sappho." Atthis said mildly. She seemed ready for Sappho's lashing out, however subtle. "Andronikos died last year. He was killed while hunting."

"I'm sorry to hear that," Sappho said sincerely. The first pangs of guilt for her selfish spewing of old anger stabbed at her conscience. "My father died this spring, and I know the pain of loss."

Atthis nodded. "I poured libations onto the bare earth for him, and I do so weekly, that he won't thirst in the darkness of the houses of death."

"You pour libations for Scamandronymus?" Sappho asked incredulously.

"We were as sisters, Sappho," Atthis said. "I haven't forgotten that. Nor have I forgotten that your father cared for me as if I was his own child. I owe him all the duties and honors that any daughter owes." Her eyes were moist when she finished, but she didn't cry.

Atthis's sister-in-law had wandered away, leaving the two women to discuss these old hurts privately. Neither had noticed her absence, just as they'd ceased to give attention to her presence for the moment.

"I have wronged you, Atthis," Sappho said. "To me, you seemed a small and ungrateful child. I have held a bitterness against you in my heart since you left me. A bitterness mixed with a love I cannot shake off, and both have hurt me."

"I never left you," Atthis said. "I was bound by honor to do your father's will. Bound by law and custom, too."

The women were looking at each other with hope of forgiveness, hope of understanding long overdue. They embraced and became conscious again of the *symposium* and its guests. They sat next to each other, hands clasped and fingers entwined, as they had done at the temple. Anactoria, Sappho noted, was lounging against a young woman, too, and everyone seemed very comfortable with this intimate sharing of women's space.

When Sappho delivered her poem, pantomiming a man and speaking directly to Atthis, the women laughed, cheered, clapped, and whistled.

> *Peer of the Gods, the happiest man, I seem*
> *Sitting before you, enraptured at your sight,*
> *Hearing your soft laughter and most gentle voice,*
> *Speaking so sweetly.*

Chapter 80

"I hate that man!"

Sappho had never seen Alkaeus angry. Not truly angry. She'd seen him sulk a time or two, and he'd been testy on occasion, but he was livid with rage now, and she quailed at the fury that was shaking within him.

Another couple of weeks had passed since the symposium, and Sappho still hadn't seen either Pittakos or Alkaeus until now. She hadn't been able to share her successes with her poet, either, since he'd clearly been so upset when he arrived.

"You and I haven't discussed politics and the general state of Lesvian affairs much, Sappho," he said as he paced the room like a caged leopard. "I know you're capable and trained in such dialog, but I've wanted and needed something softer and gentler from you." Sappho didn't interrupt. She knew he needed to speak weighty, unsaid things.

"You should know, though," he continued. "You have a right to know. You have family here, and when tyrants begin throwing around their political weight, any and all are likely to be crushed by it."

Sappho felt that cold prickle along her back that told her something was worse even than it seemed. "Alkaeus, I can't make sense of this. Please slow down and tell me what has happened."

He slumped into a chair. "I've made an enemy of a powerful man, Sappho. He mocks my heritage and the reputations of many men of wealth and good family reputation. He craves power for himself, and I have challenged him through my poetry. Perhaps I've been too public in my disdain for him because now I think that he is taking this enmity further than a public debate of ideas. He has forced some men of position into exile, banished them from Lesvos. Sappho," he sounded close to panic, "I think he means to banish me and my family as well."

Disbelief coursed through her. "No, no he wouldn't..."

"He would, Sappho," Alkaeus said firmly. "You don't know Pittakos, the tyrant. He is capable of this and worse."

Sappho gulped air. "I do know Pittakos, my love," she said, gently but firmly. "I have known him since I was of an age to marry. I was his *hetaera* for two years and sailed through the Aegean with him while he -"

"While he won the support of neighboring cities and islands," Alkaeus was snarling again. "So, you are his lover? Still?"

She looked at the floor and then quickly met his eyes again. Her own eyes held pain and grief, but they also spoke the truth to Alkaeus. "I haven't stopped being Aphrodite's priestess, Alkaeus. You know that."

"I do know," he said simply. He wasn't softening, as she'd hoped. He was breaking. He was crumbling before her. He slumped into the chair nearest him. His shoulders were slack.

"I won't leave," he said, but only a shadow of defiance colored his voice, and Sappho wasn't convinced. "He can kill me, if he must."

"Don't be ridiculous," she scolded. "It's better to live, even away from your home, than to be killed."

438

"I could live far from home, but not far from my heart," he said, looking her in the eyes. "I can't leave you, nor Kleis. I die either way."

She fell at his feet and put her head in his lap. "We can go with you," she suggested. "We can go to Lydia or Aegyptos, and we can stay together."

"You would leave with me?" he asked, stronger now.

"Of course."

He kissed her as he stood. "Be ready, then. I'll come for you and the babe when it's time. We'll leave with our freedom, before he has the chance to banish me."

Chapter 81

They had made love that night, but if Sappho had known it would be her last time to hold Alkaeus, to touch him, kiss him, look at him, she would have done all of these things until sense and reason completely left her; and she would have been content to wander the world delirious and insensible, keeping the sight of Alkaeus in her eyes and his touch in her skin.

She expected him within a few days. She was hesitant to send Fotis with a message because she didn't want to draw any attention to their elopement. By week's end, she decided to go to the market and see what she could discover.

One of the poets from her recent performance was there orating for a group of interested men. Sappho was impressed by the number of people listening to him, especially since she didn't remember him as a very talented poet or speaker. He was the one she had dubbed Urania, with his shining pate sweating in the sun. His real name was Platon, which had struck her as just as funny since that name referred to a high, flat place. She edged closer to listen, hoping she could get some information after he finished.

"We are lucky, men of Lesvos," he was saying. "Very fortunate, indeed. Pittakos is nothing less than a man of genius, a protector of this island and its people. He has improved our trade with neighboring islands, negotiated peace with our neighbors, and acted on our behalf in every way that a man who isn't a king could do."

"That's what he wants," grumbled a man in the middle of

the crowd. "He wants to be king." Grumbles of agreement echoed around him.

Platon said quickly, "No! He despises the aristocracy and all that goes with it. He's been outspoken enough about that."

"Yes, and he's done away with them that opposed him too strenuously," said the crowd's vocal dissenter. "Where is young Alkaeus now? He's been out here for months, railing against Pittakos, but he's been absent for too long."

Good question, Sappho thought. She was starting to worry even more about her young poet.

Another voice, one closer to Platon, said loudly, "He didn't keep his malcontent discreet enough for Pittakos's liking. Alkaeus was escorted away from Lesvos in the middle of the night, probably three days ago. And if you don't harness your tongue, Manasses, the same or worse may happen to you."

Manasses opened and then snapped shut his mouth, apparently deciding that his retort could wait.

"Friends," Platon said in an attempt to regain control of his oration, "we need not argue amongst ourselves. Enough conflict brews around our beautiful and peace-loving island. Let us gather around and support the man who has proven so capable of supporting us."

He continued, with cheers of ascent from many within the crowd and growing approval from most. The dissenters stayed silent, now, and Sappho turned her fearful heart and tremulous body back toward home.

She was holding Kleis, a fact she'd momentarily forgotten

until she felt the baby squirm in her arms. "Oh, my girl," she whispered as she walked, her eyes blurry with a veil of tears. "What are we going to do?"

"You'll not be leaving Lesvos, I hope."

The voice behind her startled her. She knew it instantly, of course, but she wasn't expecting to hear the man so close to the scene of rhetoric being spoken in his honor. Pittakos was watching her closely, waiting for her reaction.

She turned her back on him and forced him to follow as she continued her walk home. This also gave her some protection from his observations. "I just heard Platon singing your gracious lordship to the crowd in the marketplace," she said. "Did you hear him?"

"A bit," he said evasively. "You had to know my influence would grow, Sappho. It was the reason we sailed."

She didn't answer. She was walking as quickly as she could, and she could feel the heat rising in her face.

"Are you angry with me, Sappho?" He asked a direct question knowing that they hadn't yet spoken directly of Alkaeus. Would she answer as directly?

"Do I have reason to be?" she said.

"I think you are upset regarding my political choices – one choice, in particular. You know I've banished your poet friend." He stopped her walk by standing abruptly in her path. "I'm sorry if that hurt you, but I have to consider the welfare of all of Lesvos. Alkaeus was a thorn in the lion's paw. He had to be pulled loose and set safely aside."

Sappho's eyes narrowed. "And who has appointed you the

protector of Lesvian well-being? Are you now our king, Pittakos?"

He was doing a marvelous job of staying calm in the face of her growing anger, she noted. He must have anticipated that. *He usually does*, she thought.

"Not king," he said. "No kings, no aristocracy for Lesvos. As for my appointment, I have done that myself, with your help, of course, and the support of many influential men here and abroad."

"So, you'll be our tyrant?" she said.

"If a tyrant, then a wise and judicious one," he said. "Lesvos will have prosperity and peace under my rule, Sappho, down to every woman and child." He put his hand on Kleis's curly head and pinched the dimple in Sappho's chin.

"What you promise sounds lovely, Pittakos; but at what cost?"

"Only the removal of thorns," he said.

She shook her head sadly and walked around him. "There are always thorns hidden among the roses." This time, he didn't follow her.

Chapter 82

Word had reached Anassa and Kharaxus about Alkaeus, and they came within a day or two of Sappho's visit to the market. Reah was with them, as was Kastor. Sappho had managed to care for Kleis, but she had not fed herself or tidied her own hair. Her face and hands were unwashed, and her eyes were swollen and shot through with red lines from hours of crying.

Gentle Adonis lies wounded, dying, dying.
What message, O Kythera, do you send?
Beat, beat your white breasts,
O you weeping maidens,
And in wild grief your mourning garments rend!

She cried and screamed these lines again and again, tugging and tearing at her own hair and clothes as she did so.

Anassa took charge immediately. "Reah, make a brew of belladonna and mix it with a cup of wine. Bring it to me hot. You'll be nursing Kleis the remainder of the day. In fact, after you've made the drink, take the babe and return to my house with her. Stay with the small children until I return. Kastor, help her. Keep the boys occupied. Put them to work helping you, if necessary." They nodded and got to work on the sedative wine.

"Aphrodite has forsaken me," said Sappho. "Love has left me to go mad in despair."

Anassa wrapped her arms around the weeping woman and

444

rocked her gently. "Quiet your mind, my child. I do not believe that."

Sappho's grief poured out from her, and Anassa allowed it to wash over her. When Reah returned with the cup of hot wine, she convinced Sappho to drink it. Sappho sipped it until it cooled enough to gulp down the rest.

"What will I do?" she asked Anassa through hazy eyes. "Do I find him and go to him, abandoning all my life here to be with the man, or do I stay and continue in what I have begun. I am of two minds and don't know what to do."

"Now isn't the right time to make hard choices," said Anassa. "We don't even know where he's gone. The choice may not be yours to make."

They sat silently, Sappho's eyes drooping. She finally fell heavily asleep on her stepmother's shoulder. As they were already sitting on the bed, Anassa easily got Sappho into a comfortable position. She occupied herself with tidying and then took a nap of her own. It might be a long night.

Chapter 83

The next eight days passed with no word from Alkaeus, and Sappho's emotional state flitted quickly and without warning from anxious to lethargic to melancholic to angry. Her rage was the hardest for her family to bear since they knew they were undeserving of the venom she spat at them during these times. Of course, her anger was also beyond her control, or so it felt, and she hadn't realized the volcano within her was rumbling until she'd spewed lava and hot ash on the heads of the people she loved.

Because of this, she wished they would leave her alone. Wild emotion was punching holes in her, and she was a leaky vessel. The only way to keep her mess off of Anassa, Reah, and Kharaxus was for them to stop trying to handle her.

They wouldn't, though. They were worried for her. Worried for Alkaeus, too. Kharaxus had formed an attachment to the poet, and he was clearly disturbed by his banishment.

On the ninth day of his exile, a letter from Alkaeus arrived by messenger at Sappho's gate.

"My love, I hope you know I didn't leave you by my own choice. It was made clear to me, by our mutual friend, that you and your family are better off if I endure my exile in seclusion. I hate that it must be this way, and I will long for you until my last breath. I hope I won't be forgotten on Lesvos, least of all by you."

She studied his letter. Had Pittakos threatened her family? Is that why Alkaeus had agreed to leave her behind?

"I'll never forget our vagabond friendship," she whispered to herself. "Though what we said in poetry is only breath, I do think men will remember us, even hereafter."

For weeks, she continued grieving for a love that had slipped beyond her reach, but she grew steadier as time passed. Eventually, she packed his letter into her box of papers and stepped into the fresh air of the courtyard to eat. It was the first time she had chosen food over sleep in weeks.

Chapter 84

Early summer that year brought a heavy and heady blossoming to the jewel of an island, so close to purpled Lydia. Gamelion, the month of the sacred marriage of Zeus and Hera, was the favorite month for mortal unions, as well. As foretold by Anactoria, Dica was marrying a young man that month, and Sappho happily attended the rites with her friends.

She dance and sang as part of the happy procession that followed the cart bearing Dica and her goods from one household to the other. Sappho wore a garland of rosemary and lilacs woven together as a coronet atop her curly head, and she wore her hair loose, as maidens were known to do.

During the celebration at the groom's home, the wine flowed freely and the food was ample. One of the guests, recognizing Sappho, shouted, "Let the Muse of Lesvos bless the new couple with a song!" Resounding cheers of support drove Sappho to her feet and in front of the crowd. She stood near Dica and Hymenaeus, her new husband.

She held her wine goblet high in the air until all the room was silent. "Hail bride, and all hail noble bridegroom!" A cheer rose around her as everyone shouted, "Hail!"

"In mighty Olympos, the bowl of ambrosia was mixed, and Hermes took the ladle to pour it out for the Gods," Sappho began. "And then all held goblets and made libation and wished good fortune to the bridegroom." She poured a libation of wine to the floor and set the goblet down.

448

The bride comes rejoicing, let the bridegroom also rejoice.
For like her, O bridegroom, there was no other maiden.
A most tender maiden, gathering flowers
And now she gathers petals of joy
      For you.

We will give, says the father,
And childhood is put away.
Maidenhood, maidenhood, where have you gone from me?
Never, o never again shall I return to thee?

Maidenhood lost, and marriage bed gained,
A sweet expression spreads over her fair face.
Happiness comes to the girl who becomes a   woman.
All my joy to thee, daughter of Polyanax.

To what may I compare you, dear bridegroom?
Best to a tender shoot, may I liken thee.
Growing ever stronger and more sturdy
In the sun and rich soil of your
      Lover's garden.

O happy bridegroom! Now has dawned
That day of days supreme,
when in your arms at last you'll hold
      The maiden of your dream.

A house of mortal size cannot contain such love.
Raise high the roof beams, workmen! Hymenaeus!
Like Ares comes the bridegroom! Hymenaeus!
Taller than all tall men! Hymeneaeus!

And to the bridal chamber, following the feast,
Outside the door set the keeper, his feet seven fathoms long
With sandals of five bulls' hides, to keep out the guests.
Sleep safely, then in the bosom of your sweetheart.

Hail, bride, and all hail noble bridegroom!

The cheers and clattering of cups and plates, the hoots and whistles, stomping and clapping were deafening for a moment. As music began to play again from drums and flutes, both Dica and Hymenaeus thanked and hugged Sappho for her gift. Dica, Sappho noticed, was flushed and a little breathless. Sappho wondered how much she was anticipating her bridal night.

At length, Sappho returned to Atthis and Reah and Kleis. She took the growing babe from its nurse and bounced her on her hip.

"Do you ever long for the days of your youth, your maidenhood?" Atthis asked her after watching younger women dance for several minutes.

"Do I long for maidenhood?" Sappho repeated. She twisted her mouth as if trying to remove a piece of meat from between her teeth and then said, "I'll always be a maid. I'll never marry."

"You are not a woman to be overlooked, Sappho," Atthis said. "You could marry, if you wanted."

"I'm the apple at the end of the bough – its uttermost end," she said. "I am missed by the harvesters, though not overlooked. But far out of reach, I ripen."

They stood silently again until Sappho handed Kleis back to Reah and joined a circle dance where she linked arms with other women and stepped the pattern of the dance until she was too tired and breathless to continue.

Chapter 85

The men and women of Mytiline knew Sappho as a priestess of Aphrodite, one of the temple maidens from Hiera; and some came to visit her as such as the summer melted into autumn and autumn blew into winter. She found friends and lovers in the city of her birth, and she was easily able to support herself from the gifts the devotees bore to their *hierodule panagia*, the all-holy embodiment of Aphrodite.

Pittakos kept his distance, and Sappho was glad for this. She saw him at erratic times, and they were cordial. To the outside eye, they even seemed friendly. Sappho didn't want to cross the "Tyrant of Lesvos," as he was now known by all, for worry of what that might mean for her brothers, Anassa, and little Iantha. Nor did she want to hurt him. Not really.

But she had already been hurt by him in her own right, and she didn't care to risk that pain again. So she remained content to maintain a cordial distance.

She was a *hetaera*, again, to a man named Kerkolos. He was not a handsome man, but he was thoughtful and sweet. He doted on Sappho, and she fulfilled her role appropriately.

She cared for him, as any friend cares for another, but she didn't reciprocate the nearly worshipful adoration that he lavished on her. She gave him attention in full measure when they were together, of course, and she never withheld any manner of physical favors from him. But she had the uneasy feeling that he filled much of their time apart with thoughts and plans revolving around her,

452

whereas she went about other business with her mind free from Kerkolos when they weren't together. She didn't know why his consuming affection made her uneasy, but it did.

Kleis and Iantha were walking by the spring of their first year. Sappho and Kleis had developed the routine of walking to Anassa's house with Reah each morning, Kleis bouncing along on the hip of one of the women. Sappho would visit with Anassa for a while, give Kharaxus any goods that would increase the family's stores and walk back alone to her own home before the midday meal. Her own visitors came to call in the afternoon and evening, and Reah returned with Kleis for dinner.

Sappho enjoyed her routine, and part of it involved reciting a welcoming verse every time Reah walked back into the courtyard with Kleis:

> *Hail, gentle Evening, that brings back*
> *All things that bright Dawn has beguiled.*
> *You bring back the lamb, you bring back the kid,*
> *And to its mother, her drowsy child.*

Kleis would squirm down from Reah's hold and toddle across the dusty paving stones to her mother's arms. Being lifted once high in the air and brought back down into her sweet smelling bosom, the tired babe rubbed her little face on the soft fabric of Sappho's *peplos*.

Reah and Sappho enjoyed a dinner of chickpeas, cheeses, cucumbers, herbed grains, and wine, while Kleis focused all her attention on the juicy cucumbers and mild cheese. Seeds stuck to her pudgy face by a thin layer of dried juice, Kleis fell asleep in her mother's arms while the women talked of the day's events and the morrow's plans.

Sappho's arm growing numb from the motionless child was the queue to clean her and put her to bed. Reah cleared and cleaned the plates and cups while Sappho attended to the child.

This schedule was easy enough to adjust when duty called Sappho to Kerkolos's side for a *symposium* or other function, but Sappho had come to prefer the predictable simplicity of her ordered days. They had a cadence, a rhythm, a meter that indicated a poetry of their own. And she couldn't deny their beauty.

Among her lovers was Atthis, though the raging fire of their youth had turned to a smoldering heat in their maturity. Anactoria was also a lover, though their romps were very infrequent and always very playful. Several men came to her as devotees of Aphrodite, along with a handful of women, but she didn't form personal relationships with any of these as she had done with Alkaeus. *No man can take his place in my heart*, she thought, which she knew was foolish since each lover makes a new place in the heart of the beloved. *Perhaps, I was a fool for loving him.* This thought always brought tears, though, and she didn't dare to explore it too closely.

Neither Kerkolos, nor Atthis, nor Anactoria, nor any devotee was her constant lover, though, excepting Reah. She and Reah had slipped silently and comfortably into a life built on partnership, compassion, tenderness, and joy. Reah was her helpmate, her partner. She was a second mother to her daughter, and she was the one to whom Sappho confided all her hopes, worries, bad poems, bitter thoughts, brilliant ideas, and every hidden aspect of her soul. It was Reah who nursed Sappho through the pain of persistent headaches and heartaches, as they made their vicious cycles through Sappho's world.

Sappho had dreamed one night, as she lay next to Reah in the bed they always shared, that she was touching and stroking the woman's hair, her face, her breasts, her belly, her thighs. When she woke, she realized she was indeed doing these things, and Reah had turned toward her to touch her in return. They were kissing, soft and wet and sweet, when Reah rolled Sappho onto her back, straddled her hips and clasped her hands together on the cushions above Sappho's head. Reah's hair spilled down like a curtain around both of their faces.

She lowered herself close to Sappho's ear, her breasts grazing Sappho's, as she whispered, "I have wanted this every night since I first slept in this bed."

The women had woken the next morning, twisted together and twined heart to heart.

Chapter 86

The women of the *symposium* came to Sappho's home at least once each month, on the fourth day following the new moon. It was the day to honor the birth of Aphrodite, and it was a sacred gathering for Sappho. To her, it was a *thiasos*, a school, a celebration of Aphrodite.

They arranged themselves around the visiting room on chairs and couches with food spread before them on small tables. Wine and water stood in large jugs, and they talked easily amongst each other.

"To you, fair maidens, my mind doesn't change," Sappho said one night while looking at her friends. "With rosy cheeks and glancing eyes and voices sweet as honey, the women of Lesvos are the most beautiful in all the world."

Each woman shared the poem or dance that was within her until they called with one voice for Sappho to sing of Aphrodite.

"Once when I was deeply troubled, I cried to Aphrodite within an apple grove," she began, "pouring out libations of thick honey and burning sweet myrrh. And she came from the heavens, clad in a purple mantle."

> *What rustic girl bewitches thee,*
> *Who cannot even draw*
> *Her garments neat as they should be*
> *Roundabout her ankles?*

"My friends know me well. I love refinement in all things, and for me, Love herself has all the splendor and beauty of the sun; but the brightness of her face does not destroy the sight. So, long I gazed upon the fairest face that ever was."

"What would you have of me, Sappho, for to you and my servant, Eros, I can deny nothing."

"Then lightly, in an enfolding garment, I sprang, and I set down the cushion. She wrapped herself well in gossamer garments, and upon that soft cushion she did dispose her limbs."

> *A golden pulse grew along the shores.*
> *Now Love, the ineluctable, with bitter sweetness*
> *Fills me, overwhelms me, and shakes my being.*

> *By the cool water, the breeze murmurs,*
> *Rustling through apple branches,*
> *While from quivering leaves*
> *Streams down deep slumber.*

Several women sighed deeply. "Yes," breathed Anactoria, nearly as sated as the Sappho in the poem, "the best lovemaking can be just like that."

Chapter 87

Kleis, as she approached two years old, began babbling like a noisy brook. The child, like her mother, had much to say. She had her own words for mother, Reah, Anassa, Iantha, cheese, carrot, bread, chair. Essentially, if she touched it on a daily basis, she knew its name and attempted to say it. Of course, since Reah, Iantha, and hello all sounded roughly the same in Kleis's little accent, her communication couldn't quite be described as clear.

As much as Sappho loved talking and playing with her daughter, there were nights when she wept herself to sleep in Reah's arms, convinced that she was a horrible mother.

"I'm not patient like you or Anassa," she hiccupped. "Kleis has a stubborn streak that angers me, and she's only two! But you seem completely unruffled."

Reah had learned not to argue with Sappho when the crying started. It did no good. Logic held no sway, and sometimes Sappho had to experience days of melancholy and tears before the sunshine of her smile would reappear.

"It's a good thing for you that I am so patient," Reah said in her exasperation. "The child screams. The mother wails. If I didn't love you both so much, I'd return to my father's house and beg him to find me a husband to replace the one that died."

"I don't deserve my beautiful daughter," cried Sappho, "and I don't deserve you." She snuggled into Reah's arms and slept, at last.

The worst nights, though, as Kleis grew, were the ones that featured screaming contests between mother and child. If Kleis refused to sleep despite her drooping eyes, or refused to eat, refused to pick up the cup she'd thrown on the floor as a childish protest to whatever request had just been made, the battle might begin. Though little Kleis only reached to the thighs of her mother, her spirit and will were huge. She never backed down. Beating, cajoling, bribery, and negotiation all had the same effect. None. Kleis did exactly as she chose, just as she had done the night her mother tried to convince the three day old girl to nurse when she wasn't hungry.

Sappho adored her daughter, was in awe of her; but she also feared her in some ways. She feared the rage that the tiny girl could unleash, and she feared that she might hurt Kleis through word or deed when her own anger shook her.

Guilt gripped Sappho in its steely claws each time her temper broke. Guilt washed over her every time she lost patience and asked Reah to fix the emotional mess she'd stirred up. Shame poured through her every time she secretly thought that Kleis would be better off with Reah as her only mother while Sappho stole back to the temple.

Sometimes when both Reah and Kleis were sleeping, their soft snores filling the little bedroom, Sappho would draw a chair beside the child's bed and watch her chest rise and fall with each easy breath. "I'm sorry that you have to struggle with me as your mother," she whispered, tears sliding silently down her face. "I only hope having me is better than having none at all."

Chapter 88

Rumors of Phaon reached Sappho months before his presence did. As *hetaera* to Kerkolos, Sappho met and mingled with men of all sorts – and their evening companions. The *hetaerae* sometimes shared whispers about other lovers when their current men were senseless with wine or deeply absorbed in a conversation that didn't involve their consorts. Of course, the women were always discreet about these little indulgences, since discussion of men not present would have aroused jealousy among the participants of the *symposium*.

"He is like Dionysos walking among mortals," one woman said dreamily.

"Yes," agreed a second courtesan. "A wildness, a storminess lurks under that slightly drunken surface. You want to unleash it, but you fear it, too."

"Have you been with him?" asked the first.

The second shook her head. "No, but not for lack of my own desire. He's an incorrigible flirt, too. But he took delight with a plump little thing that night."

The first *hetaera* nodded, a knowing smile sneaking across her lips. "That seems to be his taste."

A third woman contributed to the quick round of gossip with, "I wasn't certain he had any taste at all. I've known of him romping with three different *hetaerae*, several tavern whores, and a merchant's wife."

"He's going to get himself killed if he isn't more discreet,"

Sappho said. Phaon sounded boorish to her.

"Hmph," grunted one of the women. "The men love their soldier turned ferryman, Phaon. They only know about his escapades with courtesans and tavern girls. I think they encourage his madness, wishing their luck was as universally good."

The conversation ended there, on the first night. Kerkolos had turned his attention back to his prize, and he beckoned her close so he could reclaim his transient hold on her.

Sappho didn't necessarily dislike Kerkolos, but she found that she tolerated him best in certain settings. She wanted him to be happy. Her training and her nature both called for pleasing those around her. The trouble with Kerkolos was that he would never tell her precisely what he wanted. Most of the time, he just stared at her and grinned.

"Perhaps he's fantasizing or playing out a conversation in his head," suggested Reah, who had been witness to Kerkolus's slaving devotion to Sappho. "It's sweet in its way."

"It's idiotic," Sappho said grumpily. "I'd like to talk with him, but he just watches me and smiles like a fool." When Sappho looked up, Reah was looking at her blankly with a syrupy smile plastered to her face. Sappho threw a pear at her, which Reah caught and bit.

"At least I'm lucky that we are normally in larger groups of people where conversation is the norm," sighed Sappho. "When he doesn't contribute anything but silent quips behind that silly facade, I don't notice because the room is lively with talk and music and frivolity. And when he does offer some audible nugget, we can all enjoy it."

Reah laughed a little but said, "Do you think you might be judging him too harshly, my love?"

Sappho slouched in her seat and bit her lips. "It's possible. Everyone else seems to enjoy his company well enough, but he makes me uncomfortable. I don't part ways with him because he's done nothing blatantly wrong, though."

Because she was critical of Kerkolos, though, she began watching the way the *symposium* guests interacted with him. Kerkolos had a swagger, a pompous little affectation. He must have practiced it in his youth, and Sappho knew its root. Kerkolos was not truly a confident man. He'd been born with a deformity, a misshapen ear. It was just a small thing to anyone else, but he'd been teased as a child. His hearing was poor on the left, and he'd taken to wearing his hair longer than the fashion to cover it. As a grown man, a wealthy one who could do as he pleased, he'd overcompensated for the embarrassment of his youth by acting like a strutting cock in the hen's yard.

Kerkolos wooed and flirted freely with the other courtesans, when he wasn't wearing Sappho on his arm like a prized new cloak. He was only tongue-tied and silent with her. With everyone else, men and women, he had the goal of being witty, clever, unique. And always, there was a sexual undercurrent to his quips.

Sappho was actually quite shocked by the personality she discovered in Kerkolos as she watched him. He was such a contradiction to the Kerkolos who fawned on her. She wondered if anyone else saw the way he was with her, or what they thought of it if they did.

So, she watched. Sappho became a clever observer of his interactions when they were together publicly, and she found that Kerkolos received a rather mixed reaction from people, though he didn't seem aware at all of how he was perceived. Men like himself, strutting peacocks and boorish brutes trying loudly to cover the inadequacies they perceived in themselves, seemed to like him. Perhaps they recognized a kindred spirit, though Sappho doubted any of them thought too long or hard about why they acted like this.

More moderate men seemed to alternate between enjoying Kerkolos's company and merely tolerating him. They laughed at his jokes, though not as loudly as he did himself. They listened to his stories, politely, and engaged him in conversation often enough, but they didn't seem to enjoy his company as thoroughly or as genuinely as they did that of less self-possessed men.

As for the women, courtesans would be a hard group for an outsider to evaluate. These women were skilled at lavishing attention on the men around them. They knew how to make men feel important, loved, handsome, interesting, sophisticated, and more. For the most part, they only attached themselves to men for whom they naturally felt some attraction, so they weren't inherently lying with every word, every look, every touch, and every moan of pleasure. In fact, Sappho was one of the rare women who found it within her scope to love and give love freely to the unlovely. This was probably one of the reasons Kerkolos was so devoted to her. In her role as Aphrodite's priestess, she gave herself to him completely and sincerely, and in that role she was able to accept him just as completely.

Hmm..., she thought, distracted for a moment from her observations of the other women. *Do I not accept and love Kerkolos outside of the sacred bedchamber? Outside my role as Aphrodite's daughter?* There was nothing about him that was repellant. Why was she experiencing an aversion to him?

Struggling to define it, she watched to see if the other *hetaerae* could give her any answers. Behind the flirting, the touching, the sly looks and the blatant intercourse that they might have shared with Kerkolos, Sappho noted that some of them avoided him or playfully maneuvered out of his range. After catching a couple of stealth signals that were common among the women, she knew that she wasn't the only one with a subtle aversion.

Sappho's heart cried a little for Kerkolos, though. He craved acceptance. All his posturing and preening were ill-conceived tools to bring it to him. And his desperate need combined with those mannerisms, were driving him further from the true intimacy that he wanted. He was surrounded with people, but he was completely ignorant of his own isolation.

Chapter 89

Her time alone was spent in partial seclusion in her house, where she wrote poems and sometimes spent hours ruminating over a tangle of questions that bothered her. Reah called this brooding; and in truth, it often was. Some of her time was given to devotees there at the house as well. But part of the routine she'd developed for herself was a regular trip to the *agora*.

She had made friends with some of the vendors, and she could sometimes trade a song for a meal among them if they were feeling generous. Otherwise, she happily paid for the bit of bread, cheese, and spinach that she liked to eat at these luncheons in the crowd.

Watching people from the shade of the colonnade had become a favorite pastime, and she found that some of her poems echoed the lives and personalities of those she watched. The merchants, grocers, tinkers, and prostitutes who spent their long days in this square fascinated her. What were their homes like? Did they have families who loved them and were glad to see them at the end of the day? Surely, that must be the case for most of these people, but it couldn't be true for everyone. Who was lonely? Who was hungry? Who slept on a cold floor or in the dusty alley?

Sappho watched. She listened. And she made friends. She bought sandals from the cobbler whose work was overlooked and asked him where he learned his trade. She sat with the prostitute whose feet were sore from walking, and together they speculated about the political future of the island and its tyrant. With the physician, she discussed drama and the role he had recently played in a tragic play.

On some days, she merely sat in her favorite place, eating her food and purveying the crowd. On some, she did the marketing for her small household, visiting with new-found friends as she went. Of course, there were days when she was goaded into public performance, and she was usually prepared enough to oblige with a new poem or an old favorite.

Sitting with a fruit peddler under a shady awning one sweltering summer day, Sappho bit messily into a very wet plum, its juice spilling down her chin as she greedily slurped the pulp. She was already feeling flushed and sticky when one of the most beautiful men she'd ever seen walked by the booth where she crouched with her companion.

He wasn't a tall man, maybe slightly taller than her. He wasn't massively built, but he had a muscular strength that reminded her of a large, sleek cat. A black cat, for his hair was a straight, thick, silky black that reflected the sun, and his skin was a polished bronze that had clearly absorbed that same light and heat. His dark eyes seemed to penetrate whatever they looked upon, and Sappho was both relieved and disappointed that they hadn't seen her. As he saw someone he knew, his mouth flashed into a brilliant smile, and the focused, hunter's expression that had given his handsome face depth and intensity broke into a wicked playfulness that made Sappho glad she was already sitting. Her knees would've buckled at least a little, she knew.

As he moved past her, toward his sighted destination, her

whole head turned in the process of watching him.

"By Pan's cloven feet, girl," the fruit dealer said, sitting next to her, "you'd think you never saw a man before, and I know that's a far reach." She chuckled at her own humor and Sappho's attempt to stop her goggling.

"I wonder who that was," said Sappho, a little more breathily than she would have chosen. *Compose yourself, priestess,* she thought.

"Phaon," said the woman simply.

Sappho caught herself straining to see where he was in the crowd and vowed to be less conspicuous. "I heard he was handsome, but few men take me by surprise like that."

The fruit vendor made a face of mild disinterest. "Meh."

"You don't think so?" Sappho was surprised.

"Oh, he's fine, I suppose," her hearty companion said. "I prefer more to a man, though. Big men. With furry chests." She giggled. "I might break a little man like that."

Sappho giggled with her. They continued talking, watching the people in the *agora*, and Sappho kept a stealthy awareness of Phaon's progress. When he reached a vendor she knew very well, but hadn't visited yet that day, she excused herself from the fruit stand, adjusted her skirts and veil, and walked that direction.

The vendor knew Phaon, too, it seemed, as they were clasping arms and offering cheerful greetings. Since nobody noticed Sappho when she first made her approach, she busied herself with the wares and tried to look unassuming but still present.

She picked up some bundled paper, the reason she'd gotten to know this particular vendor so well, and then waited for an opportunity to interject herself into the conversation. Payment for product was a legitimate and inconspicuous topic, so she felt safe. A minute passed, though, before the merchant realized she was there. Uncomfortable as she was, leaving might have drawn odd looks and unpleasant attention.

"Oh, Sappho," he said at last. "More paper? You aren't burning it, are you?"

"By Olympos, no!" Sappho said. "This commodity is every bit as precious as gold or jewels to me."

He accepted her payment, and she thought the merchant might skip the introductions, despite the fact that Sappho and Phaon were standing practically nose to nose in the bustling market.

"Thank you," she said and turned to go.

"Phaon, have you met Sappho before now?" the paper seller asked.

"No," he said simply. He nodded courteously, but she got no brilliant smile.

"She's the Muse of Mytiline," the merchant added.

Phaon smiled, but there was still no flash for her.

"'Phaon', is it?" Sappho asked innocently. "I believe I've heard your name spoken a time or two. I'm glad to meet you." She tried to match his cool reserve even though she felt like she was shaking like a flower petal in a stiff breeze.

He grinned a little at that.

Before she turned to leave, she noticed the tattoo on his arm. It was crudely done, but the ram's horns of Ares were clearly visible.

"I see you are marked by Ares," she said with a smile,

pointing at the tattoo. "That's an honorable thing."

Phaon stiffened a little and then shrugged off both his tension and her comment. "That mark is from a part of my life that is over. I wish the ink no longer remained."

With such an inauspicious first meeting, Sappho should have known to leave Phaon alone.

Chapter 90

Sappho analyzed, chewed on, and otherwise labored over her afternoon's encounter with Phaon for the rest of that day. She recognized the instantaneous infatuation that had sprung up inside her, and she simultaneously reveled in it and reviled it.

Her initial opinion of him based on the *hetaerae's* gossip really hadn't changed. After meeting him, she still thought he was arrogant and self-possessed, but he was also undeniably handsome. There was something beneath that handsomeness, too, that drew her, but she couldn't identify it.

If I could figure it out, she thought, *I could probably dismiss it.* As it was, she spent the first few hours after their introduction indulging in fantasies spun around Phaon. Later, though she tried to banish him from her mind, he roughly intruded when her guard was weak. She woke from her dream that night feeling plundered and sulky, hating that she was obsessing over a man who had barely acknowledged their introduction.

The Fates, those meddlesome weavers, brought Phaon to Sappho again a few days later at a *symposium*. She made a point of paying him no special attention. In her opinion, he got quite enough female attention already. The other *hetaera* present that night, while paying appropriate respect to her own escort, was clearly trying to win the eye of Phaon.

She had it, too, Sappho noticed. The girl was ample in every bodily area, and Phaon pursued her with lusty eyes. Noticing, and hoping to gain the young man's favor, her consort leaned over and whispered something in Phaon's ear. The two quickly fell into hearty chuckles and clapped each other's shoulders in camaraderie. Phaon left the men's chamber not long after that exchange with the soft, rounded *hetaera* in tow. All the men chuckled at this and toasted the good fortune of their young friend.

"Dance for us, Sappho!" Kerkolos declared. She didn't like being commanded to do anything, but she was happy enough to get up and move. The musicians, following her cues, played slow and sensual music that she was easily able to pour her own lust into.

When Phaon and his *maenad* returned, Sappho was still dancing. Sappho's dance had taken an undulating pattern of rhythm, cycling from the sultry and intensely passionate to the lighter, bouncier swirling that echoed men's happy intoxication. She was now at a part in her dance where she was spending a little time dancing for each man in turn, making eye contact enough to boil the blood and stir desire, to make enough of a connection that when she danced the climax, it would seem like a simultaneous release between just two partners – Sappho and the man watching her.

Phaon obviously got a turn within Sappho's dance. To ignore any man would be unthinkably rude. When she turned and took long, languid steps to stand in front of him, she danced for a few moments without looking into his eyes. He was sitting next to Kerkolos, and they had been whispering together while Sappho's attention had been on the other side of the room. Had Kerkolos been offering her to Phaon? She wouldn't have been surprised. Anything to win friends.

Sappho was consumed with the music, and she was filled

with her own passion combined with what had been poured into her body through the eyes of her expectant audience. Phaon could have done nothing but watch every move, and he could have responded with nothing but aching desire. The drunken Bacchante yearned for Aphrodite's daughter in that moment.

When her eyes sought his at last, she was scorched with the burning desire that raged there. Her knees didn't buckle this time, and she felt no weakness in her body or mind. There was, however, a pleasant softness and a heat. She was simmering in response to him.

She turned her back on him and returned to the middle of the room where she began her steady rise to the crescendo. The final throes of the dance burst from her, leaving her gasping and dreamy-eyed. She'd ended the dance with the breathless drop to the floor she'd seen in parts of Lydia, her legs tucked under her from the knee down, lying on her back with her arms, hair, and skirt spread fan-like around her.

After a breath, the men stomped, clapped, cheered, and poured libations on the ground. Sappho rose like a snake and accepted the coins they were now tossing gently to her feet. She tucked them into a pouch and then excused herself for some air, taking a cup of wine with her.

She walked to the far end of the host's courtyard, to a corner that was dark with the lateness of the hour. The household altar stood nearby. She steadied herself with deep breaths of the balmy air and planted her feet solidly on the paving stones.

"Hail, Dionysos," she said, "thundering, twice-born God of the vine! I honor you, despite the maddening men of yours that you

472

send to entice and confuse me." She poured her libation of wine on the altar and was startled by the male voice not far behind her.

"Hail, Aphrodite," the voice said from the short distance, the face belonging to it obscured by shadows, though Sappho knew who it was, "violet-crowned, foam-born Goddess of the sea! I honor you, and give thanks for the women you send to tempt me." He, too, poured a libation, now that he had stepped close enough to the altar.

She didn't speak, but she watched his every move. He circled around her, stalking her like a hunter stalks prey. She dimly thought that she ought to offer some resistance, but no part of her body or mind actually wanted to do that. In fact, she stopped his progress around her and put her hands on his shoulders.

Aware of Aphrodite's presence, she welcomed the Goddess into her body quickly and completely. In that moment, she realized that the lover standing before her was both Phaon and the twice-born Dionysos. That was the last of their interlude that she remembered clearly. The rest of that moment's bliss consisted of snatches of sensation – swirling darkness streaked with gold, the sweet pressure of being caught between a man and a wall, and the jeweled flower that she saw so clearly when Dionysos and Aphrodite found the peak of their mingled ecstasy.

She slipped sideways back into normal consciousness and gathered her scattered wits. Looking around the dark courtyard, she saw an area that was blacker than it should have been. There, she saw the silhouette of Kerkolos.

Chapter 91

Kerkolos shot irritated comments to Sappho all the way home. Long stretches of silence as their sandals clipped the streets were punctuated with bits of venom.

"You could barely control yourself" … "Couldn't control yourself at all" … "Never show that sort of shameless lust for me" … "Your dance was wanton and embarrassing" … and more.

Sappho bore it as long as she could, but her patience wore thin very quickly.

"My dance was no different than you've had me do on a dozen such occasions," she snapped. "You are simply unwilling to see any lust for another man in my eyes. And on that point, Kerkolos, I had little more lust for Phaon while I danced than I did for any other man."

"Just more than for me," he sulked. "You share your bed with me as often as I ask it of you, but you have never looked at me the way you did at him. There is a wrongness in that, Sappho."

"I've given you all I could, Kerkolos," she said simply. They had reached her courtyard now, and she was trying to keep from waking Reah and Kleis.

"You haven't given enough," he said. "It isn't your best. It isn't the depths of you. I want that, too."

Sappho's mind was racing. She wanted to say more words than would fit in a human breath.

"Kerkolos, I can give you no more than I already have." She drew a deep breath. "In fact, I believe that you were best to seek the company of another *hetaera* and priestess for a while. I need some time to myself, to make sense of things."

He looked both stunned and angry. "No, I refuse. You won't just push me aside like that."

Straining to control herself, and knowing she was losing the battle, Sappho thought momentarily of halting this conversation until daylight and rest brought both sides into clearer focus. She was agitated, though, and it felt more gratifying to settle this now. Her face was growing hot, and she knew that was a dangerous sign that her temper was nearly lost.

"It's not really for you to say, Kerkolos," she said. "No man commands me, including you. If I wish to end our business association, I'm within my rights."

"Is that all I am to you? A transaction?" His voice wasn't pleading. He wasn't, on the surface, a man begging for her love. To the contrary, his manner was taunting. He was daring her to confirm all the worst ideas he'd been harboring about her and all women.

Rashly, she obliged. She stared at him with a growing hardness, blinked once and then offered a careless shrug with one shoulder.

"Fine," he said. "Then this ends it."

"At long last," she said the words to his turned back, and she felt them sink in there like a knife plunged to the hilt.

After he had left, and Sappho was sure she was alone, she dissolved into salty tears in her courtyard. Ending the relationship with Kerkolos didn't necessarily cut her very deeply. *But why did I resort to such cruelty to do it?* She wept until morning's light for the darkness and villainy that she was now sure dwelt within her.

Chapter 92

Her departure from Kerkolos was all she talked about for weeks. She recounted every detail to Reah, who mostly felt that Sappho had been right for ending the relationship, but she nearly scolded Sappho for her lack of decorum or compassion.

"There had to have been some other way," she'd said to Sappho, who argued and sank further into obsessive melancholy.

Kerkolos, meanwhile, was telling anyone who would listen about the many wrongs Sappho had done him. Some were imagined and others were enhanced, but all created shockwaves of gossip through Mytiline.

Sappho hid away in her home. As much as she talked about Kerkolos, she also thought about Alkaeus and dreamed of Phaon. One was a past she could never reclaim, and the other was an obsession that haunted her brooding. Peppered into thoughts of these men were images of Pittakos, another heart she'd managed to mangle.

It's no surprise that I didn't fit at the temple, she thought. *My love affairs are brutal.*

Taking stock of her relationships with women, she didn't feel much better. She and Atthis had endured years of separation. She's abandoned Daphne at the temple without a backward glance. Reah was a solid love, but Sappho felt that she probably took this closest partner for granted.

The guilt consumed her. When Reah was home, Sappho begged for her assurances that she'd been treating Reah well. More than anything, though, she apologized all too frequently for her perceived shortcomings.

"I'm not as kind as I should be," she'd say with her eyes full of tears. "Please forgive me my short temper."

She began apologizing for her nights out at *symposia*, and then she stopped going. She made apologies for her looks, her schedule, her malaise. Eventually, she began to apologize for her incessant apologies.

Reah was worried for Sappho, but she was also at a loss for how to handle the situation. Riding out the storm seemed the best choice.

Sappho's poetry was mournful, too. When she wrote. Many poems started well, but then Sappho couldn't find endings that suited her. Her half-written poems frustrated and angered her, and she wondered if her Muses had finally forsaken her.

She turned away devotees who came calling on her before she stopped making even an appearance at the gate when they knocked. Eventually, she lay in the bed and pretended she wasn't home until she heard them leave. She hoped, in that sorrowful seclusion, that they would stop seeking her company altogether.

Anassa arrived one morning and let herself in. Sappho had sent Reah and Kleis to the family home every morning that week, but she hadn't joined them. Despite her growing malaise, she hadn't failed to see her family in the mornings until the last few days.

Sappho was curled in her bed when Anassa came into her room. She was awake, but she didn't respond to her stepmother's approach. She continued facing the wall, looking at the shadows and the cracks and tracing similar blemishes within her own being.

Anassa stood looking at her before finally taking a chair nearby. She was shocked by how frail and thin Sappho was. She hadn't been eating much, Reah had told her, and Anassa thought Sappho looked worse than she had even one week earlier. If she'd eaten even one meal in that time, Anassa would have been shocked to know it.

Thinking of Sappho's obvious need for food, Anassa got up and prepared something light and plain and then returned. Bread and mild cheese shouldn't upset her starved belly too much.

"Sappho," she said gently.

At first there was no response, but after a moment, Sappho rolled toward Anassa and looked at her tearfully. She said nothing.

Anassa's heart broke. Everything about Sappho was beginning to look skeletal and dull.

"Sappho, you need to eat something," she said, setting the food on a table by the bed. "You'll starve to death where you lay, my dear one. Is that what you want?"

Sappho looked at the food, obviously uninterested, and she looked away again. Her eyes fluttered shut, and silent tears slid from beneath the lids. With great effort, she pulled herself up to a sitting position. She took the bead and nibbled a little then sipped the cool water Anassa had brought.

Anassa, feeling slightly more hopeful, asked Sappho, "Would you like a touch of honey to sweeten your bread?"

In a hollow voice, Sappho said, "Neither honey nor bee for me."

"What?" Anassa asked. "Sappho, what do you mean? What's wrong? Please talk to me. I'm very frightened for you."

Sappho was silent again, and Anassa thought she wouldn't answer. Then, in a tone of warning, Sappho said, "You don't want to see the debris and detritus, the crawling and squirming things under the surface of the peaceful and lovely beach, Anassa. Stir not the pebbles."

Anassa now sat silently for several moments. What she was about to say was hard, and she was trying to find the best way to say it.

"I can't pretend to know what is hurting you, Sappho, but I know that Kleis is acting out because of it. She is scared, and she misses the mother she knew. You're wasting away in front of her," Anassa was almost pleading. If Sappho would agree to be Sappho again, she wouldn't have to continue with what she needed to say. A pause brought no response from Sappho except more tears.

Anassa pushed on. "I think it would be best for Kleis if she stayed with me and Iantha until you are recovered." Another pause and no response. "I hope that is soon, my love, but your child is welcome as one of my own for as long as needed." Tenderly, she added, "I'll need Reah's help, though."

Sappho nodded. She held very still for a moment, and then something broke. The tears and sobs flooded forth, and she fell into hyperventilation. "I …'ve failed … everything!... My poor Kleis … and …. Reah…" Her chest was spasming, and it hurt to breathe. The words she was fighting to say were like knives slicing through her lungs and mind. In her gasping, she clenched her fists in an angry attempt to control her breath.

Anassa jumped to the bed and wrapped her arms around her shuddering stepdaughter. She handed her a soft handkerchief and whispered, "Shhhh…" repeatedly until Sappho's breathing stabilized.

After long, silent, tear-filled moments, Sappho pulled away a little and held up the little cloth, saying, "This is what I am. A napkin, dripping. Soggy and used up." She set the thing aside.

"Nobody else sees you that way," Anassa said.

Sappho laughed harshly. "Pittakos, Kerkolos, even Phaon."

"I don't know what these men think or feel, Sappho," Anassa said. "But I know you are a true and gifted priestess. You seem lost right now, and I know you are not far from your path." She sat and thought for a moment and then offered the suggestion that had been forming. "Maybe you need to go to the temple for a while."

"I don't think I belong there," Sappho moaned.

"Maybe not," said Anassa, practically, "but you might do well with a visit. Stand in the temples and the groves, walk among the women. Talk with your friends. Seek counsel from your *hiereia*."

Sappho nodded. There was no enthusiasm in her agreement, but there was acceptance.

"And," Anassa added, "you may find that you do belong."

"What about Kleis?" asked Sappho, her eyes filling with tears again. "I can't abandon my girl. I love her so much!"

"You are leaving her in the care of family, not abandoning her," Anassa said. "If you decide to stay, we can bring her to you. She would surely be welcome there. Or, she can stay here with Iantha until both girls are ready to attend as students. That's not so many years away, you know."

Sappho smiled, and she realized it was the first smile she'd had in a long while. Anassa, encouraged and hopeful, helped Sappho make the arrangements for the journey.

Chapter 93

She was glad that she had recovered herself somewhat when she saw Kleis. Sappho spent two days with her daughter before she left for the temple again, and she wouldn't let anyone else take care of the little girl during that time. The little mother was hyper-vigilant in her care for the child, playing with her throughout the day, preparing every morsel that she ate, and watching her sleep long into the night.

Sappho laughed and felt giddy, and she wasn't sure she'd ever felt so elated before in all her life. She giggled and rolled with Kleis on the tiled floor of the courtyard and chased her throughout the house. Sappho was still weak from her recent lack of food and movement, but she felt like her strength might be returning.

When Sappho was tired, Kleis climbed into her lap and begged for stories and songs. Sappho always obliged, telling herself that she had to make up for the poor effort she had given to motherhood in recent weeks.

Kleis brought Sappho's heart soothing balm. Her laughter and her kisses kindled a fire in Sappho that she knew had almost gone out.

"You're the best Mama in the world," the tired little voice would say as she was drifting to sleep.

"Oh, Kleis," Sappho would reply, "you're the most precious daughter I ever could have imagined."

Of course, in the quiet hours of the night, while she watched her slumbering child, she found herself crying for the wasted days and nights that she had spent in despair.

When the morning came to go to the temple, Kleis clutched her mother's legs and begged to come with her. "Please, Mama, let me go to your temple."

"You will come to me in just a little while, my darling girl." Sappho was kneeling in front of Kleis and holding the girl's pudgy hands in her own. Kleis's straight and shining hair was blowing into her face with the little breeze that was grazing them as they looked at each other. Sappho took in every detail of her daughter's sparkling eyes, the cleft in her little chin that was a perfect replica of Sappho's, and the sweaty little palms that clutched her mother's hands.

Sappho threw her arms around her daughter's waist and squeezed her until the little girl giggled.

"Your laughter makes me brave, my girl," Sappho said. "Your smile makes me strong. Keep smiling for me, bright Kleis, until Kastor and Kharaxus bring you to me at the temple. It won't be long, my little love. I can't be gone from you for long."

Kleis clung to her mother even when Anassa pulled her away. She cried, and Sappho cried in return. But she tried to keep her own smile in place so that Kleis would be brave and strong, too.

Chapter 94

Sappho hired Fotis, the young man who lived in her street and had served as messenger for her so often, to escort her to the temple and to bring the mounts they were using back to Mytiline. She hired the mules at a stable and wished vaguely that she could ride a horse this time instead.

Her own house was barren of food for the short trip, and she hadn't wanted to take food from Anassa's stores, so she stopped in the *agora* before leaving Mytiline. She bought enough for them both to share on the way to Hiera, for their dinner at the temple that night, and for Fotis's return trip the next day. She had decided to stay at least two weeks, maybe longer.

Almost upon her arrival in the *agora*, people began asking if she would share a poem that day. She was evasive initially. "Maybe." She felt uncomfortable around all the people, even those with whom she had been friendly. She felt tainted somehow, like she might do or say something that would hurt them. She wanted to leave as quickly as possible.

She wasn't at all surprised when she saw Phaon. He saw her, too. She knew it. They made eye contact for a moment, and then he turned his attention to the pudgy prostitute who had sidled up to him.

"Oh, gold-throned Muse of Mytiline, will you sing for us as you have so often done before now?" A pleasant man was asking for a song from near her, and she decided to oblige the city of her birth, the place that had honored her, before she left it again.

She took her place and made her invocation to the Muses. The busy marketplace grew still and quiet, and she knew that even Phaon was listening. Good.

> *O careless reveler, bright torch before the host,*
> *You drain innumerable drinking cups.*
> *For you to whom I do the most good,*
> *You harm me the most,*
> *And with your touch, burn me.*

> *Over the hills the heedless shepherd,*
> *Heavy-footed, plods his way.*
> *Crushed behind him lies the iris,*
> *Soon empurpling in decay.*

Her voice was clear but filled with agony, and some of those listening to her wiped away tears, whether for her pain or their own, they couldn't know.

Sappho left the *agora*, not daring to see if her words had made any affect in Phaon, and she never returned to the city where they called her Muse.

Chapter 95

Sappho arrived in Hiera unannounced, and, feeling self-conscious, she didn't seek announcement. She paid Fotis and sent him with food, money, and horses into the village below the temple. He would return home tomorrow. She would make her way to her favorite places within the temple grounds and eventually seek Eugenia for counsel.

She dressed like a priestess, and she had traveled lightly. Walking through the buildings and the trees, she went unnoticed. Another priestess going about her business.

She sat in the apple grove, burning incense that she'd brought with her upon the altar that stood amongst the tress for that purpose. Though there were no apple blossoms on the trees, she was sure she smelled their sweet fragrance mixing with the swirling smoke of the smoldering myrrh tears.

She sat on the grass under the twisted trees, writing poems, her heart and soul at peace as they hadn't been in months. She didn't feel the sting of tears. Instead, her heart was filled with calm.

The sun was setting when she left the grove, the memory of Aphrodite's touch upon her skin from a night so many years ago. She wasn't ready to see Eugenia or anyone else, and she passed through the grounds like a ghost. Nobody took notice of her as she approached that high place above the sea where she had sat and watched the water and the birds playing on the wind when she had been so ill. She saw in her mind the image of Timas's letter to her fluttering over the edge of the cliff where it soared before being sucked down to the waves and rocks below.

The warmth was ebbing out of the day as the sun sank into the eastern sea. Sappho stood and watched until a single star appeared in the deepening indigo. "You are the evening star, the fairest of all the stars, I think. Ah, Hesperus!"

"Hesperus," a melodic voice repeated behind her. "His daughters guard my apples, and that star bears my name in some places." Aphrodite looked as she usually did to Sappho, like Sappho's self, only perfected and glowing.

Sappho turned and knelt before Aphrodite, her back to the cliff's edge. The Goddess gestured her to stand again.

"As I did at our first meeting, Sappho, I ask for a song. Can you give me one?"

She nodded. "I've just written it." She proceeded to recite it from memory.

Then, soon after hearing my cry,
You arrived, blessed Goddess,
With divine and smiling countenance, and asked me
What new woe had befallen me now, and why
  I had called thee.

What in my mad heart was my greatest desire?
Who was it that must feel my allurements?
Who was the fair one that must be persuaded?
  Who wronged you, Sappho?

But it is none of these, for I am one of your doves soaring.
But when the spirit within them turns chill, down drops their
wings.
        And this I feel myself.

Come then, I pray, grant me surcease from sorrow,
Drive away care, I beseech you, O Goddess.
Fulfill for me what I yearn to accomplish.
        Be my ally.

Aphrodite looked on Sappho with gentle eyes and said, "A heart so tender is easily ripped and broken. Life in this world brings joys and pleasures, but cares and sorrows are their promised price. From what would you find relief, dear one?"

"From my distress," Sappho cried out. "Let the buffeting winds bear it and all care away." Heavy drops fell from her eyes, obscuring her vision. She tried to blink the water back, but the cold wind stung her eyes. The wind on the high cliff rushed in her ears, and she could neither see nor hear the Goddess she so loved.

She thought she heard someone calling her name from far away. She shook her head and used the heels of her hands to push the tears out of her eyes. Aphrodite was gone. She searched the cliffs for her, but the Goddess was gone. Two men were approaching her, , running and calling her name. There was something in the way they said her name that frightened her. Was it urgency? Panic?

Fotis reached her first, but he didn't know what to do with himself once he got there. The look he gave her froze her to her core, and her palms were sweating. The cold sweat that she had come to hate was breaking out on her brow and neck.

She had barely had time to force the question, "What's wrong?" from her lips when the other man caught up to them. It was Kastor, and he was both exhausted and sickened. Worse than that, Sappho saw, he was weeping.

"Kastor …?" She was so frightened that she couldn't ask for information coherently. She knew that no good news could be borne by a messenger in such a state.

"I came as quickly --" he broke off. He looked lost. He didn't want to say what he'd come to say. "I'm so sorry, Sappho – "

"What?" she shrieked. "What's happened, Kastor?"

"Kleis," he said, dropping Sappho to her knees with the word. He sobbed, "Kleis fell. A great height for a little girl. Anassa tried, but there was nothing to do for her. She's gone."

Her screams and moans cut the two men standing near her. They tried to reach out to her, but she lashed out at them in rage and pain that consumed her mind, body, and soul. She pulled at her hair and ripped at her garment, and the endless cry poured out of her body. She hugged her arms to her chest, anguished that she would never again hold her bright and beautiful child.

Kastor again tried to approach her, to hold her, but she hit and pushed him away, screaming, "Don't touch me. Leave me! Leave me!"

"Come back with us," Kastor pleaded. "Come to your child."

"My girl is gone," she moaned. Her throat felt raw, and she wanted to be done with her own voice. She wanted never to hear it again.

Kastor looked like a broken man. Sappho pitied him, even from the depths of her own desolation. "Give me a moment, and then you may take me back, Kastor. Wait for me, there," she said, pointing to a large rock not far away where he could sit.

When she had regained some aspect of privacy, Sappho looked back out over the cliff's edge, and there she saw Aphrodite. The daughter of the heavens stood solidly upon the insubstantial air.

Sappho stood, trembling, her torn garment hanging in ragged folds around her shoulders and torso. Her life raged in her ears with the pounding of her heart, but her breath felt stolen away. She took shaking steps toward the Goddess, who held out her arms toward the forlorn woman on the cliff's edge.

Sappho looked down at the rocks far below and then back at the Kyprian. "With my two arms, I do not aspire to touch the sky."

Visions of her daughter's fall came to her eyes. She knew her baby's cry, and she imagined the terrified scream of her precious girl as she fell through air. Oh, the agony of the mother who couldn't save her child! Tears of pain mingled with the hope of relief as she looked at the rocks and waves below. Her hurts were soul-deep, and only oblivion could obscure them. Both pain and the promise relief shone in Sappho's bright eyes as she looked to her Goddess.

"The hurts you feel now, on that cliff, are the last you will ever know. I'll not let you feel the fall into my sea." Aphrodite took a step backward, creating more distance between the rock wall and her ethereal self.

Sappho was blinded by her tears, but she felt herself

steadying again. Her darling girl had been her joy, and now life was without sunshine or laughter. Her pain lingered but something inside Sappho's heart turned to iron as she saw her next few steps with brilliant clarity.

She wiped the salty water away from her eyes. Her bag, the one that held her new poems and writing materials, was lying on the ground. She didn't remember removing it from her shoulder, but she was somehow glad that her words would stay behind and not drown in the sea beneath her.

"Love conquers all things, Sappho. Find rest and peace in the arms of Love."

Sappho ran into the arms of her beloved Kyprian, unaware of her body's long descent as her spirit melted into that eternal embrace.

Printed in Great Britain
by Amazon

32039549R00278